*L*adies and gentlemen," began the stranger. He was not a tall man, neither did he unduly raise his voice, but I'll swear he was seen and heard in every corner of the restaurant. "Ladies and gentlemen—allow me to introduce myself. I am Deveraux. Captain Edward Deveraux. I am, as you must know, a scientist, an engineer, an aerial wayfarer. Tomorrow I ascend into the higher air for your instruction and delight. But now, today, in less than a moment's time, I propose to offer—an unique spectacle."

The words flowed as smooth as silk. He was indeed handsome and fine, this mountebank captain. For all that I could recognise and distrust his masher's eye, his roaring way with words, his showmanship, he held me breathless, mermerised. In that moment I'll swear he held us all so. He was a powerful weaver of spells, this fine and handsome captain.

The
FINE AND HANDSOME CAPTAIN

A Novel by

Frances Lynch

A FAWCETT CREST BOOK

Fawcett Publications, Inc., Greenwich, Connecticut

THE FINE AND HANDSOME CAPTAIN

THIS BOOK CONTAINS THE COMPLETE TEXT OF
THE ORIGINAL HARDCOVER EDITION.

A Fawcett Crest Book reprinted by arrangement with St.
Martin's Press, Inc.

Copyright © 1975 by Juque Ltd. and Souvenir Press Ltd.

All rights reserved

ISBN 0-449-23269-7

All the characters in this book are fictitious, and any resemblance to actual persons living or dead is purely coincidental.

Printed in the United States of America

10 9 8 7 6 5 4 3 2 1

ONE

As I sit down now, twenty years after, to recall exactly as they happened the events of that early summer in 1885 when I first met my fine and handsome Captain, I could wish there was something special to be remembered about the dawning of that day on which they all began. Certainly it should have been a moment of unforgettable significance. It was, after all, to be the last morning of my stay under Mrs Skues' frugal roof; the ending, also, of six weary years in the service of the passengers of the Great Western and Southern Railways. And the beginning of all that has been new and exciting in my life since.

An auspicious morning, then—no doubt one full of omens of change. One that surely should have been heralded by an eclipse, a firework display, or a roll of drums at the very least.

Yet in all honesty it was not so. It was a morning about as drear as any other. A Sunday morning, admittedly—a Whit Sunday morning, to be precise, the 24th May—and all we restaurant girls much excited at the prospect of the Grand Fete and Gala coming to the city on the morrow. Experience told us that famous *artistes* arriving in Bristol by rail often passed through our refreshment rooms and might even order soup from us across our counters. It was a morning also that happened to begin for me a day on Late Call, which depressing thought probably sobered what foolish thrills the coming fete might otherwise have caused me. A morning, in fact, about as drear as any other, and quite lacking in omens of whatever kind.

For the sad fact was that, since the death of my parents in the Ross Bridge disaster, I had been in Mrs Skues' employ long enough to have known six Whit Sundays and any number of Late Call days, and never once had either brought me any alteration—let alone improvement—to my circumstances.

To begin the day then on a note of wearisome normality, at six-thirty Barty Hambro came knocking with his strong right arm, the only arm he had, against our dormitory door. Seven days a week, twelve months a year, his night's work done, Barty would rouse us thus before trudging on up to his own slant-roofed nook close under the tiles. His routine was thus: the morning mail train from London arrived at four-thirty, and the First Class Refreshments Room must stay open till then, tended by him and the girl from our number listed for Late Call by Mrs Skues. At four thirty-five or so he would escort her back here to the hostel through the early morning city—it was no great distance—and then return to the station. By the fine generosity of Mrs Skues this girl was then allowed to lie abed in the dormitory until ten, in recompense for her previous day's full twenty-two hours of duty.

Barty, meanwhile, would work on alone in the great empty station, cleaning both refreshment rooms, scalding through the tea and coffee urns and milk pans, receiving fresh supplies from the Pipe Lane bakery, and generally making ready for the new day. Even with his one arm he could still fold with marvellous dexterity the paper rosettes for the First Class tables. It seemed to me shabby work for a soldier wounded in the service of Her Majesty, but he never complained.

As was his habit, Barty beat on our door, paused, then beat again. I woke, as always, at the first touch of his knuckles. There is something in me, I fear, that remembers still that knocking, that terrible knocking early in the morning on the very day of my twelfth birthday, bringing to Bristol news of the disaster, news that Papa and my dearest Mama had cruelly been taken from me. A knocking that tumbled all of life mercilessly about my ears. Even today, I still wake at the smallest sound, at the slightest touch on my shoulder, no doubt in dread that further calamity may have crept up on me while I have lain sleeping.

I started up, afraid, then lay back again, reassured by the familiar scene and the calm sound of Barty's departing footsteps. A sliver of early morning sunlight shone on the wall opposite. It reminded me to hope that the weather would stay fine. Since the early part of summer, when the sun had shone so hotly that the pitch had risen in bubbles between the stones of Temple Street, the weather had not been good, with cold winds and much rain. This was hard on us girls, who had long looked forward to the easier months of summer when lemonade was much drunk in place of troublesome tea, and the press of people at our counters markedly lessened by the simple absence of Inverness capes and Ulsters and dripping umbrellas.

This, in the main, was what fine weather meant to us: easier conditions in our work. This and the chance, on our fortnightly half-day, to walk in the Clifton Zoological Gardens to take an outside seat on a tram to Clevedon or one of the estuary villages. I do not mean to sound self-pitying, for I now know of many infinitely more wretched places of employment than Mrs Skues' to which I might have been put on the death of my parents and the total loss of my family's fortune. But at the time I felt as any girl of spirit must do, that the precious days of my youth were being stolen from me in ugly drudgery. Admittedly I had a plan for my own eventual liberation, but all too often its fulfillment seemed quite impossibly distant.

Along the small dormitory with its eight neat beds, the girls were beginning to stir. The room was low and bare, papered with brown flowers older by far than the six years of my own residence, faded to muddy yellow around the gas jets, worn quite bald at door and window. But there was a pretty curtain at the window, such as an ordinary house, even a family home, might have, its little blue flowers repeated in the wash basins and huge water jugs provided for our use. Mrs Skues had provided a picture also, well-meant if not wholly suitable: an oleograph depicting some fearful moment in the American Wild West. The savage treachery of the Indians was powerfully delineated as they fell upon the covered wagons of the brave frontiersmen and their womenfolk. Childish though it was, this picture fed the restlessness in my bones. It reminded me that women could be strong and courageous, and could lead lives of high adventure. And here was I ...

I sighed, and pushed back the bedclothes. The girl in the bed to my right was still sleeping. "Amy!" I called to her. "Amy—it's half past six. Time to get up."

She rolled over, screwed her eyes more tightly shut. "Leave me be. It'll be time enough when Barty comes. I ain't moving just on your say-so. It'll be time enough when Barty comes."

"He's already been," I told her.

Kate, in the bed beyond little Amy, laughed bitterly. "Though you'd never know it—tapping like a frightened mouse the way he does whenever it's Bella's turn for a lay-in." She sat up, felt behind her head for thick locks of her beautiful dark hair, and angrily began plaiting them. "Hear what I'm saying, Bella? Ain't that so, Bella? The rest of us could sleep over and get chewed to rags by Skuesy, and your Barty'd not care a fig! Ain't that so?"

Poor Bella. The current story in the dormitory was that Barty Hambro was soft on Bella, and some of the girls allowed her hardly a moment's peace from their teasing. Personally I doubted if there was any truth in the matter—Barty was a good, quiet young man and not much given to favorites— but our little community always seemed to need some piece of gossip to keep it entertained. Indeed, had Bella been in better straits to deal with her companions' raillery I would have welcomed this particular fiction, for it diverted the others from myself.

But Bella was scarcely fifteen, and newly come from Doctor Barnado in London, and as yet quite without defenses. Her only response now was to hide her head under the blanket and—I don't doubt—wish that she were dead.

I got out of bed and began pouring water noisily into one of the china bowls. "He knocked loudly enough to waken the dead," I said. "Some of you would sleep through the trumpet of the Archangel Gabriel himself."

It was a poor joke, but it served its purpose. Big-boned Kate, her hair pushed up all anyhow, arrived at my side to jostle me as I bathed. "But not Miss Hester. Oh no. Our Miss Hester Malpass is halfway to the Golden Gates already, if the holy way she carries on is anything to go by."

Others joined in. "Not that she's got all that much to be so holy about, not all things considered . . . not when you think why she's here in the first place. . . ."

Their words were familiar enough. Putting them out of my mind I stooped in front of the spotted mirror above our long washstand and concentrated on the difficult daily task of subduing my hair: it was dark—I would indeed have called it black had not that color carried the disgraceful possibility of "a touch of the tar brush"—and of a thickness that rebelled continually against the scrimping up decreed by Mrs Skues. My jaw was hardly to her liking either, being square enough to be open to the accusation of obstinacy. Otherwise, however, I was mercifully unremarkable—well-formed but no more. Certainly nothing as dangerous as a beauty. And if I was privately a little more than satisfied with the unusual amber-brown of my eyes, it was an excess of satisfaction I kept discreetly to myself.

I dressed myself carefully, and let the girls' taunting words drift over me, being well used to them. Although we were orphans all, in our little grey world the gulf between them and me was immense. For they were *respectable* orphans, come either from Doctor Barnardo or from a certain Methodist foundation run by a relation of Mrs Skues in Wales, while I was a *disreputable* orphan, child of that most dreadful of men—a gentleman of pretensions, a failed genius even, a person who had clearly lived beyond his means and been saved from the bankruptcy courts only by the untimely landslide that had taken him and that ill-fated railway embankment down into the river together....

All this no doubt was true enough. They seemed to consider, however, that the terrible Ross Bridge disaster had been some sort of merciful dispensation. As if my orphaning on that cruel day had been a stroke of good fortune for me. As if a father dead were preferable to one publicly disgraced.

Furthermore, since—unlike them—I had endured paid schooling up to the age of twelve, a degree of learning stood between us that they found difficult to forgive. It made my speech different, and gave me the manner of someone putting on airs. I was thus, in their eyes, fair game.

Yet they were not cruel people: only unthinking, like puppies perhaps, instinctively baiting the outsider, not yet knowing or caring how sharp their teeth were grown. And if I remained, even after six years as one of their number, still mostly an outsider, this was a matter for which I doubt if either side could wholly be blamed.

I hope I will not be thought too fanciful if I trace the blame back to the restless nature of my poor Papa. Failed genius or not, he was a man always pursuing some new vision, his mind impatient of the family circle, and the memories I have of him are sadly not of the happiest sort. In particular I recall a winter's evening when I found myself —being aged nine or thereabouts—for some reason alone with him in the drawing office behind his shabby workshop. Possibly it was a day in the school holidays, and Mama had detailed him to amuse me for a short time while she went out into the city on some unavoidable errand. He was not, as I have already said, a man good with children. Be that as it may, once the necessity of entertaining his small daughter became inevitable he set about the task with a good enough grace.

He need not have had a difficult time of it. Simply to be allowed in his office was for me a rare thrill. I did not perhaps pay much heed to the dusty engravings on the walls, pictures of engineering marvels, viaducts, bridges, great pumping engines; nor to the misted cabinets containing models of incomprehensible things that smelled sharply of copper and machine oil, and served seemingly no interesting purpose whatsoever. But he had beside his desk a stool, a stool that revolved, screwing its little round leather seat either up or down as it did so, and to sit on this was one of the great excitements of my little life.

But Papa had no understanding of such small joys. Determined upon entertaining me and at the same time testing my abilities, he pushed aside his own mysterious designs and set me drawing from memory various commonplace household devices: the towering shape of the curate's new bicycle, Mrs Pitts' mangle out in the steamy wash-house, the hansom cab in which I sometimes rode about Bristol with Mama. . . . I screwed up my eyes, trying to picture in my mind these simple, everyday things—but I'm afraid my crabbed little drawings were not to Papa's liking.

I can remember even now my cold anxiety as I felt his good-will towards me fade. To be sure, he made a great show of having fun, imagining the strange sort of animal able to ride my topsy-turvy bicycle, and what would happen to old Mrs Pitts if she tried to use my mangle, or to Mama if she tried to sit in my hansom cab. But there was little kindness in his teasing, and I do not think that either of us was much amused. I can hear his voice still, and smell the fine sandalwood pencil he had placed in my hand, one of his very own pencils of which I was so clearly unworthy. Even the twirly stool lost its magic that evening, and I kicked my frilled legs wretchedly against its ugly metal frame and never to my recollection sat upon it again.

But I will be brief, for the point of this memory is not Papa's impatience. The point is that his impatience grew out of his own great sympathy with mechanisms of every kind and his recurring dissatisfaction with the irretrievably female sex of me, his only child. The simple fact of my sex, he considered, would make me always incapable of sharing with him his only abiding interest. . . .

The femaleness of my mother he accepted, I believe, as a necessary evil. Certainly I never saw him be anything but patient with his Mary, though she was, I now suspect, a dear but somewhat foolish person. Of practicality she had little. Her passion was for nature, her skills with the sick wild things she rescued and tended from time to time. In my days at Mrs Skues' I had her likeness with me, and stared at it often. We shared the same dark hair and eyes, she and I. In character, I was determined that we were utterly dissimilar.

I had, after all, lived with Papa's dissatisfaction quite long enough for it to shape my nature. His dissatisfaction became by degrees my own, with the girl I was and with the woman I would become. It became also the constant spur for me to transcend the limitations of my sex. I would *not* grow up like soft, uncomprehending Mama. In pursuit of this aim I once for several weeks shot catapults and had the grocer's lad play cricket with me in our patch of garden when he should have been out on his deliveries. There was even a period when I sought education in many daunting subjects not provided by my teachers, such as mathematics and chemistry, turning instead to the books on Papa's shelves for guidance. The period was brief, the guidance negligible.

I also read Papa's copy of the *Times*, with much self-importance if little understanding, taking care that he should see me. By the age of twelve I seem to recall being privately determined upon a career in politics at the very least. Though precisely what politics were I would have been hard put to it to say.

Such then was the scope of the expectations I brought with me to Mrs Skues' establishment in December 1879, to the situation finally found for me by Mr Margulies, my father's distrait solicitor. They were expectations that later life taught me to modify, but never abandon altogether. Indeed, it was of these that was born my plan of escape, the secret ambition that gave me continuous hope and purpose through the dreariest of days.

But it was these expectations also that made me intolerant of the other girls' more frivolous concerns, and gained for me a reputation for priggishness and conceit.

Perhaps the reputation was just. Perhaps I did in truth feel myself superior. Certainly the critical eye I directed upon those around me was but rarely applied to my own failings. But at this moment of writing I find myself still too partial to remember truthfully, as they happened, the strange events of that spring and summer, and set them down here as honestly as may be, and leave them to speak of me as they will.

We were allowed fifteen minutes for rising and washing and dressing ourselves. As I tightened my apron and tied it behind me in the even bow that Mrs Skues demanded, little Amy came to stand in front of me, her back to me, up on tip-toe so that I could reach to help her, as was my custom, with the last few buttons at the top of her dress. The girls' taunting had run down for lack of interest some minutes before and was, I think, genuinely forgotten by them. And by myself also, so little did it really signify between us. I leaned forward to deal with Amy's buttons.

She whispered urgently at me over her shoulder, "Hessie love—put in a good word for me with Skuesy, will you? About tomorrow's half-day off, I mean. I've got to get it. I've just *got* to...."

It was natural enough that Amy should return to me in this—if my background made me the group's butt, it also made me its spokesman. Besides, I could well understand that the question of the Monday half-day was far too important to Amy for her to dare to raise it herself. Naturally we would all of us have liked time off on the day of the Fete, but for Amy the need was especially urgent. She claimed intimate acquaintance with a member of the Bristol Reed and Brass Band which was to play on the green during the festivities, and she must see him there in his fine blue uniform and wave to him, or surely die of a broken heart.

Rich indeed had been the selection of back-stage gossip relayed to us by Amy on the strength of her bandsman sweetheart. There was, for example, the wife of Gus Gauntlett the vocal comedian and Canadian skate dancer, who had arrived a full week ahead of her husband and entered into financial agreements with the keepers of Clifton's drinking houses not to serve Mr Gauntlett at any time on the all-important Monday of his performance. On the other hand—and Amy claimed her bandsman had this on the highest authority—there was the dashing balloonist Captain Deveraux and his wife Kitty, neither of whom would be putting in any sort of appearance whatsoever. Their courage, it seemed, had quite deserted them since an experience at the Hereford Conservative Gala some eleven days before when Madam Deveraux' parachute, by which she was about to descend, blowing kisses graciously down upon the assembled multitude, was clearly seen to be struck by lightning and utterly destroyed.

Altogether, Amy's narrations had brought the coming events of the Fete alive for us as never before. And although I might have my private doubts as to the real intimacy of her relationship with the bandsman in question—to my uncharitable way of thinking it was probably confined to a masher's routine attentions across the counter, or at best to a contact of hands during the purchase of a chaste plate of Ha'penny Fingers—I had no doubts at all as to its importance in poor Amy's limited scheme of things.

I wished sincerely that I might be of some use to her. Usually our half-days were posted on the notice-board well in advance. On the subject of the Whit Monday afternoon, however, Mrs Skues had been ominously reticent. When work had ended at ten o'clock the previous evening the space on the board had remained unfilled.

I finished Amy's buttons and patted her shoulder. She turned to me anxiously: even in her drab grey uniform she had a bright-eyed prettiness that I could well see going straight to any bandsman's roving heart. "I'll do what I can," I told her. "Last year Mrs S was in a good mood and let us off in shifts. All of us. Perhaps that's why she's left the—"

My optimistic words were cut abruptly short by the arrival of Mrs Skues herself, bursting headlong through the dormitory door. Mrs Skues never entered a room, or indeed went anywhere at all, in the manner of an ordinary person. Always she seemed to be contending with a strong head wind that only she could feel, battling head down into it with very much the disjointed air of an inside-out umbrella. Disjointed also was her speech, and the assembly of her dress, and her habit of mind.

The door burst open before her, banged shut behind her. "Best in the West," she announced, braking abruptly and clutching her Sunday black straw hat. "Best for Provender, best for Service, best for General Amenity. Cup-winners last year. Cup-winners the year before that. And don't you forget it."

As we scuttled to our positions beside our beds she moved

rapidly between us the length of the room and back. To some she might have seemed a comic figure, but seldom to us. Such was her power over us and the uncertainty of her temper.

"My fingers to the bone," she proclaimed. "And all for what? Eight hundred pounds per annum the Concession do cost me. Eight hundred pounds. I shudder to think."

We—those of us who had been with Mrs Skues long enough to know the signs—shuddered also. We knew that for her to invoke the Concession never boded anything but ill. And certainly a group of girls worth six pounds a year each, all found, must consider eight hundred pounds a fearful sum to be made responsible for.

"Impervious vigilance, ladies, that's what do's it. You knows that, I know that, Mr Hambro knows that. Impervious vigilance...."

She strode back down the room to where Bella, as was her right after Late Call, lay quietly trying to sleep, and pulled the bedclothes into an untidy heap on the floor at the foot of her bed.

"Now, ladies, this one's new here, mind, so us won't make all that much of it. All the same, served tea, this one did, to a gentleman travelling on his Railways Pass. Smart gentleman, he was, in our line of business too." She leaned over the bed, raised her voice. "Steward in a Restaurant Car, wasn't he Bella? Talked to Mr Hambro about the inspectors, didn't he Bella? The *company* inspectors didn't he Bella?"

The poor girl was clutching her nightdress round her knees, her face quite blank with uncomprehending terror. And Mrs Skues not yet into her stride. I took a small step forward, grateful, for Bella's sake, that my years at the hostel had encouraged a certain quick-mindedness.

"Excuse me, ma'am," I said. "Bella Parsons roused me this morning, told me about the inspectors, asked me what she should do. I thought it best, ma'am, not to disturb your sleep at that very early hour, I told her I'd see you were informed as soon as possible."

Mrs Skues stared at me. For a moment I thought she was going to challenge me for the liar I was. Even if she did, I thought I was safe enough—not even Bella Parsons would be fool enough to deny my story. Mrs Skues' pale eyes narrowed in her deceptively apple-cheeked face as she grappled with the possibilities. Her real problem—and ours—was that she had a mind suited to the complexities of little more than keeping a few yard hens. Occasionally this could be used to our advantage. Mostly, however, it simply bred confusion and ill temper.

On this occasion her gaze faltered, and she fussed uncertainly with the feathery collar of her coat. "Well then ... Well then, like I said, us won't make all that much of it. ... Which isn't to say there ain't p's and q's to be minded all the same." She was stoking up her indignation. "Impervious vigilance, ladies, and don't you forget it."

She returned to the door. I was glad to see the girls on either side of Bella replace the covers on her bed and make some show of tucking them in. "There it be then, ladies. Company inspectors on the prowl. Mr Hambro was good enough to tell me not fifteen minutes gone. You won't know them, but they'll know you fine enough." She paused to peer (closely) at the large silver watch she carried on a long chain about her neck. "My dear soul—another minute and us'll be late opening, near as drabbit."

The door banged open and she was gone, we girls in hot pursuit, snatching our shawls about us as best we could. At the head of the stairs she brought up short, causing a sudden breathless jam behind her, and turned to face us. "P's and q's, mind. Win the cup third time around, and it's ours in perpetuity. Best for Provender, best for Service, best for General Amenity. Ours in perpetuity...."

Suddenly she smiled, engulfing us all in the warm feeling that we were forgiven. Though for exactly what I don't believe we asked ourselves. "And, tell you what, it's five shillings each, apiece, all around, if us makes it."

And there we were, at that moment, willing to follow Mrs Skues to the ends of the earth—not for the five shillings she had promised us, but for the radiance of her smile. So, I believe, do many tyrants rule, not so much by fear of their wrath as by desire for their approval.

And it was I of course, the priggish one, remembering my promise to Amy, who had to spoil the moment's false comfort. "Excuse me, ma'am," I said. "Excuse me, Mrs Skues, but the girls were wondering if you had come to any decision, ma'am, about tomorrow's half-holiday. Some of us, ma'am, have a natural anxiety, for we have had hopes that ... hopes that...."

I caught myself sounding humble, against my express intentions. My request was reasonable, not something I need grovel for. But that was not the true reason why my words tailed off so weakly. It must be admitted that I fell mute from sheer panic at Mrs Skues' outraged expression, which but a moment before had been so sunny.

I was terrified. I'm sure we all were. Looking back on it, I think that a large part of the fierceness of Mrs Skues' glare could have been attributed to her extreme shortness of vision. Comforting explanations like that, however, have a sad habit of turning up only after their moment of usefulness is long past.

"Half-holiday, Hester Malpass?" The aitches were breathed with infinite menace. "Has your fancy airs turned your brain, then? Half-holiday? With half the company inspectors in England a-prowl? Not to mention incoming excursions, four extra on Monday afternoon as you well know—Swansea, Weymouth, Tintern *and* Chepstow. . . . Not to mention the Guv'ment's new liquor tax, paring me profit to the bone? Eight hundred pound per annum, the Concession do cost me. Where's the profit gone if I lets you girls off a-gadding? I shudder to think."

To which, of course, there was no answer. I hung my head. With even Mr Gladstone and his new liquor tax arrayed against us, what chance did we poor girls have?

It was then a subdued party that hurried in its usual helter-skelter crocodile behind Mrs Skues, down Temple Parade to Temple Meads Station. And there, as we turned into the station approaches, there on the wall a Fete poster was prominently placed, beside a faded advertisement for Mrs Allen's Hair Restorer, to taunt us with the exciting particulars. Performing dogs, a tight-rope walker, clowns, double trapeze artistes, dancing on the green, refreshments of the finest quality . . . and—as yet uncancelled—the daring exploits of Captain Edward Deveraux and his wife Kitty.

The climax of their performance was to be an ascent at dusk, discharging fireworks and coloured fires, while at a certain height his intrepid wife would parachute down carrying a magnesium light capable of illuminating the countryside for miles around. Surely such an enterprising pair would never allow a mere bolt of lightning to discourage them!

Being Sunday morning, the station platforms were quieter than usual. The weather was bright, but by no means warm, with clouds already gathering away to the west. The seven-ten for Reading, getting up steam on Platform One, had attracted few passengers, and no train was expected in for twenty minutes. With little to do, therefore, the porters leaning on their barrows had time to turn, and stare after us, and whistle —though surely a duller lot of girls than we in our plain white aprons and drab grey dresses would have been hard to imagine. Today their impertinence sparked off no flirtatious giggles, no side-long glances, no secret blushes. We were, I think, even the most susceptible of us, too wretched for that.

Even I, who had secretly vowed not to visit the Fete on account of the financial temptations it would offer, even I was bitterly disappointed. Fireworks, the music of the band, perhaps a glimpse of the balloon, even the cheerful bustle and sense of general festivity—these were things that could have been enjoyed from outside the grounds without cheating my china savings Pig of even the sixpenny entrance fee. Life was grey enough. And now even these small pleasures were to be denied me.

But as always the thought of Pig—old Mr Margulies' parting present to me—comforted me. By means of the strictest economy Pig's little treasure had grown steadily over the years. The sum I needed, the sum my plan needed, the sum I had decided would be enough to set me free, was twenty pounds. Of these Pig now guarded a full eleven, lying safely wrapped in my spare pinafore in the corner of the small tin box at the foot of my bed. There was little else in the box: an outgrown pair of silk slippers kept for remembrance's sake; a bundle of my father's papers and rough drawings similarly hoarded; a little silver picture frame containing my mother's likeness. I rebuked myself for my childish disappointment and determined that from now on Pig would receive an even larger portion of my slender resources. I was nearly nineteen and life was slipping away between my fingers.

Once inside the refreshment rooms Mrs Skues lined us up on the black-and-white tiles of the First Class for a brief Sunday morning prayer. We folded our hands together and bowed our heads. In her prayer that morning I remember Mrs Skues referred to us as *cup-bearers of the Lord*—no doubt a subtle reminder to the Almighty of her own cup-bearing aspirations. I certainly hoped it would not pass unnoticed: apart from the five extra shillings for Pig that success would bring, it was after all quite nice to be Best in the West. And the cup in question—prominently displayed on a mahogany bracket over the First Class counter—was a

17

fine, eye-catching affair. And even a refreshment room girl, I thought wryly, could have her pride.

The prayer over, we were despatched to our various duties. As always, mine were with Kate and Amy in the First Class, the one place where my faded gentility was thought by Mrs Skues to be of some small advantage. Mercifully this caused less resentment among my companions than might be thought, since serving the nobs was generally a far more troublesome task than serving the decent, ordinary folk. For one thing, they were assumed—quite wrongly, in my experience—to have more sensitive palates. The matter of the mustard pots was a case in point. While it sufficed for the girls next door to stir in whatever slight skin as might have formed on the mustard overnight and shuffle the pots out around the tables again, my first task each morning was to empty completely the ten First Class pots—saving the contents, of course, for later Second Class use—clean them and polish them, and fill them anew, each with four spoonsful of the freshly-mixed condiment. Yet I swear that the result was in no humanly detectable way superior.

And so the distinctions went on throughout the day. Our floor, being polished tiles, required constant attention in rainy weather, while the Second and Third Class customers trudged contentedly in and out on friendly sawdust. Our tables had cloths while the girls next door could whisk around smart brown marble. And to cap it all, our customers behaved with an imperiousness that the few odd extra pence they paid seemed hardly to warrant. There were times, in fact, when to be Best in the West seemed scarcely worth it.

I moved off and settled resentfully over my tray of little mustard pots. It was a bad start to the day that for me must continue without respite till four the next morning. Amy went to unlock the public doors and behind me Kate banged about, setting the water to boil in the tea and coffee urns. Whatever Kate did was noisy, and frequently things got broken. I sighed, and wiped ten small mustard spoons, and put them on one side for washing.

A chirrup from Amy caused me to look up. The station cat had appeared in the doorway, and Amy was passing the time of day. But it hurried on, too wise in the ways of Mrs Skues ever to dare linger. We'd put out milk for it later, behind one of the weighing machines, when no one was looking.

The seven-ten for Reading left in a last minute flurry of

banging doors and shrilling whistles. Its smoke hung about the platform, drifting slowly. The lad from W.H. Smiths sauntered past, ostentatiously reading one of his own stall's newspapers. The sun must already have gone behind a cloud, for the light that filtered down through the sooty glass of the station roof was sad and grey. As sad and grey as our spirits that Whit Sunday morning.

Amy returned behind the counter and began lining up bottles of porter. "I'm going," she said. "No matter what."

Kate and I both knew she was referring to the Fete. "You'll never dare," Kate said.

Amy glared at her. "I will so. And if she gets on at me I'll run away to my brother Patrick on the barge."

"You'll never dare," Kate said again, clashing teacups till I wondered at any of them retaining their handles.

"I will so."

I was glad Kate let the matter drop then. It was going to be a long day. Soon we served our first customer, a young army officer who had clearly been out all night and loudly demanded the blackest cup of coffee we could provide. Mrs Skues shot through from next door in a moment and chaperoned us all the time he was on the premises. In the face of her suspicious stare it cannot have been a cup of coffee either enjoyable or particularly restorative.

Quickly the morning settled down to the usual trickle of out-going trade—no heavy drinking, but the most troublesome sort all the same. Customers catching trains are always in a hurry, the nobs jostling each other quite as much as the ordinary folk, the occasional manservant demanding preferential service for his master lounging elaborately at the farthest table. And Mrs Skues continually in and out berating us through the fixed joviality of her public face. When not doing this she was assessing each customer for his potential as a company inspector in disguise... "That's a possible over there by the door, Amy—the one looking at his watch.... It's by their watches you can spot them, often as not. Their watches, I say. Big silver watches. Company watches. You mind what I'm telling...."

I'd heard it all before, of course. And the only company inspector I'd ever spotted, having caught him making notes on the bill of fare, hadn't had a watch of any kind at all that I could see. A fair-minded sort of man he'd been, who'd promised not to mention my hem where I'd caught my heel and left it hanging.

Around eleven the pattern changed: arrivals then, and more leisurely, ordering shilling bowls of soup and willing to wait their turn. I'd learnt to spot arrivals quite well: even the most-travelled of them had a certain timidity, none of that brassy grab-what-you-can-and-be-off, lingering over their food as if the station was the last safe place before they launched out into the city. I learnt a lot about people, and not all of it bad, in those quiet years of my innocence, so soon to be shattered.

On this particular day, of course, arrivals were especially interesting for the chance that any one might be a personage or world-famous *artiste*. Many such would be crowding into Bristol in preparation for the morrow, and in this matter a degree of friendly rivalry had grown up between us girls. I can remember my chagrin when I realised it was the girls next door who had set the ball rolling.

The first Kate and Amy and I knew of this was when the high level of conversation coming over the partition was interrupted by a piercing whistle, followed by a succession of short yaps such as are made by the smaller kind of dog. At the time I was serving chops to a gentleman in the company of a lady young enough to be his daughter but almost certainly nothing of the sort. This person affected to be much startled by the noises off, at which her elderly knight errant grandly ordered me to discover what they signified and immediately stop them. They were, he assumed, my personal responsibility. Glad of the excuse, I retired from their table.

Amy was ahead of me, and Kate not far behind. Such is the power of curiosity that I think even had the Queen herself been lunching at our tables, we would have found some excuse to spy upon the happenings next door.

The sight that met our eyes in the Second and Third Class refreshment room was astonishing. A space had been cleared among the people in the middle of the floor, and around it paraded six little dogs of a breed I did not immediately recognise, all of them dressed in red cut-away jackets and walking upon their hind legs. Standing at one side of the circle was a thin, immensely tall old gentleman, obviously their trainer, dressed in lemon yellow breeches and a smart hacking jacket, a high-crowned topper upon his head. In one hand he held a silver-mounted riding crop and in the other a small ivory whistle. Just as I pushed my way in among Mrs Skues and the other girls behind the counter, he blew a short blast on his whistle and rapped twice with his little whip on his thigh. At this the dogs neatly reversed the direction of their circling and paired off, for all the world as if they were dancing. It was a charming spectacle, and brought applause from all sides.

On a second whistle blast the dogs dropped obediently onto all fours, then sat, wagging their stumpy tails and panting, while their master went down the line and solemnly shook the front paw of each. He was so tall, and they were so tiny, that there was much kindly laughter at this courteous gesture. I looked carefully for any sign of fear in the dogs or of the whip being used as an aid to discipline, but saw none. Clearly this old man ruled by love rather than by terror.

During his passage down their line the dog trainer must unobtrusively have attached some sort of ribbon to their collars, for now, at a final command, the dogs leapt up and resumed their former parade. And strung between them this time was a yellow satin banner emblazoned in red with the words:

* Professor * Morrell's *
* Unrivalled * Performing * Poodles *

To my surprise no collection was taken. Doubtless Professor Morrell considered the advertisement well worth a few moments of his time, for he now bowed, distributed a number of handbills, and then led his talented troupe out through the open doors of the refreshment room.

Beyond, on the platform, a truck loaded with theatrical hampers was waiting, and an assistant with any number of other little dogs on leashes about him. The six leading performers of our brief show leapt nimbly up onto the truck, and the entire party moved slowly out of sight.

I turned to Amy. "I'm glad I'm not the one who'll have to untangle them all when they get where they're going."

But she did not laugh. Her face was fixed in a glower of determination. "I'm going," she whispered fiercely. "I'm going to the Fete, whatever Mrs. S has to say."

"But how my dear? If she finds out she'll discharge you surely."

"I don't care...."

I might have reasoned with her longer, had not Mrs Skues herself suddenly discovered us there and trodden briskly upon my foot to remind me of my duties. Back we trooped, Amy and Kate and I, back to our various impatient customers. I told my irritable gentleman of the little performance I had just seen and was immediately berated for not having stopped it sooner. Was there not, he demanded, some law to prevent such vulgarity from occurring in a public place?

In reply, of course, I had no alternative but to murmur meek nothings and wait for him to finish. Out of the corner of my eye, however, I saw the little lady's attention quickly begin to wander, and with it her gaze—now here, now there ... and suddenly becoming rivetted. Curious, I edged around —still filling the gaps in her companion's tirade with appropriate noises—till I could identify the object of her fascinated attention.

It was, predictably, a gentleman ... or rather, to be accurate, a person not exactly a gentleman, the green of his bowler and matching waistcoat a little bright for that, his cravat a little daring, the raven curl of his moustaches a little too luxuriant. Clearly a man of style, however, and flair, and most appealing, I thought, to a young lady definitely not the daughter of her elderly consort.

The fine newcomer quickly noticed her interest as he surveyed the restaurant, and tipped his hat very civilly in return. Then he picked up a largish basket that had been out of sight on the floor beside him, and eased himself through the crowd toward us. Arriving at the table, he swept his hat from his head and bowed deeply, allowing his glance in passing to linger on me in a brief smile of seeming complicity. Unbidden, the thought entered my head that it was me he had noticed from the door, and not the young lady at all. ... Then his eyes were lowered, his mouth solemn, his whole attitude one of respectful supplication to my two customers.

"Madam? Sir? A moment of your time, I beg! It will not be wasted, I promise you."

Clearly the young lady had all the time in the world. And before her friend could protest, the handsome stranger had lifted his basket and placed it firmly on the table. A silver plate vase of folded serviettes went flying, and one of my mustard pots as well. Cutlery was scrambled, and my customers' plates of food much endangered.

"Madam? Sir? A moment of your time, I say ... And do not fear—the simple, rustic delights of performing dogs are not within my competence. Rather I bear in my basket here a phenonemon more fitted to the diversion of sophisticated minds." He gestured widely, spared me a minute but unmistakable wink. "Sophisticated, I say... tasteful, unique, instructive... and never before seen in this noble city."

The basket was about two feet square, with a carrying handle on its lid, and no grille or aperture around its sides whatsoever. It contents, thus, were completely mysterious. The newcomer placed his hand upon its catch with a flourish. My elderly gentleman was too occupied with keeping his disordered lunch plate out of his lap to be concerned, but I must confess I stepped back a pace. Anything at all, I felt, might be forthcoming. Not surprisingly, our little group was beginning to attract the attention of the whole restaurant. Even the most exemplary gentlemen craned vulgarly to see. Our fine stranger's hand remained poised upon the basket's catch. Evidently our curiosity was to be screwed up still further.

"Ladies and gentlemen...." He was not a tall man, neither did he unduly raise his voice, but I'll swear he was seen and heard in every corner of the restaurant. "Ladies and gentlemen—allow me to introduce myself. I am Deveraux. Captain Edward Deveraux. I am, as you must know, a scientist, an engineer, an aërial wayfarer. Tomorrow I ascend into the higher air for your instruction and delight. But now, today, in less than a moment's time, I propose to offer—quite without charge and entirely for the general good—a rare, an unique spectacle. Ladies—be assured my small entertainment is both tasteful and discreet. Gentlemen—be assured it will commend itself to your most serious attention."

He tapped lightly upon the basket. "In this humble skip, ladies and gentlemen, is emprisoned the embodiment of a prophetic vision, *my* prophetic vision, a glimpse of future felicities without bounds...."

The words flowed as smooth as silk. He paused on the up-flow of his peroration. He was indeed handsome and fine, this mountebank Captain. For all that I could recognise and distrust his masher's eye, his roaring way with words, his showmanship, he held me breathless, mesmerized. In that moment I'll swear he held us all so. He was a powerful weaver of spells, this fine and handsome Captain.

TWO

"Ladies and gentlemen—ladies and gentlemen, I give you Josephine. I give you Josephine, my little treasure!"

The Captain flung back the lid of the basket. Immediately there was a puff of smoke, contrived I know not how. Out of this smoke there rose, with a whirring of released clockwork, a most delicate and pretty device. It was clearly a miniature balloon, but elongated and turned on its side, for all the world like a neat little vegetable marrow, with, suspended below it, a tiny aërial carriage, windows and doors being painted skilfully upon the sides. At either end of this carriage air paddles rotated, driven by some clockwork mechanism concealed within. And along the delicate blue of the balloon, in big silver letters, the single word: *Josephine*.

The apparatus spiralled up to within a few feet of the restaurant ceiling, and then commenced to travel in wide level figures-of-eight, its paddles churning the air to very good purpose. From many tables spontaneous applause broke out —though not, it need hardly be said, from the table so cheerfully invaded by the Captain, his ingenious basket, and its noisesome puff of smoke. No, my elderly gentleman customer was so much not amused that his young lady companion was obliged—though less vocally—to disapprove also.

The Captain's way of dealing with them was disarmingly simple. He appeared to hear not a word that was said. In a flash, however, he had whipped the basket from off their table, had straightened the cutlery and plates, restored the mustard and the vase of folded serviettes, and was offering each of the astonished diners a beautiful crimson carnation produced from I know not where. A carnation, and the most winning smile you could imagine.

Meanwhile, the *Josephine* continued to cruise majestically above our heads. One by one a succession of containers within the carriage opened, letting down rose petals, and a veritable snowstorm of confetti. And finally, as the paddles slowed, the craft descended to head height, hovered, and let down a tiny rope ladder. So perfect was the illusion that for a moment I half expected a suitably tiny man to emerge and climb jauntily down.

The implication was clear enough. Now Captain Deveraux moved between the tables to where the *Josephine* hung motionless in the still air, recaptured her, and returned her adroitly to his basket. Only then, her deeds having spoken far louder than any words of his could, only then did he address us.

"I promise you I am no mere toy maker," he said. "My little *Josephine* here embodies all that is newest in aeronautical practice. Her purpose is serious, and strictly scientific. One day very soon I shall build her again—but ten, a hundred, a thousand times bigger. Then at last mankind will truly have conquered the aërial elements...."

He talked on in this entranced manner for some short time more, but I will confess that I hardly heard him. It was rather the brightness of his eye that held me enthralled, the breadth of his gesture, the fervour of his whole being. Assuredly, here was no man to be discouraged by a mere bolt of lightning. And the wife of such a man—surely she must be of like spirit!

Suddenly he was preparing to go, and his words were nearly over. "... Tomorrow as you must know, I ascend into the higher air for your instruction and delight. Indeed, now, at this very moment, my *monstre* balloon, the *Emperor*, is being unloaded from the train that brought it hither. Tomorrow the intrepid Madam Kitty and I will ascend together, and all of Bristol will marvel. But remember—" he was at the door now, basket in one hand, the other tapping his bowler matter-of-factly onto his head—"remember, it is the free balloon drifting at the mercy of the elements that is really the toy. My little Josephine may seem to you today no more than a pretty conceit. But tomorrow her like will span the skies, just as today ships of steam span the oceans."

"And what'll push 'em along?" shouted some hard-faced, practical man. "More clockwork?"

There was a murmur of laughter. But the Captain was already gone, the door swinging shut behind him.

It was as if a light burning brightly in the room had suddenly been extinguished. The place was shabbier for his going, more wearisome. The disbeliever was nothing to me. Captain Deveraux was no man to be confounded by mere practicalities; he had a vision, and faith in his vision—the faith of a Stephenson, the faith of a Brunel. I swear I could have warmed my soul for ever in the blaze of his words, and my heart in the brightness of his presence.

The couple at my table soon departed, the old gentleman still somewhat enraged, the young lady strangely absent-minded—seemingly quite entranced by the scent of the Captain's carnation....

Sadly I turned back to my petty tasks. The day wore on, dragging me gradually back to the smaller preoccupations of my life. The first of these being to keep out of Mrs Skues' way for another nine hours.

Starting at two-thirty we were each allowed, in turn, fifteen minutes' break back in the kitchen with Cookie, stoking up on gravy and vegetables, plus generous slices of bread and any broken pies that the Pipe Lane Bakery might have delivered. It was Mrs Skues herself, of course, who examined the pies and pronounced upon them. Yet the strange thing was that there were always enough genuinely broken pies for each of us girls to have at least one.... Now, even Mrs Skues might have been forgiven for thinking this too convenient a coincidence. But delivery of the pies was taken early in the morning by Barty Hambro, and he—for all his youth, being scarcely five and twenty—was a man with a formidable dignity. He had marched with General Roberts to Kabul. He had given an arm in the service of the Queen. To think that such a man might break pies himself, dishonestly, with malice aforethought, was beyond even Mrs Skues' suspicious nature. So we lunched well, we girls, and asked no questions.

My lunch break with Cookie was always a welcome break. She was an Irishwoman, a cheerful bag of bones with six children, her carter husband dead three years before in a level-crossing accident, and she lived a life of courage and independence that was a daily example to me. There were always, so she said, so many people worse off than she: "Remember, Missie, back in old Ireland there's thousands starving this very moment minute. When they're not after killing the British sojers. I just thank the Holy Mother for finding me a man to take me safe out of it. Seven years we had, himself and me, and such a loving he gave me as will last me out me time...."

Today, however, Mrs Skues was there even, lurking in the kitchen, putting poor Cookie in a great fluster, her hair in a frizz, the cabbage burning, and nothing going right at all, at all, and the lunch plate she handed me (out of deference to her employer) but meagrely filled. I smiled at her as understandingly as I dared, crossed to the table, and sat myself warily down.

For Mrs Skues the day had started badly, with rumors of company inspectors, and had gone from bad to worse: the performance of the dogs followed by the extraordinary behavior of the gentleman with the balloon had convinced her that total anarchy was about to overtake her respectable establishment. Clearly she was in need of a scapegoat and I, with what she thought of as my airs and graces, the most suitable candidate.

plumped herself down at the table opposite me and began

After charging disconnectedly about the kitchen for some moments, muttering furiously beneath her breath, she wildly berating me for not at once reporting to her the outrageous goings-on in the first class dining room. Why had I stood there gawping instead of doing my duty? Besotted, no doubt, by a pair of fine moustaches and a grand green waistcoat....

To answer her with excuses would have made matters worse. Yet my meek silence was hardly better. What would Mr Margulies think? she ranted. What would my *benefactor* think, come to that, him as had paid thirty golden sovereigns to find a place for a worthless orphan girl who . . . ?

I interrupted her in full flight. "Mr. Margulies gave you thirty pounds to take me?" I asked incredulously.

Brought up short, Mrs Skues had the grace to look embarrassed. No doubt in her agitation she had said more than had been her intention. "Well, no. Not exactly. Twasn't his money exactly ... Anyways, what's more to the point, my girl, is the proper gratitude you should show to folks as—"

But I was not so easily to be put off. "Well, whose money was it, then? Mrs Skues—I have a right to know. You *must* tell me." If I really had a benefactor, if I wasn't as totally alone in the world as I thought, then I had to know.

"Can't tell you his name, girl, for I don't know it. But thirty sovereigns I asked, and thirty sovereigns I got...." Possibly my steady gaze shamed her, for she looked down, examined her pale lumpy fingers. When she continued, her

27

tone was altogether more subdued. "What was I to do? Chit of a girl coming to me out of the blue, no better nor she oughter been, full of Lord knows what ideas—what was I to do to protect myself?"

At any other time her assessment of the immorality of my background might have provoked me to protest. Just at that moment, however, other matters were of far greater importance. "Why have you never told me this before?"

"What would've been the odds?... Anyways," she conceded, after more consideration of her fingers, "anyways, I was asked not to. Asked most particular, I was."

I turned to my food and was silent for a time. I understood old Mr Margulies' kindness in keeping this from me. To be told that a bribe was needed before I could be employed in even this humble capacity would not have been heartening. A phrase of my mother's came to mind—*you couldn't give it away with a pound of tea*. That had been my position exactly: too worthless to be given away with a pound of tea. Rather had thirty golden sovereigns been demanded.

Resentment stirred in me, an angry determination to repay the money and rid myself of the burden of past charity if it was the last thing I did. But then I saw the false pride in this, and tried instead to feel gratitude to my unknown patron.

"And did Mr Margulies never tell you the person's name? Or why the money was given?"

"Never a word. Thirty pounds I said, and away he went. Came back with them the very next day. Gentleman as didn't want his name to be knowed. Most particular, he was. Just that a certain person took an interest." She fussed with the muddled frills of her Sunday blouse. "And there's no call for you to go off to his office in the city, pestering him with questions. Only get me into trouble, and he won't tell you nothing."

She was probably right. I remembered little of Mr Margulies except that he had a sharp way with him, and smelt of cachou sweets, and carried a stick with an eagle's head handle. All in all, I fancied, not a man lightly to break a client's confidence.

"But you believe this person to be still alive?"

"No reason why he shouldn't be."

In the world I knew, where people died as easily as birds in winter, there were a dozen reasons why he shouldn't be. Clearly Mrs Skues had no real idea whether he was alive or not. Neither was she much interested. Yet I was grateful at least for the foolish impulsiveness of her tongue, for I could now feel in some strange way less deserted, less alone. I was indeed deeply moved by the thought that, though of family I might have none, yet somewhere out in the city there was perhaps a person still living who had once cared enough about me to give full thirty golden sovereigns for my welfare....

Short-sighted though she might have been, Mrs Skues didn't need the despised wares of the spectacles vendor on the corner of Old Market Street to see that I was near to tears. Not unkindly she reached across the table and put her hand on mine. "Now then, you shouldn't take on so. It's all water under the bridge. You're the best girl I got, and that's a fact."

For a moment there was genuine warmth between us. Then she took her hand sharply away. "And you mind you eat up quick, Hessie Malpass. Sitting there chatting like I don't know what. As if we hadn't had troubles enough today. And the inspectors a-prowling. I shudder to think."

I left my pie half-eaten and stumbled to my feet. My eyes were still blurred. Her voice followed me out through the swinging bead curtain: "Impervious vigilance, and don't you forget it. Best for Provender, Best for Service, Best for General Amenity...."

I leaned upon the counter, wondering at the sudden intensity of my emotion. Perhaps this was why I gave thought to my past so very seldom—because there was pain in it I still could not bear to remember. It was her distant ranting that brought me to my senses, and the "impervious vigilance" that I would never dare correct her for. I straightened my shoulders and quickly wiped my eyes. Then I sent Kate back for her lunch, and wished her luck of it, and set myself to buttering buns for the afternoon trade. I was no longer utterly alone. And if we did not win the cup it would not be for want of my trying.

Barty Hambro came on duty at three. He looked in on us first, but we were enjoying a quiet period with the end of the set lunches, no more than two customers in the place, both of them business gentlemen with newspapers, so he didn't linger. He smiled in his slow, gentle way, and then went next door where there was always more general cleaning and carrying away of empties to be done.

Amy and I were dusting glasses at the counter. After

Barty had gone she paused in her work. "What's he like?" she asked me. "I promise I won't tell."

"Who?" Her question puzzled me. "You mean Barty?"

"That's right—Barty." She moved closer and nudged me. "To go out with, I mean."

"How should I know?"

"Give over. We all know he's soft on you."

I stared at her. "I thought it was Bella he was supposed to be soft on."

"Don't be so stuck up. You know that's just our talk. It's been you all along, right from the very start."

Barty and me—the idea was ridiculous... I could easily have been angry with her. But this was all they ever thought about, who was soft on whom. I shook my head. "If that's true, I promise you he's never said a word. And I've never been out with him, not once. After all—how often are we free on the same day? Once a year?"

"That's true." She didn't appear to have thought of this. "Then where *does* he go in his time off?"

I shrugged my shoulders. He was nice enough, but where he spent his meagre free time didn't really interest me... It was odd, though, that I didn't remember him even mentioning where he'd been or what he'd done. He was often quite chatty, in the general way.

I might have wondered about this further, had not our whispered conversation been interrupted at that moment by the quiet arrival of a new customer—new, that is, in that he was a man I did not immediately recognize. Certainly his clothes were familiar enough, the green bowler and matching waistcoat, the daring cravat. And even his moustaches had a familiar curl to them. But his manner was so different, so muted, so retiring, that it was a full five seconds before I recognized the person standing at our counter as Captain Edward Deveraux.

His words, too, were unexpected. "A pie and pickled onions, please."

So mundane? And even the voice his, yet not his... I must have been gaping at him—and Amy also—for he smiled deprecatingly. "I'm afraid I made a bit of a racket last time I was here. You don't want to take any notice of that. I'm quite a decent chap really."

He took off his bowler and placed it on the counter. Amy giggled. "Handsome is as handsome does," she said pertly. Her bandsman sweetheart, it seemed, was quite bringing her on. "We liked your show, Captain. Fair stirred up the place, it did."

"That *was* its intention." He sighed. "Though to be honest with you it pains me to make a cheap sideshow of my precious Josephine."

She giggled again, not quite sure of his meaning, and primped her hair. "Pie and onions, was it? And a nice cup of tea?"

"Heaven forfend!" He held up his hands in mock horror. "The pie will do very nicely. But no railway tea, thank 'ee. I fear I have not the constitution."

Amy turned away to the kitchen, leaving me alone at the counter. It will be noticed that up to now I had taken no part in the conversation. I had been struck dumb. I must admit at once that, even without its showman's dazzle, I found his countenance quite disarmingly well-formed. His forehead was finely-boned, his jaw firm, his nose too manly for mere prettiness. His hair, eyebrows and moustaches were all astonishingly black and sleek. His ears, neither too large nor too small, lay fittingly in his elegant side whiskers. His age was of the best, being thirty or thereabouts.

He smiled at me. I disciplined my thoughts. Clearly my scrutiny disturbed him not in the slightest. Indeed, he expected it. For all his present effacing manner I saw he was still a vain extravagant person, and well aware of the confusion he caused me. He was, I told myself, no more than a mountebank after all, and almost certainly a rogue. But he was Captain Deveraux, a man whose exploits high above the earth's surface had thrilled half the nation. And he was there, at our counter. And talking to *me*.

"The thing is," he said, "my aërostat—my balloon, that is —is taking longer than I thought to unload. Besides, I am expecting a friend. And station platforms are draughty places to wait upon.... Is the weather always so unwelcoming here in Bristol?"

I lowered my gaze. "The summer has been bad, sir. The sun has hardly shone since early April."

Something in my words caught his interest. "Then you think the forecast may be correct?" He produced a folded newspaper from his pocket, leaned closer, read aloud. *"Winds south-westerly, fresh or strong. Possibility of rain. Outlook unsettled....* The weather means a lot to me, you understand."

"I could not say, sir." The forecasts were only recently

started in the paper. I thought them a joke. "But the outlook is bad if today is anything to go by."

Again the curious look. "You speak well, child. You have had some schooling, I think." His interest astonished me as much as his gaze disturbed me. "Might I know your name?"

So that was it—his true nature stood revealed. He dared desire to know my name! He was more than a mountebank, he was a rake, seeking some pretext for a dangerous liaison. For so long I had listened to Mrs Skues' warnings in disbelief. Now I might well be in need of her protection. I looked around wildly—for once she was nowhere to be seen. But the two gentlemen were still there, available no doubt behind their newspapers. And now Amy was returning, pie in hand; and Kate also, still chewing, evidently dragged from her lunch by whispered news of the Captain.

I spoke to myself severely. Even had I been quite alone I was still quite safe. I was not a mere instrument to vibrate to the Captain's will. I was my own person. I drew myself up, therefore, to my fullest height, and looked him straight in the eye, much as I had read a hunter must do with a charging rhinoceros. "Captain Deveraux," I began—

But Amy was by me now, and my dignity quite spoiled by her chatter. "Your pie, sir, and hot from the oven. I've give you three onions, sir, though by rights it's only two."

As Captain Deveraux took the pie with a courteous word I moved away, determined that the hot-water gas burners should require my earnest attention. But he was undisconcerted by my back, and spoke to me again. "You know *my* name," he said. "Am I then not to know yours?"

And before I could stop her, Amy was at it once more. "Her name's Hessie Malpass, sir. And I'm Amy Dobbs. And this—" reaching behind her for some part of Kate that she could pull forward "—this is Kate Sillitow."

There was a long pause, I turned slowly, not to appear childishly put out, and curious to see how he took his small triumph. I had to admit he took it very well, very gently, quite as if it were no triumph at all.

He bowed slightly, but equally, and with great propriety, to each of us in turn. "Hessie Malpass ... Amy Dobbs ... Kate Sillitow ... I'm pleased to make your acquaintances. If the rest of the population of Bristol is even half so charming, then my stay cannot but be a happy one."

My distrust faded. So he was a rogue, and a rake, and a dozen things worse. So his flattery was but the emptiest formality and his smile scrupulously impartial. Yet my name on his lips was enough to drive out all sanity. Though he was gentleman enough to include us all in his civility, it was *my* name only he had wanted to know, not Amy's or Kate's... He was fine and he was handsome, and he had spoken my name as if it were in some way beautiful to him.

I would not have had him see my confusion, yet I knew not how I might conceal it. Mercifully at that moment Fate came to my rescue, causing the attention of all of us to be diverted to the open door at the far end of the restaurant. In it, swaying ever so slightly, stood a most remarkable apparition: an old man whose shabby appearance would normally have sent me running for Barty's assistance. Not only was he mildly drunk, but he was also obviously in the wrong refreshment room. His suit, to be sure, was spanking new, and in the highest fashion. His straw hat displayed the gayest ribbon. His shoes fairly creaked with newness. But the man inside all this... well, the man himself was not new at all. Indeed, he was so ancient and limp, and the turnout he wore so fresh and stiff, that I might almost say rather that it wore *him*. And with no advantage at all to either party.

Before I could make any move, however, Captain Deveraux had let out a cheerful cry. "Jowker! My dear Mr Jowker. Come on in—I've been waiting for you."

Mr Jowker steadied himself, and advanced towards us with great dignity. Upon closer inspection it seemed that the skin of his face and hands was almost as ill-fitting as his clothes. And rather less clean. He came to a halt in front of the Captain, produced a large white handkerchief, ran it carefully around inside the inch or so's leeway between his collar and his scraggy neck, replaced the handkerchief, cleared his throat, and spoke. "Procrastination, Capting, is the thief of time." The words seemed to sadden him. "I am late, Capting. There's no denying it. *H'un*-doubtedly and *h'in*excusably late...."

But the Captain had already taken his hand (which had not been offered) and was shaking it handsomely. "My dear fellow—it doesn't matter in the least. You're here now. And in the meantime I've been making the acquaintance of these young ladies."

He paused, almost as if this might be significant in some way. If it was, then its significance was quite lost on Mr. Jowker—he was lugubriously examining the hand that had just been shaken, as if to check it was all still there. The Captain beamed at him, not in the least put out. "Jowker, my friend, you look famished. Let me get you some food."

Mr Jowker brightened. "A toddy would be the thing, I think. A toddy would do the job."

"But I'll wager you went short on your lunch, my poor fellow. What say to a meat pie? They're of the best, I'll warrant."

"... Not that a glass of porter wouldn't go down just as well, Capting, if you've a mind that way."

Captain Deveraux frowned, became aware of us three girls, still standing like stuffed dummies. He gave up trying to be entirely his boozy friend's conscience. "A pie then, for my sake—and a pint of porter to wash it down with."

Amy was first to get her hand to the tankard. Kate blundered off for the pie. I stood bemused, the contrast between my fine and handsome Captain and this bleary new arrival more than I could rightly encompass. Yet Mr Jowker was not entirely a joke—though his clothes fitted him nowhere, and were almost certainly bought the previous day, there was a sense of rightness about the outfit, a matching of components that on a man thirty years younger would have looked the very thing. Clearly he had been given five pounds —probably by the Captain—and told to tog himself up. Now he was being given pie and porter. And for what reason I could not imagine.

Captain Deveraux guided his friend carefully away to a distant table and saw him safely settled. Then he returned to the counter. He took the porter Amy had ready, and paid the reckoning. While he waited for Kate to bring the pie he appeared to seek some idle topic of conversation.

"Did you say *Hessie* Malpass?" he murmured. "It's a strange name, *Hessie* . . . What would that Hessie signify? Would it be Hester in short?"

I nodded. Amy nodded. But his lightness of tone had fooled me not in the least, and I was content. More than content, that is, till the recollection came to me of his wife, of the intrepid Kitty, driving into my soul like a nail. Then I was near to death.

"*Hester* . . ." He smiled absently. "Good. Good. I thought that must be it."

Then Kate arrived with Mr Jowker's pie. Amy would have helped the Captain but he waved her away, placing the one pie plate upon the tankard and carrying this and the other plate safely away to his table... Pies, pie plates, tankards—how unappealing were the tools of my simple trade! And there always, clouding the sky with her rightful presence, there always was the interpid Kitty. I'll swear I wished that I were dead.

In the circumstances, the arrival just then of Mrs Skues on one of her random inspections was almost a relief. At least it spared me the coy nudgings of Amy which I could not have been borne. There were smears to be removed from immaculate glasses, and chairs to be straightened that were already straight, and Barty to be summoned to sweep up crumbs visible to nobody but Mrs Skues herself. And I more than others, perhaps because I had recently known a moment's tenderness at her hands, was bullied from here to Michaelmas and back... The three-thirty left, taking my two business gentlemen with it. And still the Captain and his strange companion lingered, deep in conversation. Then the four-ten arrived, bringing a gaggle of customers bound for an evening on the city and cursing the weather as they fortified themselves with tea and toasted buns. By now gawky Kate was put in such a state of nerves by Mrs. Skues that she spilled milk, dropped spoons, stumbled over her skirts, and finally cut her hand quite badly with a breadknife. As I was calming her and applying a suitable court plaster, word come from next door that they had a suspected acrobat at one of their tables—almost positively a double trapeze artiste.

Amy paused in her work long enough to sneer. "Tell 'em not to bother," she said. "Tell 'em just who we've got at one of *our* tables!"

I said nothing. If points were to be scored it should not be off the unattainable Captain. Anyway, news came almost at once that Barty had discovered the "acrobat" to be a humble apprentice jockey on his way to the Whit Monday Cheltenham Races.

And through all this Captain Deveraux and his ancient protégé sat on. Occasionally Mr. Jowker appeared at the counter, buying porter for himself, clearly spending his own money, and not with the Captain's approval. But mostly they sat and talked, their heads close together, and sometimes argued.

For the rest, I had little chance to observe their conversation in any detail. Except when, just once, I experienced an overpowering sensation that someone was looking at me, and turned from what I was doing to catch the two of them both staring intently in my direction, a piece of paper, a letter of some kind, spread out on the table between them.

Intercepting my glance, Captain Deveraux had the grace to turn away confused. But Mr. Jowker was unabashed and waved at me, fluttering his fingers. I glared at him. For the Captain to know my name was one thing—for Mr. Jowker to think he could wave at me was quite another.

The next time I looked in their direction it was because everybody was doing so. Captain Deveraux was on his feet, laughing, one hand held high above his head, Mr. Jowker protesting in a petulant whine and scrabbling at his sleeve. And the cause of his agitation was the letter I had seen, or one very like it, that the Captain was holding up in the air while it burned steadily down to his fingers. In his other hand he still had the vesta with which he had lit it.

Suddenly Mr Jowker broke away. He grabbed his empty tankard from the table, smashed it violently against the wall, and advanced on Captain Deveraux with the jagged handle flickering dangerously in his boney fist. He was shouting now, almost incoherent in his drunken rage. "Where I been... where I been they learn you to look after yourself. And you so clever. I may be old... I may be old, but I'll not be taken advantage of."

There was a moment's screaming hubbub, then all was still, nobody daring to move, all eyes on the two men. The Captain's laughter had died. He lowered his arm and crouched watchfully, the scorched fragment of paper that remained drifting idly to the floor. The old man darted at him, dagger edges of glass flashing. He stepped back, kicking aside the chair that hampered him. The other lurched unsteadily, but recovered himself and came on.

There was something utterly pathetic in the old man's raging. The contest was unequal, and could not last long. And it was quite without dignity. Mr Jowker darted forward again. The Captain feinted. Then, in a movement quicker than the eye could follow, he had his opponent's wrist held fast between his own two hands. They tightened. There was a moment's pause as the two men sweated. Then Mr Jowker's fingers relaxed, and the jagged shard of glass fell harmlessly to the ground.

Of the confusion that followed, only two pictures stand out clearly in my mind. One is of Barty, summoned by the tumult, thrusting powerfully through the crowd into the empty circle that had instantly been created, as if by magic, around Captain Deveraux' table. The other is of an old man, a foolish, drunken old man, quite harmless now, sitting in a sprawl of knobby joints and uncomfortable new clothes, and crying into a large white handkerchief.

The police were not sent for—Captain Deveraux would not hear of it. He righted the upset chair and paid for the broken tankard. He apologized handsomely for the disturbance. And then he went away, he and Mr. Jowker together.

But before he went away, he left the old man briefly and came to the counter.

"Miss Malpass," he said. "Miss Malpass—I wouldn't want you to think that poor Mr Jowker is often like this. Possibly it is I who am partly to blame... Neither would I want you to think that I make a habit of being involved in drunken brawls...."

He tailed off. *Drunken brawls*—he had spoken the phrase himself. I stared at him. What could he want? The rights and the wrongs of the matter were no concern of mine. Perhaps the letter had been his to destroy—perhaps it had not. But the brawl was his, just as Mr Jowker was his. This, then, was what it was to lead a showman's life, to be subject to the vulgarest of passions in the full sight of the world. Suddenly I felt tears in my eyes. Disappointment, disillusion overpowering. His Kitty was welcome to him ... No doubt she was vulgar too, with her vulgar magnesium light illuminating the earth for miles around.

To have fallen in love and to have had that love shattered, all within the space of an hour, is a chastening experience. I make no apology here for my foolishness, but simply state things truthfully, as they happened.

I stared at him coldly, without a word, then turned and went calmly on my way, calmly past the end of the counter, calmly the length of the servery, calmly through into Cookie's kitchen.

She looked up from the stove. "Great doings, so I hear. Sure but it's hard, being always out of things and missing all the fun."

I stood very straight, not I speaking but a stranger. "Six more toasted buns," I said, for want of better. "And be quick about it."

She stared at me, scratching her hot arms, not moving. I turned, as calm as ever, and left her kitchen.

And in the brief moment of my absence, though it hardly

seemed possible, Captain Deveraux had gone, vanished, and Mr Jowker with him. I felt almost faint with relief. He was dangerous, dangerous... Then I looked anxiously round the remaining customers, aware that soon I would have six toasted buns, and no one to serve them to.

Amy came up to me, gaping. "You cut him dead, Hessie Malpass," she whispered. "And him such a handsome feller."

A phrase of her own flashed into my mind. "Handsome is as handsome does, Amy Dobbs," I retorted.

In due course, from a still slightly puzzled Cookie, the buns arrived. And in due course, mercifully, they were disposed of, four to a stuck-up nursemaid trailing a fat, peevish little boy in a sailor suit, and two to a whispy curate almost certainly travelling beyond his means.

Then, just as I was placing the curate's few pence safely in the cash till, all at once, quite without warning and quite without apparent reason, I felt overcome with a strange dizziness and found I had to lean heavily upon the counter to keep myself from falling. The whole restaurant seemed to lurch about me, and there was a roaring in my ears. Such faintness was terrifying and—since I was not a girl much given to vapours—quite foreign to my experience.

As the worst of the spasm eased I lifted my head. "Kate —Amy—I feel dreadfully ill," I gasped. The ceaseless chatter and clatter of the restaurant, the heat, the smells ... suddenly I felt they would drive me mad. "Fresh air— cool—I'll feel better if—just a breath, a breather outside...."

Amy was at my side now but I eluded her grasp. The last thing I wanted was a fuss. I staggered away. At the side door I paused. Amy had followed me, her peaky little face really quite anxious. "I'll be all right," I said, managing a smile. "And please—if Skuesy comes in, try to keep her happy. I'm sure it will pass."

And pass it did. Even as I closed the restaurant door behind me the echoing tranquillity of the empty station folded me in its soothing, cool embrace. And the breeze that blew in moistly under the huge vault of the roof, that too was balm to my troubled spirit. Feeling already much improved, I moved slowly from iron pillar to iron pillar, going nowhere in particular, just glad to be quiet, and alone.

Instead of smells of food in the air there was faint smoke, and the bitter smell of wet stones, and on the breeze even something, I fancied, of the distant countryside. Sometimes it seemed to me that if I was to spend just one more day in the refreshment rooms I would indeed quite lose my reason.

Suddenly I found myself at the entrance to the goods loading bay, and instinctively drew back into the shelter of a pile of crates. This was no place for one of Mrs. Skues' young ladies to be unaccompanied. From my hiding place I heard clearly a wagon just leaving the bay, its horses' hooves clashing and slithering on the cobbles. The pungency of sweat drifted out to me, and with it something I was slower to identify—the sweet sickliness of coal gas. I peered round the crates, saw a flat-base cart moving away, loaded high with mysterious objects: a large, square basket open at one end and a huge mound of something covered in a gay tarpaulin. And on the tarpaulin words were stencilled: *The Emperor. Monstre Balloon.* And walking beside the wagon, his hand stretched out to touch it, as if he could not bear to be long parted from it, was Captain Edward Deveraux.

Looking more closely, I saw a figure cradled in a hollow of the tarpaulin, a skinny figure in a smart, uncomfortable suit, straw hat close beside him, sleeping peacefully.

I watched them go, and not without a pang of sadness. They were another life, another world.... Perhaps this was the thought, and not faintness at all, that had drawn me from the refreshment rooms. A final farewell? In my mind I waved to the Captain. I was safe enough, for he would certainly not look back. I knew I would never see him, like this, again. When his engagement at the Fete was over he would surely make certain he did not have time to kill here at the station again. And if he did come, why then we would surely only regard each other as the utter strangers we were.

THREE

It was scarcely five o'clock when I waved my little, secret, sentimental good-bye to the Captain. I waited on quietly in the entrance to the loading bay until the rumble of his heavy wagon was quite lost in the Sunday afternoon sounds of the city. A pair of sparrows twittered in under the high arches. Two old ladies on a seat behind me decided their train was overdue and moved off down the platform. And still I lingered. The only place for me to go was back to the refreshment room—where nearly twelve full hours of my working day were still to be served. It was no wonder that I did not hurry.

Barty it was who came after me. I felt a hand on my arm and turned to find him gazing anxiously down at me. "They said you was took poorly. I didn't like the sound of it."

I shrugged lightly, not wishing to be forced into any long explanations. "Oh—it gets so hot in there. I just felt a bit faint and came out for a breather."

"I'll bet that do with the old man upset you more nor what you reckoned."

"Perhaps it did . . ." I sought a little wildly for a change of subject. Barty was so concerned, so *earnest*. "Perhaps it was just excitement about the Fete. Shall you be going to it tomorrow, Barty?"

He shook his head. "Don't reckon so. Not or else I give up sleeping time and go in the morning."

"When you *do* have a half day, Barty, what do you do with it?" Now I had the conversation going nicely.

He stared at his boots. "This and that. Visit family mostly."

"You have family nearby? That's nice. Where do they live?"

"Here and there . . ." He turned away. "Time we were getting back, if we don't want trouble with Mrs. S."

Clearly he was reluctant to tell me about his family. Suddenly I remembered Amy's earlier cross-questioning and felt a bit like her—nosey and importunate. I followed him meekly back into the restaurant.

Mercifully Mrs Skues was still recovering from the nervous palpitations caused by Mr Jowker's drunken brawling, and my short absence went unnoticed. I thanked Amy for carrying on without me. She eyed Barty, waited till he was out of ear-shot, then nudged me delightedly. "Rushing after you like that," she whispered delightedly. "And you *still* say he's not soft on you?"

I didn't answer her. Poor romantic little Amy—she had her own version of the truth, and it made her happy, so why should I try to convince her otherwise?

The Captain I put briskly out of my mind—just as I was most certainly put out of his. For me to grieve at losing what I had never possessed was ridiculous. Indeed, I had myself so very well in hand that when the time came for tidying around the tables, I was able to approach his—the chair on which he'd sat, the table on which he'd rested his elbows—without the smallest qualm. I dusted the cloth, straightened it, then ducked under it to make sure that all the broken glass had been safely swept up. Barty had done his usual good job, and I could not see a single sliver. I was about to rise again when something else caught my eye—a scorched curl of paper that had shifted with the draft of my movements. Apparently it was the remains of the letter with which Captain Deveraux had taunted Mr Jowker, the letter that had been all but burned away.

I stared at it. There was writing on it. I told myself that such writing was no concern of mine. It was entirely a personal matter between the two men. There was no excuse whatever for me to pick it up and read it.

Except that . . . except that, well it *had* been thrown away. Nobody else wanted it. And if I didn't read it then someone else, less discreet, might. And I was, it had to be said, quite extraordinarily curious.

The decision took a shorter time than the telling. With a quick glance around the restaurant I leaned under the table and snatched the piece of paper up. Some of it was so charred that it broke away even as I touched it. The remainder I nursed in my hands as I rose and sauntered—very casually—away. I positioned myself—even more casually—in the restaurant doorway, as if staring idly down the platform. Most casually of all I raised my hands into a convenient position and peered with difficulty down the sides of my nose at what they held.

At first glance I seemed to have wasted my effort. It was the top of a letter that remained to me, headed with the name and address of some dull firm of solicitors. The scorch marks up the right hand side of the sheet had risen high enough to obliterate completely the date written beneath this heading. On the left, however, the letter began clearly enough, in a formal lawyer's copperplate. *My dear Ted*, it began, *as we probably both anticipated, no reply has been received from Orme. In the circumstances*—The rest of the line was burned away. Back on the left of the page a few words of the second line remained: *that Mordello is hardly* ... And that was all, the ink becoming rust-colored with the heat, and fading, and ending abruptly in an uneven brown edge.

A letter to Captain Deveraux, then—Captain *Edward* Deveraux—and his to dispose of how he wished. So, whatever justification Mr Jowker might have had for his fury, the letter was probably not a part of it. Apart from providing that small inference, however, the letter was a great disappointment. It meant nothing to me, as well it might not ... Except that I found my eye returning continually to one small word, uncertain why, yet drawn back to it by some faint chord struck in my memory.... *no reply has been received from Orme* ... *from Orme* ... Orme—it was a name, of course, of a person or possibly of a place. And it had something to do with my father, something long ago, something not pleasant. More than that I could not determine. And as I concentrated, even that small certainty faded, till not even the memory of a memory was left; no more, in fact, than a shiver down the spine, tiny and quite unexplained.

Besides, to imagine that a letter to Captain Deveraux might have the slightest connection with myself was the utmost in conceit. And what, moreover, was this sinister *Mordello*? These matters like the rest of his life, were simply inexplicable, and would remain so. And yet, for no reason at all —for no reason that I cared to admit—I folded the brittle fragment of paper as best I could and put it carefully in my apron pocket. And felt a moment's real sickness of heart when I looked for it not ten minutes later and found nothing but dry brown dust.

On the stroke of ten Mrs Skues assembled the other

girls. Supper and bed awaited them, but for me six more hours on duty remained, and already ached with that tiredness that is far more than simply of the body. They were left in a fidgeting line while she totted up the contents of the First Class till, counting mightily upon her fingers. Once the total had come out three times the same I signed for it, and the finances of her mighty business enterprise became my awesome responsibility. Then the Second and Third class section was locked and barred. Finally Barty and I had to stand by the outer door, rather like visiting dignitaries, while she wheeled her tiny battalion and steamed away at its head through the dim summer twilight.

When they had all gone the restaurant was suddenly very quiet. Barty turned to me. "It's been a hard day," he said. "Why not go out back—have a bit of a rest?"

This suggestion was against regulations, which said that neither of us should stand duty alone. Usually Barty was a stickler for regulations, but tonight he seemed to sense the weariness of my disturbed spirit. "Till the cabbies come in around midnight," he went on, "there's only three locals and the Birmingham Express. Nothing I can't manage on my own."

I shook my head. Grateful though I was, "out back" meant Cookie's kitchen, and to tell the truth it was not so much breaking regulations I feared as Cookie's kitchen and her not in it. I suspected black beetles and worse. "Thank you, Barty, but I'd rather stay out here and keep busy. The fact is...."

I hesitated. Barty was soft-spoken and kind, but not a man I'd ever thought to confide in. "... The fact is, Barty, I'm quite undone. I feel I can't breathe. Don't you ever feel suffocated, Barty—with all this, I mean?"

I gestured around the deserted refreshment room, garish under its flaring gasoliers. He chuckled and rubbed his chin. "Fed up and far from home, eh? Course I do—reckon everybody do. Still, we're none of us as alone as we think—just you remember that, Miss Hessie."

"What do you mean?" I stared at him. Could he have overheard Mrs Skues telling me about my "benefactor"?

"Mean? Nothing much. Just a manner of speaking..." He hugged his armless side in embarrassment. "Besides, we all got ships what'll come in one day. I tell you—the day my ship comes in I'll be out of this like a shot. Little cottage out in the wilds somewhere, row of cages out back, breeding ferrets."

A manner of speaking...? Well, perhaps it was. And we'd all heard of Barty Hambro's ambition to live in the country and breed enough ferrets for all the poachers in Gloucestershire. A strange ambition, I thought, for an ex-soldier of the Queen. But then, the way I felt that night none of it mattered: his ship—like mine if I had one—was five thousand miles away at least, and probably sunk.

I kept such thoughts to myself. "Don't get a cottage that's too far out in the wilds," I said. "Otherwise I won't be able to come and see you."

"You'd like that? You'd like to come out and see me?"

"Of course I would."

I spoke lightly, turning away to pick up a newspaper some customer had left on a chair. He started to say something more, but a late traveller came in from the platform and I had to move back behind the counter. Barty watched me for a moment, then got out his cloth and began polishing the brass mountings of the hat-stand by the door.

Somehow the hours passed. The occasional customer, impatient, bringing with him a great air of the big world; long periods on my own spent staring at my reflection in the black glass of the windows. And, I confess, seeing another figure there as well as my own: a dark-haired figure, in green waistcoat, who smiled at me, spread his arms wide, flaunting his reckless freedom....

At midnight the cabmen trooped in for a nightcap: a cheerful, shabby lot who shuffled their feet and supped their whiskey and joked quietly among themselves, and were careful not to spit on the marble tiles.

When they had gone at last to whatever lodgings they might possess the waiting of the night really began. I nodded off at the counter, my head on my arms, and dreamed of freedom, till cramp jerked me awake. Nothing had changed, or ever would. Barty was standing now at the door, talking quietly with the night porter, their men's voices murmuring of the war in Egypt, of the things men talk about, of cricket, of loose women.... I picked up the newspaper I had tidied, intending to throw it away. An advertisement caught my eye—an advertisement for a parlourmaid. The wages offered were twelve pounds, exclusive of tea and sugar. Twelve pounds! Double what Mrs Skues was paying me!

A parlourmaid—why had I never thought of that before?

I ran my eye on down the column. There were many such advertisements. There was even Morgan's Registry, appealing for Servants Male and Female—to go to Noblemen's families, Clergy, Schools, Asylums... It seemed that half the world desired just those services I could provide.

Except that I was not quite certain what those services might be.

"Barty," I called. "Barty—isn't your sister a parlourmaid in a grand house somewhere?"

He turned from the door. "Effie a parlourmaid? That'll be a year or two yet. She's still below stairs. There's a mort to be learnt, so she tells me."

"What has to be learnt, Barty? What sort of things?"

"This and that. Frillies and dillies. Not quite in my department, I'd say." He paused. "Didn't you have maids when you was young, Miss Hessie? I'd reckon you're in a better state to say what they did nor ever I am."

I wasn't, of course. To be sure, there had been a maid, just one. But I remembered her, shamefully, as no more than a starched white apron and a pasted-on smile. Of what she did, of what she was, of *who* she was, I had no idea at all. Her name had been Kathleen, I thought.... Barty watched me for a moment, a curious sadness in his eyes as if he were guessing my thoughts. Then he turned back to his conversation.

I went humbly back to the paper, found a post more suited to my inexperience: Below-stairs maid, good character, early riser, churchwoman essential, must have been out before.... I flung the paper down—I could readily picture the mistress who had penned those words and I withered. The cold hours of the night bred such fantasies, and killed them as readily.

In due course the porter wandered away and I joined Barty at the door. We gazed out into the pillared vault of the station, lit murkily with flickering yellow lines of gas flames. The station cat mewed, or it might have been an owl. In the night's stillness mice came out to rummage in the platform's litter of paper bags and straw, easy prey for the hungry hunter.

In time a goods train rumbled through, showering sparks and leaving the station quieter and more empty even than before.

I went back to the counter, poured coffee for me and Barty. We talked. We talked even, for a moment or two, about my fine and handsome Captain. And then, suddenly, in the way time has when you've quite despaired of its passing, suddenly it was nearly four o'clock, and the London mail expected, and dawn just beginning to lighten the sky above the sleeping city.

Barty was along at the end of the platform, beyond the station buildings, watching the first stirring of the new day. I quitted the safe shelter of the refreshment rooms and went quietly to join him. The rain had stopped some hours before, leaving the air cool and clean, and breathlessly still. Smoke rose in straight columns from the chimneys of the blacking factory up on the skyline. And away to the east the faintest green streaks of the sunrise were just spreading against the pale, layered clouds. Somewhere not too far away a horse whinnied and kicked his stall. A dog was set barking. Gradually silence returned.

"Might just be in the country," Barty murmured. "Save for them blessed chimneys."

I took his arm in simple friendship and sudden joy at the beauty of the morning. "You'll get your cottage one day, Barty. We'll all get our dreams one day."

He sighed. "Maybe I will, at that... What's your dreams then, Miss Hessie? A country cottage too, maybe? A few hens?"

I was silent, thinking of my dream. It was a dream I had told nobody, for fear of ridicule or worse. As Barty went on speaking I hardly listened, caught up with my own thoughts instead. "Small beginnings, mind," he said. "But they needn't stay that way. I got my pension—ninepence a day. And I got a bit put by from when I quit the service. The Major thought kindly of me, give me something, a gratuity like, out of company funds. I never spent a penny of it...." He shifted his feet. "I mayn't be a whole man, exactly, nor all that fancy, but I daresay I'll never be at a loss to turn an honest penny—"

I should have been paying him proper attention. I should have remembered Amy's words. But I had my own dream and was not disposed to understand another's.

Abruptly he turned to face me. "Thing is, Miss Hessie— though I'm not talking, mind, of this week, nor next, most like—still, the thing is—" He seemed in some difficulty. I dragged myself back to the present. He ruffled his hair distractedly. "The thing is... well, I don't reckon you're fixing to stay your whole life hereabouts, are you?"

"My whole life, Barty? Of course not."

"I didn't reckon you were. You and me's alike in too many things. So—"

Suddenly I felt enormously fond of Barty Hambro, his tanned, honest face, his countryman's way of speaking, the strength of him. I would tell him my secret plan. He was the one person in the world I could trust.

So I did not wait for him to finish. "The thing I'm fixing to do," I burst in, "the thing I'm fixing to do one day is to work a typewriting machine. I'm going to be a typewriter girl."

The words, spoken aloud for the first time, were like poetry. They carried me along. "I'm saving money, Barty. When I've saved enough I'm going away from here—I'm going to have typewriting lessons—there's a school on Commercial Street. I'm going to be a typewriter girl, I'm going to work in a grand office, I'm going to typewrite important letters, even the books of famous men. I'm going to live on my own, in lodgings, and be an independent, self-supporting young lady."

In front of us the sun was coming up, now in a blaze of glory. I laughed aloud. "And when that happens, Barty, I'm never going to have to butter a bun again in all the days of my life."

I ran out of words then, and out of breath too. I turned to him in the innocence of my joy—not a shadow of what he must have been thinking showed on his face as he took my hand and pumped it up and down. "A typewriter girl— that's the very thing! I'd lay a hundred to one you makes a go of it. You'll earn good money—and find a fine husband into the bargain!"

To be honest, a husband was not an idea I had given much thought to—not even in connection with a certain handsome Captain. The possibility of falling in love was often in my mind, but the husband and home that went with it got quite lost in the gay round of my future typewriting life. Once my independence had been gained, could I ever seriously think of giving it up? All the same, I nodded happily at Barty, delighted beyond words by his simple enthusiasm, not thinking at all what it must have cost him.

Now he released me and ran his hand, this time thoughtfully, through his short, soldier-style haircut. "These lessons mind, and your keep while you're taking them—it'll need a mort of money. There's a bit I got put by. I'd be very happy if you would—"

What a dear, generous man he was! I hugged him impulsively. "Bless you, Barty, but I couldn't possibly take your money. Besides, I've saved more than half of what I need already."

In my mood of optimism I wasn't going to tell him—or even remember myself—how long those eleven pounds had taken me to gather. "And anyway," I went on, "you'll need every penny of your savings one day soon—for that little cottage and a pretty wife to share it with you."

A shadow of pain crossed his face, and briefly he turned away. And still I had no inkling of his pain. For such cruel blindness there can be no excuse, its cause being simply the easy selfishness of youth. But he understood, even if I did not. When he turned back to me his face was calm again, and happy. "You're right of course, Miss Hessie. Get there under your own steam. There's no better way. I reckon you know I wish you well."

"And you won't tell my secret?"

"Not if you say so. Not to a soul."

We stayed a moment or two longer, watching the gold in the sky turn slowly to an ominous red, a shepherd's warning indeed. Then a faint thrumming in the rails warned us of the approaching London mail, and we made our way quickly back to the refreshment room.

It seemed that nothing in it had changed—indeed, how could it be otherwise?—that its chairs and tables and ornaments and long mahogany counter were fixed for ever immovable under the harsh lights, that nothing in the world could change the exact disposition of a single item. And yet ... and yet something made me pause in the doorway, momentarily uneasy. The moment passed, but the feeling stayed with me as I moved on in across the shining marble tiles, stayed with me so that I was not wholly unprepared for the surprise that greeted me as I rounded the end of the counter.

Crouched on the floor in the far corner, among the empty wooden skips waiting to go back to the Pipe Lane bakery, and staring piteously up at me, was a handsome young woman, not ill-dressed, in straw boater and shawl and neat blue bombazine. She had a shabby carpet bag clutched against her chest, and an umbrella half-concealed in the rucked-up folds of her skirt. I observed her closely and calmly, for certainly from her attitude there seemed no danger of her launching an immediate attack upon my person. She had, I decided, the broad, well-rounded face of a fashionable beauty, marred only by a slight sharpness of nose and jaw.

Barty was standing in the restaurant entrance, watching the London mail draw in. I called to him above its clatter. "The oddest thing, Barty. Come and see what we've got here."

The girl didn't move, except to press herself more firmly back into the corner. Barty joined me, followed the line of my gaze. "Now there's a to-do." He clucked his tongue disapprovingly. "What's got her so scared, d'you reckon?"

I had no answer. Neither of us approached any nearer to the cowering girl. It was as if we had found a frightened animal and did not want to put it to further terror. Outside on the platform trolleys rattled by on their way to be loaded with the heavy red mail bags. Carriage doors banged, men shouted, the mysterious stillness of the station was so shattered it might never have been.

I knew we should never have left the refreshment room untended. Then the problem of the girl would never have offered itself. Although she presented no obvious threat, her piteousness did not wholly disarm me. Lodged as I had been for six long years in Temple Street, I had seen too many of the ruses humanity could get up to: not only the most poorly-dressed were thieves, not only the most destitute were beggars.

But our indecision could be prolonged no further. The first priority was to get this girl on her feet and looking half-way presentable, in case some customer should appear and, seeing her in her present state, feel obliged to concern himself with her. I moved slowly forward. "There's no need to be afraid," I said. "If you've not done anything wrong we'd like to help."

Even if you have, I thought, and it's not *very* wrong, I doubt you'll find us over-righteous.

Perhaps some of this warmth got into my voice, for the young woman seemed reassured, and struggled to her feet. "I didn't know who was coming. See? I hid away because I didn't know who was coming."

Her sharp tones were a curious contrast to her ladylike clothes and features. "Who did you think might be coming?" I asked her.

She peered about her. "*Him*," she whispered, cowering most theatrically.

Barty stared at her, perplexed. "What sort of '*him*' would that be, then?"

"*Him*—me husband, of course." As the bustle out on the platform died down, and no passenger came to disturb us, so our night visitor began perking up. "I've run away. See? I tell you—first train out of here and you won't see my heels for dust."

She was a strange creature, her appearance at odds with her brassy speech, her aggressiveness hiding only thinly, I thought, a very real fear. There was something about her, too, that was curiously larger than life.

Barty made up his mind more quickly than me, and in his usual no-nonsense way. "What's between you and your husband, missus, is no concern of ours. But the next train's not due out for two hours and more, and we'll be closing this restaurant any minute now. Looks like you'll have a good long wait alone on the platform to think about the rights and wrongs of what you're on."

He started to ease her along to the end of the counter. She wriggled away, made a great play of straightening her hat. "You let me be. I'll go when I'm ready. And I don't really care if he *does* find me here. I've made up my mind —I'm not going up in that thing again, not no matter *what* he says."

It took a moment for her words to make any kind of sense. And when they did, I could only stare at her incredulously. At least the staginess was explained. But could this young woman really be the wife of such a man as that?

She was gaining confidence steadily. Her next words strengthened my suspicions. "Then we'll see who the public really pays their money to gawp at—him or me."

"You're Mrs Deveraux," I said, still not quite believing it.

"Mrs Kitty Deveraux." She preened herself in the big mirror behind the counter. "*Madam* Kitty, if you don't mind. My husband being a Continental. It's on all the posters."

This irritated me. The Captain certainly hadn't sounded like a Continental, not when we'd talked together that very afternoon. "You won't be *Madam* Kitty much longer," I pointed out sharply, "not if you're planning to run away and leave him."

At this all her bravado suddenly faded. She burst into tears. "But what can I do? You don't know what it's like.

You don't know how scared a person gets." Her sobs grew wilder. "You're a kind girl. A good girl. What's a person to do, then? Tell me that...."

This then was the other side to the smiles and the tinsel. This was the truth behind Amy's bandsman's gossip. Barty, quite out of his depth, retired from the situation and went to lock up. The station was quiet now. Evidently there were going to be no callers other than Kitty Deveraux that night.

Her distress seemed so genuine that I led her to a table, sat her down, fetched her hot milk with even a little brandy in it. My own tiredness was quite forgotten. I could only think with compassion of what desperate straits she must have been in, to have fled her husband like this, at the weary, dead hour of the night. I wanted to understand. "Surely he won't force you to go up with him," I said, "not if you tell him how it troubles you?"

She looked up at me, pushing the tear-damped hair back out of her eyes. "What use am I to him else? I bring him good bookings, fat fees, big audiences. He doesn't love me. He couldn't love me, else he'd never...."

Her crying threatened to take over again. But could I really believe my fine and handsome Captain to be such a heartless monster? "You've been doing these jumps for some time," I said with slight asperity. "Have you always found them so difficult?"

"Wasn't so bad at first." She fumbled in her sleeve, produced a minute handkerchief. "Then you gets to hear about other girls. All burnt up down a factory chimney, one girl was. Hit by a train, another. You gets to have nightmares, even when you're awake."

"And Captain Deveraux refuses to listen to you?"

She laughed bitterly. "Take Hereford," she said. "Week before last, that was. Let go in a flaming thunder storm. Lightning flashing hither and yon, and the Captain fair enjoying himself.... 'Kitty,' he says, 'Kitty, we'll get a bob or two extra for this—you'll see. They thinks it's dangerous, but it's not...' Then he goes into some yarn about lightning needing an earth, which makes no sense to me, my hair standing on end with the stuff."

She told a good story—I had to give her that. "Was this the time when your parachute was destroyed?"

"Not *destroyed*, exactly." She began drawing patterns on the tablecloth with the end of her spoon. "Tell the truth, I let it go. Let it go without me. So would you of. The cold up there—you wouldn't credit it. And me just in my tights and my thingummies."

I looked around quickly, relieved to find Barty nowhere in earshot. She was a forward, foolish, saucy creature. All the same, these were hardly grounds for the Captain's seeming cruelty. "The thing is," she went on, "I don't think he's ever been the littlest bit afraid himself so I don't suppose it comes all that easily, understanding them as are."

In spite of his faults, imagined or otherwise, obviously she was proud of him. There was a warmth in her voice now, and a tenderness that told me she'd run from him about as far as she was going to run, and a very few of the right words from me would send her running back.

"What are you going to do now?" I said, as anxiously as I could. "A runaway wife, quite alone, little money, no references... what *are* you going to do?"

She gazed at me with round, innocent eyes. "I daren't go back to him—at least not all on my own." So little it had needed to persuade her. "Will you come with me? Will you? He'll never be so cross if he sees there's two of us. I know you're a kind girl... will you come?"

I held my breath. It was one of those moments of decision when time seems willing to stand still, when the whole universe seems placidly to stop and await the outcome. A multitude of considerations flashed through my mind. There were aspects of Kitty's story I thought overplayed. At the outset of our strange encounter, however, there had seemed to be no doubting her genuine terror of being discovered by her husband. If I went with her, therefore, I would be performing a noble, a charitable act. An unconventional act also—one for which Mrs Skues might never forgive me. An act, moreover, that would bring me to see Captain Edward Deveraux again. And not as a stranger but as his wife's defender....

I should have known that even the universe would finally lose patience. Behind me Barty Hambro shifted his feet in the doorway and cleared his throat. "What's to do, then?" he said. "Are we off, or are you two young ladies going to stay here gassing till all hours? It's time all decent folk but me was fast in bed."

That little joke—*all decent folk but me*—was a part of my life. He'd made it at the end of every Late Call I could remember. It spoke to me poignantly of the safeness of established ways. But there was more to life than mere safeness, and I did not turn to him. "Come with you, Kitty Deveraux?" I said. "At this hour of the morning? I doubt the Captain would welcome either of us for an hour or two yet."

"You'll come then?" She did not wait for confirmation, but bounced to her feet, gathering up her bag and umbrella, all her fears and tears forgotten. "Oh, he never sleeps much on the night before a show, not with the site to prepare and the inflation to see to. We'll find him hard at it along in the Zoo Gardens, or I'm a Dutchman."

I didn't meet Barty's astonished eyes as I took my shawl from its peg behind the door and followed her out past him. The break with six years of secure routine was too prodigious. "I'm going first to the Zoological Gardens with Madam Deveraux," I told him grandly. "The visit won't take long. I'll make my own way back to the hostel from there."

Even then, even as soon as that, I believe I knew I would do no such thing. How it was to come about I had no idea, but I set forth on that cold, forbidding morning with the fantastic notion firmly in my mind that my life was about to begin anew. I left the refreshment rooms, the hostel, Mrs Skues, much as I would leave a suit of ugly, worn-out clothes, without a moment's sorrow. And Barty, who stood and watched me go—I could not grieve for him since I knew with equal certainty that he and I would meet again. Our destinies were interwoven—I was his friend, and he was mine.

Indeed, as I reflected on my way at Kitty's side through the deserted ticket halls and out into the slowly waking city, Barty Hambro was in truth the one and only friend I had.

FOUR

Kitty Deveraux was right. We found the Captain on an open space outside the Lion House, spreading out the huge collapsed envelope of his balloon. And he was by no means the only early riser that morning in the Zoological Gardens.

Everywhere construction gangs were busy, and traction engines puffing and slithering as they manoeuvred wagons onto position, and the Zoo's animals in their houses objecting most vociferously to such goings on.

At the very outset, on leaving the station, I had been astonished to find a horse tram able to take us up Blackboys Hill, being myself fully prepared for the three-mile walk. Kitty informed me that the tram company had run a service for workmen all through the night, by arrangement with the Fete proprietor. She also scoffed mightily at the trams themselves, being a much travelled person and accustomed to the *steam* trams of Britain's more enlightened cities. I briskly told her that we Bristolians had tried such vehicles—they set fire to the trees and terrified the horses for miles around. If that was enlightenment, then we wanted none of it.

Our entrance to the Gardens, however, was contrived to put me firmly back in my place. We were stopped by the man at the gate, a coarse individual in cloth cap and long red muffler.

"How's it going then, Kitty-puss?" he bellowed.

She tossed her head. "I reckon it's nearly gone," she shrieked back.

At this meaningless sally the two of them entered into such raucous laughter as to scare the rooks from the trees above. I sought to pass them, lightly, as if Kitty were nothing to me. Immediately a grubby serge arm shot out across my path and the laughter was turned off like a tap.

"What's this? Sneaking in, is it?" His voice was deafening. "Don't yer read? Hasn't yer learned? Want me to tell what's on the bleeding sign, do yer?"

He pointed to a notice board. UNAUTHORIZED ENTRY FORBIDDEN. Then he caught my wrist and insisted on leading my eye along the notice, like a child, letter by letter.

"No—bleeding—strangers," he declaimed. "That means you. No bleeding strangers—that's what it says. That means you!"

I struggled vainly in his grasp. Workmen were beginning to gather for the show. At last I found my tongue. "I'm with Madam Kitty," I gasped. "She asked me to come with her. I'm her friend. . . ."

At last Kitty condescended to rescue me. "You'd better let her go, Bert," she said. "I suppose she *is* a sort of friend of mine."

Still Bert was jostling me. "She needs a pass. Can't 'ave all sorts tramplin' in and out."

"Come off it—honest as the day is long, that one. Let her in—there's a pet."

"Don't know why I should...." He considered. "Tell you what, Kitty-puss—give us a kiss and I'll let 'er in."

To my shocked amazement she did exactly that, without a moment's hesitation, right in front of all the workmen. A ragged cheer went up. Freed now, I scuttled past the pair of them, terrified that I too might become involved in the crude Postman's Knock.

A moment later Kitty joined me, straightening her hat. "The things I do for you, love," she said.

But she giggled, clearly not much put out, so I forbore to mention who was really doing what for whom. And wondered anyway if my errand was really the one of mercy it had suited me to believe. Certainly my pulse beat shamefully fast at the prospect of seeing my fine and handsome Captain again.

Once inside the grounds we made our way gingerly between half-erected marquees, boxing booths, a wax works, even something claiming to be a *Roller Skating Arena, Fresh from Brooklyn, USA*—In many places naphtha flares still burned, pale now against the gray morning light. A wind was getting up. The red of the dawn was living up to its warning. I saw a gypsy caravan, painted yellow and green, its panels decorated with sprays of bright flowers. Everywhere big angry men with hammers were rushing to and fro. It seemed impossible that more than half of the Fete would be assembled and ready in time for the Mayor's opening at ten.

Captain Deveraux himself was clearly in no better condition than the rest, his balloon still only a flat crumpled mass of ropes and red-and-gold varnished silk. Real progress appeared to have been limited to a strong gaseous smell and the presence of a worried-looking official of the Bristol United Gas Company.

Kitty pushed me forward. "Edward," she called from somewhere in my rear. "Edward—I've come back."

Captain Deveraux looked up from what he was doing, frowned, wiped his hands on his trousers, and circled the untidyness of his balloon to where we were standing. He was in his waistcoat, his shirt sleeves gathered up with rubber bands, his sleek dark hair tousled. I found him as handsome as before, and far more handsome than was proper. Suddenly

I was not quite sure why I was there.

He seemed wholly unsurprised to see me, regarded me neutrally for a moment, and then turned to his wife. "You've come back?" he said, as if not wholly aware that she had ever gone.

She had nothing to say to this. It seemed time for me to perform my errand of mercy. I gulped. "She's come back. But she's not going up in that balloon again. And you mustn't try to make her."

He looked at me again, now with a little more attention. "Ain't I seen you before somewhere?" he said mildly.

For a moment his indifference came as a blow to me. But this was salutary, and drove out my childish fancies. Indeed, reflection told me that this must be its purpose, since I could not believe that he had sincerely so soon forgotten me. "If you do not remember me, sir, it does not matter." I met his eyes boldly. "I'm here on your wife's account, nothing more."

"My wife's account? What's this, then?" He reached past me and dragged her forward, half-playfully. "Where have you been, Kitty my love? And what have you been saying?"

She shook him off with a show of defiance. "Only saying the truth, Edward. I've risked my neck one time too many, You're not catching me up in no balloon, not ever again."

"You go too far, Kitty." His face hardened, and his voice also. "We've been through this a dozen times. I'll hear no more of it."

"This time I mean it."

He sighed with insulting boredom. "You always do mean it. Now run along, there's a good girl. I've a hundred things to see to." To me he bowed perfunctorily. "Your servant, ma'am." He strode off.

Kitty was at my side, and near to tears. Now was the moment for me to come to her aid. But Captain Deveraux was clearly no easy man to cross. In fact, he frightened me so that I was left quite without words.

A few paces off, however, he hesitated and turned. "I remember you now," he said. "You're Hessie Malpass from the station restaurant."

The admission seemed a significant weakening. I walked towards him with new confidence. He smiled warmly.

"And you've come to take Kitty's place for just this once."

I stopped, transfixed.

He held out his hand. "Don't be shy. I should have heard you out at the start. Impatience is a bad habit of mine. You see yourself flying high above the earth. You would like—"

"No!" The word burst from me, a strangled cry. "No, I would not like." Nothing could have been further from my mind. A balloon...a parachute...me in tights and thingummies...the idea was quite preposterous, and my denial positive. "No!" I said again.

"No?" He looked down at me, his head on one side. "So I mistook you? A pity...I swear you would quite capture all their hearts. Two guineas for the fee is fair, I think. You still say no?...It is no matter. Madam Kitty will have second thoughts. She always does."

He bowed again, and went on his way. Other questions immediately claimed his attention: the setting up of a perimeter fence to keep the public at a safe distance, the anxieties of the gas official. Perhaps he knew he could safely leave me to my thoughts. Perhaps he knew I had already succumbed in my heart.

My intellect was to take a little longer. I thought of Kitty. Had this possibility been in her mind also? If so, I did not blame her for the deception. In her frightened condition I might have done the same...Perhaps I was by then in that state of wide-eyed tiredness that borders on insanity. Take her place for just this once? Fly high above the earth? For just this once? I thought of Mrs Skues. Already I had stayed away too long to be back in Temple Street before my absence was discovered. I found I did not care about Mrs Skues. The boldness and novelty of the prospect ahead was already quickening the blood in my veins.

Finally the Captain's words came to me...*a pity... capture all their hearts...two guineas for the fee*...Even now, at this sober distance, I like to believe it was the fee, and a mental picture of the grateful face of Pig, that finally made up my mind for me. The fee, then, and not just the promise of a continued relationship with the dashing Captain Deveraux.

I took Madam Kitty by the arm and led her away to a place out of the wind, a seat in the shelter of a half-assembled carousel. From the nearby Lion House came restive snarls, and a sudden tearing roar magnified by the resonance of the surrounding walls. A tiny midget ran out from under the frames of the carousel, threw his hat in the air, did a little dance, and ran back again. Nobody seemed in the least surprised. Clearly the world was mad, and I with it.

"I think you had better tell me," I said carefully, "exactly what I have to do when I go up with the Captain in his aerostat."

And Kitty laughed and threw her arms about me, and I laughed also.

The next few hours are confused in my mind, not so much hazy as over-vivid, like blurred colour pictures in a children's book. I talked with Kitty. I talked with Captain Deveraux. I was no longer one of Mrs Skues' young ladies—I was an *artiste*. The idea had a certain reckless charm to it.

I wandered off. At some time or other—when much of the Fete seemed still not ready—the Mayor arrived to perform the opening ceremony and the public came surging in. Their roughness unsettled me and I returned—not without several wrong directions—to the balloon enclosure. There I was taken by Kitty into a tent in which there was a camp bed, and permitted to sleep—though for how long I cannot say. But I emerged from the tent refreshed, and aware rather more forcefully of what I had undertaken. Not exactly frightened, I believe, but maybe just a mite apprehensive.

It was early afternoon, and the Fete in full flood about me. Screams and laughter assailed my ears, shouting, the sounds of the alarmed Zoo animals, music from at least two bands and innumerable steam organs. Briefly I remembered Amy and her bandsman sweetheart—I'd never find her in all this, nor she me. Against the stormy skyline a man was performing shakily on a high wire. A group of young working men ambled by, singing coarsely, already rather drunk. And in front of me a large circular barrier of ropes had been erected with, in the middle of it, Captain Deveraux's balloon, the *Emperor*, still hardly a quarter inflated, wallowing on the grass like some stranded sea monster.

The basket was attached now, and lying on its side, well hung about with little bags of sand. I ducked through the ropes and approached it, interested to come to terms with this unimpressive vehicle. It was no more than six feet square at the most, its sides to a height I reckoned would come approximately to my waist. From its open top a profusion of ropes, none too new-looking, trailed away across the grass, tugging occasionally as some small swelling of the balloon caught the wind.

Captain Deveraux was on his hands and knees a few yards away, busy with a needle and cotton. "She's safer than she looks," he said. "Scores of ascents, hundreds of hours of flying time—and not a bone broken." He got to his feet. "It's the landings that are the tricky part, y'see. Basketwork cushions you. Anything else would break up in little bits."

I remarked with a calm show of wit that from the sound of balloon landings I was glad to be coming down by parachute. He was deceived not in the least. "You're worried," he said. "Here—let me show you your harness. It's of the very best—I designed it myself."

He led me into another tent, filled with apparatus of various kinds—ropes, boxes of fireworks, a mound of yellow-and-black striped silk, assorted bundles of string netting. He rummaged and produced a large wooden ring from which various leather straps depended.

"Now, here's a professional secret," he said. "The public thinks you're hanging from this ring by your hands, but you ain't. Not at all. These straps lie under your arms and keep you safe as houses. You just cast off and float down on the breeze. Spare the people below a wave and they're yours for ever."

How simple it all sounded! But I was rested now, and just a little wiser. "What about the girl burnt up down a chimney? And the one hit by a train?"

"You've been listening to Kitty. I tell you, it's as safe as houses. Look—you live in Bristol, surely you read of that good lady who fell from the suspension bridge not two months ago and floated to safety by her skirts alone?" I had indeed read of poor Miss Henley, and sorely pitied her the experience. Captain Deveraux started to laugh, then changed his mind. He laid the wooden ring to one side, sat down on a packing case, motioned me to sit beside him, and took my hands. When he spoke his voice was lower, gentler.

"I won't pretend there ain't risks, Hessie. Of course there are risks. It's not a ride on the railway you're taking—it's a ride in the unpredictable ethereal elements ... But ain't risks what makes life worth living, Hessie? Don't you feel that? To take risks is to be *free*—not trapped in the safe, niminy-piminy lives of ordinary people. Isn't that what matters? Don't you feel that, Hessie?"

I nodded dumbly. I didn't know what I felt. Except that when he took me seriously, and forgot his showmanship, and took my hands in his, then I could listen to him for ever, and follow him clear over the moon if he so desired.

He leaned forward earnestly. "Besides, risks are mainly a matter of common sense. They're halved at once if you can keep from getting rattled. Up there in the air there's things you can do—ropes you can pull upon, for instance. I'll swear you don't *have* to float straight down into a factory chimney, not if you keep your head and don't get rattled."

"Is Kitty," I asked quietly, "is your wife one to get rattled?"

I suppose I was wondering why it was I and not she who was there at that moment. In my absence would he really have forced her up with him against her will? What sort of a man was he?

"Kitty? Well—you've seen her, talked to her..." He was less easy—understandably so, I thought. "She's done some good things... In Leeds, for example, she was so popular that the students pulled her through the streets in an open carriage. With her help we've made the headlines in the scandal sheets often enough. But she gets... over-excited." He gestured vaguely. "And she's tired. A long rest is what she needs—possibly to go away for a while."

He paused. A long rest—how did that place me? My jump was to be for just this once he'd said at the beginning, and I had avoided thinking past it. Hardly muted by the canvas of the tent, the Fete blared on about us. Just this once, and then what? Return to Temple Meads and throw myself on Mrs Skues' mercy? Mrs Skues, whose mercy at the best of times was a variable commodity?

Or just this once, and then again. And again....

"We'll have to see how you shape," he went on. "It's a grand life, if you've the spirit I think you have." He sat back and tweaked at his cuffs. "By the way, there's just one thing you ought to know. Kitty and I ain't married. Not in the least married. It just looks better on the posters."

I felt my ears go hot and I think I must have blushed, for he peered at me closely and then burst out laughing. "Lord bless us, Hessie Malpass, there's nothing for you to look so shocked about. We travel together, that's all. It's a purely professional arrangement. The *Madam* Kitty is just to keep the small-town Mrs Grundys happy."

I believed him. But I was still troubled. "It's more than that to Kitty, sir," I said as boldly as I dared.

He got up, took a pace or two across the tent and back. "She's a rough girl—I don't blame her for wanting to be other than she is. Her life was a hard one before I found her and took pity on her. And she's done well—I'll not deny that. If she gives herself a few airs, likes to think of herself as my wife, why, it harms no one and I'd not want to take it from her."

And no more would I. Her pride in her "husband" who was a "Continental" had been too touching. "What will happen to her now, sir?" I asked.

"She'll make her way. I've paid her well—if she's wise she's put a pretty penny by." He stopped in front of me, hands deep in his trouser pockets. "Your concern becomes you, Hessie. But tell me—what's a man to do? She'd made her choice. You heard her. If she don't care to go up in the dear old *Emperor* any more, then what's a man to do?"

To this, of course, I had no answer. Only time would tell if I was that much braver than she. He lifted me to my feet. "Talk with her, Hessie. Satisfy yourself. You have to get together about the costume, so there'll be plenty of opportunity." He would have said more, but for the sudden sound of creaking and confused shouts close outside the tent. "I must go. I've left the aerostat far too long unattended as it is."

He turned away, then paused, his hand on the tent flap. "There's things about her and me I shouldn't have told you, maybe. Things she might not have wanted me to tell. But we needed to start straight, you and I, cards on the table... You know what I'm asking you?"

I nodded. "If Madam Kitty wants me to know the truth I'm sure she'll tell me soon enough. Till then...."

"Bless you, Hessie. And thank you for your understanding."

Without further word he left the tent. But his gratitude stayed with me, warming me like summer sunshine. I followed him a moment later, after I had calmed my beating heart.

During our conversation the strength of the wind had increased yet more. Also the *Emperor*—already I had begun to think of it by its proud name—had gained somewhat in volume, so that it now lumbered, sometimes fully clear of the grass, in an elephantine fashion from side to side against its restraining ropes. Several men were occupied in tying it down more firmly.

Furthermore, some sort of crisis appeared to be in progress. While the monster was being tamed a heavy black rubber pipe had sprung loose from its lower vent and was thrashing about, filling the air with a heavy smell of coal gas. Shouts were going up for pipes and cigarettes to be doused, while the gas official was struggling with a giant stop-cock mounted on a massive wooden block. Crowds of spectators had gathered to cheer and laugh and generally get in the way. Such alarums and excursions were quite beyond my competence, and anyway no doubt an accepted part of the balloonist's life, so I left them and went in search of Kitty.

I found her easily, for she was in the nearest beer tent, and singing loud enough to be heard out in the open above the popping of the rifle range close by. My work in the refreshment rooms had given me experience of those who had taken drink. She had a good voice, and I did not think her seriously intoxicated, but rather just a cheerful person who liked to sing—and especially, perhaps, when there were other cheerful persons to hear her. I joined her in the tent, and she came with me willingly enough when I suggested that I try on the costume in case alterations might be necessary. It was then half past two or so, the Captain's first tethered ascent tabled for four thirty, my own escapade for six.

Kitty took me to a tiny shed put up for her use near the balloon enclosure. Inside there was a vast clutter, and scarcely room for two of us as well. There was a long broad shelf screwed to one wall, a stool in front of it, a long mirror, a huge, barrel-topped trunk, and any number of smaller valises, some open and spilling their contents every which way.

Kitty perched on the shelf, knocking over a glass and several empty porter bottles as she did so, and swung her legs. "So you're really going to do it," she said. "Straight, I never thought you'd have the nerve."

She could not have given me a better opening if she had tried. "There's still time for you to change your mind, Kitty," I urged. "After all—it's your name on the posters. It's you the people are coming to see."

"Having second thoughts, are you, love?"

I shook my head. "No. But I'd understand it if *you* were."

She leaned back against the wall, stretched her arms luxuriously. "Look, lovey—it's a pair of legs they're coming to see. A pair of legs and a pretty face. . . ." This was an aspect of the affair I'd avoided thinking about. She sighed. "Believe me, pet, I've had enough. First three or four times was alright. It's only later it begins to get you. It's only later you start thinking. . . . The Captain's different, of course. He's got his factory, he's got his blessed research. Them's what keeps him at it—always needing money for his blessed research."

The mention of legs had set me looking fearfully round

the shed for the costume I was to wear. Its probable nature was suddenly horribly clear to me. I dragged my attention back to what Kitty had been saying. "Research? You mean, scientific research? I didn't know Captain Deveraux was a scientist?"

"Beats me what he is." She slid down off her shelf and began fumbling with the straps of the big trunk. "He's got this balloon and tent factory, see, away in Brimscombe. It's over by Stroud, not far—maybe thirty miles or so. But there's things go on there as he don't let nobody know a blind thing about—not nobody, not even me." The straps fell away, and she lifted the lid of the trunk. "Here we are, then. Lucky we're of a size, you and me."

"Kitty," I said desperately, trying to put off the moment of sartorial revelation, "Kitty—tell me ... tell me about the balloon factory. Does that Mr Jowker work there?"

"Jowker?" For a moment she was puzzled. "Oh, you mean the old gent who's sleeping it off round the back. No—he's a new one on me. Wrote the Captain a letter a week or so back. Never did see what was in it." She looked up from rummaging in the trunk and threw out an unmistakable pair of pink tights, followed by something that resembled one of those intimate corset advertisements in the *Woman's Friend*. "Well now, I've gained a bit of weight since I first took up this ballooning lark, so there's a smaller size here if it's needed."

She stood up and eyed me from head to toe. I blushed at her frank appraisal. The shed was suddenly very small indeed, and dusty, and full of the smell of cheap scent and moth balls. Only the asking of questions remained to me.

"Kitty—where does Mr Orme fit in to all this?" I remembered the fragment of letter now dust in my pocket. "And what is Mordello?"

"The things you ask ... Well, there's never been no Mr Orme, not as I've heard of. And Mordello is an old gypsy fortune teller. I expect he's around here somewhere. You often see him at the fairs and fetes." She advanced upon me. "Well now, Hessie Malpass, are you going to get into these here things, or aren't you?"

Having quite run out of questions, Hessie Malpass had no real alternative. It wasn't as if either name really interested me. Though a letter from a solicitor that mentioned a gypsy fortune teller was perhaps a mild curiosity....

Of those female matters that followed, little need—or

indeed should—be said. Suffice it to mention that what I had taken to be merely an undergarment turned out to be the costume more or less in its entirety. And to add that for my face there was the fearful promise of grease-paint, and sequins to be attached with gum arabic to my eyelids. The Whore of Babylon could not have been accoutred worse.

The thought of appearing outside the modest confines of the shed in such a garb was almost beyond contemplation. But then the grateful, virtuous face of Pig appeared in my mind's eye to persuade me, together with the virtuous typewriting future that would now so much more quickly be mine. Strict truthfulness forces me to admit that another face appeared, at least fleetingly—the approving face of my fine and handsome *bachelor* Captain.

Against such persuasions, what chance had I?

Kitty, of course, was hardened to immodesty, and utterly businesslike. "You're better built nor I thought. Just a tiny tuck in the back and this one'll do you a treat." She got out her needle, sucked the end of her thread. "There'll have to be an announcement, mind."

"An announcement?" I was a little breathless, rebuttoning the back of my dress.

"Of course. You're the stand-in. I mean, it's only fair." One eye closed, her tongue sticking out, she threaded the needle. "Though what the Fete Proprietor's going to say I tremble to think ... After all, it's Madam Kitty's the draw, not some inexperienced little nobody. If you'll pardon the expression."

I pardoned the expression. It was rather the thought of the announcement that disturbed. Everybody would know. It would get back to Mrs Skues—Mrs Skues, whose girls always did so well for theirselves. It might even get back to my secret benefactor—it was the way of benefactors, I suspected strongly, to be stuffy about such matters.

I dealt with the last button. "Need the Proprietor know?" I began tentatively. "I know I'm not nearly as pretty as you, and a complete beginner, but perhaps—with the costume and all—people wouldn't notice...."

However reasonable, I could see the idea did not please. Mercifully, I had a sudden better one. "No—no, I'm sure you're right," I said craftily. "After all, once the Proprietor's heard your reasons, he's bound to understand."

Kitty's needle stopped moving. "Easy enough to say I been took sick," she offered.

"And I'd support you, of course. But the trouble with that is, you've been seen out and about...." A further refinement occurred to me. "And having such a good time, too."

Slowly she caught my meaning. "You're saying there's them as would like to believe it was the drink?"

I sighed piously. "The world is full of mean-minded people."

"True word you said there, alright." She stitched in silence for some seconds. Suddenly she glared across to me. "Look here, Hessie Malpass, it's no use—I'm not allowing no announcements, and that's flat. You can go on up, seeing you're so set on it, but there I draw the line. I'm sorry, pet, but I got myself to think of. And if you don't like it you can do the other thing."

I did like it. I liked it enough to let her browbeat me into accepting it. And felt hardly a twinge of shame.

All afternoon the weather worsened. As the time for Captain Deveraux' tether ascent approached, showers of rain became frequent, the wind during them gusting till the grass was flattened and loose tent walls snapped like whips. The carousel closed down, and the high wire walker moved his show into a neighboring marquee. At four fifteen Kitty and I joined the Captain in the balloon enclosure, our heads bowed to the elements.

He was attired now in clothes of a vaguely nautical design —dark blue reefer jacket and peaked cap over knickerbockers and smartly-striped hose. His shirt was white, with a loosely tied red-and-white spotted neckerchief. Looking about me, I was surprised at the large number of people who had stayed to brave the elements in the hope of an ascent.

"Not surprising at all," the Captain told me. "They know just how dangerous ballooning is in this kind of weather. They're hoping for a spill. And if I was mad enough to attempt an ascent in this they'd almost certainly get one!"

That I could well imagine. Close above our heads the Emperor, though restrained by many ropes, was leaping and flailing from side to side, its basket clattering beneath it enough to shake any poor occupant to pieces. "But they've paid their money," I said. "What'll you do if you have to cancel?"

"Give it to them back." He shrugged. "They won't like it —and neither will I. But what can I do? Just put off the decision as long as possible in the hope that things improve. Which they won't."

He looked up anxiously at the balloon, shielding his eyes

from a sharp flurry of rain. "I only wish I could get some more gas in. When the Emperor's full and round and sleek he rides the wind like a bird...."

Kitty stepped forward, tugged at his sleeve. "I'm pushing off now," she said. "I've fixed up Hessie, now I'm making myself scarce. It'll save a lot of talk—the minds some people have. She'll tell you."

I moved away a pace, but covertly watched their parting for what it might tell me of their feelings for each other.

They stood regarding each other for some moments. "You're going on up, then?" she finally asked.

"Wind and weather permitting," he replied.

"Don't expect me to visit you in the hospital," she said.

"I won't."

He got out a notebook, and began absently leafing through it. Dismissed, she walked away. Was there really to be nothing more? I watched her go to the shed, fetch her umbrella and carpet bag, and wander quietly off. A strictly business relationship, he'd told me. Yet it seemed a little too casual, even for that. Would they not meet again, and say their farewells more properly?

He closed his notebook with a snap. "Well, Hessie Malpass? What's this Kitty said you're to tell me?"

I explained what Kitty and I had agreed, raising my voice to make myself heard above the creaking of the balloon's ropes and its angry buffeting. But he did not seem particularly interested—more than half his attention being understandably elsewhere, surveying the low, scurrying clouds, testing with his eyes the strained fabric of his aerostat. I wound up my resumé as quickly as I could: the costume was altered to perfection and I myself ready for final instruction at any time he might find convenient.

He waved me impatiently to one side. "Later, child. Later...."

But he caught my arm as I was turning a little sadly to go. "You need do none of this, Hester. Do you understand that? You owe me nothing—nothing at all." He spoke intently, peering into my face. "Tell me, child—are you not afraid?"

His sudden concern, after such an abrupt dismissal, confused me. But I answered truthfully enough. "No sir, I'm not afraid. I don't believe you would make an ascent with me if there were any very great danger."

"Quite right... You do well to remind me of my duty." He shook my arm up and down several times, as though there were other matters of which he would have spoken, had the occasion been right. But the crowd around us was becoming restive. He frowned at its noise, released me, and went to whisper urgently with one of the men who were guarding the balloon's mooring ropes. The man moved quietly away, and Captain Deveraux took his place.

At the Captain's appearance the crowd fell momentarily silent, no doubt expecting some immediate excitement. But when he did nothing but stand by the rope, staring anxiously up at the angry heavens, its restlessness soon returned. Jeers were offered, fists were shaken, and a few bottles were thrown. Still he ignored them. He appeared to be waiting for something. And this indeed proved to be the case, for it was not until the man he had sent on the mysterious errand returned and caught his eye and nodded that he squared his shoulders and stepped forward to address the raucous onlookers.

His decision made, he carried it through boldly. In a voice loud enough to carry to the very back of the assemblage he explained that owing to the very bad weather the first balloon ascent of the afternoon must regrettably be abandoned. The British climate, he reminded them with a small attempt at humour, was one of the few things not susceptible to reasoned argument. Spectators' money would be returned to them.

The response was immediate, and ugly. Muttering broke out, the jeers intensified, and fists were shaken more fiercely across the flimsy rope barrier. Worse would certainly have occurred, had not the two policemen wisely sent for by Captain Deveraux appeared in ponderous disapproval by the ticket booth. Thus intimidated, the audience—though still shouting coarse abuse—left in reasonably good order, collecting their refunded entrance money at the gate in the high canvas screens that had been erected round the balloon enclosure.

Above us the red-and-gold bulk of the Emperor continued to strain to be away. Captain Deveraux turned to me, laughing, his tiredness vanished, his dynamism quite restored by the small crisis. He was clearly a man who thrived on danger. "We'll never make ourselves rich that way, Hessie. There's half the day's profit gone! So pray for a break in the weather. Besides, I warrant we'll never get away with things as easily a second time."

I asked him what he meant.

He frowned, and swept his hair back out of his eyes.

"Y'see, Hessie, there's no knowing what a crowd'll do.... There was a balloonist up in Manchester—a good man too —who refused to go up on account of the weather. By all reports it was blowing a gale and a half. He offered them their money back, but they weren't satisfied. They broke through the barriers, destroyed his aerostat, trampled it to pieces. He only got away safely himself after a tussle, and with strong police protection...."

He sighed, then recovered himself and waved jauntily at the last of his departing audience. "They're a rum lot, Hessie. One moment they love you, the next moment they'd gladly murder you. We live in violent times. It's part of the fascination of the job."

He looked down at me, an encouraging smile wrinkling the corners of his eyes. "But as for you, little Hessie, be sure they'd never harm a hair of your head. So young and pretty, they'll take you to their hearts. You'll be their queen, their goddess...."

There was a moment's silence between us, his hand resting gently on my shoulder, his presence infinitely warm and reassuring. A queen, a goddess—was this the showman in him speaking? At times he seemed so serious, so earnestly concerned for me—at others the merest spinner of words. Would I ever know his true nature? One thing alone I knew, that I must not fail him: he was a man possessed of a rare certainty, a courageous man, a man who wrung from life the very most it had to offer. And his good opinion was worth more to me than anything in the world.

The moment passed, and the Fete blared on about us. Captain Deveraux removed his hand from my shoulder and consulted a fine gold watch from the pocket of his reefer jacket. "I must leave you, Hessie. There's a man I need to see.... If the weather improves we'll be making our grand ascent in about an hour and a half. I suggest you take a bite to eat—there's some sandwiches and fruit in the tent."

Dismissing me thus with typical abruptness now that his mind was back on the day's practicalities, he strode away, circled the men on the tethering ropes, gave them their instructions, and briskly left the balloon enclosure. The world was a drabber place without him.

In the hour that followed the weather lightened: the sky cleared a little and the wind abated. More gas was fed into the balloon so that it rode huge and serene, tugging but gently at its moorings. I tried to feel whole-heartedly glad at this marked improvement, and to put out of my mind the sneaking regret that natural causes were clearly not about to spare me my final fearful moment of truth.

As the time drew near I went to the little shed where I must change. I dressed myself in my fairground finery, avoiding as best I could my reflection in the cracked mirror on the wall. In particular, any sight of my lower limbs, for their pink brazenness was a source of great shame to me. Indeed, it was the thought of exhibiting these to the rude public gaze far more than fear for the future that filled me with misgivings.

Once clothed as much as I was going to be, I seated myself on the rough stool, took up a small hand mirror, and essayed the next stage in my transformation—the application of greasepaint in the manner Kitty had indicated. Although she had presented this as a simple task, the early results of my efforts were quite astonishing. No Judy could ever have faced her Punch with cheeks as improbably carmined as mine. With experience, however, and the soiling of many face towels, my skill improved. Time passed and finally I allowed myself to be satisfied.

As I surveyed the result in the little spotted oval of glass the strong impression came over me that this face was not, could not be mine, that it had nothing to do with me at all. Comforted, emboldened, I stood up and turned for the first time fully to the mirror on the wall. I revolved slowly in front of it. And again the image was not mine, could not possibly be mine. This brassy, half-naked creature in the glass—she had nothing in common with Hester Malpass. Even the hair was different, fluffed up, with a sparkling paste comb in it. She wasn't me, she was some quite different person altogether.

My misgivings disappeared. I felt strangely free. Suddenly greatly excited, I grabbed a crimson velvet cloak from the bottom of the trunk, shook the moth balls from it, wrapped it about me, and stepped boldly from the shed.

It cannot be said that this thrilling apparition's first arrival on the stage of life was an unqualified success. Truth to tell, it went wholly unnoticed. A considerable crowd had gathered, both inside the balloon enclosure and in the area immediately outside where the sixpenny ticket was saved and the view almost equally rewarding. All attention, however, was upon the balloon itself, and rested on me not at all—which I saw at once to be a substantial mercy, since the people were almost as impatient and angry as I had seen them once before, and I would not have cared to be the butt of their unfriendliness. My Captain still being nowhere to be seen, I thought it wise to go in search of him.

I knew not where to go, of course. But, as chance would have it, I had not wandered long between the tents and gaudy fairground booths before voices came to me, familiar voices raised even above the surrounding Babel.

The first was hoarse, the unmistakable tones of Mr Jowker. So he then was the "friend" my Captain had needed to see. "... but the wind, dear Capting—you'd never trust it, surely? The game, sir, ain't surely worth the candle?"

Then the Captain's reply. "Nonsense, man. It's my best chance in months, I tell you."

I circled the nearest tent, trying to find the two men. And still their voices came to me. "But the plans has changed, Capting. There's the girl to think of now. I must humbly remind you, sir, of your responsibilities. If she was to come to harm, then what—"

"You think I'm a fool, Jowker? It's just that we do not yet know for certain if—"

What they did not yet know for certain I was not at that moment to discover, for I came upon them then, standing together in the sheltered lee of a waxwork show. Mr Jowker saw me first, touched the Captain's sleeve, and pointed.

The Captain turned, looked me up and down, and made an effort to calm himself. "Hessie, I do declare. And girded for the fray. That cloak becomes you mighty well." Was his smile false? I could not tell. He gestured in the direction of his companion. "You probably guessed, my dear, friend Jowker and I were just having a little argument. But you haven't met. Hessie Malpass, this is Mr Ambrose Jowker, an honoured friend and helper."

I curtsied slightly, keeping the velvet cloak tight about me. Mr Jowker bowed as discreetly as any butler. He was wearing the previous day's clothes, now the worse for a night evidently spent in some hay.

"Miss Malpass—my pleasure h'entirely." He sought his shirt cuffs in the depths of his coat sleeves, found them, and pulled them grandly down over his boney wrists. "And as for any little argument, far be it from me to—"

Captain Deveraux interrupted with little civility his "honoured friend and helper." "We were discussing the ascent, my dear. Jowker thinks I should cancel."

That had been at least a part of what they had been

discussing. "The day does seem a lot brighter, sir," I said, not knowing quite what would please him. "And the wind less fierce."

"A doubtful blessing," intoned Mr Jowker. "A veritable snare and a delusion."

Captain Deveraux stared up at the sky. "You've been out in the open, Hessie. This wind—what would be its direction?"

I thought back carefully to the conditions in the balloon enclosure. "It comes from behind the Lion House, sir, and goes on down across the valley."

"There you are, Jowker." Captain Deveraux sighed. "A temptation—you must admit it's a sore temptation."

"A humble question, Capting—who would require two birds in the bush when one is already safely in the hand?"

Their unmannerly mysteries angered me. If I myself was the bird referred to, then I was in no one's hand at all. I was my own property, come what may. "You may not have a choice, Captain," I said with some acerbity. "There's a big crowd along at the balloon enclosure. They've been kept waiting and they're not at all pleased. I would not like to be the one to tell them if you decide to cancel."

Captain Deveraux squared his shoulders, rammed his cap more firmly down upon his head. "I must go to them at once ..." He turned to me, adventure flashing in his eyes. "Good flying weather, eh? A clear sky and a steady breeze? You're not put out with me, are you, Hessie? We'll do it then, you and I?"

His eagerness was irresistible. Of course I was not put out with him. How could anyone long remain put out with such innocent enthusiasm? Hardly daring to speak, I nodded my joyful willingness.

"Good girl. Then I'll go ahead. Just give me five minutes to make ready for your grand entrance." He whirled round, clapped Mr Jowker's shoulder so that the old man staggered. "A simple ascent, friend Jowker. Nothing more—I promise."

Then he was gone, striding away between the tent stays, Mr Ambrose Jowker scrabbling after him. "Not wise, dear Capting.... Two birds in the bush, I say, when...."

I watched them out of sight, Mr Jowker taking three steps to the Captain's one, tacking to and fro behind him and bleating as he went. A strange associate, this "honoured friend and helper," this man Kitty had clearly not seen before today.... And why his great concern for my safety? Was it perhaps just that the Captain, in his vigour and the rareness of his certainty, frightened the battered old man just a little?

I followed them slowly, thoughtfully, taking a detour to fill out the five minutes of preparations necessary before my grand entrance, my way leading me past a gypsy caravan, green and yellow, painted with flowers. Insensibly my steps slowed, then halted altogether. Though my mind had been far away, yet I knew in some strange way that I had not stopped entirely of my own free will. I found myself close by the caravan steps, held fast in my tracks, transfixed, quite unable to move.

The sense of being without a will of my own intensified. Yet with it came no fear. I waited, quite at peace, while the little door above me opened and an elderly gypsy in shabby moleskins came slowly down the steps.

"You wanted me?" he asked, his voice deep and low.

I knew not how to answer. Briefly, inexplicably, it seemed to me that I had indeed wanted him.

He regarded me calmly. "You wanted Mordello," he said, this time no trace of question in his voice.

At the sound of his name I panicked, and would have fled had not some force still held me there. "No—no, I wanted nobody. I must go. Captain Deveraux is waiting. I must—"

"Captain Deveraux can wait a moment longer." He seated himself tranquilly upon an upturned bucket. "You would not have come to me, Hester, if there had not been a good and sufficient reason." He closed his eyes. "I know your name, you see—as I know the name of Edmund your father. Mordello knows many things. You would be wise to listen."

"I have no time. The crowd is angry. I—"

"You think I seek out of vanity to impress. That is not so. Mordello has no need. But when he knows, he must speak...." He opened his eyes. My gaze was drawn to them. They were as black and empty as pits. "There has been tragedy in your life, Hester, tragedy six years past and not of your doing. See that you do not soon bring about a tragedy as great."

He moved his head slowly from side to side, as if he were trying to recall some long-forgotten memory. "Once there was a man who gave, in order that he might withhold. Now there is a man again, this time with the false glint of guineas in his hand. See that you do not—"

At last I broke away, common sense coming to my rescue. *A man with the false glint of guineas* ... it was really too ridiculous. It reminded me of advertisements in the papers: Your future for 9d. Dangers to be Avoided, 2/6d. Send Age. Numerous Testimonials....

"Thank you, Mr Mordello," I said firmly. "I'm sure you're very clever. But the past is best forgotten—and the future, if fixed and certain, is best not known."

I was pleased with that, and began to walk away. I *could* walk away. The whole episode had been a nonsense, half a dream perhaps. Yet as I went the gypsy's voice followed me, distant yet clear, as if down a long tunnel. "... the secret Orme seeks is yours and none other's. Remember that. And when you find it—see that you do not share it unwisely."

Then, almost—at the mention of Orme—almost I went back to him. How could he know what had been written on that letter's charred fragment? But I kept walking—the man was a charlatan, up to all the tricks. It was a name he could have picked up anywhere, a hook on which to snare my reluctant credulity. If I went back to him, in a moment I'd be asked to cross his palm with silver. He had nothing for me, nothing but superstitious mumbo-jumbo....

And yet. And yet he had not been like other fortune tellers, ogling crystal balls and promising journeys across the sea.... My pace slowed again. And in that instant, with all within me muddled and uncertain, I raised my head and saw, towering above the surrounding tents and fairground gimcrackery, the giant red-and gold bulk of the Emperor. It waited for me, silent and magnificent. And, hanging from its side, the huge umbrella stripes of my parachute, stretched over its bamboo frame, waiting for me also.

At such a sight all indecision ceased. I could delay no longer.

As I ran towards the balloon enclosure a sudden gust of wind tore at my velvet cloak. The sky was ominous, and darkening with every step I took. I pushed through the crowd, which was silent now, expectant. The inner barrier was ringed with policemen, but no more than the merest handful. Mr Jowker had obviously abandoned his arguments and retired, for he was nowhere to be seen. Captain Deveraux was already in the basket of the balloon, lurching a few feet above the ground. He called to the policemen and they let me through.

My appearance in the central cleared arena was greeted by a subdued murmur that quickly spread and rose to a strange, almost animal roar. This, then, was my audience. I turned to them, that they should not think me afraid, and swept the cloak from my shoulders. The wind, gusting now, nearly ripped the fabric from my fingers. The noise about me increased. The ring of policemen staggered, then held firm. I stared at the faces lining the ropes: their expressions were like nothing I had ever seen—gloating, angry, fiercely laughing, men and women alike. Children too, pointing, shouting I knew not what. I backed towards the balloon, bowing and smiling, bowing and smiling....

Suddenly I was close to the basket, and Captain Deveraux' voice sounded in my ear. "Well done, Hessie. We'll make a star of you yet. Never show 'em you're scared.... Now get in quick, for God's sake. They're in an ugly mood—if we delay much longer there'll be no holding 'em."

Still my eyes were on their faces, trying to see humanity in them, trying to understand what it was they wanted. The Captain was pulling at me, urging me to hurry. I stood in a daze.

Then, all at once, a waving arm attracted my attention, and below it at last—thank God—a friendly face, a familiar face. There, fighting tenaciously for his position by the rope, was Barty Hambro.

A moment later he had broken through the rope, even through the cordon of police. I ran towards him: I needed him—more than anything I needed a friend in this hell of gaping faces. "Barty—dear Barty... how is it you're here? Has Mrs Skues let you come?"

He shook his head. "I've risked it. I had to warn you."

"Warn me? Warn me of what?"

The noise all around was deafening. We were bawling at each other. At any moment the police would be engulfed.

"Warn you there's a warrant out for your arrest." He seemed near to weeping. "The contents of the till, the silver cup—they're gone. And with you gone too, Miss Hessie, it's as if you must of took them."

I did not believe him. "But that's impossible. How could—"

"It don't look so good, Miss Hessie. I had to warn you...."

I was pulled away. Captain Deveraux had left the balloon, was at my side, dragging me back. His words were lost to me. Above us the sky was whirling by like an angry sea. Rain was beginning to fall. Somehow I scrambled up over the swaying side of the basket and collapsed in a heap on the bottom. Behind me the Captain was shouting instructions.

The basket staggered sideways, his feet arrived close by my head. I struggled to get up.

"It's madness," he was saying. "But we'll give them this show, you and I...."

Around us the cordon had completely disintegrated, and people were streaming across the beaten grass, jostling the men on the ends of the tethering ropes. The balloon rose jerkily till it was restrained a few feet above their gaping faces. It leaned steeply in the wind. I collected myself, remembered my duties, began to smile and wave. The Captain, too, was calmer now. He stood beside me and smiled and waved also.

"One of my closer shaves," he murmured. "Though unless I'm much mistaken our real troubles are only just beginning."

Close above my head were the cords from my parachute, and the wooden ring. Captain Deveraux signalled magnificently with his arm and the tethering ropes were released. The upturned faces below us fell away, dwindled with astonishing rapidity. And with them the noises of the Fete dwindled also. We were carried on the wind, silently and effortlessly, out across the valley.

FIVE

Looking back on it, I could wish that my first experience of the miracle of flight could have been undertaken with a mind unagitated, fully receptive to the many new and exciting experiences crowding in upon me. In the event, however, my mind could scarcely have been more agitated or less receptive.

I had, so it seemed, but barely escaped with my life from a ravening horde. I was suddenly an accused thief, and without the wherewithal to prove my innocence. I had been seriously distressed by the cheap trickery of a fairground soothsayer. I was dressed like a vulgar music hall entertainer.

I was masquerading under another's name, and I was embarked all unthinking upon a career both disreputable and quite immoderately dangerous. In addition, I was alone, several hundred feet above the surface of the earth, in the company of a man who, wholly fascinating though I might find him, had but twelve short hours before been a total stranger to me.

In such circumstances the miracle of flight seemed no miracle at all. I closed my mind to everything—to past and future, to the stranger at my side, to the swaying of the basket, to the intermittent rattle of raindrops on the envelope above my head, to the steady circling of trees and rooftops beneath my feet—and concentrated instead upon a more prosaic matter: the proper disposition of the parachute harness straps under my arms.

The Captain, too, was occupied with practicalities—hauling up ropes, examining certain scientific instruments, adjusting minutely the lower vent of our supportive envelope: so occupied, in fact, that it was not until I had completed the attachment of the harness to my satisfaction that he took sufficient note of me to see what I was doing.

"Good heavens, child," he exclaimed. "What *are* you up to?"

I was affronted. "Making myself ready, sir. I would not have you think me a laggard."

"Ready? Ready to jump, you mean? Why, bless you, that won't be necessary this trip at all." He directed my gaze downwards, over the edge of the basket. "Look there, Hessie. Do you see the Gardens? Do you see the people that we left behind?"

Stare as I might, I had to confess that I did not. He put an arm round my shoulder.

"And no more, I warrant, can they see you. This madcap wind has carried us far beyond their vision. Save your courage for another day, Hessie. Once clear of the city I'll see what can be done about bringing us safely to the ground."

In the stillness of the air about us it was hard to believe that we could have journeyed any distance at all. I searched the city below for the tents and open spaces of the Gardens we had so recently left, sure that it was but some trick of unfamiliarity that hid them from me. Only then, as I saw how the buildings sped by, did I realise that we were indeed travelling with the rapidity of the wind—that the air about us was still only because we were one with the wind, on it and in it and truly a part of it.

The sensation was enthralling. I felt I could sail on thus across the face of the earth for ever. Away to the north was the thrilling sweep of the Avon gorge, spanned by Brunel's new bridge on which I could incredibly look down and see carriages and even the tiny figures of foot travellers; while below me attic windows, inner courtyards, gardens undreamt-of behind high walls, all were revealed to me. I gazed down upon a hansom cab toiling up a cobbled hill. I made out the dark sweep of the railway line, and longed to see a train upon it. I saw the silver ribbon of the estuary far ahead, and the Welsh hills beyond, their summits hidden in the clouds. I was riding the ethereal elements. I remembered the Captain's words and felt myself indeed a queen, a goddess. . . .

A shout from him as he struggled with bags of ballast sand brought me back to my senses. Directly in our path lay a rise in the land, topped by a confusion of factory chimneys. I was still so unafraid and bemused by the seeming sureness of our progress that I believe I would have sailed straight into them without lifting a finger. Fortunately the Captain was no such dreamer. He tore at canvas fastenings and sand trailed away like smoke beneath us, a new phenomenon for me to watch and marvel at.

"We're rising." He gripped the side of the basket. "We're going to clear them, Hessie. I think we're going to clear them. . . ."

For myself, I had no doubt whatsoever that we would clear them. And clear them we did, with a margin so thrilling that for one brief second I was able to stare directly into a soot-caked orifice as black and terrible as some gigantic cannon-mouth. Then, suddenly, we were in cloud, and I was cold and wet, and there was nothing to see on every side but chill grey mist.

The stillness was uncanny. Our frail craft of ropes and basket-work became a ship, a becalmed Spanish galleon, drifting, fog-bound, powerless. I shivered, and dared not move for the fierce loud creakings I made. Above, below, and on every side the greyness was uniform, and without end.

"Are we still going up?" I whispered.

"I don't know." He pored over his instruments. "I don't think so. But if we are, the weight of the condensation on the gas bag will soon bring us down again."

I stared up at the huge, silent globe. Moisture clung in pearls to its crimson silk, merged into tiny rivulets, dripped soundlessly. The Captain spoke again, his voice thrown back hollowly from all sides by the surrounding walls of mist. "Times like this, Hessie, how one longs for a dirigible...." He spoke as if entranced, in a dream. "How one longs to be master... even here, to be master of one's destiny...."

"A *dirigible?*" I had lost his meaning. "What is that?"

"Don't you remember? Don't you remember my little Josephine? To be able to travel at will, Hessie—up, down; right, left; forwards, backwards... All at one's own whim, Hessie. Power, child, power to vanquish even the ethereal elements...." He gestured languorously. "There's a Frenchman, Hessie—he's offering a prize, a prize of fifty thousand francs. Fifty thousand francs for a single flight—just one negotiation of a prepared course, there and back within the thirty minutes. To be master of one's destiny... now, wouldn't that *really* be ballooning, my dear? Wouldn't it?"

I made no answer. His trance-like enthusiasm passed me by. Just at that moment ballooning—in whatever direction —had suddenly lost its charm for me. I felt overwhelmingly alone, as if he and I were the only persons left alive, poised for all eternity in a world of drifting grey vapours and rustling quiet.

I shivered again, not only from fear, and wished prosaically for the velvet cloak left on the ground somehow in the scramble to be off. Captain Deveraux saw, and took off his jacket, and placed it about my naked shoulders. "We'll be out of this soon, Hessie," he murmured gently. "The earth's still down there where it always was. There's nothing to be afraid of."

As though to belie his words, the basket gave an abrupt lurch and the cloud appeared to boil about us. Shreds of mist tore by, and the silence was filled with loud squeaks and whispers as the ropes above us shifted minutely against the belled silk. I felt a wind on my cheeks, though from what direction it came I could not determine.

The Captain remained calm, standing, legs astride, his hands resting lightly on the basket's edge. Gossamers of dew had formed on his eyebrows and moustache. "Nothing to worry about," he said. "Just a boundary layer between two air currents. We're certainly going down now, and quickly."

Almost at once the mist above us thinned, gave way to a curiously dead grey light, and we were in clear air again. The outskirts of the city were below us now, the panorama no longer magical but drab and faintly menacing. The estuary was now much nearer. And as if to cap our miseries, rain began to fall steadily on all sides.

Captain Deveraux remained untroubled. Indeed, he had produced a telescope and was interestedly scanning the rooftops. "Incredible," he muttered. "I could not have done better if I had tried...."

For myself, I could see no reason to rejoice. He would put us down, he had said, once clear of the city—yet we appeared to be descending rapidly into a suburban area thickly set with trees and large, turretted houses. I reassured myself with the thought that any minute he would shed some ballast to take us skyward again.... But still we fell, angling steeply down on the wind, till it seemed certain that we must crash, that he had lost his reason and was plummetting us to disaster.

I shouted to him but he made no move. I knew that time was running out—the weight of the rain that cascaded about us made our descent only the more inexorable.

Blind instinct drove me to action. I clutched at sodden, slippery ropes and dragged myself up till I was crouched on the edge of the basket. At least I would be able to jump clear at the moment of impact. Perhaps I had some innocent notion that the parachute to which I was still attached might bear me up and break my fall.

Then, at last, when surely it was too late, the shining rooftops so near I could see their leaf-clogged gutters, then, miraculously, he acted. "Don't jump, Hessie!" he cried. "For God's sake, don't jump—you'll be dashed to pieces!"

I clung therefore, frozen with fear, not daring to move a muscle. He tore at sandbags, shed ballast in great gouts of sodden sand. The balloon checked sickeningly, bounded upwards with a jerk that dragged one of the ropes I held clear from my hand. I swung out dizzily, scrabbled for a new hand hold, swayed for an eternity above the circling void.... Then my hand found a new rope and locked round it with the tenacity of a drowning man's. The Captain was by me now, gripping my ankles. The ground beneath me diminished faster and faster, as if I was falling from it, falling helplessly out into the limitless depths of the sky.

Gradually his voice came to me, soothing my mindless terror. "Hessie, my dear ... Hessie, my pet ... There was no danger. I'd never have let you come to any harm. We were clear by five hundred feet at least—I'd never have let you come to any harm...."

The falling slowed, then stopped. The earth no longer diminished like a stone cast down a well. I could tear my eyes from it, could remember where I was, what I must do. I listened to the Captain's gentle voice, coaxing me to come down, to come back into safety. I felt more ashamed of myself than I could say. But still it took strength to break the grip my fingers had on the ropes about me, and determination to move my feet even an inch on the canvas-bound upper rim of the basket.

It was at this crucial moment that a contrary gust of wind caught the Emperor, spinning us sideways and down, in an evil, cork-screwing motion. My senses, only just then adjusted to security, were slow to react. My balance went, I kicked out wildly, quite breaking the Captain's safe grasp on my ankles. I snatched too late at ropes that seemed to leap maliciously beyond my reach. I fell, and screamed in the extremity of my terror.

I fell outwards, in an arc, on the cords of my parachute. For a moment I dangled. Then, far above my head, the parachute release mechanism went into operation, severing my link with the balloon, and I floated free. Free of the balloon, free of my fine and handsome Captain, free of everything but the sighing, vertiginous acres of the upper air. And around me the rain drifted slowly, almost caressingly down onto the earth below.

To say that I retained my sanity during the timeless period of my descent would be presumptuous. Certainly I was beyond fear then. Indeed, at one moment I think I laughed aloud and showered kisses down upon an assembled, invisible multitude. Certainly I was capable of receiving vivid and, I believe, accurate impressions: principally of the total emptiness of the sky around—which I worked out to be on account of the sudden release of my weight lifting the Captain's balloon abruptly into the clouds close above. Certainly I was able to feel both cold and wet, my eyes stinging with greasepaint running down from smeared lids. But I made no plans, contemplating not at all the inevitable moment when my leaflike descent must terminate. And I was aware not in the least of the perilous and utter solitude that now in retrospect appalls me, suspended there, beyond all succour, between a leaden, hurrying sky and the indifferent earth below.

A proper sense of my predicament came late, and agonisingly, forced on me by the sudden realisation that all was not right with the disposition of my harness straps. The cause, no doubt, was my unskilful fastening. The effect was a painful constriction of my chest and shoulder-blades, and the inescapable impression that I was, slowly but helplessly, slipping out.

Although my height by then was not great, I could very well see that the time had positively not come when my parachute and I could safely part company. That much being clear, blind instinct again took control. And for the second time in a very few minutes, blind instinct was wrong.

It had me grasp convulsively at the wooden ring above my head. Immediately the harness slid easily up past my narrowed shoulders, upwards till I was hanging only by my arms.

That I am here to tell the tale is proof conclusive that my arms did not fail me. The final moments of my descent, therefore, shall be as brief in the telling as they were in the event.

I drifted, treetop high, across a lane, over a wall, the length of a lawn and shrubbery, blundering now into pine branches as I passed, then above a low line of grey-stone buildings, sinking steadily, till I was brought up sharp against the upper storey of the imposing house beyond. There I stuck for a moment, like a human fly, aware of shouting and agitation in the courtyard below, before I slithered down to the convenient roof of a ground floor bay window. On its sloping tiles I lingered very briefly. Of my arrival on the wet paving stones of the courtyard itself I know nothing: except that it must have happened, and that I was assuredly very fortunate to do myself no lasting injury thereby.

I remember little of the next several hours, just fleeting moments of consciousness accompanied by pain and nausea and the heavy smell of ether. Mostly I inhabited an uneasy dream world, reliving previous events confusedly, as in a distorting mirror. In these visions the gypsy Mordello played an unreasonably large part, his swarthy face reduplicated in the crowds that jeered, his deep voice echoing through deserted station concourses, his caravan bearing me and innocent Barty Hambro at a breakneck, runaway pace down Blackboy's Hill at dead of night into a wall of unseen, ice-grey mist. This last moment, when the mist closed about me and Mordello's laughter rang in my ears, I remember most acutely, for it was then that I cried out in terror and became in that instant fully awake, sweating, tossing my head from side to side, clutching the cold metal uprights of the bed on which I lay.

In that instant, also, I recognized the dizzying ride of my dream: it was a ride I had conjured countless times before, that last fearful ride endured by my father and mother, down from the broken embankment, down into the surging, murderous waters of the Wye river far below. And in that instant, furthermore, a recollection that had eluded me came strangely into my mind, quite unsought. I remembered the name Orme, and the place it had occupied in my childish fears. The whole scene needly sharp: my father, huge, standing by a lace-curtained window; someone else—Mama, I think —seated out of sight, in the shadows. And my father's voice, as loud as he was huge: "Orme? Don't talk to me of Orme. That man would strangle us if he could. Strangle us and leave us for the crows...."

That those were Papa's exact words I had no doubt at all. Such half-understood horrors linger long in a child's memory. And even now, now that I knew of metaphor and of the exaggerations folk may use in their daily speech, even now it had the power to bring a shiver to my spine. *Strangle us and leave us for the crows....*

My cry on waking had been loud enough to attract attention. Hardly had I adjusted myself to consciousness and put intrusive memory from me before the noise of a door opening brought my head up from the pillow. The door I saw was totally unfamiliar, large and finely-panelled, with a handsome crystal door knob. Round its edge appeared an elderly woman, big-boned and thick of body, wearing a very plain dark blue dress, its austerity lightened only by white linen collar and cuffs, and a small gold locket hanging round her neck. Her features were large, her hair was straight and uncompromisingly cropped, and a detectable moustache lay upon her upper lip.

She regarded me sourly, then came further into the room. "You're awake, then," she said.

"No answer to this seemed necessary. I smiled uncertainly and struggled to sit up.

She approached to the side of the bed. "Do that and you'll be sorry," she remarked conversationally.

And indeed, even as she spoke a wave of nausea swept over me that I could scarce control. Also a curious sense of constriction to my legs, almost of immovability. I lay back weakly. I was wearing, so I now discovered, a simple white flannel nightdress. "Am I ill?" I asked her.

She grunted and circled the bed, pushing and patting at the covers. "It's the ether," she said. "Turns the stomach, clouds the brain." She took my wrist and felt for my pulse. "The effect will pass," she coldly added.

For the moment this satisfied me. I gazed past her, at the massive furnishings of the room—wardrobe, tallboy, dressing table, easy chairs, all of an overpowering darkness and size. The pictures on the walls were huge and murky also: storm-swept seas and ruined cliffs by moonlight. A fearsome fire burned in a monumental grate. And the curtains over the windows formed a wall of brown and purple damask, sheer from floor to ceiling. From somewhere a memory came to me: a turreted mansion, dark and forbidding under a leaden sky, increasing in size with terrifying speed as I sank towards it. Such a house, I knew, might well conceal within its walls so grim a room as this.

"Ether?" Suddenly there were things I did not understand. "Why should I be given ether?"

"Why indeed. There's plenty wouldn't get such consideration. For the like of Madam Deveraux, though, it seems nothing's good enough."

She tightened her lips. There were puzzles here too many for my fuddled brain. Kitty? Was she here also? I tried to move again, and came upon the same disturbing obstruction, the same leaden immobility below my waist. Kitty...the balloon...the parachute...the wet stones of a courtyard ...ether...Possibilities emerged, terrible possibilities. I struggled up onto my elbows, fought with the feelings of sickness, tore back the bedclothes.

Still my legs were concealed from me, hidden beneath a wicker cage. Frantically I tipped that off also.

The nurse, for such she must be, folded her arms, massaged her elbows, looked calmly down at the obscene contraption of splints and straps and bandages that encased my right leg. "The doctor's done a pretty job," she said. "The way you fell it's a wonder you're still alive. The Devil looks after his own, and no mistake."

The house, the courtyard, my fall, now this room—all these came together in an unmistakable sequence. Anxiously I looked up into the nurse's coarse, unfriendly face. "What ...please tell me, what...?" I choked, unable properly to voice my terrible fears.

She raised a heavy, sardonic eyebrow. "Broken ankle—

bumps and bruises—nothing more."

Weak with relief, I returned my gaze to my poor damaged leg. It was not a comfortable sight. And at the end of it my naked foot projected, utterly alien to me, from the swathed rods and buckles. It was hard to believe that the foot was mine even. As if she had read my thoughts, the nurse reached down and tweaked it sharply. The pain she caused hurled me back on the bed, rigid. I cried out in agony. The foot was mine—there could be no doubt of that.

My nurse frowned. "What a lot of fuss," she said. "These things have to be done, you know. Doctor Craggan's orders." She repositioned the cage, and drew my bedclothes back into place. "I expect the doctor will want to see you for himself, now you're awake and uppitty."

Awake I might be, but I had seldom in my life felt less uppitty. And too many questions remained unanswered. "Whose house is this?" I asked.

My nurse laughed shortly. "There now, Madam Deveraux, aren't you the little innocent?"

She left the room then, evidently considering she had given me answer enough. For a big woman, not young, she had a way of moving that was strangely smooth, as if on oiled wheels. And she did not like me.

Alone now, I attempted to take stock of my position. If my nurse believed me to be Kitty—a reasonable enough mistake in anyone exposed to the Fete posters—then possibly this error might be put to my advantage. For if I was Kitty Deveraux, wife of the fine and handsome Captain, then I could not be Hessie Malpass, fugitive from justice. Instinct, to be sure, told me that such a deception was folly, and that the correct—indeed, the only possible—course of action was to contact the police immediately and rely on their wisdom and just dealing. Hard common sense, however, counted the cards stacked against me: I was an orphan, daughter of a bankrupt, a disgraced man, a failure; I had fled the scene of my crime in the most scandalous manner any magistrate could surely imagine; I had disguised myself and taken another's name; furthermore, I had consorted with gypsies and showmen, any of whom, it was well known, would deal in stolen goods and ask no questions.... To prove my innocence in the face of such compromising circumstances would be difficult indeed.

I remembered a little ragged lad who had been about the station for a time, touting the cabmen. Scarcely ten years of age, he was convicted of stealing a shirt worth two-and-a-penny from a stall, They sent him for ten weeks prison and five years in the boys' reformatory. How much more then for me, stealing a silver cup and the several pounds in the First Class till?

One thing was dazzlingly clear: the young woman I was now mistaken for was the person in fact guilty of the theft. It was a strange irony—I remembered vividly her capacious carpet bag, and the terrified, exaggeratedly innocent look in her eyes: exactly the look, I now realised, of a young thief, caught red-handed. This was the girl I had befriended, the girl who had so coolly taken advantage of me. I remembered the feel of the carpet bag against my leg on the tram up Blackboy's Hill, and Kitty's bright prattle. She was a rough girl, the Captain had said. My own feeling at that moment was that she belonged back in the gutter whence he had lifted her.

The best way out of my present predicament was for me to leave my bed as soon as might be, decently and quietly, as Madam Deveraux, and immediately seek out the Captain. His influence over Kitty, the undoubted affection she had for him, was my strongest hope. If the stolen property were regained, then a careful word with Mrs Skues might bring about the desired accommodation.

I sighed. To remain Madam Deveraux was to continue to suffer the manifest dislike of my nurse. And for what reason I could not tell. Unless... But at this moment my thoughts were interrupted. The door of my room opened a few inches, then a few inches more, and through this crack a young man diffidently entered. I gaped at him. Though his face was smudged and he wore brown workman's overalls, he seemed to be no common workman. His complexion was pale and scholarly. There was a fumbling grace, a sensitivity, about his whole demeanour. His forehead was high beneath tousled reddish hair, his features were lean, his eyes deep-set and now most troubled.

He shuffled his feet awkwardly, then managed a sort of bow. "Mrs. Deveraux—I find you much improved, I trust?"

I clutched the sheet about me. He seemed harmless enough. Yet his question was one I could not truthfully answer, hardly knowing in what earlier condition he might have found me. "Are you the doctor?" I asked instead.

"Lord, no." He drew the back of one hand across his brow, thereby contributing a further greasy mark to his grubby visage. "Lord no—that's my guardian. He'll be here in a minute. I just wanted to tell you not to mind him. Not to mind his manner... When I've had time I'm sure I'll get him to see the innocence of your part in the matter."

I hesitated. As Madam Deveraux perhaps I should know the matter to which he referred. I tried a more general enquiry. "A nurse was here just now—I asked her if this was the doctor's house. She didn't seem to want to answer."

He stared at me. "You're not pretending? You mean you really don't know?" He edged a little further into the room. "I did tell the guv'nor—I did warn him he might be jumping to all the wrong conclusions...." He broke off, confused, then straightened his back and took refuge in stiff formality. "This house belongs to my guardian, Mrs Deveraux. He is Doctor Cashel Craggan. My name is Quennel—Peter Quennel."

He brought his heels together, bowed again timidly from where he stood. I fear I must have been still a little lightheaded, for I began to laugh helplessly, both at the incongruous spectacle he presented and at my strange good fortune —for if I *had* to parachute into the side of a house and break my ankle then it was luck indeed that the house should be that of a doctor.

Mr Quennel came forward to the side of my bed, evidently seriously alarmed. "Please, Mrs Deveraux, please.... However we may look at your presence here, it's still a pretty serious matter. If the guv'nor were to hear you laughing, he—"

"A verra serious matter indeed, Mrs Deveraux." This new voice was abrasively Scottish, and issued from a gaunt, whitebearded figure in the now wide open doorway behind my young companion. "A matter of criminal trespass, I fancy...." My laughter died as quickly as it had begun. "Criminal trespass, I say!"

Dr Cashel Craggan—for this must surely be he—strode impressively into the room, followed by my nurse who came to stand at the foot of my bed. He was a giant of a man, eyes gleaming darkly from caverns beneath straggled white eyebrows, clad immaculately in frock coat and striped trousers. He held in one hand a pair of gold-rimmed pincenez which he tapped irritably upon the palm of the other. "Peter—get back to your work. It is not proper that you should be in this young person's room unattended. It is also against my express instructions. I shall speak with you later."

He stared his ward out of the room, waited till the door

was closed behind him. Then he turned to me. I will confess that I trembled before the blast of his displeasure. "Your laughter is unseemly, marm. As is the rest of your behaviour. ... But I am a medical man, and merciful." He swung his pince-nez upon their thin black ribbon. "There should be an understanding between us, I think. It seems, Mrs Deveraux, that you are to be a guest in my house for a while and a bit. I ken well that this will no be to your liking—neither, I promise you, is it to mine. None the less—"

I could not let this pass. "Then I will leave immediately, Dr Craggan. If I am unwelcome, then I cannot—"

"Your medical condition does not allow of it." He moved to the bed, pointed dramatically at the covers domed over the wicker cage. "You would walk again, I take it?"

I stared at him appalled.

"Certainly you are unwelcome, Mrs Deveraux. Indeed, I marvel that you should expect aught else. But if you would walk again, then your leg must not be moved. The ends of the bone must be allowed to knit. Disturb them, Mrs Deveraux, and I'll no answer for the consequences."

Was I helpless, then? Was I, as Kitty Deveraux, really so helpless? "Dr Craggan, I would not for the world be a burden to you. I'm certain my husband"—I spoke the word boldly—"will make provision."

"Your husband, is it? And where is he? I tell you, marm, had a wife of mine disappeared under such circumstances I would have been scouring the district for her long ere now." He strode to the fireplace and there turned to face me, roasting his coat tails. "Not a cheep, Mrs Deveraux. Never a cheep. ... One might almost conclude—" he placed his pince-nez upon his nose and eyed me sarcastically "—one might conclude that for the present he considers his connection with you a mite embarrassing."

This allusion was evidently another of those I was supposed to understand. Having just reminded myself that I was Kitty Deveraux, I now had to remind myself that I was not. And that the Captain knew I was not. Even so, surely he must feel *some* concern for my fate?

My eye was caught by the tomb-like clock on the mantel at Dr Craggan's shoulder: its hands stood at five past one. This, together with the drawn curtains, told me that the time was still in the middle of the night. There, perhaps, was the explanation for Captain Deveraux' seeming callousness.

"If the clock behind you is correct, sir," I said, "then

Captain Deveraux has scarcely had time to land and properly secure his aerostat and return from whatever place he may have been carried."

I was guessing, of course, but the doctor was not to know that. He regarded me sardonically, one whiskery eyebrow raised. "You are argumentative, marm. But no doubt it was foolish of me to expect a fair spirit of contrition.... So be it, then—your husband will be informed of the situation. And if he dare come for you he will be in no way molested."

"Molested, Dr Craggan? Why should he be molested?"

At this seemingly harmless question the rage that I had sensed always not far below Dr Craggan's surface flared so brightly that it seemed about to break all bounds. "She asks me that! You hear, Nurse Buckingham? You hear how she taunts me? Dear God, but such false innocence is more than I can rightly endure...." He bore down upon me. "Should I cast you out, marm? Should I return you to the gutter where you belong? What is it to me whether you live or die?"

Surprisingly it was the woman, Nurse Buckingham as I now knew, who came to my rescue, though in the most inexplicable way. Not moving a fraction from her station at the foot of my bed, she was heard minutely to clear her throat. "The courtyard, Doctor," she murmured. "Remember the courtyard."

Abruptly Doctor Craggan came at last partially to his senses. Though his anger remained as fierce as ever, the nurse's words placed some mysterious restraint upon him. My small relief at this was tempered by the vivid realization that the world I now inhabited was as fraught, as unpredictable, as sinister, as the dream world from which I had but recently escaped.

When the doctor spoke again, it was with a calm almost more frightening. "Search your heart, Mrs Deveraux, and you'll see far better than I can ever tell you just what your husband deserves at my hands. You know of his scheming. You know of his insane ambition. Possibly it was you who picked the buckshot from him after his last burglarious attempt upon my property.... He and I have never met, Mrs Deveraux. But there is war between us as surely as if we were brothers. That too you know—or you would never be where you are now. So let us have no more innocence, Mrs Deveraux. No more lies. Let us have silence, rather."

He fixed me with his piercing eyes, challenging me to reply and at the same time forbidding me. Yet the choice was none at all, for I had no words to offer, not even my very real innocence to protest. He waited, hunched over me, eyes boring into me, for a timeless eternity. Then he turned from my bed and was gone, his fury finding but poor release on the door, so that the whole room shuddered to its banging.

Nurse Buckingham remained unimpressed. She came to me and eased the edge of the sheet from my terrified fingers. "The doctor's quick to anger," she remarked mildly. "Always was." Then, lest I should think this showed a softening in her, she gave the sheet a vicious tweak. "Not that you didn't ask for it.... But there's just one thing I'll say, so you know where you stand. It's just that your Captain isn't the only one with an ambition. And if you're caught between the two of them—well, I'm sorry for you."

I could have wished that she sounded sorrier. Brusquely she bent over me, plumped my pillow, made me ready to sleep. I was terribly tired, and my leg ached abominably. I was haunted by a vivid mental picture of shattered bone-ends grating one against the other. Helplessly I watched my nurse as she went round the room turning down the lights till only the fire remained, its drowsy comfort wasted on my wakeful spirit. Sleep that night I knew would be impossible, the strangeness of the house huge and frightening about me....

And then, suddenly, it was morning, and sunlight streaming in around the room's heavy damask curtains. And my cruel stay in Doctor Cashel Craggan's house but hardly begun.

SIX

My next few days under Dr Craggan's sinister roof were spent in an increasing agony of expectation. On each of the doctor's visits he did not fail to make clear that the enmity between him and my fine and handsome Captain was extended to exist between him and me also. Of the young and more affable Mr Quennel I saw nothing at all, though there were sometimes mutterings in the corridor between him and his guardian, and on one occasion distantly raised voices. I did not know whether to hope that I was the subject of this family dissension or to hope that I was not. Either way, the reason that young Mr Quennel had believed he could get his guardian to see was slow in coming.

As for Nurse Buckingham, she remained efficient but remote, giving just enough of herself to keep me in passable spirits, but never so much that I might over-excite myself with the notion that someone actually liked me. In such drear circumstances it is not surprising that my thoughts were principally directed towards the moment when my Captain should learn of my whereabouts and ride to my rescue.

My days were uneventful. Reading matter of a somewhat earnest nature was provided—I discovered, for example, that the stories of Mr Dickens were considered too highly coloured for the sick room. I received no news of the outside world, and indeed I thought to ask for none, being much absorbed with the smaller world of my own situation. What medical attention I received was confined to a dish of Condy's fluid in the room to disinfect the over-heated atmosphere, and a small dosage of St Jacob's Oil to combat the considerable pain following Dr Craggan's single daily examination of my damaged limb. Apart from my leg, my injuries were slight: a grazed arm and a twisted shoulder, neither of which mercifully required the doctor's brisk attentions.

Only once did Nurse Buckingham's dislike of me falter. It was on my third morning, I think, when she wished to change the sheets upon my bed, and permitted me therefore to rise, and supported me grudgingly to the broad window seat where I could rest my leg. I found those moments by the window precious, an assurance that the old world of grass and trees that I had almost ceased to believe in still existed, as free and green as ever, beyond the heavy confines of my room.

I stared and stared. To be sure, the view was not distinguished—a ragged lawn, bounded by impenetrable poplars, the rear corner of a shabby summer house—but it was real, and the birds that flew between lawn and trees and summer house were free.

I leaned the side of my head against the window pane. Behind me Nurse Buckingham was thumping pillows. "You've been with the doctor a long time?" I asked her, wanting to be friendly and believing this a friendly question, for I had found people took pride in length of service.

For once my good intentions succeeded. "Thirty-nine years," Nurse said, not altogether unwillingly. "Brought in for Mrs Craggan when she was carrying, I was. Stayed on to tend the baby after she was taken—and a skinny scrap he was in those days. The baby and the master both—it was my promise to her as she lay dying."

I gained the strong impression that it was this death-bed promise rather than any great personal charm of Dr Cashel Craggan that had kept her so loyal. The mention of a son, however, intrigued me. "The baby you brought up, Nurse— where is he now?"

For a moment her hands were stilled. "Dr Craggan's son is dead," she said. "You'll do well not to mention him— Mr Peter is the doctor's son now in all but name."

She was still for a moment longer. Then she unfolded my new top sheet and flicked it out, so that it billowed like a great sail and settled slowly, neatly, exactly in place. I watched her quietly from my window seat, thinking of the doctor and of the sad canker of bereavement somewhere in his soul. Perhaps he would be now an altogether different man if his son had lived, and brought him joy.

Nurse Buckingham paused again, leant on the foot of the bed, remembering. "I'd have done anything for Mrs Craggan," she said. "To look at her, you'd hardly have said there was anything there. But she had more strength in her little finger than he had in his whole body. Terrible thing, her going like that." Her fingers moved up to the locket about her neck. "She gave me her likeness. Thanked me for what I'd done. . . ."

She hesitated, glanced towards me, then left the bed and came to where I sat propped in the window recess. She stooped awkwardly beside me and held out the open locket for me to see. The silhouette within was of a determined little person, fine-featured, with softly-piled hair. And the son, born of the one, nursed by the other—what of him?

In most families there were memories best left undisturbed. I questioned her no more, simply thanked her warmly for letting me see the picture. She stayed beside me a minute longer, looking at the picture, then straightened abruptly and went stiffly back to her bed-making.

"That's right," she said, talking briskly now, covering her lapse into sentiment, "thirty-nine years I've been in this house. Thirty-nine years.... Not that there's been all that much call for a nurse, not since the master gave up his practice."

She flung on the blankets, folded the corners, tucked them under. My attention began to wander back to the world outside my window. Nurse Buckingham talked on. "Twelve years ago, that was. It was then that the bicycles got him, you see. Suddenly he thought of nothing but bicycles. Heart patients, lung patients, rheumatism patients—he'd tell them all to go out and buy bicycles. His bicycle cures made him famous. Next step was to design a bicycle himself. The first was the Craggan Jaunt—sold thousands, all over the country. In no time at all he was busier with his bicycles than he was with his patients. Bought a workshop down on the Cheltenham Road. Went into the business properly. Never looked back...."

And no particular loss, I thought, to the medical profession ... Below me a man came slowly across the lawn, a man in a Norfolk jacket, sturdy, with a large Alsatian dog at his heels. He paused to look around, then went quietly on about his business. It fascinated me that another life, another set of preoccupations, something strange and quite unknown, was going on down there, and that I could watch it and even become a tiny part of it. I would have tapped upon the glass had not Nurse come at that moment to take me back to bed.

"... Mind you, Mrs Deveraux, that was before he forgot all about his bicycles and got this other bee in his bonnet. This terrible —" She broke off as her gaze followed the direction of mine. "One of the gardeners," she said, very quickly. Then, "The place is crawling with them."

The information, unasked-for, seemed a little odd. But I was content to let her carry me back to bed. I had seen my grass, my trees, my summer house, my gardener, his dog. Though the grass, I thought briefly as my hated sickbed claimed me, the grass did him and his dog little credit.

My days were uneventful, then: their high point my journey to the window seat and back. The same could not be said for the mysterious business of the household beyond my closed door. This was eventful in the highest degree—indeed, quite shatteringly so. Not only were there periodic bursts of great activity, distant hammerings and shouts, but frequently, both in the day and the night, the peace of my room would be disturbed by sharp explosions. Bangs. Detonations.

... Mostly these came singly, but sometimes they were repeated, several in close, uneven succession.

At first these alarmed me, sounding for all the world as if the house were under some kind of attack, and about to fall to the invaders. When this thought was proved nonsensical I came to the conclusion instead that rifle practice of some kind was being carried on close by, possibly in the long single-storey building I had drifted over on my parachute. Should marksmanship indeed be the bee my host had got in his bonnet, it seemed to me indeed a strange occupation for an elderly doctor and his ward. But I could think of no other explanation.

On the day following my excursion to the window Nurse Buckingham happened to come into my room bringing coal for the fire shortly after a particularly brisk outburst. Although I had learned that such questions were unwelcome, I dared ask her what all the noise was about. And in doing so lost all the ground I had gained with her, the intimacy she had offered by showing me the portrait of her beloved mistress, for her whole demeanour towards me instantly changed.

She set the coal scuttle abruptly down in the middle of the hearth rug. "The Doctor's right—you're not to be trusted. Not to be trusted an inch. Poking and prying as if we were all fools. And it's no use pretending, *Madam* Deveraux. You know what those noises are just as well as I do."

By now she was only calling me that when she was seriously out of sorts with me. Before I could protest she had banged out of the room, forgetting altogether the fire she had come to tend.

I stared after her, bewildered. Evidently the house held secrets, secrets Kitty and the Captain were unwelcome parties to. This, then, would explain the coolness of my reception. Possibly I was considered some sort of spy.... All sorts of suppositions rushed into my mind. Was the doctor testing some new firearm? Or might he not be engaged in the training of a secret army? Certainly the house was large enough, and the Irish troubles a possible reason. And Ireland but a few hours away by fast packet boat....

My thoughts were interrupted by a further succession of detonations. I covered my head with the bedclothes. Only a few days before my life had been simple—circumscribed perhaps, but orderly, and progressing in an orderly direction. My aspirations then had been orderly too, tied to the humble skills of a typewriter girl. What folly could have possessed me to cast such orderliness aside? The greatest aspiration I dared entertain at that moment was simply to be allowed to stay alive.

And so five days passed, and then six. It seemed incredible that the Captain should have received news of my whereabouts from the doctor and yet not come to find me. A terrible suspicion began to form in my mind. On the seventh day I summoned the courage to ask Dr Craggan during his morning visit exactly how and in what terms news of me had been sent.

His fingers were on my pulse, and they tightened perceptibly. His reply was—for him—unusually smooth and melodious. "A letter was sent, Mrs Deveraux, addressed to your husband by way of the Fete Proprietor. Captain Deveraux would surely have left a forwarding address, so there can be no doubt as to his receiving the letter." He released my wrist, straightened his back and replaced his watch in his waistcoat pocket. "You have an accelerated heartbeat, Mrs Deveraux. You should avoid agitation. No doubt the Captain will come when his fear of me is outweighed by his desire to be parted from you no longer."

His smoothness told me he was lying. I knew then, with terrifying certainty, that no letter had been sent, and none would be. For some inexplicable reason my presence in the doctor's house was being kept secret. Had I possessed proof of this I would have challenged him at once. But without proof his denials were all too predictable, and all too insulting to my intelligence. So I accepted his reply with dignity, and let the matter rest.

The proof I needed came to me the very next day, the eighth of what I had now come to regard as my captivity. And it came to me through the kind offices of the most unsuspected and unsuspecting person.

At around eleven in the morning, when usually I was left to my own devices, the door of my room opened to admit young Mr Quennel, clad no longer in overalls, his person excellently groomed, one hand holding something concealed behind his back. He was as pale as he had been at our first meeting, and indeed slightly haggard, as if from much work indoors and insufficient sleep, but his eyes were startlingly clear and blue beneath gingery eyebrows and an obstinately untamed shock of curly hair. He closed the door swiftly and tiptoed exaggeratedly to my bedside.

"Mrs Deveraux—do I intrude?"

But before I could reply, and just as if he expected some scandalised protest from me, he blundered on. "You see, I hoped that if we called my presence here 'sick-visiting', then it might seem quite proper."

I smiled at him, and primly adjusted the high collar of my nightdress. "Sick-visiting," I said carefully, "is I'm sure the most proper activity in the world, Mr Quennel."

In fact, of course, I was so delighted to see a new face in my dismal room that such a thing as propriety or its lack was quite unimportant to me.

He laughed pleasedly. "In that case I'm a sick visitor. And sick visitors are quite properly expected to bring presents."

With a flourish he produced from behind his back a large bunch of marigolds, wrapped in a neat cone of newspaper. "The gardens are pretty neglected," he said, "but these seem to be coming up all over the place. And they make a brave show."

They did indeed make a brave show. In that over-furnished, over-heated, over-stuffed prison of a room their bright, careless petals made the bravest show I could imagine. His kindness touched me. I took the flowers from him, buried my face in their sharp, summery smell.

"Thank you, Mr Quennel. They're the best present in the world." Then I looked up at him, a new thought clouding my pleasure. "But you'd better not leave them. Your guardian will be sure to find out where they came from. And he—"

"I'm not a child, Mrs Deveraux." Looking at him, at the squareness of his jaw and the determined line of his mouth, I saw that he was not. "Last week, when I was ordered out of your room and went so obediently, it was because you were feverish and sick—an argument in your presence was to be avoided. But I'm not always quite so meek, I promise you."

His words made as brave a show as his flowers. There was in them, moreover, and in the tilt of his head as he spoke them, more than a hint of his guardian's obstinacy—learned from him, no doubt, but more wisely and gently employed, so that courage rather than arrogance would be the outcome, compassion rather than brute force.

But that same courage and compassion, I judged, would ultimately allow him few weapons against his own ageing, domineering benefactor. "I wouldn't want to be the cause of trouble between you," I murmured.

He laughed ruefully. "There'll always be that, I fear. Underneath it all, though, we understand each other very well. After all, I owe him everything. And we do share the same dream...." Even as he said this I could see that it wasn't quite true. He broke off, strode to the window. "Dash it all—I came here to cheer you up. I wanted you to tell me all about your parachuting adventures—you must be extraordinarily brave—and all I do is go on about me and the guv'nor. It's too bad!"

"But you've cheered me up immensely." I meant it. "Just to know that I have a friend in the house is—"

"No—not a friend." He swung round from the window, frowning, deeply agitated. "No—that would be disloyal. Besides, you're that man's wife."

Not for the first time, my impulse was to end my foolish masquerade, to admit the truth at last. But it seemed unlikely that I would be any more welcome to Dr Craggan or his ward simply for a change of name: besides being still an associate of "that man" I would become additionally a person sought by the police and thereby doubly vulnerable. So I hung my head and said nothing.

Young Mr Quennel flung himself down on the window seat. "I'm sorry. Lord knows, I wish things were different. It's just that ... well, from what we'd heard of you we expected someone—well, someone rather different. Someone it would have been easier to ... to hate and all that sort of thing."

There was nothing I could say to that either. He and I were locked in a situation not of our making, our loyalties radically opposed. So, I imagined, might two men of confronting armies meet by chance in some quiet corner of the battlefield and reluctantly discover neither to be the monster the other had supposed. It was a nice, romantic thought—and not the less so for the awareness that within the hour a bugle might blow and the two soldiers be committed again to mortal combat.

"Please don't be upset," I said. "Please talk to me. There must be something we can talk about. I tell you what—I have a secret ambition. I'm sure you'll never guess what it is."

We were outside the world, outside time. All things were possible between us. I did not wait for him to guess, but blurted it out, my precious dream of being a typewriter girl. He stared at me, not laughing, scarcely seeming to understand.

"It's your turn now," I coaxed. "What's *your* secret ambition?"

For a moment he hesitated. Then he shook his head, rose, and went to the door. "I've stayed too long. I shouldn't have come. The guv'nor trusts me...." He opened the door. Then, briefly, his anxiety cleared, and was replaced by a different seriousness. "My secret ambition? I've never told a soul. They would all laugh at me. It's... it's to go to the South Seas—or India, perhaps. It's to sail in the tall ships. It's to be shot of the lot of them."

He shrugged deprecatingly. Then he was gone.

I stared at the closed door. I had hardly thought that a man like him, young, and possessed of every advantage, might still be caught in the very same frustrations as I. My heart warmed greatly towards Peter Quennel, with his innocent young dreams. What children we both were... I sighed, my mind returning sadly from future dreams to present reality.

The marigolds lay on my bed, tumbling from the newspaper in which they were wrapped. I gathered them up by their ridged, furry stems, and thrust them—for want of anywhere better—into my drinking glass on the table beside my bed. They were the first flowers ever given me, and the whole corner of the room glowed with their cheerful presence. I smoothed out the paper they had come in. And allowed my eye to wander idly down the page. And saw a small headline above a short report—a headline that in its eerie unexpectedness chilled me suddenly to the very bone: *Balloonist's Wife Dies in Aerial Escapade—Death by Drowning Assumed for Intrepid Parachutist.*

The paper was four days old, dated Thurs, 27th May. It was my own death reported there—it could be no other. For a moment I trembled uncontrollably. It was as if I had been walking in a tranquil country churchyard and come upon a gravestone with my own name on it, crisp and new. It was the very stuff of nightmare—as if I were in truth dead and knew it not.

I calmed myself as best I could, and read on down the page. A parachute, my parachute, had been discovered by a fishing vessel, floating in the fast waters of the estuary off Portishead Point. Of its burden, of me, no sign had been found. It had to be concluded that the body, my body, had been taken on the treacherous currents out to sea. A watch for it was being kept on the Welsh and Somerset coasts. Little hope was entertained, however....

Slowly sanity returned. The mechanics of what had happened were simple. No body had been found because there was none to be found. I was here in bed, and by no means drowned at all. Clearly my parachute, relieved of my weight, had risen again into the air and been carried on across the countryside like a dandelion seed on the wind, to settle finally in the tideway beyond. From that freakish accident it was easy to see how the mistake had arisen. But it was the implications of the mistake that set my mind in a whirl.

Clear thinking did not readily come to me. First of all there was Doctor Craggan's part to be considered. Obviously he had sent no letter, or the truth would be known outside the four walls of my room and the newspaper report would never have been printed. That much was unequivocal. Furthermore, he must now believe that as far as the outside world was concerned Kitty Deveraux was dead. And I was Kitty Deveraux. So he could do with me whatever his intense dislike of me prompted him to. And I, crippled as I was, lay totally at his mercy.... It was a painful thought. I found reassurance, however, in remembering the care that had been lavished upon me—a man with murder in his heart would scarcely have been so generous. What, then, was in his mind?

What, also, was in the mind of my fine and handsome Captain? I will confess he seemed a little tarnished in my eyes. He must now believe Hessie Malpass dead—as must Kitty and the eccentric Mr Jowker. Why should they, in allowing the newspaper report, obviously have kept my identity a secret? And dear Barty—must he believe me dead also? What reason could all these people have for not telling what they knew?"

And would my Captain have grieved for me? Grieved for me just a little...?

Questions... so many questions, all without answers. And the problems of Hessie Malpass, accused thief, now doubly confounded. To be confined in bed at such a time of perilous uncertainty was an agony to me. If only I *knew*—if only I could somehow unravel the web of lies that had been woven about me. Yet to hope for the truth from my captors at this late stage was folly. Even young Mr Peter would be silent, kept so by an understandable loyalty to his guardian. My one chance lay in confronting Dr Craggan with my now certain knowledge of his deceit—with that much established, perhaps he would be willing to disclose his further intentions.

For the rest, all that remained was for me to wait with what patience I could muster until my leg be healed again and myself fit to travel. Then the winning of my freedom would only be a matter of determination. I would discreetly seek out Captain Deveraux and gain from him solutions to my other uncertainties. He might be tarnished in my eyes, but he was not—I felt sure—the monster Dr Craggan made him out to be.

This, then, was what I must clearly do now. And what I must hope to do in the future.

The making of decisions—even simple-minded ones—has always had a calming effect on me. I lay back on my bed and turned my mind to immediate practicalities. I wanted to protect young Mr Peter from the worst of his guardian's anger, for his loyalty to the older man touched my heart. His radiant honesty was a great comfort to me in that secretive place. Clearly he was no newspaper reader: I feared for him, that his bringing of the paper might cause him far greater trouble than a mere gift of marigolds might have prepared him for, and cast about me for some means of disposing of the incriminating material.

The fire was the only really safe answer. I pushed back bedclothes and wicker frame, and lowered first my good leg and then my splinted leg carefully to the carpet. I stood on my good leg, the other dangling free. In this manner I hopped to the fireplace. I put the wad of newspaper on the fire and watched it burn until it was the merest filigree of black ash. I would have beat it flat with the monstrous poker had it not then obligingly risen of its own accord and disappeared, like smoke, up the chimney. The return journey to my bed was less adroit: I staggered, and nearly fell, and saved myself at least in part with my poor bandaged leg. I was encouraged by the small degree of pain this caused. I knew nothing of the treatment of broken limbs, but could not imagine I would remain much longer so utterly incapable.

Once back in bed I could survey my brave little odyssey with some satisfaction, for Mr Peter was made safely innocent of all indiscretion. It was Nurse Buckingham now who must be saddled with the guilt: she must be persuaded to think she had let the truth slip out—assuming, of course, that she knew it. I believed that she did. Even if Dr Craggan had not told her, I judged her to be the sort of person who read the daily paper from cover to cover, elbows on the kitchen table, over her breakfast cup of tea.

Nurse Buckingham arrived punctually at one o'clock, bearing my lunch tray. She laid it across my knees, removed the silver cover, and revealed a fine mutton chop for my delight, and spring carrots, and green peas so extravagantly tiny as would have broken Mrs Skues' heart. Whatever else I might have against Dr Craggan, he had never skimped my food—indeed, the nourishment I received under his roof was the finest I could remember in my whole life, the meals of my more prosperous childhood having merged in my mind into jam pudding which I liked and tapioca which I did not.

"Nurse Buckingham," I said, taking a mouthful, "I've been thinking about my parachute—what happened to it after I landed?"

I was relieved to see her start guiltily, and cover the movement with an irritated shrug of her shoulders. She knew the truth well enough. "How should I know what happened to it?" she said. "Blew away, most like."

"Blew away?" I continued to attack my chop with innocent good cheer. "Where to? They're very expensive—couldn't we get it back?"

"Might have gone anywhere." She hesitated, then—like all good liars—took refuge in the truth. "Out into the Bristol Channel, I wouldn't be surprised."

I looked at her, wide-eyed. "But that's terrible. I mean—if someone found it floating there, what would they think?"

She saw the trap too late. "Maybe it didn't get that far then. Maybe it—"

"They'd think I'd been on it. They'd think I'd been drowned."

She looked at me sharply. "Somebody's been talking to you," she said. "You can't fool me. Come on now—who's been saying things? I'd have sworn there wasn't anybody knew."

So then I had her. To make my simulated astonishment appear more real I clutched at her, spilling my tray, my lovely plate of food in pretended horror on the floor. "You mean it's true? You mean that's what really happened?"

"I mean nothing of the sort." She glared at me, anger battling with uncertainty. "You ought to be ashamed of yourself, making all this mess."

"But Nurse—you just said. . . ."

"I said nothing. I'm saying nothing, nothing at all."

But she had already said too much, and we both knew it. In furious silence she stooped to clear the spilled food as best she could. It was a menial task, and I would have apologised had not her face forbidden it.

When she spoke again, it was almost sadly. "You take advantage of me, Madam Deveraux. You poke and pry. Why can't you believe that things are kept from you simply for your own peace of mind?"

Indeed, I felt a mite ashamed so to have tricked the poor woman, though still rebellious. "I'm not a child, Nurse Buckingham. I have a right to know the truth."

She straightened her back. "A fine lot of good may it do you," she said. Then she gathered up the tray and stormed out, leaving me to my thoughts.

My excitement faded. All that I had gained by my trickery was cold certainty where before there had been supposition and the lurking possibility of doubt. The truth of my situation was no longer some intellectual exercise, it was harsh reality— in the eyes of the world I was dead. I had ceased to exist. Therefore I was quite at Dr Craggan's mercy. My room, for all its dark magnificence, was no more than a cell. And I could expect no help from outside it.

I was given, however, little opportunity for anxious meditation. My nurse must have gone straight to her master, for I was left alone but a very short time before he came to me, filling the whole space about my bed with his overpowering presence.

"What's this I hear?" he demanded, rubbing his hands together till the knuckles cracked. "Spilling your food? Distressing your good nurse? Have you no grown out of tantrums then, Mrs Deveraux?"

I kept very still, gathering my courage. This, then, was the confrontation I had desired. "There is the matter of your letter to Captain Deveraux," I said boldly. "I do not believe that any such letter was sent."

He controlled himself and reached down to take my wrist, humming mildly into his beard as he did so. No doubt he wished to maintain the illusion that we were no more than doctor and patient.

I hid my arm resolutely beneath the bedclothes. "Captain Deveraux will have been told by the authorities that I am dead," I persisted. "Drowned in the estuary. With no letter from you he will have believed this story. That is the reason he has not come to search for me. That and none other."

"Drowned in the estuary? What nonsense is this?"

"It's too late to pretend—Nurse Buckingham admitted it."

"I know the good nurse unco' well, Mrs Deveraux. I'll swear she admitted no such thing."

He shot his cuffs and consulted his watch, as if anxious to be elsewhere. I too had no wish to prolong the charade. "But you do not deny the truth of what I say, Dr Craggan?"

He drew in a deep breath, hissing between constricted nostrils, controlling the violence of his displeasure. "You forget your position, young woman. You are my patient—I need deny nothing, I need admit nothing. You came here unasked, yet I have showed you every consideration. You—"

I dared interrupt the harsh flow of his rhetoric. "Am I really your patient? Or am I not rather your prisoner?"

"Prisoner?" He expanded. Clearly it was a word for which he had had an answer long prepared. "Prisoner? You are no prisoner. Do you see bars upon the windows? Are there bolts upon the door?" He gestured widely. "Does not yon good nurse even bring you flowers for your bedside? Are you not showered with every comfort?"

Of the flowers I was glad enough to say nothing. For the rest—"Then I may go? I may leave your house?"

"Aye—of course you may." He strode to the door, flung it wide open. "A pair of crutches will be brought this instant." He made as if to call for them down the corridor. Then he hesitated, and peered at me doubtfully over the gold rims of his pince-nez. "Though I should warn you, maybe, that if you were to remain upright for any length of time it is my opinion that the blood would rush to your damaged limb in a flux. The pain would be considerable, and the healing process seriously endangered. That is my opinion. But the choice, of course, remains yours entirely."

He knew well that the choice he offered was no choice at all. I was indeed a prisoner, if not of him then of my own infirmity. For all the contrived theatricality of his reply it was only too possible that he spoke the truth. It was in my mind to demand an ambulance, but the story, I knew, would be the same—a shaking of the head at the danger of movement, the jolting on the long road to find my Captain. Vainly I cursed the idiot fall that had brought me to this. Was there no admission I could get from him, none at all?

"If I am no prisoner, then why do you keep me isolated, Dr Craggan? Even the coal for the fire is brought by my nurse. What is it you fear your other servants might tell me?"

I was desperate, the walls of the room seeming to close around me. "Please, Dr Craggan—please tell me your purpose."

He came back into the room, and gently closed the door. "Might I not rather ask you *your* purpose, Mrs Deveraux?" His voice was quiet now, his evasions suffocating me. "Am I to believe that your arrival here—at this house of all houses—was the merest accident? Might I not suggest instead that you came here as a spy?"

The word shocked me into silence. If it had been in his mind since the outset, then many things were explained. It was a possibility I had but toyed with and dismissed. To hear it spoken aloud, and with such venom, was a cruel blow. I could only stare at him, and shake my head, protesting dumbly.

He sighed. "I see you deny it, marm. But you are damned by your associates. You ken well how your husband and his crew would like to see my work here set at nothing. So it's best we talk no more of 'purposes', you and I. And put your thought to this—there's folk who would kill for what lies between us. So be thankful I'm a medical man, and for the moment merciful."

With that, he left me to my thoughts.

Not for nothing had he reminded me that his mercy was "for the moment," and could at any time be withdrawn. That much at least was clearer than ever before. I lay in the trapped silence of my room and wondered what else my confrontation, so bravely begun, had gained me. Certainly no concrete admission, and even less any clue to his future intentions. Only the accusation that I might be a spy, openly made, was new. And this brought to my mind with painful clarity the telescope Captain Deveraux had so busily employed during our eventful flight. Furthermore, I could not help thinking of a bright, leather-covered telescope possessed once by my father and referred to by him more usually as a "spy-glass." A *spy*-glass... the word chimed disturbingly well with Dr Craggan's accusation. As did certain oblique remarks made earlier between the Captain and Mr Ambrose Jowker.

Perhaps then the doctor was closer to the truth than I had imagined. And in that case I would remain helpless in his power, for I would never be able to convince him of my innocence of the charge. Even when my leg was healed it seemed quite possible that he would not release me.... In the face of such a dire conclusion I fell into an apathy of misdirected dread, while the long sunlit hours of the afternoon slid by unmarked.

It was a familiar sound that brought me to my senses—the explosive rattle as of distant rifle fire. For a day or so I had been spared this. It brought with it now a dismal recognition of my own unimportance in Dr Craggan's scheme of things. There were other far weightier concerns in the house than the fate of Hessie Malpass. I could imagine its countless rooms about me, seething with mysterious activity, its workshops busy, its derelict lawns and gardens secure within the high wall that I had seen surrounding them. How easily, I thought, might I not be set to one side, forgotten, my small life dwindling, like a faint candle, to be snuffed out one day without its going disturbing in the slightest the surrounding air.

I make no apology for this melodramatic notion—when one is trapped and alone one is open to all manner of morbid fancies.

What saved me from it was not so much sober commonsense as the curiously finicky operations of my memory. Remembering the derelict lawns I had seen from my window, I remembered also that Peter Quennel had admitted that the gardens were "pretty neglected." Yet my memory chose that moment to offer the further odd fact that Nurse Buckingham had looked over my shoulder and said the place was "crawling with" gardeners. I was forced to wonder what they did with their time.

Thinking back, I realised that Nurse need never have bothered to identify the man with his dog—it was as if, by firmly naming him a gardener, she sought to prevent me thinking him anything else. But what else might he have been? If I was a spy, then what was he? A member of the army I had previously imagined, the army being prepared to go in support of the Irish Invincibles? Was the idea really so preposterous?

Beyond my window the staccato rattle continued, becoming more regular. I had never before heard it continue so long. Suddenly it terminated in a considerable explosion. I heard confused shouts, and the painful sound of breaking glass. I covered my ears, expecting I knew not what. But the walls of my room remained secure about me. The declining sun continued to shine through my window. The hands of my tomb-like clock continued their measured progress round its silver-studded dial.

I remained alarmed, however. For one thing, I realised that my supper was late in coming. My lunch had been squandered in foolish dramatics and my tea had for some reason been quite omitted. Increasingly, therefore, the discomfort of hunger was added to my other troubles.

My meal, when it finally arrived, showed worrying signs of domestic upheaval. The tray on which it rested was ill-laid and without a cloth. And it was brought, for the first time ever, not by Nurse Buckingham but by young Mr Quennel. He was apparently in a state of great agitation. He put the tray down brusquely and would have departed without a word had I not called after him.

"Mr Quennel—what's been happening?" Clearly any threat to the calm running of the house was a threat to me. "Where is my nurse? Is everything all right?"

He swung round on me, distracted. "No—everything is *not* all right!" He controlled himself. "No doubt you heard the explosion. The workshop is a shambles—and the guv'nor's been injured. He's had a finger nearly blown right off. Bucky's seeing to him. The wound's serious, but we must thank God it was no worse."

How shocking if his had been the cries I'd heard. "Oh, the poor man—what a terrible thing. I'm so very sorry, Mr Quennel!"

He seemed hardly to hear me. "Then there's our work, of course. It's been set back months. Months. . . ."

"Poor Mr Quennel—" I reached a hand out to him. "I really am sorry you and the doctor should be having all these troubles."

"Are you? Are you really?" He approached me, peered at me, took my hand. "Yes—you know, I think you truly are."

Of course I was. I could wish mutilation on none. And besides, Dr Craggan might not have been the gentlest of doctors, but then, from his point of view, neither was I the most deserving of patients.

Suddenly the mercurial young man was full of a new enthusiasm. He strode about the room. "I shall tell the Guv'nor that. I shall *make* him believe me. I knew it. I knew all along that we were mistaken about you, Mrs Deveraux."

I watched him in silence. There was nothing I could say. Only I knew just how mistaken they had been.

"Please, Mrs Deveraux, tell me something. Tell me just

one thing." He was at my bedside now, his bright blue eyes regarding me with anxious intensity. "It's most terribly important. The courtyard, Mrs Deveraux—please tell me truthfully, the day you descended in our courtyard, what did you see there?"

"See there, Mr Quennel?" I gaped at him. "I saw nothing. I thought myself as good as dead. I saw nothing—just the wall I struck and the tiles below it to which I hung."

He nodded several times, making up his mind, his piercing eyes still on my face. "Yes ... yes, it is just as I expected. In fact, I told my guardian so. I shall tell him again. And this time he *will* believe me."

He bent over me. "You've been very brave. I've seen you, Mrs Deveraux—I've known what you must be going through. I've ... come to respect you." He blushed, then hurried on. "Now you must trust me. Your ordeal will soon be over. I promise you that."

He took my hand again, and squeezed it. Then he was gone. But he left a blinding light of hope in my breast. He would be courageous and determined on my behalf. Trusting him was easy.

Hope shone in my breast, and in my mind at least the glimmerings of understanding. It seemed that I had been kept prisoner on account of what I might have seen; on account of some mysterious thing or person in the inner courtyard of the house at the moment of my precipitate arrival: some thing or person that the outside world—or perhaps simply my fine and handsome Captain—must not know about. I had been judged a spy, and, far more than that, a spy with vital information. As such I must be kept incommunicado. Now, with one simple question, and one simple answer, and one simple act of faith, all that was changed. Soon I would be free.

My joy was overwhelming. And short-lived. Twenty minutes later my supper tray was fetched, not by young Peter Quennel but by Nurse Buckingham at her angriest.

She swept into the room and snatched the tray from my knees even before I was rightly finished. "You're clever, Madam Deveraux," she said, "and I'll grant you have a way with you. You wound me round your little finger well enough. Young Mr Peter was nothing after that. To hear him talk you'd think you was some sort of angel, some poor little hardly-done-by." The cutlery on my plate rattled with the intensity of her scorn. "Maybe you reckoned that with the doctor hurt he'd be more likely to fall for your story. All I can say then is you don't know Doctor Cashel Craggan."

I stared at her, remembering another woman, stooping at my side, showing me the likeness of her long-dead mistress. Nurse Buckingham was not really this virago. But I had tricked her, and no doubt caused her great trouble with the irascible doctor. The more she had opened her heart to me, the more she would now feel bitterness; and I could not blame her for that. But before I could make any reply, any explanation at all, she was at the door, turning to deliver her triumphant parting shot.

"I can promise you one thing," she said, "you'll be with us here at Orme for a good while yet. And in less comfort too, I dare say."

"Orme?" The word struck a chill of frightened recognition down my spine and I cried in desperation after her. *"Did you say Orme?"*

But the door had slammed. And now for the first time the key was turned in the lock behind her. I was alone, and filled with a new and more complete despair. So it was in the house called Orme that I lay and where I was now to be kept openly a prisoner. Orme the grey, turreted mansion behind its high wall. Orme, the name that held such menace for my father. Orme from where the burned letter told me Captain Deveraux had awaited a reply in vain. Orme that had swallowed me just as completely as the grave. I was as good as dead. I did not exist, I lay incarcerated in the house called Orme.

Yet in that moment of my deepest distress there sprang unexpectedly into my mind the vivid picture of a man: not, as might have been predicted, a picture of my father, nor yet of my fine and handsome Captain. Rather it was singularly of the gypsy Mordello whom I had seen but for a moment, his shabby moleskins, his bright gypsy shirt, his dark, serious face with its heavy eyebrows and strangely listening expression. And with his picture came his voice, sounding again in my ears, loud above the fairground's blare: . . . *the secret Orme seeks is yours and none other's. Remember that. And when you find it, see that you do not share it unwisely.* . . .

And in that moment it was singularly the gypsy Mordello who I wished most earnestly might be with me, might be there to guide me. He had spoken of my father, he had spoken of a secret. Possibly in his veiled way he had also spoken of my mysterious benefactor and even of the Captain. Was there a link between all these, a link that he had tried to warn me of? Had he seen even where my journey that day would end? I knew not what his powers might be, this man I had taken so lightly for a mountebank. But the conviction came to me that had he been with me there, in the house called Orme, so close to the secret that was mine, he would have counselled me well.

My wish received no answer. Indeed, I had expected nothing more. I was alone, more alone than I had ever been in my whole life. If my danger was greater than it had been an hour before, I could not tell. Certainly it was no less. My nurse, my wardress, had uttered threats. The comfort she could take away was nothing to me. But the limitless imprisonment she also threatened appalled me to the depths of my soul. I knew that people did not, like wild birds, die in cages: nature was not so merciful. Perhaps—horrid thought—I would live on long enough to become well pleased with my four walls, afraid of venturing into the real world beyond.

The evening advanced, and darkened into night. No sound disturbed my room except the dusty ticking of the clock and the coal's faint shifting in the hearth as the fire settled and died. Lest I should settle also I got desperately from the bed and tottered around my room, drawing curtains, turning up the lights, making a show of the normal, routine things of life. By the time I returned to my bed I was panting from exertion. My captors need not lock my door, I thought: with my splint upon me I could not escape even as far as the end of the corridor.

So the hours of night came upon me to complete the darkness of my spirit. Against this the brightness of my room was a travesty. I wept into my pillow, beat at my crippled leg, and wept again. The bright lights taunted me. The pictures on the walls were windows into storm and torment. The massive furnishings loomed indifferently, as they had loomed before I came and would still loom long after I had gone. Even the gay marigolds by my bed only mocked at my distress. While the bright gas flames hissed and flared.

The hours passed. I sought resignation, yet feared it. Suddenly a notion, wild and foolish, came entire into my head. I saw that my captors had presented me with the means of my release. I had been staring at it till my eyes ached. Half a dozen gas flames burned about my room—just one of them provided the means by which I could fire the house.

In the resultant confusion might I not then make my escape?

It was a poor plan, the product of fevered despair, taking no account of my crippled condition, monstrously dangerous to many others than myself. But I might well have executed it, so frantic I was. Indeed, my bedclothes were already thrown back and my one good leg firmly on the Turkey carpet, when a tiny sound froze all movement. The key of the door was turning slowly in its lock. First the key, and then the door-knob. And in a rush my visitor was in the room, the door closed fast behind him.

It was young Peter Quennel. He narrowed his eyes, nearly blinded by the brilliance of my room. He was fully dressed, even though the hands of my marble clock stood at ten past two. He held in one hand a candle in a china candlestick, and in the other a pair of scissors. There was a cloak of some kind over his arm. He might have been a dream. He spoke to me. His words were of dream-like simplicity.

"I've come to set you free," he said.

Then his candle tilted, and spilled hot wax upon his hand, and he cursed most humanly, and clearly was no dream at all. And if he was no dream then I was certainly most immodestly displayed. I hauled the bedclothes up around my neck and waited, trembling, for what he might do next.

SEVEN

Young Mr Quennel blew out his candle and put the china candlestick down on my bedside table. The cloak he took from across his arm and flung onto the foot of my bed. "We must get you out of here," he said again.

My reprieve was so sudden that I still could not believe it. "But the doctor," I stammered. "Nurse Buckingham told me Dr Craggan was determined to—"

"My guardian has dosed himself with morphia for the

pain in his injured hand. He'll sleep soundly for a good few hours yet."

"Then you're doing this without his knowledge?"

He turned away, his honest face troubled. "Obedience can only be taken so far, Mrs Deveraux. Loyalty also. I . . . sometimes doubt if on the subject of his work, my guardian is completely sane."

He went to the fireplace, poked moodily at the dying embers. I said nothing. If the battle was between Peter Quennel and his conscience I had no part in it. Finally he turned to me. "The accident this afternoon, you see—it changed many things. We'd thought ourselves so near to success. When you first came here our work seemed on the very brink of triumph. The guv'nor convinced me that to keep you here for just the few remaining days was reasonable enough. Had this afternoon's trial been successful, then the whole world would have known of it. You could have gone free, and welcome."

His explanation only served to set other questions buzzing in my head. Clearly his guardian and he were engaged upon the perfection of some mechanical device. It did not surprise me that my previous improbable notion of the raising of some secret revolutionary army was proved wrong. But what device might it be that sounded like gunfire, yet was as rapid almost as a machine?

My thoughts were interrupted as Peter Quennel continued his anguished explanation. "I spoke to the guv'nor as I had promised you I would. You had seen nothing, I told him. You were innocent of all malice. . . . I'm afraid he flew into a great fury. You were to be kept here, he said, even if the redesigning and rebuilding took several months."

His face grew sad as he relived the moment. "I could see he meant what he said. No word from me would ever make him change his mind. His ambition has driven him beyond all reason, Mrs Deveraux. He is now in a place where I cannot, where I must not follow. I must act on my own, by my own standards."

Clearly this was a decision that had cost the young man much heartache. "He'll be angrier still when he finds out what you've done," I warned him.

He returned earnestly to my bedside. "Certainly he will be angry. But in the end, when he can look back, I believe he will be grateful." He took one of my hands in his, seeming almost to plead with me. "My guardian isn't a monster, Mrs

Deveraux. He's a man capable of great kindness. But he's a determined man also, a man possessed by a vision. Sometimes he lets this overcome his better judgement...." He became aware that he was holding my hand and released it, embarrassed. "I expect you understand that sort of thing very well. I expect in many ways he's quite like your husband."

My fine and handsome Captain—how could I say what he was like? The few hours we spent together had been so tumultuous, my impressions of him so brief, so thrilling.... But Peter Quennel's gentle eyes were on me, asking for reassurance. "Of course Dr Craggan isn't a monster," I said. "He's looked after me so very well. Only imagine what might have happened to me after I broke my ankle without his help. I might by now be a permanent cripple."

Rather than cheering him, my words seemed to deepen his distress. He put the scissors he had been carrying all this while onto the table by my bed and picked up his candlestick. He turned from me and lit his candle carefully at a gas jet. "There's something else I have to tell you," he said, his face still averted. "A thing of which I feel much ashamed...."

He tailed off, clearly more disturbed than I had even seen him. Seeking distraction, his eye fell gladly upon the cloak that he had brought, still lying across the foot of my bed. "That's Bucky's—I borrowed it from downstairs—if you're going to escape you'll need something to put on over your fairground clothes—they're in the chest over there—" He was babbling wildly and backing towards the door. "I'll leave you now, so that you can get dressed. We have plenty of time, of course, but you need to get dressed...."

He had his hand upon the crystal doorknob. I opened my mouth to protest, to remind him that I could not walk without crutches, let alone dress myself unaided in Kitty's tights and thingummies. But he forestalled me, found the courage to tell what had to be told. "The thing is, Mrs Deveraux, I have a confession to make—on behalf of myself and on behalf of my guardian. Your ankle was never broken, only sprained. By now it will be quite recovered."

I gaped at him, but did not interrupt as he hurried on with his explanation. "We lied to you so that it should not seem you were being kept a prisoner. Besides the splints and bandages prevented you trying to explore. And they gave us a cover story should the police for any reason come...."

He hung his head. "You'll find the bandages fall quite readily away if you use the scissors."

And still I could hardly believe what he was telling me. He opened the door. "You see, we have a lot to answer for," he whispered. "My guardian for deceiving you so cruelly, myself for acquiescing. If I can make up to you for my part in the deception, believe me I shall do so."

He went then, as silently as he had come.

For a moment I stared at the closed door, unable to move, appalled by the cunning with which I had been ensnared. My judgement of Dr Craggan as no monster now seemed unduly charitable.... Suddenly feverish haste came upon me, very much as if Peter Quennel's confession would only be true if it were acted upon in a matter of seconds. I snatched up the scissors, flung back the bedclothes, and pulled my nightdress up about my waist. There lay the bandaged limb I had come to think of as fragile, dangerously vulnerable—was I really to lay violent hands upon the poor delicate thing? Bravely I bent to my task, suppressing a shudder at the first cold touch of the scissor blade, sawing laboriously down through layer after layer.

Mr Quennel had been right—after the first few rounds of bandage were severed the whole structure rapidly loosened and fell away. I moved my toes, experimentally flexed the muscles of my foot and calf.... There was no pain. I laughed aloud, for there was no pain—only the stiffness to be expected in a limb unused for seven long days. I laughed aloud, and bent my knee, and shook my leg undecorously in the air, sending splints and irons and bandages in an untidy clutter to the floor. I stood. I stood upon my own two legs, upright, unsupported.

I walked.

And then a sudden cramp caught me, and I had to clutch the bed-head, laughing still. For the pain was a good pain: the pain of a good sound leg protesting at its long imprisonment. I tottered to the chest that Mr Quennel had indicated, hauled open its massive drawers. The sight of Kitty's clothes, unsuitable though they were, was a perfect joy to me.

When Peter Quennel tapped lightly upon the door of my room I was caught parading critically in front of the long wardrobe mirror. The cloak he had brought me reached nearly to the ground, and when it parted as I walked it revealed but a discreet glimpse of the flannel nightdress I had retained for modesty's sake beneath. To be sure, my parachutist's shoes were a little frivolous for serious night walking, but I had never been a person closely bound by the dictates of fashion. I happily bade Mr Quennel enter.

He put down his candle and surveyed me. "You need a bonnet," he said at last. "Let's hope Bucky's left something down in the hall. A girl as young and as pretty as you out in the road at such an hour needs something to hide her face."

The compliment was so matter-of-fact, and so kindly meant, that I could but thank him for it. "Look at me walking," I said—for this simplest of actions was still a novelty and a delight to me.

He clapped softly, in gentle mockery. "You do it very well. Almost as if you had been walking all your life." Then suddenly he was serious. "But now you must listen carefully, because what you're going to have to do will not be easy."

I straightened my face to suit his earnest demeanour. He motioned me to a high-backed wing chair by the fire embers, and I sat in it. If I had been inclined still to frivolity, such an inclination died abruptly with his next words.

"You must know, Mrs Deveraux, that there is a guard in the grounds here, day and night. And dogs also. By day they are kept restrained, but at night the door to their run is left open. Your escape is still possible, though, I promise you."

A coldness crept down my spine. This, then, was the explanation of the man and his dog I had seen from my window, the man Nurse Buckingham had been so eager to identify as a gardener.

"Now, the guard makes a round at two thirty," Peter Quennel continued. "He gets back to his hut at about three and returns the dogs to their run, leaving the door open. They know me well, and I ought to be able to close this door without making much of a racket. And that's your chance."

He sat down opposite me. His face was paler than ever, but calm and determined. "When you hear me whistle you leave the house and go straight down the drive. I don't have the key of the main gates, but before you reach them there's a path away to the right, leading to the little side gate. That's the one the guv'nor lets me use, and you'll find it open. The dogs will know at once there's someone about and they'll start barking. But they won't be able to get out until the guard comes to see what's up. I'll hang around to delay him as long as I can. You'll have plenty of time to get away."

I nodded, trying not to show how fearsome all this

sounded to me. "But what about you?" I said.

"Oh, I'll tell the guard some story. It's Robbins on tonight, and he's not over-blessed with brains. Nobody'll know you're gone till Bucky brings your breakfast. By then you'll be miles away and they won't be able to do a thing."

I was silent. There was no use in asking what would happen to the young man then. Dr Craggan was such a violently tempered man that almost anything was possible.

His ward must have read my thoughts. "Even if the guv'nor turns me out of house and home," he said, "it won't be too much of a disaster, I'm not without skills with which to earn a decent living. And if he won't see reason, then I wouldn't want to stay in this house anyway." I knew this was not lightly said. He allowed a moment's pause, then glanced briskly at the clock. "Five to three—that gives us roughly another ten minutes."

I felt very small in my big, buttoned leather chair. "I shouldn't let you do this for me," I said.

He was embarrassed. "Oh, it's not for you I'm doing it," he said quickly. "After all, you're still the Captain's wife. No—it's a matter of principle. The guv'nor must be shown he just can't go on trampling over people and getting away with it. There are more important things in life than our work here."

Before I could take this any further he had set off on another, safer track. "Take my mother, for instance—she always says we could have managed well enough without him. My father was an old friend, y'see, died when I was tiny, left us pretty much on the rocks. Dr Craggan roared into action, took things over, simply shouted my mother down when she said it wasn't really necessary. He'd had a bereavement of his own at about that time, so it worked out very well. And he's been wonderful to me, wonderful to both of us. . . . But he likes his own way, and just this once he has to be shown that he can't get it."

I nodded, as if in agreement. In fact I had hardly been listening, but was feeling instead most sharply the incongruity of our situation, engaged thus in family reminiscence at dead of night around a dying fire in the silent, fiercely guarded house called Orme. But I saw what he was about—the minutes had to be got through somehow.

I made an effort. "And your mother," I asked, "where is she now."

"I'm happy to say she remarried. Four years ago. She

married a corn merchant, a good kind man. They live in Bath now."

I looked for resentment behind his cheerful words, and found none. Four years ago his mother had remarried... how old was he now—twenty-three? Old enough at any rate to have accepted his mother's going without bitterness or jealousy. He would take much of life, I judged, in the same unselfish, philosophic way.

The clock struck three in its black marble tomb. Peter Quennel smiled across at me. "It's about time we were on our way. Are you frightened?"

I smiled back, admitting nothing. I do not believe myself a particularly timid person, but the unthinking savageness of large dogs has always unnerved me. I remembered the Alsatian hound I had seen from my window, heavy, thickset, watchful... all too readily a picture of gaping mouth and yellow slashing fangs came to my mind... The leap upon me in the dark... my futile efforts to protect myself.

"You'll be all right." He got up, held out his hands, lifted me to my feet. "I'll make sure the dogs don't get to you. You'll be on your own, of course, once you get out of the grounds—" He broke away, suddenly agitated. "But what will you do then? What a fool I am—I should have thought of that before. The guv'nor's always saying I never think things properly through. It's more than seven miles back to the city—what *will* you do, Mrs Deveraux?"

"I'm a great walker." I laughed encouragingly. All I wanted was to get away from Orme. What happened after that could be left to take care of itself. "And I've got lots of friends in Bristol. There'll really be no problem."

He hunted through his pockets. "You'll need money— and I'm always kept a bit short myself...." He produced half a sovereign and a handful of pence. Even in the anxiety of the moment I had to smile inwardly—what he called being "kept a bit short" would have fed a working family for a week.

"What do I need money for?" I asked, feeling that I had accepted too much from him already. "It's not as if there'll be a four-wheeler cruising by at three in the morning for me to hail."

He shook his head, pressed the half-sovereign firmly into my hand. "You never know when it mayn't come in useful. Now, don't argue—you can return it to me when you return the cloak and bonnet."

I didn't argue. Clearly more of his guardian's masterful ways had rubbed off on him than he realised.

He fetched his candle. "Now, you must listen to me carefully. No harm will come to you as long as you do everything I say. First of all you must follow me downstairs. Bucky sleeps in the old servants' wing, so there's no chance at all of her hearing us. And I looked in on the guv'nor while you were dressing—he's sound asleep, snoring like a grampus." He pushed a straggle of auburn hair back out of his eyes. "By the front door there's a hatstand where I swear Bucky keeps her everyday bonnet. I shall leave you there to get fixed up while I go to see to the dogs. Leave the front door open after I've gone, but do *not* go through it till you hear me whistle. Then, fast as you can, straight down the drive, turn right at the end of the rhododendrons, and the gate's just a few yards on. Close it behind you, and there you are. Nobody will come after you because they won't know you've gone."

It certainly seemed a simple enough enterprise. Always assuming that he really could keep those slashing fangs safely out of the way till the gate was shut behind me. He gazed into my face, making sure that I understood. Then he opened the door and went out into the darkened corridor. Briefly I turned back to look round my room: this was an unceremonious departure from the place that had for seven long days been my prison. My eyes lighted on the bunch of marigolds by my bed—so much had happened since young Mr Quennel had brought them to me, could it really only have been the previous morning? On a sudden impulse I darted across and snatched them from the glass. They would be something to remind me of his kindness. Then I followed him from the room.

The corridor was long, and broken by unexpected turns and steps up and down. The flickering candle flame cast our shadows huge on chairs and black oak linen chests and row upon row of antlers and paintings in ornately gilded frames. Everywhere thick carpets muffled our tread. My companion stayed close by me and helped me whenever I stumbled. After a very few paces I would not even have known the way back to my room correctly, so difficult was our route.

At last we came to a wide landing at the head of a great angled staircase. Below us, seeming impossibly far away, gas lights burned dimly in a black and white paved hall. Here guns and native spears hung upon the walls, and the snarling heads of lions and tigers, and at the stair's foot a great stuffed bear stood guardian. It was a place I would not have gone down into alone, not for a hundred pounds.

Peter Quennel nudged me. "The big game hunter was the guv'nor's brother," he whispered. "Got himself eaten by a Bengal tiger year of the Indian Mutiny."

I shivered. From what I knew of Dr Craggan, one of the heads upon these walls might be the very one that ate his brother. Together Mr Quennel and I went down the stairs, down and down, into this fearsome, petrified menagerie.... Once down on the tiles I clutched at his arm—our footsteps, quiet though they were, seemed to echo like a marching regiment. He comforted me. There was nobody to hear, he said. But the menacing silence must have over-awed him, too, for he whispered still, and crept—like me—on tip-toes to the double doors out into the lobby.

There I felt easier, the place of a more human scale, with a mirrored mahogany hat-stand and not a savage trophy in sight. He eased open the front door, letting in the reassuring summer smells of the garden.

"This is where we part," he said. "I'll leave you the candle —and there's a bonnet on the peg that'll just do the job. And remember—don't budge an inch till you hear me whistle. Then, straight out down the drive—it's not as dark as it looks —right at the end of the rhododendrons, through the gate and you're safe." He turned to go, then paused. "Good luck, Mrs Deveraux. And I sincerely hope we meet again one day under happier circumstances."

I looked up at him. Shadows lay across his deep-set eyes, making his expression difficult to read. "Thank you," I said. "Thank you for everything."

He laughed, suddenly boyish. "It's nice having principles," he said, "when they make you have adventures with pretty young ladies."

He squeezed my hand and went softly out into the moonless night.

For a short time after he went I was busy, putting on Nurse Buckingham's bonnet and tying its ribbons beneath my chin. I did not like so to be borrowing her clothes unasked, but I could not, I just could not face the outside world clad only in my nightdress and fairground costume. The moment I was settled again I would return her cloak and bonnet to her, as I would return the half-sovereign still clutched in my hand along with the bunch of marigolds.

Then I blew out my candle, so as to be ready to go the instant I heard Mr Quennel whistle, and at once regretted doing so. I had no idea how long I would have to wait, and the darkness closed about me utterly. If I heard a movement, any movement, I knew that I should scream. I began to count what I believed to be seconds beneath my breath, just to give shape to my waiting.

It occurred to me that I was leaving Orme with its secret still unknown to me. But I kept on counting. Yet I was at liberty now within its walls and could surely delay just long enough to investigate? I kept on counting. But then again, what a gift it would be to my fine and handsome Captain if I could only bring him the information he—the whistle came even as I was trying to persuade myself, and my count at two hundred and thirty-three. It was no signal but a tune that Peter Quennel whistled, innocent and sprightly. *A wand'ring minstrel I, a thing of rags and tatters....*

I flung wide the door of the house and stumbled down the steps onto the drive. Accustomed now to the dark, my eyes made out at once the curve of the gravelled drive away between the trees, the sky above it bright with stars. I ran. At once my leg, so long unused, began to pain me. I ignored it, as I ignored the barking and howling that broke out the minute my feet crunched upon the gravel. I ran and kept on running, my cloak billowing behind me.

Under the trees the drive was darker. I looked for rhododendrons on my right—shrubs of some kind loomed past me in a solid wall. I slowed, having no idea how long they might continue, not wishing to miss the path to the gate. Already I could hear voices mixed with the barking of the dogs, Mr Quennel's and another man's—Robbins', no doubt. So the guard was roused already, and curious.

The shrubs parted. I veered right, running on grass now, starlight showing but dimly through the leaves above my head. The path wound between high hedges. Then it widened. Suddenly there was grass, nothing beneath my feet, and I was falling forward.

I staggered, nearly saved myself, and collapsed, quite slowly, onto my hands and knees in eight or nine inches of water. I was on my feet again in an instant, stumbling on, flinging weed and lily pads from my sodden arms. The marigolds, for which I had no time to grieve, were gone, but the half-sovereign I still clutched, as we are told that drowning men may clutch at straws. My panic now was not that I was soaking wet, nor yet that I had hurt myself, for in truth my hurts were fortunately slight. My terror came in the realisation that I was clearly lost, that I must have turned from the drive too early or too late, that no path Mr Quennel might direct me along would have in its midst a lily pond, that I now had not the slightest idea which way to go next, and that in a very few moments the dogs would be released and the slavered fangs of my imagination a horrible reality.

What I might have done if pressed I know not. The need to find a strong high tree was in my mind, but the night was painfully dark and my clothes ill-suited to climbing. Mercifully, however, my initiative was not put fully to the test, for hardly had I reached the far side of the pond and staggered out before a figure came out of the shadows and Peter Quennel was at my side.

"Dear God," he said. "Here's a pretty mess." He took my arm and began to hurry me away. "Don't talk—save your breath for running. You took the wrong path, of course. My fault entirely—I quite forgot the earlier path. It leads to a tumbledown summerhouse...." We ducked round treetrunks, moving fast, Mr Quennel still whispering explanations in my ear. "I guessed what had happened when I heard the splash. I don't think Robbins heard it, though—he's too busy trying to sort out the padlock on the dog's run. The key has mysteriously got jammed all crooked in it somehow."

He managed an ironic chuckle. Then, abruptly, his grip on my arm tightened. I noticed that behind us the baying of the dogs had ceased.

"That's bad," he said. "It means Robbins has got their door open. They're trained to hunt in silence. They don't make a sound till they attack."

I stopped dead in my tracks. Our headlong flight was ludicrous—we'd never outstrip trained hunting dogs. Besides, my leg was agony by now. For seven days I had lain in bed, quite without movement, and now, suddenly, I was being expected to run some sort of nightmare marathon. "I'm safe if I'm with you, aren't I?"

His answer *had* to be yes. Yet he hesitated. "I wouldn't like to promise, he admitted. "To face them with a strange figure skulking in the bushes at dead of night ... I'm not their trainer, I wouldn't like to promise I can keep them back." He brightened, and patted my shoulder. "Still if we keep on walking, quietly and calmly, we'll find out soon enough."

And that is what we did. We walked on quietly and calmly. And Mr Quennel openly whistled the dogs to come to him.

They must have been stalking us but a few yards distant, for they were on us instantly. He addressed them by name, not a trace of the moment's tension showing in his voice for my insensitive human ear to detect. They snarled uneasily, made little rushes, backed away in front of us as we walked calmly on. They began to circle us, snapping still. I actually saw the pale flash of their bared fangs, and the starlight gleaming in their eyes.

I had always believed that if a fierce animal smelt your fear of it, then it would attack. Yet on that walk through the shadowed grounds of Orme my fear must have lain like a heavy miasma in the surrounding air. In my imagination the dogs' teeth were already ripping my flesh. I walked as if on wafers of ice, each pace my last. I stared about me till the darkness seemed to burn my eyes. I listened, deafened, to the thudding of my heart. I have never, I swear, in all my life been more afraid.

All things, even the worst nightmares, end. The animals held back, did not attack. Just as the blundering sound of footsteps and the light of a lantern among the trees behind us signalled the approach of Robbins, we came to a little gateway in the wall. It stood, as Peter had promised, invitingly open. He pushed me through, shut it softly behind me. I heard the key grate in the lock.

"Good-bye, Mrs Deveraux," he whispered. "Think kindly of me. And good luck!"

The dogs scratched at the bars of the gate, whining. He called them off and moved away. Suddenly my trembling legs would take me not a pace further. With the closing of the gate my terror had eased, and my body's reaction was to become quite helpless. I leaned against the wall close by and closed my eyes, and shook uncontrollably from head to foot.

Within the grounds of Orme the guard had caught up with my young rescuer. Light from his lantern shone out through the gate, casting long barred shadows on the grass beside me. "Mr Quennel sir, may I ask what's going on?"

"Going on, Robbins? That's just what I was going to ask you myself."

"With respect sir, Dr Craggan don't like folk wand'ring about outside the house at all hours."

"Neither, Robbins, does my guardian like the dogs to be confined when they should be free to guard his property." Young Mr Quennel spoke calmly but firmly. "I thought I heard movements here in the shrubbery so I came to investigate. By the time you'd got the dogs free if there'd been someone here I might have suffered serious injury."

"That's as may be, sir. Locking in the dogs was none of my doing."

"Dammit, man—are you suggesting it was mine?"

"May I ask, sir, what you was doing out and about in the first place?"

"Strolling, Robbins... just strolling. Today's accident in the workshops has left me with many problems on my mind...."

They moved away out of earshot. Clearly Robbins was unconvinced, as well he might be. But equally clearly he would never dare accuse openly the trusted ward of his employer. And by breakfast time, when Peter's little plot would finally be exposed, I would have placed myself safely beyond the reach of Dr Craggan, his guards, and his hellish dogs.

These lingered a few moments, snuffing and pawing the gate, then were called to heel and I was left to the silence of the night. And to the first serious thoughts about my immediate future. I had assured Peter Quennel that there were friends I could go to—a reasonable enough claim for Madam Kitty Deveraux to make but a pathetic falsehood in the mouth of Hester Malpass, accused thief. To throw myself on Mrs Skues' doubtful mercy was quite out of the question, as indeed was contact with anyone connected with the refreshment rooms, even Barty Hambro. My only hope, as I had long since decided, lay in the good offices of my fine and handsome Captain—and where he might be found I did not know, except that Kitty had said he owned a balloon and tent factory near Stroud. And in what direction?

The half-sovereign Mr Quennel had given me would buy me transport. But the hour could not yet be four in the morning. Till such a time, therefore, when a lift might be obtained I must simply decide upon a direction, and start walking. Perhaps I would come upon a signpost and be blessed with enough starlight to read it by.

My trembling abated and I moved away from the shelter

of the wall. I was in a grassy lane that must soon join the road that led past the main gate of Orme. My arrival a week before had been alas too precipitate to leave me with any impressions of overall geography. I could only set out and trust entirely to luck and mother wit.

The lane sloped down to the left, and I chose that as the easier course. And was fortunate, for it did indeed almost immediately join a considerable highway. Walking on the stones of this, however, reminded me very quickly of the thin soles of the pretty slippers into which Kitty Deveraux had compressed my feet. I took to the verge instead, but stumbled continually over unseen tussocks and had to return to the carriageway. So there I was, with scarcely a hundred yards of my journey accomplished, and my right leg cramped and aching, and my feet already sore.

I hobbled on. Above me on my left loomed the outer wall of Orme, and then pillars crowned with eagles massively black against the lesser, starlit blackness of the sky, and huge iron gates. Staring at these as I passed, I nearly blundered into the back of some high vehicle standing motionless in the road. Ahead of me a horse shifted its hooves and snorted uneasily. I stepped back, on my guard. The cart had high sides, and above them I could make out a curved canopy of some kind. What vehicle was this, to be waiting silently in the blackest hour of the night so close to Orme's chill gates? What criminality had I come upon here all unawares?

Suddenly I detected on the still night air the unmistakeable smell of woodsmoke. And almost in the same moment a voice sounded out of the darkness ahead. "You've come then," it said. "I knew you would."

I would have run, I think, had my legs been willing to carry me. I would have screamed had there been breath in my body for screaming. Not for fear in the voice, for I knew it well, but for fear of the unearthly power that had brought its owner so impossibly, so opportunely, to my aid. For the voice, of course, was Mordello's, and the vehicle I had so nearly blundered into was his gypsy caravan.

EIGHT

Mordello laughed softly. "You called me," he said, "so I came. Climb up beside me now, and we'll be away from this unhappy place."

Still bemused, but strangely unafraid, I made my way along beside his caravan. He reached a strong arm down and helped me up. Then he flicked the reins and his horse started slowly away. I sat back, clutching tightly the curved iron hand-hold. In the stillness of the night the wheels of the caravan sounded painfully loud. I expected instant pursuit, yet at the same time trusted this man utterly that no pursuit would come. For minutes we neither of us spoke.

Dark treetops heavy with summer leaf moved steadily past against the myriad stars of the sky above us. Warm smells of horse and faintly creaking harness rose up around me. For a time there was nothing I wanted to know, execpt that I was safe.

Then—"You said I called you," I queried. "How could that be? I did not even know you were near."

He took his time over answering. "I was not near. I was away on the downs. But you called Mordello. You called him as surely as if you had shouted his name from the rooftops. A cry from the heart that he could not deny. So . . . he came."

And I remembered. As if the memory were put entire into my mind, I remembered the moment of my deepest distress, I remembered my cushioned prison of a room, I remembered my nurse, my wardress, exulting over me, I remembered the name Orme burning into my mind . . . and I remembered indeed the silent cry for help that had gone up from my heart, the longing for the mysterious wisdom and counselling presence of the gypsy Mordello. No man could have heard that cry. Yet Mordello had heard it. And had answered it.

"Would you have broken in to Orme?" I asked. "If I had not been able to escape, would you have broken in and rescued me?"

I saw him turn his head sideways, quizzically, to regard me. "Mordello cannot concern himself with what might have been. He just knows what is."

Briefly I felt again my distrust of his fairground manner, of the grandiose phrases in which he cloaked his meaning. Yet it could be no fairground trickery that had brought him there, no cheapjack illusion that had enabled him to divine my need.

The horse plodded on. "Where are we going?" I asked.

"We're setting you, as is now necessary, on the road to Captain Deveraux," he said. But before I could begin to express my astonishment at this further omniscience he had raised a deprecating hand. "Just information received, Miss Malpass. No trickery, I promise you."

I was glad of the darkness to hide my blushing confusion. Could he have been reading my thoughts, even as I sat there quietly beside him?

"An old friend of yours came to see me," he went on. "My brother's son. A good, fine young man—Bartholomew Hambro."

"Barty?" My surprise robbed me of all manners. "Your brother's son? But Barty can't be a gypsy...."

"Can he not?" There was gentle mockery in Mordello's voice. "Because he went for a soldier, perhaps? Because he fought bravely for the English Queen?"

"Not because of that—no, of course not...." What could I say? Because he's gentle and hard-working? Because he doesn't cheat and lie? Because his skin is as fair as mine? And then I remembered that of course his skin was not as fair—there was a duskiness we had all attributed to the hot climates he had endured campaigning with General Roberts.

Mordello put his hand softly on my arm. "You're quite right, of course. Bartholomew is no ordinary Romany. He's given up the travelling life, you see... But then, there were reasons. I—" He came near to saying more, then changed his mind, and turned away, and encouraged the horse to a brisker pace.

Common civility suggested that I offer something more friendly on the subject. "So you're his uncle," I said. "I wonder why he never talked to me about you."

"Uncle? Not in your sense, I think. We Romany folk will

call all members of our tribe our brothers." He paused. "And as for his telling you of me, he would not do that. He has his way to make in the Georgio world. For an honest soldier wounded in the service of the Queen that is possible—for a Romany, not so much."

I remembered then how Barty had refused to be drawn on the subject of his family, or of the manner in which he passed his free time. It was sad that he had not been able to trust even me with the truth—however I searched my heart I could not believe that I would have thought worse of him for being a member of the mysterious Romany people. In my own way I felt myself quite as much of an outsider as he.

We rattled on under a lightening sky. Mordello went on to explain that Barty had gone to him for advice in his anxiety about my fate, and for help. The old man had been able to tell him with great certainty that I was alive and in no serious peril. More than that his powers had not been able to determine—tracing me to Orme had come much later, brought about by the intensity of my need for him.

As he talked the sun came up over the chimneys and spires of Bristol now visible between the hedgerows away to our right. As always, a grey haze of smoke hung over the city. He told me that he could not take me all the way to the Captain's headquarters near Stroud, for he had an engagement in Bath the next day, which was in quite the opposite direction. Instead he would take me to Sharpness harbour, from where boats ran regularly up the Thames and Severn canal to Brimscombe, the village just beyond Stroud where Captain Deveraux' balloon and tent manufactury was actually situated. He did not think, he said mildly, that canal folk would concern themselves unduly that I was Hessie Malpass, and wanted by the police.

I noticed that in discussing the everyday things of life his speech quite lost its mysterious, theatrical flavour. Periodically he stopped the caravan and went back into it to replenish the little wood stove whose black chimney pipe sent such a deliciously resinous aroma floating over the surrounding fields. When the sun was well up and we had just passed through Littleton-upon-Severn—which indeed seemed scarcely "upon" but rather several miles from the great river—he drew off the road beside a little stream and proposed breakfast. I am happy to say I was not then too far from childhood to find intense delight in the brightly polished miniature fittings of his caravan's interior, in filling his old black kettle at the crystal stream, in sitting—Nurse Buckingham's cloak long abandoned—on his trim bunk to eat the handsome plate of bread and eggs he set before me.

Looking back on that morning I cannot but marvel that at no time did I, alone in the depths of the countryside with this strange, powerful man, feel in the least afraid, nor even —clad as I was in Kitty's tights and thingummies beneath a flannel nightdress—particularly self-conscious. The tribute here must go to Mordello himself, to his quiet dignity and his air of wise acceptance. So forgetful was I indeed of matters of social rectitude that it quite surprised me when he indicated a press within the caravan where he said I might find clothes more suited to my coming journey by canal, and then discreetly left me.

The press was a treasure house of gaudy skirts and blouses such as I in previous times would never have dared to think of wearing. The times now were different, however, and I with them. It crossed my mind briefly to wonder at his having such a store, for he was not, I believed, precisely a married man, but the ways of his people were no concern of mine and I quickly set aside all scruples in the excitement of choosing myself a not too startling outfit. For all my efforts, however, as I finally descended the caravan steps dressed in a rusty-brown skirt and yellow, round-necked blouse, with a fringed shawl of darkest orange about my shoulders, I could not help but imagine Mrs Skues' face if she could but have seen me then. First, a parachutist's garb, and now this... certainly she would have thought her sober Hessie far advanced upon the road to sin.

Mordello was tending the horse. He turned, and at the sight of me he started, clearly much disturbed. I pulled the shawl more closely about me. "Will it not do? I asked anxiously.

"Do? It will do very nicely." He collected himself. But the explanation he then gave me for his doubts seemed less than the truth. "If I had fears," he said, "they were that it might do a mite *too* nicely. You will be among rough people, Miss Malpass. And Captain Deveraux himself is not—"

"But they're the plainest clothes I could find." And in truth, for all their strong colours, more than a little shabby. "And surely far better than the outfit I was wearing before?"

I had not missed the possibility that he was about to say something to the discredit of my fine and handsome Captain —whatever it was, I would rather not hear. I would go to Captain Deveraux warily—anything less would be foolish—but I would judge him only as I found him. Anything more would be unjust.

Such then was the brave determination with which I believed I could ignore the dictates of my heart.

Mordello smiled down at me. "Much better, Miss Malpass. If the effect is still striking we must blame not the clothes, but the person within them. She would be just as handsome, I fear, in the drabbest sackcloth."

The compliment was as graceful as it was unexpected—clearly this quiet, thoughtful man was no ordinary gypsy. I remembered then the neat shelves of books I had seen within his caravan, and the pen and ink stowed above his bunk. He had some learning then, beyond the grammar of his fortune-teller's art. I acknowledged his courtesy as best I could. With a grave inclination of his head, he handed me up, and we started again on our way.

The morning was radiant with the pure light of early summer, the sky palest blue and set with tiny clouds as silent and stately as swans. The lanes we drove along up the Vale of Berkeley soon became busy with brown-smocked men going to work in the fields, with carters bearing loads of lettuce and radishes for the city, with farmers and their wives in pony traps on their way to market. For every one of these Mordello had a friendly salutation, a wave of his whip, a joke or two. And they responded, cheered in their turn by his easy contentment, his happiness to be out in the countryside, and free.

Yet, for all the simple delights of the journey, and my own weariness—having had but three or four hours' sleep the previous night—I was still restless, still bothered by many questions as yet unanswered. The time came when I could contain myself no longer. "You spoke of a secret," I said. "When we met in the fairground you warned me that Orme sought a secret that was mine. You said I wasn't to share it unwisely."

"Did I?" He frowned. "Sometimes I have dreams, Miss Malpass. You cannot expect me to remember them so long after." He shifted the horse's reins from one hand to the other, then appeared to change the subject. "Would it surprise you if I told you I was once acquainted with Edmund Malpass, with your father?"

I waited. To be honest, nothing he might have said or done would have surprised me then.

"Edmund Malpass was a very special sort of man," Mordello went on. "I would not say *great*—greatness needs to be proved and he died too soon for that—but a man of brilliance and courage. Certainly his death was a tragedy for you. But it may have been a tragedy for the world also."

I shifted uncomfortably on my seat. I did not want to hear about my father: with the intolerance of eighteen years I had of him already a fixed opinion and it was not good. I remembered the little revolving leather stool. And I remembered the times when my mother and I had needed him and he had been too wrapped up in his dreams to notice. "What of my mother?" I said. "Did you know her also?"

"Well enough.... Hers was a head full of singing birds, and he loved her for it. He needed to, the trouble she brought him."

"The trouble *she* brought *him*?" I would have thought it all the other way. "What sort of trouble? You can tell me —I'm no longer a child."

He acknowledged this, but with a smile that did not accord me yet the fullest adulthood. "The worst sort of trouble, I'd say Miss Malpass—family trouble. Have you never wondered that you had no grandparents, no uncles, no aunts, no cousins?"

"They told me my grandparents were dead." I stared at his dark, expressionless profile.

He sighed, but did not question the truth of this. "And as for uncles and aunts," he said, "your parents were only children, so of course there were none." He hesitated, driven, it seemed, to say more, filling his moment of indecision with whipping up the horse for the steep hill we were approaching. At last he spoke. "You should remember, Hester Malpass, that sometimes the dead may live. And that even only children may sometimes have brothers and sisters...."

And this oracular pronouncement—irritatingly evasive though I found it—was all I could get out of him. Neither would he speak more on the circumstances of his meeting with my parents, though I persisted in my persuasions right to the top of the hill, even when we alighted from the caravan to ease the horse's load and trudged along beside it up the dusty lane. I was about to learn that his silence on any subject he wished closed could be formidable indeed.

Once at the top, however, my dissatisfactions were driven clear out of my head. The Vale of Berkeley was now behind us. We had surmounted a small ridge and now looked down upon the unfailingly noble spectacle of ships in harbour, their masts and yard-arms towering over the surrounding huddle of dockside buildings, their funnels bright in the mid-morning sun. Beyond them, beyond the harbour, the silver Severn lay broad and calm between grassy banks and softly wooded hillsides. While away on the far shore, very small, a train ran close beside the water, laying a trail of smoke like a tiny wind-blown veil in the air behind it. All this was a sight to drive from the mind everything but the simple joy of being alive.

Brake hard on, we slithered down the winding lane into town, a cloud of dust lingering in the still air behind us. Ragged children came out to run beside us through the streets. I felt myself very much the grand lady, perched up there on my seat, and thought to toss them pennies as I paraded by... till I remembered that in truth I was scarcely less poor than they, having only Peter Quennel's half-sovereign between myself and complete destitution.

So we passed through cobbled streets to the harbourside, and made our way along it to where the docks joined up with the canal that would start me on my way to Brimscombe—the Gloucester and Berkeley Ship Canal, to give it its full grand title. The docks had been newly-built but eleven years before and much of the town with them, yet already the principal commodity of their trade—coal—had left its heavy mark upon the buildings so that my first romantic hill-top impression of the place had quickly to be amended. The town of Sharpness was dirty and poor, and its drinking houses, two in every street, reminding me painfully of the Bristol I knew so well. The Bristol that a few short days in the pampered home of Dr Cashel Craggan had helped me to forget. Must men, I thought, always so devastate the places that give them their living?

A bridge crossed the canal. On it Mordello stopped the caravan and bade me stay by it while he went down to the dock. "Canal folk are easy-going," he said, "but I'd rather make my own enquiries first. I wouldn't want you taken advantage of later on."

Canal folk... the memory came to me then of Amy Dobbs, whose brother Patrick worked the Thames and Severn, carrying coal to Stroud, and through the summit tunnel to Coates and beyond. Quickly I told Mordello of him—Patrick had visited his sister more than once, and we had met, and immediately I had known him for an honest open fellow.

"I'll ask around for him," Mordello said. "We'll be lucky if he's here, though—he might be anywhere, up as far as Lechlade even."

But I had no fears. I knew that on such a day as this, when everything was going right for me, he'd be obligingly near at hand ... and I was right. Hardly five minutes passed before Mordello was back, and Patrick with him, and I was answering a dozen questions, about Amy, about myself, about dear clumsy Kate.... The day was going right indeed, for soon I learned that he and his skipper had just finished loading and were off within the hour, off for the dock at Cirencester with a full burden of coal. He knew the Brimscombe balloon and tent manufactury well—it was on their day's route. Night and day, by way of advertisement, he said, a balloon hung above the factory, a landmark for miles around.

In all the turmoil and excitement, my leave-taking of Mordello was briefer than I would have wished. He was not, however, a man for long farewells or expressions of gratitude. "I'll be near," he said. "Give me a week or two and I may even be round to see how you're doing."

We turned the caravan. I was reluctant to see him go and walked beside him as he moved off slowly on his way. I was reaching up, my hand on his arm. Suddenly he seemed very still and distant. He looked down at me, his eyes as dark as pits, just as they had been once before. And when he spoke his voice came as if down a long tunnel, everywhere and nowhere, blotting out all other sound. In that moment, as our eyes met, I was linked to him by far more than just my hand upon his arm.

"Remember, Hester, a man's destiny must be what he has the courage and the wisdom to make it. Aye, and a woman's too." I felt that he was staring into my soul. "But remember also that you are never alone—Mordello has eyes that see and ears that hear. He is close, even when he is far. Remember that also...."

The spell between us faded. I withdrew my hand. The horse gathered speed and left me. I stood for a moment, shading my eyes against the sun, watching the green and yellow caravan rattle away between the shabby houses. Courage and wisdom ... he asked more than most. But he promised more in return. Slowly the thoughtful moment passed. I turned reluctantly away, my small bundle of possessions beneath my arm, and entered again the cheerful hurly-burly of the world.

Patrick's skipper was a Mr Osgood, a rugged, coarse-visaged man, but with a thoughtfulness of speech and manner acquired no doubt in the long plodding silences of his working day. He introduced me to his wife, and she to their bonny, wriggling baby. Their way of life was of the simplest: there had been a time when longboat skippers were men of some small substance, with cottages for their families and fine Sunday clothes—but competition with the railways had changed all that. Now the Osgoods lived in a rough wooden cabin scarcely eight foot by six, and windowless, at the stern of their boat—the three of them, and Patrick also when the weather prevented him sleeping rough. It was a cramped, plain little place, but spotlessly clean, and neatly hung with their few pots and pans and a portrait of Her Majesty. A stove like Mordello's was tucked in one corner, but burning coal rather than wood, and leaking acrid fumes at every seam.

Indeed, it relieved me to hear that in their care, God willing, I would reach my destination before nightfall. To be honest, my guilt at burdening them with my presence overnight would almost have been equalled by my unwillingness to share their tumbled, airless sleeping arrangements.

Within ten minutes or so the big old horse was harnessed and our journey begun. For a while I walked with Patrick at the horse's side. Our course ran closely parallel to the river at this point, and it was strange to be up on the towpath with the canal water to my right and far below me to my left the wide reaches of the Severn now draining to sickly mud banks with the ebbing of the tide. Then the stones underfoot began to hurt me through the flimsy soles of my shoes, so I went back to ride in the barge with Mr Osgood.

He was not a man much given to light conversation. Indeed, he ignored me altogether and stood, stiff and straight, one hand upon the curving iron tiller, his cap pulled far down over his eyes, smoking a rancid clay pipe and absorbedly scanning the busy waterway ahead. To the sailing trows that passed us he would nod infinitesimally. Only in the wake of the steam tugs that occasionally blundered by, a train of scows bucking behind them, would he become animated, unleashing such a torrent of obscenities that I took to going below whenever one hove in sight.

His wife was an open, friendly soul, and much absorbed

with the wit and intelligence of her baby. The simplest of compliments from me and we were bosom companions. Such praise was easy, for he was a fine, cheerful child, and delighted to be placed upon my knee and allowed to chew the fringe of my gypsy shawl.... How easy it is to like those who are willing to like one instantly in return.

At the village of Saul there were great goings-on as we turned off the big canal and locked into the narrow Thames and Severn. There was a bridge at the junction, and a little white lock-keeper's cottage with honeysuckle and big yellow daisies just coming into flower. Mr Osgood departed into this cottage while Patrick saw to the locking, and returned in a high good humour, wiping his mouth on his sleeve and bringing welcome news of the way ahead. There was water aplenty—no shallow places, five good feet of draught through to Brimscombe and beyond. Clearly the wet summer weather that had caused us refreshment girls such disheartenment was a boon to the barge skipper.

And so I embarked upon the final stage of my journey from Orme to my fine and handsome Captain, the tranquil sunlit hours filled with the water's rustling murmur, the steady plod of our patient horse, the inconsequential chatter of mother and baby, Patrick's whistled excursions into the realms of Gilbert and Sullivan... and filled above all with the sense of gentle, unhurried progress, of gliding calmly, purposefully on, to a place that would be there waiting for us, unperturbed, no matter how long we took. What the exact o'clock might be, nobody knew or cared.

As the hours slipped away, so my years in the hectic, go-getting scramble of Temple Meads Station slipped away also, leaving me in a world where time was still the servant of man, and life was for the living.

We came to Frampton, to Leonard's Stanley, to Stroud. There were trows taking salt to Lechlade, and barges like ours with iron for the blacksmiths of Cirencester. There was wool from the spring shearing coming down out of the many mills along our course, tall, many-windowed buildings in the grey-gold Cotswold stone, tucked in among the steep surrounding hills, their sluice gates hissing, their wheels for ever turning. It was an England I had never seen before.

And when at Stroud, a railway train rushed thunderously along an embankment high above us and Mr Osgood actually removed his cap the better to swear at it, I realised this was an England I might soon not see again.

It was evening as we locked up past Stroud and came into the Golden Valley. So called, Mrs Osgood proudly told me, by Queen Victoria herself. And it seemed to me golden indeed, a contented place, filled with the fragrance of meadows. I was nearing the end of my journey—just at that moment there appeared above the trees in a turn of the valley ahead, like an eerie sunrise, the bright rim of a giant red balloon. I knew that below it, although hidden for now, lay Captain Deveraux' factory.

I was pleased, I was excited even. But a part of me wished that the journey might have gone on for ever.

The dock basin at Brimscombe was large, and boats were already crowding into it for the night. There was an inn close by, from which came sounds of singing and men's coarse laughter. Briefly the Osgoods tied up alongside for me to climb ashore—they were going on up to the mouth of the tunnel at Sapperton, to be first through in the morning. A group of leggers lived there and would work them through, lying on boards at the sides of the barge and pushing with their feet against the dripping walls of the tunnel. Patrick would lead the horse the two miles over the hill to where the tunnel ended. He stood with me for a minute on the dockside. Neither he nor the Osgoods had questioned me about my journey. Now, in the gathering dusk, he reached out awkwardly to shake my hand.

"Amy wrote me," he said. "Got a letter the other day—there's none of the girls believes you done it. Stole them things, I mean." He shook his head and frowned, "'Tis a wicked world, though, when you'm poor and got nobody to stick up for you."

His sudden sympathy, utterly genuine, moved me, brought me dangerously near to tears. For the magical duration of my journey I had forgotten my troubles, lived only in that tranquil moment. Now, before I could speak, before I could thank him, he had darted away and was chirruping up the horse for the last few weary miles. I let him go. Like Mordello, he would have little time for my gratitude. I moved off, skirted a group of urchins torturing some wretched cat, and found myself on the lane that clearly led to the group of old mill buildings above which the gaudy balloon advertising Captain Deveraux' factory drifted idly in the misty evening air.

NINE

Captain Deveraux' house lay to the right of a paved courtyard at the side of the main factory buildings. I fought down my sudden violent misgivings and knocked firmly upon its front door—having come so far with the express intention of throwing myself upon the mercy of my fine and handsome Captain, it would have been ridiculous to baulk at the final hurdle. My doubts increased fourfold, however, when the door was opened by a suspicious Mr Jowker.

He did not recognise me. "What's this?" he cried. "Hawkers and pedlars round to the back, if you don't mind. Not that we won't want nothing, not when you get there, so I'm warning you."

I could not blame him for thinking me the gypsy my clothes so clearly proclaimed me. But already the door was closing in my face, so that I had no alternative but to insert my scantily-shod foot and suffer the pain of its crushing.

"Mr Jowker," I said, "it is I, Hessie Malpass. Please tell the Captain I am here."

I should have been less abrupt, knowing that he believed me dead, that he was not a young man, and that such surprises have been known to be fatal. He weathered the shock well, however, first throwing the door wide to let the light fall fully on my face, and then hustling me in with much irritable clicking. "Where have you been then, wicked girl? Giving us all such grief and sorrow. And what's the meaning of these fancy togs? Been a-jaunting, has you?"

Hardly had I begun some small explanation before I was interrupted by a great shout from the room to the left of the staircase at the back of the hall. And in the same moment Captain Deveraux appeared in its doorway. His eyes were bright, his dark eyebrows puckered in almost comic incredulity, and his welcoming smile banished at once my every smallest fear. He was glad to see me. My perils were over.

"Hessie," he shouted, "do my ears deceive me? Can it really be Hessie Malpass, returned from the dead, the fairest ghost that ever a man beheld?"

He held out his arms. Unhesitatingly I went to him, and was received into a hug that was as warm as it was joyful. "No ghost, then" he said, releasing me and holding me at arms' length before him. "No ghost then, Jowker, but honest flesh and blood. And weary too, by the look of her. And no doubt hungry."

I could but smile and nod, for in truth I was both exhausted after my long day and quite famished, having cared to eat no more than a few mouthfuls of the Osgood's meagre fare, generously offered though it had been. Captain Deveraux led me through into the room beyond, a study with heavy leather chairs set before a window open wide onto a misty view of millpond and pale wooded hills. He fussed at me, and set me down, and bade Mr Jowker fetch me what meats their greed had left from the supper but recently over. In due course nearly half a pie arrived, and cabbage, and crusty bread, and a rich red wine.

As the light outside the window slowly faded I ate and drank, and told the two men my story. I told, that is to say, some small part of my story, for soon my weariness combined with the food and wine to dull my senses. My speech became fazed, my sentences all too often curiously unfinished.... Indeed, of the rest of that night I remember very little. One recollection stays with me, however: that of my Captain's face close beside me and his voice softly insistent in my ear. "Believe me, Hessie, I tried to find you. I called on every house for miles around. I beat on the gate of Orme, demanded to know if you were there. That swine Craggan came in person to swear he'd never seen you. To swear to set his dogs on me if I tried to force an entry. Believe me, Hessie, I did not lightly lose you...."

I woke much cramped and stiff, to find myself still in the study where I had been entertained the previous night, still fully dressed, and stretched out upon a leather-covered chaise longue of surprising hardness and discomfort. Since I could not remember choosing this uncomfortable couch for myself I could only assume that I had been supported to it while sound asleep. Or even—so my poor aching head suggested—while shamefully drunk.

The room's heavy curtains were still drawn across the windows, but enough light leaked in around them to announce another fine day already well advanced. I was alone, but from beyond the study came sounds of activity and the distant rhythmic clatter of factory machinery. Rising with great care so as not to aggravate my various aches and pains, I went to the window and drew the curtains. Their clatter and the sudden inrush of sunlight caused me to wince. But the view of terrace and mirror-smooth water beyond quickly calmed my spirits. And with this calming came recollection of my previous evening's reception, of the welcome extended me, and with it a feeling of great contentment. All my confused impressions of the Captain centred into one of tenderness and warm reassurance.

I was leaning by the window, my forehead against its blessedly cooling glass, when a door behind me opened and Mr Jowker entered. "Aha," he said, "so you've woke up. I hoped my ancient ears did not deceive me."

I made no reply. His manner unsettled me as always, being compounded of a great self opinion and a certain sly servility. As he approached me I perceived that he was wearing a green baize apron over the same crumpled trousers and grubby shirt as I had seen him in before. He cleared his throat and clicked his knobby knuckles. "You slept snug enough, I trust? This is a masculine household, Miss H—we did not think it suitable to move you far, not to divest you of more than your most respectable h'outer garments."

He was, I discovered then, referring to my shoes. Such rectitude on the part of him and Captain Deveraux was reassuring. I could not but smile. "I slept very well, thank you Mr Jowker. Indeed, I fear I must have *over*-slept."

"The Capting gave orders as you was not to be disturbed. He's about his business. I'm to take you to him as soon as you are breakfasted and ready."

I remembered Madam Kitty telling me that the Captain and Mr Jowker had been unacquainted until very recently. Evidently the old man had already made himself indispensable—adroitly filling at least some of the vacancy left by Madam Kitty's own departure. I had, of course, no illusions about the probable relationship between the Captain and his lady. But, whatever it might have been, it was now clearly at an end. I used my breakfast period with Mr Jowker to enquire about her most searchingly and became convinced that she was not only out of sight but also out of mind. This state of affairs, although comforting, brought with it problems of another kind. If I were ever to be cleared of police suspicion I needed her to be found.

After my breakfast I was taken to Captain Deveraux' office, the partitioned-off corner of a big clean work room on the ground floor of the tall mill building. I passed between rows of busy sewing machines, all driven by belts and overhead pulleys from the water wheel that creaked and shushed outside. At the machines sat a company of young women in headscarves, stitching and hauling at great furls of canvas and scarlet calico. I would not have been one of them for the world, yet they were obviously cheerful, their chatter loud above the clack and rattle of their work.

By contrast Captain Deveraux' office was strangely silent. He sat in his shirt sleeves at a plain wooden desk, poring over sheaves of invoices and order forms. It was a new man I saw: no mountebank, no theatrical, but a man who bent his mind assiduously to mundane concerns, a man with books to balance, a man—to judge from his expression—with worries much like other mortals. My heart went out to him more than ever before.

When he saw me his frown cleared. He leapt to his feet and greeted me with something of his old extravagance. He sat me opposite him, and Mr Jowker, who showed no inclination to depart about his duties, on a stool by the door. Clearly he was happy for the old man to be present. Resigning myself to this, I passed what time I must in dutiful civilities, then came quickly to the matter of Madam Kitty.

"Kitty?" the Captain said, surprised. "Why, I ain't seen her since Whit Monday—that's ten days ago. How about you, Jowker?"

The old man shook his head lugubriously and the Captain turned back to me. "What would you be wanting her for?"

I hesitated. I could not be certain how he would take the suggestion that she had been responsible for the theft of which I was accused, the theft of the money from the refreshment room till and the precious silver cup. I came to the matter as discreetly as I could.

In the event he was not at all put out. "Up to her old ways, was she? Well, I won't say I'm surprised—she always did have itchy fingers, poor child. I told you Kitty's a rough diamond. I did what I could for her while she was with me, but evidently.... He shrugged. "I'll make enquiries, of course. But she could be many miles away by now. And as for my getting back the things she stole, it seems to me most unlikely that she'd still have them."

"The cup has an inscription, sir—perhaps she'll not have dared to sell it."

He conceded this—though as much, I suspected, to give me some small measure of hope as from any great conviction. "Anyway, child," he went on, "you hardly need to worry. I'm sure your supposed offence will be no great matter to keep the authorities endlessly vigilant. You can stay here as long as you like—we'll be glad to have you, won't we Jowker?"

Mr Jowker piously bowed his head. "Speaking for myself, Capting, Miss H is as welcome as the flowers in May."

They were very kind. I was beset by doubts, however. Certainly I wanted nothing better than to be allowed to stay—but under what terms, and in what capacity? To step lightly into Kitty's shoes, for example, would be unthinkable.

A further uncertainty also existed: one that had troubled me much while still a prisoner of Dr Craggan. I braced myself for a question that must seem perilously close to impertinence. "Captain Deveraux, I must be honest with you—"

"I would misjudge you, Hester," he put in, "if I thought you capable of aught else."

I let that pass. My stay at Orme had revealed in me surprising capacities for deceit. "Then I must ask you, Captain," I ventured, "why you did not correct the newspaper report that it was Madam Kitty who had drowned in the estuary. You believed it was I who had died, yet you said nothing. I find this hard to understand."

He frowned at me, for a moment almost fiercely. Then he burst out laughing. "She finds it hard to understand, Jowker. Clearly she ain't an idea in the world of the troubles that beset a man in my profession." He leaned across his desk towards me, serious again. "Hester my dear, the public is eager for thrills. It is eager that beautiful young women like yourself risk their lives to provide such thrills. It is *not* eager, however, to take its share of the responsibility when —very occasionally—such thrills have a tragic outcome. The blame then must be shifted... in this case onto none other than myself."

He gestured bitterly. "Imagine the public outcry, Hester —an outcry. I must admit for once, with ample justice on its side—if it had become known that the poor dead girl was an untrained novice, a girl undertaking her first descent under conditions that would have daunted even the most experienced performer. Imagine—"

"It was not your fault that I jumped, Captain Deveraux. Indeed, you tried your very best to stop me."

He spread his hands. "Who would have believed a tale like that? An excuse so obvious? No Hester, it was alas far wiser to allow the lie. The loss of Kitty, veteran of a score or more descents, could not be set so resoundingly at my door. And who to suffer from the small deceit? Not you yourself, for I believed you dead. Not your family, for you have none...."

He paused. "Forgive me, Hester. Expediency tempted me. The easy lie, the lie that harmed not a soul and spared me the world's censure. The truth might well have ended my career as a performer. The lie left me to grieve for you in decent obscurity."

I would have forgiven him far worse. And not a word of blame I'd heard for my own idiocy that might have cost him so dearly. "Alive or dead," I murmured, "I would not for the world have brought you even the smallest disgrace."

His hand found mine across the cluttered desk. "Bless you, child. Bless you." Then he turned to Mr Jowker, who seemed much absorbed in smoothing the folds of his apron across his knees. "Jowker old fellow—Miss Hester I'm sure will want to make herself useful. You've been saying for days that I ask too much of you. I suggest she helps you about the house. And the two of you can dust out the guest room above the study for her use. She'll want privacy, and a place she can call her own."

Now I was completely reassured. I was to have a decent function in the household: my position was made clear. I was even, for the first time since I was a child, to have a place I could call my own. And as for a chaperone, I felt sure that Mr Jowker was sufficient of an old woman to qualify for the post.

Before I could express my gratitude however, Captain Deveraux had turned back to me and pinned me in the rare intensity of his gaze. A new tension entered the proceedings. "And as for making yourself useful, Hester, I'm much interested to hear what news you may have gathered of old Craggan's work. I'm willing to swear the old fool's not a day ahead of me—still, I'd be greatly obliged to have that opinion confirmed."

"Dr Craggan's work?" I thought back over the alarums and excursions of my week's captivity. "You mean that explosive device? That mechanical gun that used to go off at all hours of the day and night?"

"Explosive device? Mechanical gun?" This time Captain Deveraux' laughter was quite uncontrollable. He pounded the top of his desk in his glee. Even Mr Jowker essayed a discreet titter behind his hand. For myself, I felt confused and more than a little foolish.

As soon as the Captain saw my discomfort he pulled himself together. "Forgive me, my dear—how deucedly uncivil I must seem. But 'explosive device'—you've no idea how comical that sounds."

He struggled with a recurrence of his helpless laughter, and won. "May I take it," he said, his face very straight, "that you never actually *saw* this 'explosive device'?"

He mocked me still, so that I found myself being sharp with him, almost to the point of rudeness. "Last night, sir, I described to you most precisely the conditions of my imprisonment. I would have thought it must be perfectly clear that—"

"Hester... Hester, clearly my thoughtlessness has angered you. I would not have had that happen for the worlds...." He hesitated, then came to a decision and stood up. "I owe you recompense, my dear. Your association with me has caused you great suffering." He moved to the door of his office. "In return I shall let you into secrets that not even my friend Jowker here is privy to. I shall give you my trust because you deserve it. And because I know you will not abuse it."

Leaving Mr Jowker, he led me through the sewing machine shop, down steps and along a stone passage to a heavily padlocked oak door. There I waited, somewhat bewildered, while he sorted through keys on a ring attached by a chain to his belt. "Behind this door, Hester, is the project that absorbs me above all other. It has driven me to the very brink of bankruptcy, it has forced me into the mould of vulgar showman just to keep my creditors at bay. But one day, Hester, it will bring me greatness. It will bring me mastery of the ethereal elements.... My life's work, child —the greatest single benefaction mankind will ever know."

There had crept into his voice a dream-like quality that I

recognised: he had spoken thus of mastering the ethereal elements before. In another man I would have thought it an ambition wild enough to border on madness. But Captain Deveraux seemed surely no madman. He fitted the chosen key into the lock and swung open the heavy door. Beyond was a long room with shuttered windows the length of one wall. He strode from window to window, throwing back the shutters. I was momentarily afraid, knowing not what I might expect to see in the light that flooded in.

What I did see was a low, white-washed, cellar-like workshop, with gas brackets at frequent intervals along its walls, filled with racks and benches, tools, and machinery of the most incomprehensible kind. He closed the door behind us, and bolted it, and led me forward by the hand. At the far end of the room we halted. We halted before an intricate construction of metal: wheels and axles and copper tubes and heavy iron devices the purpose of which was quite beyond my limited understanding. It was not big—apart from one large wheel it could reasonably have been contained in an ordinary tea-chest. A curious smell hung about it, a smell I could not identify.

The Captain released my hand. He spun the wheel of his machine, watched entranced as components slid and meshed, engaged and disengaged. When he spoke, it was in a voice scarcely above a whisper. "Five years' work, Hester ... and the theory is right, I'll swear it is." Under his hand the components slid and meshed, engaged and disengaged. "It's the relationship, Hester—the exact relationships elude me. Trial and error...." He sighed. "But I'll have it, you mark my words. One day very soon my petroleum engine will be a reality."

Groping for his meaning, I picked out the one quite unfamiliar word. "Petroleum?" I queried.

"The logical step—first steam, then gas, and now the compression of petroleum vapor.... One uses the Otto four-stroke principle, with external flame ignition." He turned to me, his face shining with an almost holy fervour. "It will be so compact, you see. So light, so powerful.... The Germans have been working in the field for years, of course. Not that we've not had our own bright men, mind After all, wasn't it—?"

He broke off. Possibly he thought he was boring me. Possibly he thought, like my father, that a poor silly woman such as I could have no interest in such things. He was wrong—if the dream was his, then I wished to make it mine also.

"You want to make this engine," I said, determined to understand the purpose at least, if not the theory, "so that you can power a balloon with it, a balloon like that little model you demonstrated in the Refreshment Room? Like Josephine?"

"What else, child?" He went to the nearest window, stared hungrily out at the patch of sky visible above the surrounding trees. "Imagine it, Hester—imagine possessing the power to ride the wind just as the steamship rides the sea, to thrust your aerostat relentlessly forward, obeying *your* will and none other!"

His eyes moved across the blue of the sky as if he were already watching the flight of just such a craft. If this then was his dream, then I could understand it well.

"Five long years on this engine, child," he murmured. "Five long years... and before that, how long? A life-time of scheming, of research, of earnest study. Sails, paddles, steam propulsion—I tell you, I once even thought to rocket myself about the heavens!"

He laughed, then quickly was solemn again, staring still up at the limitless blue of the sky. "They tell me, Hester, that all children dream of flying. Well, so they may. They dream of many things, and each dream passes. But with me the dream of flying did not pass. It lingered, gained in power till its fulfillment became my whole reason for living. Can you understand that?"

I thought I could—I who had a smaller, humbler dream. But he gave me no time for a reply, indeed, desired none. "My first ascent was made when I was scarcely twelve," he went on, talking now half to himself. "A fairground affair, in a tethered balloon, it satisfied me not at all. How could it? But it told me at least that I'd been right—that flying was the thing, the only thing for me. I determined then, that day in the fairground, that one day—one day I would ride the wind as a bird, reckless of its currents, indifferent to its moods, free for ever of earth and earth's petty ways...." Suddenly he pounded the frame of the window with his fist. "And now, Hester, that day has almost come. My engine will set me free. It will set all earth-bound men free. All the glory and beauty of the world will be there for the taking."

He turned back to me. Slowly the fire died in his eyes, to

be replaced by something close to disgust. "And what, I ask you, would that footling old schemer Dr Craggan use *his* engine for—always assuming that he ever made it work? Can you guess the extent of that idiot's pitiful ambition? No? Then I'll tell you. He has set his heart on a petroleum engine simply so that he can propel one of his ludicrous little tricycles slightly faster along the public high road than all the other ludicrous little tricycles. There's vision for you! There's scope! There's man's questing spirit at its widest stretch!"

If that was Dr Cashel Craggan's ambition, then it did not seem to me nearly as ignoble as my fine and handsome Captain would have had it. But I gladly allowed that he was not the most disinterested of commentators. And I was certainly very pleased to have learned at last the real nature of the doctor's mysterious work. Though in truth if this then was the secret of Orme that Mordello had spoken of, then I could not for the life of me see how it could possibly be mine, as he had suggested. Neither did I see what connection it could have with the gun-like detonations that had shaken the big house to its very foundations.

This last was the question I pressed on Captain Deveraux. Readers today may wonder at my innocency. They will certainly be able to anticipate the answers Captain Deveraux gave me. But I ask them to remember that this was 1885, and words like *compression* and *exhaust* and *ignition* by no means a part of everyday vocabulary. Besides, by the time his explanation was finished it seemed to me that my much-mocked description of the petroleum engine as an "explosive device" was amply justified—and to bring home this very point I told him of the accident on the day preceding my escape, the accident that had reportedly cost Dr Craggan a portion of his hand.

At this Captain Deveraux became thoughtful. "Poor Craggan—I would wish such an injury on no man, not even him." He paused, then looked at me sideways. "The detonations continued for quite some time, you say? Regularly? Close, one upon the other?"

"So close that I could not readily distinguish each from its fellow."

"Growing faster, you said? Terminating in a sound louder than any?"

I nodded.

"Ah, so... It was the flywheel that broke, I swear. Or else the cylinder heated till it split...." He spun the wheel of his own machine again, watching closely, listening to the curious suck and hiss it made. "Set him back, I think you said? A month or more? Hm?"

I nodded again. Clearly his sympathy for Dr Craggan had been the merest matter of form, his real emotion one of curiosity, even of relief. Was he then a monster after all? Or was this not what the pioneering spirit must entail—the determination to think objectively, to learn from others' failure, others' tragedy? And the terrible human determination to be first, to be best, to win outright whatever race was being won.

Satisfied by my nod, he led me away, shuttered the windows, locked the door fast behind us. "The good doctor, poor fool, is trying tube ignition. To his cost, I fear—it can't be controlled, y'see. External flame's the only answer."

I wondered that he knew so much of Dr Craggan's work. "He told me you broke in," I said. "Did you really?"

He shrugged. "Let's say I was curious. It's a rash man who don't sound out the opposition. He let go a shot-gun at me —both barrels." He smiled ruefully. "In his place I daresay I'd have done the same."

We made our way upstairs. "There's one thing I don't understand," I said. "He planned to release me when his work was completed. How could he do that, thinking me Kitty who would have had no reason at all not to go to the police at once and accuse him of keeping her prisoner?"

"Wasn't your ankle his perfect alibi? Who would be able to prove it had never in truth been broken? After all, from what you've told me he treated you much like a favoured guest. In fact, if he's any style at all he'll send me before long an account for his professional services."

At the thought of such cheerful effrontery I had to laugh. "And will you pay for it?"

"To have Hester Malpass safe and sound? Cheap at a hundred sovereigns!"

But he became serious again as we reached his office. "What you've seen today, child, will one day transform the world. Speak of it to no one, I beg you. People know, of course, the nature of the work I'm doing here. But the details, the particular path I'm taking—that must remain a closely-kept secret. There are those, my dear Hester, who would try to get it from you."

I promised the utmost discretion. Though in truth I would have been a singularly poor informant, since the Captain's "particular path" was as much a mystery to me as it had ever been. Still, he thanked me for my promise, and regretfully bade me seek out Mr Jowker.

"I must get back to my desk," he said. "The time that I spend on my engine must be earned. And money, too, for its development. For that I must work, my factory must produce... we have a contract for two hundred bell-tents —tents for soldiers who must fight and suffer and die in the far corners of the world. You see the irony, child, that I should spend my hours thus? One day... one day the world will be ruled and shaped and pacified from machines in the air above—from *my* machines—and not one soldier will ever need to bear the burden of Empire again."

It was an inspiring vision—I thought of poor one-armed Barty Hambro, and other men even less fortunate than he, once soldiers of the Queen, now beggars on the streets of Bristol. A world where honest men need not suffer so would be noble indeed.

I left Captain Deveraux to his work and made my way back to the house. By daylight I saw it to be a fine, rambling edifice in dusty golden Cotswold stone, with stone-tiled roof to match, and thick comfortable chimney stacks and deeply mullionned windows. It nestled in the narrow bottom of the valley between high wooded hillsides, hard up against the mill building that spanned the stream and was its livelihood, even its reason. On one side of the mill lay the canal, and on the other the railway. And above it hung the huge balloon that was Captain Deveraux' own distinctive trade mark, trailing a banner with proud letters red on gold: *Deveraux Balloon and Tent Manufactury*. It seemed, all in all, a far more sporting, far more cheerful enterprise than ever Dr Cashel Craggan's bicycle factory on the Cheltenham Road could be.

I found the back door of the house, and went through it into the kitchen. A smell of roasting lamb hung in the air. Mr Jowker was peeling potatoes in a bowl at the table. For a moment I watched him, bent over this humble task, trying to recognise in him the drink-crazed creature that had brandished a broken bottle in the station Refreshment Room. It was hard, I decided, but not impossible.

Some small sound from me caused him to look up. Seeing me, he got at once to his feet. It was not, however, gentlemanly good manners that prompted this action. "I like a girl what volunteers," he said, firmly giving me his vegetable knife. "You can take over peeling the pertaters and welcome. I'll not say as it's a job that's beneath me, for all my classical h'education, but it's one as I don't have the calling for, nor yet the vocation."

I was about to protest a similar lack of sympathy when a sample of Mr Jowker's work caught my eye and I saw that we would clearly eat far more and throw away far less if I relieved him of the alien task. Besides, when I had disregarded the feeling of being put-upon I immediately realized that to peel the potatoes for my fine and handsome Captain's dinner was the very least that he might reasonably expect of me.

Mr Jowker watched me settle at the table, and rubbed his knobbed purple hands approvingly. "Tea and coffee, now, is my department all over. I bakes a nice pie, and my cabbage comes up a treat. Contrariwise, my gravey's like hotted-up porridge and my Yorkshire just don't bear thinking on."

As for myself, we refreshment room girls had left all the cooking to Cookie, so I had no idea whether my Yorkshire would bear thinking on or not. Still, he seemed to be proposing a fairly reasonable division of labour and I had already identified a dog-eared Mrs Beeton on the shelf above the range, so I reassured him on the subject. He then proceeded to apportion the various basic household tasks with a similarly quirkish selectivity. He would make beds, it seemed, but not change pillow slips. He would polish silver, but broke every glass he ever laid hands on. He would polish floors, but detested the new, more amenable linoleum. Doorsteps he would scrub, and happy to. Cleaning windows, however, was a degradation to which he had never yet sunk.

I agreed to all this willingly enough, having neither the inclination nor the right to do otherwise. The main difficulty I foresaw would be to remember exactly which tasks Mr Jowker's vocation extended to, and which it did not. Apart from this I could not see that my energies were to be unduly taxed. Certainly not when I remembered my days in the service of the Great Western and Southern Railways.

The domestic list completed, Mr Jowker tucked his thumbs under the straps of his apron and bent his knees portentously. "And now, Miss Hester, to sartorial matters." He eyed as much of me as was visible above the mounting pile of potato peel. "The Romany touch is out, I'd say right out. I venture to suggest it would give the h'establishment a bad name. No offence meant, Miss Hester, but I'm a respectable gent, always has been, and there'd be comments sure as fate."

I kept a straight face. "Won't there be comments anyway, Mr Jowker?" I asked innocently. "A young girl like me alone in the house with two gentlemen?"

He struck a defiant attitude. "Comments the like of that would have no justice, Miss Hester. They would be unjust. Injustice we can live with. Injustice is man's lot."

From which I could only deduce that he would consider comments about my gypsy clothes abundantly just, and therefore quite unsupportable. I was at a loss. "All I own is what you see," I said. "And I would not have the Captain buy me more."

The propriety of this sentiment appealed to him. He nodded solemnly. "You have not, I take it, the wherewithal to purchase fresh attire?"

I shook my head meekly, being in no position at all to resent his impertinence. Then an idea occurred to me. "Madam Kitty lived here once, didn't she? If there were things of hers remaining, then perhaps I might...."

"The room is cleared." He was quite sharp. "Not a trace remains."

This seemed to me a curious circumstance—unless of course she had returned here from the Fete in Bristol and undertaken a wholesale removal. Or unless—an even more curious circumstance—Captain Deveraux himself had wished to rid the house of every reminder of her presence.

Mr Jowker interrupted my thoughts. "Have you nothink, then? No savings? Not nothink at all, not nowhere?"

"Only a half sovereign," I said. "I have savings also, but I cannot get at them. Not ... just at the moment."

Not, indeed, till Kitty was found, and the stolen property regained, and I could return to Mrs Skues and set things right, and claim in return my few possessions, my small tin trunk and my darling Pig, the china guardian of my slender wealth.

Mr Jowker was heavily thoughtful. "What a great pity," he murmured. "In that case we'll just have to see what can't be arranged."

I said no more. As long as I fairly earned my keep I was content: the clothes I put on my back were truly of little concern to me. I finished the potatoes, put them to boil in a great black pan, and then inspected the meat that was roasting in the oven. It looked frizzled and at the same time raw. Basting it in the manner I remembered Cookie employ on the joints for the First Class dinners improved it enormously.

Mr Jowker, I saw, was busy now with the cabbage that was to "come up a treat." I was curious about him, and the moment seemed ripe for me to return at least in some degree his searching inquisition of me and my affairs.

"Mr Jowker," I asked, "you've not known Captain Deveraux long, have you? What were you doing before that time?"

He turned from his chopping board. "That's a fair question, Miss Hester, and a question as I knew was bound to come." He sighed lugubriously and seemed about to weep. Even so, I was unprepared for what followed. "Ambrose Jowker cannot tell a lie—those were the days when he was tucked safe away in a jail. Six years he served, and all for picking a person's pocket or two."

I was horrified, and knew not what to say. Certainly he was no man to make a joke of such a matter. "Six years...." I echoed. "How terrible!"

"Ah yes." He seemed about to burst into tears. "But then, the persons concerned was drowned, you see."

I recoiled. Such frankness seemed to me not only unnecessary but also positively shocking. To have robbed the dead was so extraordinarily squalid an admission. It was almost as if, for all his expression of regret, there was somewhere in Mr Jowker a secret pride at the enormity of his crime. Though such was not unheard-of, I knew, among criminals of the more depraved sort, I preferred not to be reminded of it. I questioned him no more, for fear of further revelations.

At least this explained the incongruity of Mr Jowker's get-up on the day I had first seen him—all bought brand new with Captain Deveraux' money, no doubt. But what did that make my fine and handsome Captain? The willing associate of a known criminal, or simply a noble spirit lending a helping hand to a fellow creature down on his luck? It needed, of course, little effort for me to believe the latter—after all, was he not being equally generous with me at that very moment? From my own experience I knew him to be a person not bound by the narrow moral judgements of the age, but I could not think the worse of him for that. If he had considered Mr Jowker's debt to society amply paid, then so must I.

Captain Deveraux came in for his dinner at two o'clock. The three of us sat down together to eat at the kitchen table, much as a family might, in a comfortably informal manner. In just such a manner also did Mr Jowker bring up the matter of my distressing insolvency, both he and the Captain sparing me quite any embarrassment by the calm good sense of their concern.

"Your savings can wait," Captain Deveraux observed, unconcernedly munching his roast mutton. "It's a problem easily solved—and justly too, with the two full guineas I owe you as the agreed fee for your Whit Monday appearance."

I protested that my descent had hardly been the theatrical tour de force I had been hired to provide.

He laughed. "Blame the weather for that. You showed willing, and you pacified the crowd. Believe me, you earned your money a hundred times over, just by not being afraid...." He paused, and stared across the table at me. "But I'm being insensitive. It ain't just the savings you're after, I'll be bound. There'll be other things—personal things you want to recover?"

I admitted that was so: my mother's portrait, my father's papers, my few treasures. I mentioned these with shame for their insignificance. Yet to me these simple reminders of my past were important, these trivial links with happier days were precious.

The Captain seemed to understand completely. "Of course you want them. They're a part of you. We'll just have to see what can be arranged—won't we Jowker old lad?"

Mr Jowker agreed, then with some mumbling brought up the question of my clothes. Captain Deveraux sat back and surveyed me. "Pretty as a picture—what an old woman you are, Jowker.... Still, if you're really worried I don't doubt there's something of Kitty's around we can put her in."

Mr Jowker stood heavily to cut himself some more mutton. "I don't think so, Capting. I'd say the cupboard was bare, in a manner of speaking."

"You think so?" The Captain was momentarily perplexed. "Well, if you say so... Not that it signifies—there's bound to be that grey fribbit somewhere around, that dress she came in from the station. Though I warrant that'll not bring her the happiest of memories." He surveyed me again. "I declare, friend Jowker, she must stay as she is. If she's mistaken for some gypsy wench, then so much the better. We must not forget that the police may still have some sort of watch out for her."

Though I would rather not have been discussed in this manner, as if I were some child to be attired at their whim, yet I was glad of the decision reached. The little money I possessed would be ill-spent on the sort of wardrobe Mr Jowker would think fit. And I had little confidence in even Captain Deveraux' powers of arrangement when it came to the regaining of my property still in Mrs Skues' possession.

In this I had underestimated him, of course, for he at once turned his attention to precisely this problem, questioning me closely about the hostel, and Mrs Skues, and where my small tin trunk might now be situated. At first I mistook his intention, protesting that she'd never part with it to him or any other man.

He laid down his knife and fork and regarded me earnestly. "The trunk is yours, you say? Your property and none other's?" I nodded. "In that case you must agree there can be no harm in taking it, with or without this Mrs Skues' permission."

"Break in, you mean?" I was aghast. "But that's thieving!"

"Where's the theft if you only take that which is yours?"

"But we'll get caught."

He roared with laughter. "There's my sensible Hester—always an eye for the really important things of life...." But before I could feel shame for the truth of what he said, he had leaned across the table and taken my hand. "We won't get caught if we go about it wisely, child, at dead of night when all are sleeping."

I drew back, disengaged myself. "I cannot. I would not dare."

"Not dare?" He flung his arms wide, containing the whole world in his exuberant embrace. "Of course you'll dare. It's the best adventure I can think of—a spice of danger coupled with the friendly righting of a wrong. No time to waste—we'll go this very night. My carriage isn't much, but Jowker here will spruce it up ... and accompany us too, I daresay, to make sure we don't come to harm."

My will was weakening. "But the hostel door is kept locked."

"I have a positive talent for locks." He snapped his fingers.

"And the inside will be dark. You'll blunder into things. You won't know your way from room to room."

Suddenly he was very still. "Of course I won't. That's why you must go in alone, Hester Malpass. That's only fair. If a wrong is done to you, then it's for you to right it. You must see that?"

The challenge was unmistakeable. If I felt only fear—and what need had I to feel compunction?—then fear was an emotion able to be overcome. And indeed the risk would not be very great, so soundly did the girls in the hostel sleep. ... Captain Deveraux was watching me, his head on one side, his eyes bright. To him the whole adventure was but a game. He knew I would not refuse him.

TEN

The night was moonless, the sky thickly clouded, and the first stage of our journey to Bristol painfully slow, along steeply winding Cotswold lanes no wider than the carriage itself. I tried to contain my impatience. Our margin of time was slight. Clearly we were to be late arriving, perhaps too late.

Captain Deveraux drove the two reluctant chestnuts while I sat inside on musty, uncomfortable cushions beside Mr Jowker, watching the yellow glow of the carriage lamps flick endlessly over the still half-naked pleaching of the high hedgerows. We spoke not at all, Mr Jowker and I, even after Wootton-under-Edge was reached and the going improved across the more open countryside beyond.

My afternoon and evening had passed in growing apprehension, for I could not wholly share Captain Deveraux' boyish delight in the coming enterprise. So much depended on Mrs Skues. If she had found a replacement for me, then my trunk would have been taken from its position under my bed and stored in the box room at the very top of the house. If she had not, then I would be obliged to brave the dormitory full of sleeping girls. If one of these woke, she would inevitably give the alarm. And what would be my situation then, a person already a thief in the eyes of the Law, discovered at dead of night in the commission of no doubt some further crime?

It was a possibility not cheerfully to be contemplated—and surely not one to be risked for the small reward of some family mementoes and the eleven pounds saved in my china pig....

Looking back twenty years to that time, I still cannot say precisely why I held my peace and went along with the Captain in his excited preparations. Except that the reward may not then have seemed so small, for the mementoes were all I had that joined me to my past, while the money joined me to my future—to my dreamed of independence as a typewriting girl. And the Captain, of course, with his generous enthusiasm, made it hard for me to play the coward.

For a time after Wootton-under-Edge the road ran clear along a ridge and the moon shone through the clouds to speed us on our way, so that it seemed we might after all reach Temple Street by the time I had decided. Three o'clock in the morning I had thought best, with everyone sleeping their soundest and an hour or so in hand before the girl on Late Call was brought back from the station by Barty Hambro. But then the sky darkened again, and Captain Deveraux was forced to rein the horses back to a sober trot. I had to admit some relief at this, since the carriage was indeed (as he had said) "not much" and the brisker pace along the rutted highway had thrown Mr Jowker and myself very much the one upon the other, and had seemed to threaten the whole structure's imminent destruction. Now however it again became possible that we might reach our destination, though late, at least entire.

In spite of my anxieties I dozed, I think. Mr. Jowker fell heavily asleep and snored abominably, but I merely elegantly dozed. I woke to the sound of a church clock striking three. I struggled the glass of the window down and leaned out. Country hedgerows were streaming by, just as they had done seemingly for as long as I could remember.

"Where are we?" I called.

"Just past Winterbourne," the Captain answered. "It may be another hour before we are there."

Still fuddled, I carefully added one and three and made four. This jerked me awake. "We mustn't get there at four," I cried. "Barty returns just after four with the girl who's been on Late Call."

For a moment I thought he hadn't heard me. Then he checked the horses to a gentle amble. "I'll take my time," he said. Then he laughed. "By five the sun will be well up —at least you'll be able to see what you're doing."

So it was that our clandestine expedition entered Bristol

in broad daylight, clattering cheerfully along streets already stirring. I was up beside Captain Deveraux now, closely swathed in Nurse Buckingham's cloak and bonnet, directing him along by-ways to St. Phillip's Bridge and the Temple Backs. To have him lose his path and scarcely an hour remaining before the girls were roused, would have been the final folly.

In Temple Backs we stopped the carriage. Mr Jowker, who was snoring still, we woke to mind the horses. The morning air was filled with yeasty smells from the Pipe Lane bakery just a few hundred yards down the road. The Captain and I cut through an alley into Temple street. He looked about him, much interested, as we hurried along.

"I never thought of you living in a place like this," he murmured. "Not a girl like you."

"They're good folk," I told him, defensively, almost angrily. "Good and bad, like anywhere else."

We passed the Crabbe's Well Inn—a bearded man was lying drunkenly asleep in the low doorway. "Like anywhere else," I repeated. "Only too poor to put a respectable front on their dissipations."

I led him up the iron-bannistered hostel steps just on past the inn. He didn't argue with my moralizing—indeed, he could hardly do so being himself where he was for the doubtful purpose of picking the lock of the hostel door.

It was a task he performed with great speed and efficiency. Hardly had I turned away to glance anxiously up and down the street before the door swung open and he pulled me inside. It clicked shut behind us. The house was cold, and smelled of well-remembered cheap carbolic soap. I left him as arranged in the shadowed entrance hall and made my way cautiously up the stairs. Each step seemed to provide a symphony of creaks and groans almost loud enough to wake the dead. Yet, on the first landing where I paused, the sound of Mrs Skues' untroubled snores came to me reassuringly through her closed bedroom door. I continued on up. Like a mountaineer I knew that if I once looked back my courage would surely fail me.

The stairs above Mrs Skues' room were uncarpetted, and noisier still. The house seemed strangely different, quite alien to me. Even after such a short absence I found it somehow smaller and shabbier, the paper on the walls more faded, the paint more chipped. For six years it had been my home, yet now I entered it as a stranger.

Outside the dormitory I paused again to listen. What I heard best was the thudding of my own heart, the rasping of my own breath. A girl cried out, flattening me momentarily in terror against the wall. Slowly her complaints subsided, first to whimpering, then to silence. The work of her day was hard and long—it took more than uneasy dreams to rouse such sleepers as she. I eased open the dormitory door, peered round its edge. Early morning light shone dimly in through the thin, blue-flowered curtains, showing me eight beds, all occupied. So I was already replaced, some poor twelve-year-old girl from the Methodist orphan's home in Wales, no doubt. Some girl to take the place of Bella as the humblest and most frightened inmate. Just as I myself had one time been.

This was no moment for reminiscence, nor yet for nostalgia. If my bed was taken then my trunk would no longer be beneath it. I must go on up to the attic floor, to Barty Hambro's room and the box room opposite.

The stairs were even steeper, and all the time the distance growing between myself and safety. Barty's door was open, his room deserted. Glancing in, I was surprised to see a Bible open on the bed, and newspapers on the ricketty chair: I had not known that Barty could read. In fact, I was sure he could not. Dismissing the thought, I turned quickly away and stooped into the box room close under the roof.

How long I searched in the cobwebby gloom I do not know, for mounting panic sets all notions of time awry. It seems now that I knew at once my box was not there, that I searched thereafter from purest obstinacy, from an angry refusal to believe the unwelcome truth. Finally I desisted. If the box were not there, then I knew not where it might be. I could have wept. And at the same time perhaps I felt the tiniest twinge of relief that the theft I had come to commit, the theft that was no theft, was no longer possible.

I made my way down the stairs, dust-streaked now and near to fainting with the fear that I might at this late stage be discovered. As I came in sight of the Captain he beckoned me impatiently down. We spoke not a word within the house, for so it had been agreed. Neither did he show curiosity that I came empty-handed, but bundled me unceremoniously out through the door. Mercifully there was no one to see our departure down the outside steps to the pavement below.

In the entrance to the Crabbe's Well drinking house the

poor bearded fellow still lay uncomfortably asleep. I walked ahead of the Captain, still too breathless to speak, to offer the sad story of my failure. We turned into the alley leading to Temple Backs. There I gasped, stifling only barely a cry of sheerest terror. Ahead of us a massive policeman was approaching ponderously between the high warehouse walls. We were utterly trapped.

I will confess that only the pressure of the Captain behind me kept me walking. We closed with the Peeler, stood to one side to let him pass. Captain Deveraux raised his hat and wished the constable good day. My heart stopped beating as the other eyed us grimly, saying not a word. Clearly I was a grubby little thing to be out walking with such as the Captain, and at such an hour. The constable continued to observe us for a moment that seemed to stretch to the end of time. Then he grunted ungraciously, touched his helmet, and trudged resentfully on his way.

We too kept our pace moderate, though for my part with great difficulty, down the remaining length of the alley and left into Temple Backs. Only then, safely out of sight, did Captain Deveraux let out a great sigh, and begin to laugh quietly, and lean helplessly against the wall, his cloak falling open to reveal held discreetly before him, a small black tin trunk with the initials H.M. in gold upon its lid.

I could have kissed him. I could have cursed him also, for not telling me sooner—though in truth our encounter with the constabulary would have been past all enduring had I known the full extent of the danger.

As his laughter subsided he began to explain. "I found the trunk almost as soon as I was left alone," he told me. "Knowing I might have some time to wait, I poked about for something snug to sit upon. And, dammit, there it was, close by the door, the very thing. I might easily have used it and gone all unknowing on my way, had not I seen them initials glinting...." He rested the box on the ground and mopped his brow. "What was I to do? Wake half the house by tramping up to find you?"

"But why was my box down by the door? It should have been up in—"

"There's a label tied to one handle, Hester. Maybe that's your answer."

I stooped and read Mrs Skues' writing upon it. "For Jacob Fish—to be collected." The words filled me with a great anger. Yet they made me glad also, for they spared me any shame or compunction for what I had done that day. Jacob Fish was a pawnbroker and secondhand dealer down Redcliff Hill, his establishment well known among the inhabitants of Temple Street and the like. Even my companions had visited him with sad little trinkets now and then, for which he would give insultingly little. And now Mrs Skues would have shipped off my few poor belongings to his murky store—in repayment, no doubt she would have said, for the goods I had stolen. Yet was not I, a British citizen, considered innocent until I was proved guilty? And was not therefore her action the clearest theft that was ever known?

All this I would have said to Captain Deveraux and more, but he was hurrying me on now to where the carriage waited. "I would not have you think me accustomed to such enterprises," he murmured, "but something tells me we should linger hereabouts as short a time as may be."

We reached the carriage and tumbled gratefully into its musty interior. Mr Jowker whipped up the horses. We clattered away at a breakneck pace. For a time I simply sat, my precious box clutched closely to me, while the Captain kept a shrewd eye out of the window and advised our wild coachman upon the route we should take. We did not pause to give the horses breath until the outskirts of the city were reached. There, with the coach now still, I could examine my treasure in greater detail. Mr Jowker came down from his seat to join in the happy reunion.

I found to my horror that the key I had brought from my grey uniform pocket would not be needed, for the lock mechanism had been crudely forced. With trembling fingers I prised back the catch. I opened the lid. And discovered what I should have known all along, that Mrs Skues would never have sent the contents unexamined to Jacob Fish, that the eleven pounds contained in my china pig would certainly first have been extracted. There, beneath my hands, by way of final insult, were his broken china fragments.

I wept. I'll swear I wept as much for the loss of an old childhood friend as for the mere money he had guarded.

My companions were at a loss, aghast. Mr Jowker would have leaned across to rummage for himself, perhaps to discover the reason for my grief, but Captain Deveraux restrained him.

"What is it, child?" he said, his voice very gentle. "Is something spoiled? Not there?"

I pulled myself together. Only Pig was damaged. The rest—the papers, my mother's picture in its silver frame, my party slippers, the few small remembrances—all these had been thought of little worth and left for Jacob Fish's haggling attentions. And these, I reminded myself, were in truth my greatest treasures, the humble, inconsequent things that gave me a past, an identity.

So I smiled as best I could, and explained what had happened. Captain Deveraux glanced but briefly in the box, then bade me close it and keep it safe. If I now had at least the things I treasured most, then he was happy.

He looked across at me, his eyes wrinkling above his now familiar, wicked smile. "And wasn't it worth it?" he whispered. "Wasn't it living? Hasn't this been a grand adventure?"

Then he swung away, climbed down from the carriage and took his place up on the driving seat. He summoned Mr Jowker beside him, and we set off back on the long journey home. I was grateful for his thought that I might wish to be alone, for indeed the alarums of the day had been no grand adventure for me, but worrying and wearisome in the extreme. I could have borne at that time neither Mr Jowker's heavy conversation, nor his heavy silence, nor his even heavier snores.

Left to myself, I slept the entire way back to Brimscombe which we reached in the late morning, not waking till the sudden stillness of the carriage on its ancient springs disturbed me. The door banged open, and Captain Deveraux was there to help me down. His two hands grasped my waist and whisked me laughing to the ground. Once safely landed, however, he did not at once release me. The laughter between us died.

His eyes sought mine and I met them as candidly as I might, not daring to breathe for what might happen next. "You're a brave girl, Hessie," he said softly, "to fall in with all my mad-cap schemes."

"Why should I not?" I lightly answered, "when all the gain was mine?"

"Would you not be brave then if the gain were another's?" I hesitated, seeking a truthful answer. He kissed me on the forehead, then let me go. "Come now—I'll not press you on that. Bravery should not be lightly given. Yours must be earned as carefully as any man's."

He turned and went with Mr Jowker to lead the horses away to their stable. Still trembling from the magic of his closeness, I lifted my trunk and carried it dazedly to the house. In the doorway I paused to look back at him. At the head of the shabby equipage the chestnuts were drooping, tired out. He had driven them hard, but now he coaxed them gently on across the mossy paving. Clearly he expected much of all about him. But the rewards of his praise and tender care were clear also. The sight of his stocky, purposeful figure stirred me deeply. And frightened me too a little.

Something else frightened me also in that moment—the sudden sensation that I myself was closely observed. Quickly I scanned the whole prospect, the wall surrounding the courtyard, the section of lane visible through the open gate, the nearby houses, the sides of the valley beyond. I saw, of course, no secret watcher. It was easy in fact to dismiss the sensation—now passed—as purest fancy. Or guilt, more like, for my own sly scrutiny of the Captain.

As I bore my box away to my room another thought struck me. Though I was not schooled in the ways of men of property, I did think it strange that a famous balloonist and busy factory owner such as Captain Deveraux should travel so shabbily, should tend his horses himself, should employ none of the army of servants his position might be expected to demand. Possibly his protestations of poverty that I had thought mere drama were all too justified. Possibly his unimpressive little engine had absorbed more of its resources than its size would suggest.... Indeed, I felt a moment's remorse at being an extra burden on him at such a time. But I quickly comforted myself with the thought that if he wanted seriously to be rid of me, then he had better devote rather more of his abundant energy to finding the errant Kitty. Until she were discovered, I must inevitably remain a fugitive from justice, dependent for my freedom on a slight gypsy disguise and the goodwill of two ill-assorted gentlemen. It was not a position to be relished, or prolonged a second longer than was necessary.

Later that afternoon the Captain came to me while I was in my room, sitting idly by the window, staring out at the hillside beyond the railway line and the little path that led up through the trees, pondering my situation. His thoughts, it seemed, had mirrored mine exactly. Indeed, it struck me then how close we were, even when apart.

He seated himself and came, in typical fashion, immediately to the point. "Tell me, child—you set much store by finding my poor light-fingered Kitty?"

I nodded. "What other hope have I to prove myself innocent?"

He frowned. "I feared as much.... Hester, my dear, this much has to be said. Even if Kitty were found, the chance of establishing anything against her is remote. Surely you must see that?"

"It's not that I want to see her in jail, sir. But if I can recover the engraved cup and—"

"But there are fences, child, wicked men who would take such a cup and melt it down within the hour. For Kitty to retain such clear evidence of her guilt would be folly indeed."

Though his words were harsh, their truth could not be denied. It was a truth that I could long before have worked out for myself, had I not preferred instead to delude myself with false hopes. Face to face now with bleak reality, I was for a moment silent. "What do you suggest?" I said at last.

"I suggest that the past be forgotten." He took my hands in his. "Already a new start has been made. You're a girl after my own heart, honest and brave. I suggest that you stay in my house, that we work together. There's a hundred ways you can help me. Success with my engine cannot be far distant—with it will come the new exciting life we both deserve."

Deserve? He who had known me such a short time, how could he claim to know what I deserved? The bargain he proposed seemed from his point of view poor indeed and I told him so.

He did not laugh my words away as I had feared. Instead he answered me with great seriousness. "If I've made this sound simply a business agreement, Hester, then that's my cowardice. You know so little of me I dare not propose more. Just stay awhile. Just give yourself time fairly to judge my qualities. Then we will talk again, you and I."

His meaning was clear enough, and too close to my secret dreams to be viewed without suspicion. For I loved him then as never before. And dared not let my love blind me. "You had a business agreement once before," I said, taking my hands away from him because I had to. "An agreement with someone" (I could not bring myself to say her name) "who called herself Madam Deveraux."

His gaze stayed on me, as steady as ever. "That's why I ask for time, my dear. You and she are as different as sun and earth. It is for me to show you in a thousand ways that difference."

He stood up then, and would have left me. But so tumultuous were the emotions in my breast I could not yet bear to see him go. "You ask me to forget the past," I said, "yet the past is what made me. You cannot think forgetting it an easy task."

He paused beside the bed on which my black tin box lay open. "That word *forget* was ill-chosen," he said. "The past is our strength, its lessons a springboard into the future. It teaches, Hester, but it must never rule...." He tailed off, glanced down, shrugged self-deprecatingly. "I'm a pompous ass. Forgive me."

To tell him that his words had seemed to me both wise and true would have sounded, though honest, like the rankest sycophancy. And anyway he might not have heard me, for his down-cast gaze had fastened in curiosity on the contents of my trunk. A silence descended upon us, of which he was not for some moments aware. When at last he realized his unmannerliness his confusion was such that I could not but laugh aloud.

He managed to laugh also. "These sheets of calculations," he explained. "You did not tell me you were a mathematician."

"Neither am I. Those papers belonged to my father. There are drawings also. I've no idea what they signify, but they came to me at my father's death. I've kept them because they show better than anything the sort of man he was. The drawings are so careful, the sums so neat."

Tentatively he reached out a hand, then looked to me for permission. I nodded gladly. "He was an engineer, sir. Maybe someone very like yourself."

I watched with pride as he turned the first few pages over one by one. The tiny blocks of figures marched and countermarched with such military precision across the paper. And the diagrams lay so crisp and delicate. I felt a small disappointment when the Captain ended his perusal less than halfway down the pile.

"Fine draughtsmanship," he said. "And I wish I had your father's head for abstruse reckoning. But the field is electrical, I think, and not mine at all."

He tapped the sheets together and seemed about to return them to my box. Then he caught perhaps a shadow of my disappointment on my face. "Another time? When I have several hours at my disposal I'll certainly be most interested...." He smiled at me. "There'll be other times, won't there? You'll not be leaving us too quickly? There'll be other times?"

He knew I could not be leaving, having nowhere to go. Therefore his question had another meaning, one on which I dared not yet commit myself. "If I can be useful, Captain Deveraux, I'll stay."

With that he had to be content. And I also, loving him yet knowing him so little.

The evening meal was late, the Captain occupied with factory matters long after his workers had all gone home. After eating he sat for a short while dozing by the fire, and then excused himself for bed. Mr Jowker and I were not long following him, once the table had been cleared and the kitchen made ready for the morning.

For once sleep was slow in coming to me. Thoughts of the future troubled me greatly. The man I had thought of as my fine and handsome Captain had been a simplified fantasy figure—the reality was far more complex and disturbing. I knew that if I stayed in his house long enough, he would ask me to marry him. And I had no idea how I might answer. I remembered my brave ambition to become a typewriter girl. Mordello had said my destiny was what I had the courage and the wisdom to make it. He had said also—and my whole body tingled at the recollection—that the secret Orme sought was mine and none other's. Yet it was a secret Captain Deveraux sought also. What could this signify? Had the gypsy foreseen my marriage? Was that how I was to make the secret mine? The thought was tempting indeed.

The night sky was clear and the moon high, shining between the cracks in my closed curtains, shining on the friendly, cottagey furnishings of the room Captain Deveraux had said I must call my own. I remembered another room, heavy and menacing, with dogs that roamed beneath its windows. And I gave a thought to the young man my rescuer. Ashamed that I had not done so before, I wondered how he had fared when his part in my escape had become known to his irascible guardian....

I tossed my head upon the pillow, feeling moment by moment more awake. Finally I could bear it no longer. I left my bed and went to the window, hoping the tranquil moonlight scene might calm my spirits. The grass was silver, the black trees as motionless as sleeping birds. The stillness, though, was so utter as to have a nightmare quality. It calmed me not at all.

As I watched, however, a distant rumble heralded an approaching train. It rushed beneath my window, showering soot and sparks, the people behind its lighted windows doubtless no braver than I, set upon paths no more daring than mine, hurtling on through the night to destinations hardly more predictable. And its passing left me strangely comforted, strangely less alone.

Then, as I was about to return to my bed, a tiny movement in the hedgerow beside the railway track alerted me, setting a shiver down my spine. Below me a man swung over a gate there, strode easily over the still humming rails, and disappeared into the shadows on the far side. Slung over one shoulder he carried a cloak, or possibly a sack. A moment later he reappeared, moving briskly up the path between the trees. The figure was unmistakeably that of Captain Deveraux: the pace was my love's, and the confident tilt of his head.

The night's surprises were not yet ended. While the Captain was still clearly in sight up the hillside path, a further movement in the shadows of the hedge beneath me betrayed the presence of a second man. He came to the gate, but did not climb it. Instead he lingered evidently watching Captain Deveraux on his way. I could see him only dimly, his attitude of attention, one hand resting on the gate. He was not, I felt sure, the only man I could reasonably have expected him to be—Mr Jowker. Besides, the memory of another watcher came to me, the watcher I had sensed that very afternoon with Mr Jowker's unctuous voice still to be heard within the stables. These two watchers must be the same, they *must* be.

The figure in the shadows below did not cross the track in pursuit of the Captain. Instead he seemed satisfied simply to know the direction of the other's moonlit journey, for once that was established he vanished from my sight and presumably departed the way he had come.

The house, then, was observed. The menace, though less crude than Orme's, remained. Was my life never again to be simple and unthreatened?

Back in the warmth of my bed I felt myself more awake than ever. I knew that the Captain should be warned that his movements were observed. But this must be done discreetly, for he might not be pleased at my own part in the discovery. I did not yet own him—he had a right to his secrets. I wanted to believe that he had gone walking at dead of night simply because, like myself, he had been unable to sleep. Yet there had been an air of purpose in his stride that betokened some more serious intention. Not to mention the sack over his shoulder, or had it simply been a cloak? Besides, it was hard to believe in his undesired wakefulness after a full forty-eight hours away from his bed.... There was so much I did not understand. Finally the comfort of my sheets and feather mattress claimed me, and I slept.

By the time I reached the breakfast table next morning, the Captain and Mr Jowker were already well embarked upon their meal, and decidedly unconversational. Such, I have since discovered, is the way of men at the breakfast table. I poured myself coffee and buttered a slice of bread. However threatening the silence might be, if I was to mention the night's events it must be now or never. I ate in silence awhile, seeking a suitably noncommittal opening.

"There's a path up through the woods outside my window," I said at last. "It looks intriguing—where does it lead?"

There was, I saw, no rush to answer. Slowly Captain Deveraux set down his cup. "A path up through the woods?" He appeared to find difficulty in understanding to what I referred. Then his brow cleared. "Oh *that*.... It's disused, I think. Hasn't been used for years, has it Jowker?"

Mr Jowker, who had been at the house scarcely longer than I, shook his head emphatically. "Not used at all, Capting. Far too steep and narrer."

"Just so." Captain Deveraux cut himself more bread. "There's a quarry up there, long worked out and rather dangerous. I fancy local quarrymen once used the path as a short cut to and from work." The bread knife paused in mid-stroke. "If you're thinking of taking a walk, Hester, there are plenty of other routes easier and far more pretty."

I thanked him for the advice, and said no more. But my heart ached that he should deceive me so crassly, and even enlist Mr Jowker's aid in the deception. If things were to be so between us then my love had best be stifled and allowed to die.

I decided then, out of the great hurt he had done me, to leave him in ignorance of the secret watcher. And further, to find out for myself as soon as possible what might be up at the end of the path he was so determined I should avoid. If the secret were innocent, then it would remain locked in my heart. And if it were not innocent, then I had best know it and be done.

Throughout the morning no opportunity to get away presented itself. After the Captain's departure to his factory office I was kept continually under Mr Jowker's eye, helping him about the house. While he skinned and prepared a rabbit in the kitchen, I was set to boil sheets and pillowcases out in the scullery copper: a task that I had to admit as I examined them was not before time. On my journeys to the drying ground beside the house I felt sure hidden eyes were on me, observing my every action. But I told myself I was by then over-sensitive, fearing bogeys behind every tree. And besides, if watcher there was, then his attentions were far more probably on the Captain than on me.

At lunch Captain Deveraux was in rather better spirits. His morning's office work had gone well, he said. The afternoon, therefore, could be devoted to final adjustments on his petroleum engine.

"Why don't you come and watch?" he said. "You'd bring me luck, child. It's run before, of course, but falteringly. I'd like you to be there when it shows its true paces."

I hesitated, having other plans for my afternoon. "I'm sure I'd only be in the way." I fluttered my hands. For once being a poor silly woman had its advantages. "I thought of taking a short walk down the valley. Perhaps I could come and watch you later."

He smiled indulgently. "You think it too fine a day to be cooped up in some old workshop."

I agreed with some show of shame. "Just a *short* walk— you could tell me the best way to go. I don't want to be out very long."

My deviousness disgusted me, and besides sounded quite transparent. But the Captain was perhaps too excited by the prospect of his afternoon's work to notice such nuances. I did however observe that, directions given, he lingered in the gateway to the courtyard for some minutes, taking friendly care that I followed the prescribed path and none other.

I walked on briskly enough—with the railway line close by I knew I could have no difficulty in finding my way back to where the path up through the woods began. I travelled that sunny afternoon hopefully, using every minute, every stride to convince myself that my Captain's secret would be some poor innocent thing, kept out of pride or tender foolishness, and of no possible consequence in the world.

Above Brimscombe harbour the valley narrowed, bringing canal and railway close together, the road crossing the water and rising a little between rows of terraced stone cottages. It was here, far out of sight of the house and the factory building that I found a well-beaten gap in the hedge and dodged through, up the railway embankment, across the track and down the other side. For most of the return journey the embankment hid me completely, so that but for the balloon bobbing cheerfully above the factory I would have had no idea how soon I might expect to arrive. The last few hundred yards were less well shielded, but by then only the upstairs of the house showed over the boundary wall. My bedroom window was there, and others I could not identify. I walked on bravely. The risk of being observed was slight, I decided, having no other alternative.

I found the gate into the woods and climbed it. No angry cries pursued me. I ascended the path. It was steeper even than it had seemed from my window. When I paused to regain my breath the whole valley was spread out beneath me, little toy houses among painted fields, little toy boats upon a looking glass canal. And the factory water wheel turning as if by clockwork above a crumpled silver paper stream. Even the balloon, though still huge, was below me. I could look down upon its shining silk, and the web of ropes that restrained it.

Up another hundred feet or so I began to wonder if the Captain had indeed told me nothing but the truth, for the path levelled there and skirted a great chasm, clearly an over-grown quarry. The way was dangerous also, in many places perilously close to the crumbling edge—so close, in fact, that more than once I came near to turning back. Yet I persisted, for surely no man would come up here at dead of night, as I had seen the Captain, simply for the view or the exercise.

I pressed on. Suddenly a rustling in the low undergrowth close by stopped me in my tracks. I waited, listening, trying to still my breathing and the tumult of my heart beats. No other sound came. I moved sideways, stooped, and curiously parted the leaves. There, frozen against the ground, crouched a wide-eyed buck rabbit, whiskers quivering, sides pulsing with terror. For a moment I could not tell what held it there, why it had not fled long before. Then I saw one back leg stretched out behind, caught in a wire snare. The running noose had tightened, cutting deeply into the muscle, so that the whole leg was now terribly swollen. It was also, judging from the angle it lay at, almost certainly broken.

I did not like to think how long the poor creature had lain thus, suffering and afraid. I knelt down, filled with compassion ... and saddened also for the cruelty inevitable when animals must be caught so that humans might eat. In a flash I remembered the rabbit Mr Jowker had worked on that very morning—was this then the reason for my Captain's small deception? If he were setting snares on this hillside might he now wish to spare my feelings, spare the delicate sensibilities of the innocent young girl he must still think me? I thought back to his night excursion, and the coat or sack he had carried over one shoulder. Here then must be the explanation I had come to find.

As I moved closer to the poor creature it juddered convulsively, but made no real attempt to get away. I looked again at the damaged leg and judged its case to be beyond saving. No animal so crippled could survive long in the wild state. I knew I was in no position to set up a rabbit's hospital. Neither had I the skill to do so. The brutal truth was that only one course remained open to me.

I stood up. Bracing myself, I went back to the quarry and sought a stone large enough and heavy enough to do what was necessary instantly, painlessly, and without risk of failure.

ELEVEN

As I carried the dead rabbit back down the hillside my thoughts were interrupted by a faint sound ... a sound similar to one I had heard many times before; similar, yet curiously different, slower and more rounded, blunted somehow. Not a sound to be mistaken for that of some rapid-firing rifle, but rather that of a larger, more cannon-like device. Even as I paused to listen it faltered and ceased. Faltered so quickly in fact that I could not feel it augured well for the Captain's progress. His petroleum engine, to be honest, sounded a poor thing beside the brave rat-a-tat of its rival in the workshops of Orme.

I sighed, then continued down the path between the trees. The engine started again, laboured, gasped, died, and was restarted. I came to the railway track, crossed it, and made my way up to the house. Once indoors the sounds were almost inaudible, more a sporadic vibration to be felt through the stone flags of the kitchen floor. I laid the rabbit on the table and went to wash my hands.

Mr Jowker came, attracted by the sound of the pump. "I hates to sound ungrateful, Miss H., but did our little furry friend come and give hisself up? There's one of his h'aunties on the hob this very minute."

I dried my hands, and turned to him. "As a matter of fact, Mr Jowker, I've been up through the woods to the old quarry." I watched him closely. "The way Captain Deveraux said was dangerous."

His hand crept up to ease unnecessarily his stringy neck in its vastly oversize collar. "Did you now... the Capting don't like his advice not being took. He don't like it at all." His tone was poised between outrage and threat. He cleared his throat. "And what did you find on this dangerous walk of yourn?"

"I found that rabbit."

"Did you now?" He turned the limp body over, but offered no further comment. For all his shameful past, he was evidently now the most loyal and circumspect of servants.

"It was caught," I told him, "in one of the Captain's snares. I had to kill it, to put it out of its misery. Then I brought it down."

His eyes met mine but briefly. "Finders keepers," he murmured.

I persisted in trying for some more positive reaction. "Those wire loops are cruel things, Mr Jowker. The animal was suffering terribly—if I hadn't happened by, it might have been left so for days."

"Quick and sharp mostly, Miss H. Coming a fair clip... head through loop... neck broke... never knows what hit it." He demonstrated, running one hand along the table top, catching it with the other.

But he was still evading the real point at issue. "Either way, Mr Jowker, I think you and the Captain should have been honest with me. I'm not a child. I do know that such things happen. It's not really going to shock me if Captain Deveraux goes out to set his traps at dead of night. Or at any other time, for that matter."

It seemed that I could almost see the cogs working in Mr Jowker's brain as he decided whether or not an admission of any kind would be safe yet. "It might be called poaching...?" he ventured experimentally.

"Poaching?" I had to laugh. But it was sad really, for now he was betraying the nature of his mind, and the difference between it and my Captain's. His was a self-interested reason for security, petty and ill thought-out, while Captain Deveraux would rather have had consideration for my feelings in mind. It would have been unkind, however, to point this out. And at least the truth was now out in the open. "You must think me a very righteous person, Mr Jowker, to object to a little harmless poaching. And besides—what could I do about it, even if I did?"

He appeared not to have thought of that. He sighed. "The Capting won't be pleased, Miss, not that you've found him out." He picked up the dead rabbit and carried it through into the cool stone larder. Clearly, even with its auntie already stewing, it would not be wasted—a pie perhaps, one of Mr Jowker's "nice pies."

As the afternoon wore on the vibration beneath our feet continued in fits and starts. Eventually I became curious to see my Captain's odd little machine actually in action. "If you've nothing more for me to do, Mr Jowker, I think I'll go down and watch the Captain at work." Being anxious to remain on good terms with him, I concluded, "Why don't you come with me?"

He drew the bag of ancient bones that passed for his body up very straight. "That invite is not yours to give, Miss H. We can't all be favoured. Never let it be said that Ambrose Jowker didn't know his place."

He sniffed, and departed. I let him go. Place-knowing was a quality much approved by Mrs Skues, but hardly one very high on my own list of priorities. After all, it sorted ill with my ambition, still undimmed, to become a typewriter girl one day when all the present alarums were past, to become, in a man's world, that most outrageous of beings, an independent woman.

I found my way through the factory sewing room and down the stairs to the workshop door. The girls who stitched from morn till night—I wondered how content they were with their place in the scheme of things. I wondered also if the Captain for whom they worked ever realized just how much of his precious petroleum engine was owed directly to the labour of their poor calloused fingers.... The workshop was silent. I tapped on the door, received no answer, so lifted the latch. The door would not open: though not padlocked, it was evidently bolted from within. I knocked again, and called out above the clatter of the machinery in the factory above. "Captain Deveraux—it is I. Hester. Please let me in!"

He did not answer, though I called several times more. Suddenly the silence within took on a sinister aspect. I beat on the door till it rattled on its hinges, but still to no avail.

Beside me was an exit to the garden. I went through this, found a rusty bucket close by to stand upon, and approached the high workshop windows. I peered through the dusty glass, cupping my hands about my eyes against the light. At first I could make out nothing inside but vague mechanical shapes. Then my vision became adjusted to the dimness of the room. I saw shelves, and lathes, and other less identifiable equipment. And I saw also—catching my breath in horror as I did so—I saw also the figure of Captain Deveraux, sprawled across a cluttered workbench.

My first fear, of course, was that he lay there dead. But then I made out how his shoulders moved, lifted slightly, rhythmically, as he breathed. He might indeed have been peacefully asleep, had not his face been lying sideways in an open metal tray piled high with rusty nails.

I beat upon the glass, but did not rouse him—and could not reasonably expect to do so. I made a great effort to remain calm and sensible. I stepped down from the bucket. I cannot now recall any thought of going for assistance— if my fine and handsome Captain were in some manner sick, then it was for me to go to him. It was for me to minister to his sickness. I lifted the bucket and swung it repeatedly against the window, showering glass inwards, breaking the slender glazing bars, making at last a hole large enough for me to climb through safely. I found a stick with which to batter down the few remaining shards along the bottom edge of the frame. I climbed upon the bucket again and heaved myself breathlessly through, falling clumsily onto the floor within. I stumbled to my feet.

Immediately a strange vapour in the air invaded my mouth and nostrils, fumes that caught sickeningly at my lungs. The whole workshop was clouded with a drifting bluish haze. If this miasma were poisonous, then my Captain's sickness was explained, and he must be transported into fresh air with the greatest possible speed. I went quickly to the door, drew its bolts, and flung it wide. Around me the deadly vapour shifted only sluggishly, drifting like slow autumn smoke.

Only then did I go to Captain Deveraux. I tried to rouse him, shaking his shoulders, lifting his poor face from its pillow of nails, even slapping it in my desperation. By now I was gasping myself, and near to fainting. He was heavier than I would have dreamed possible, yet somehow I had to move him. Wincing, I toppled him off the bench, scarcely able to watch as he fell in a bruised heap to the floor. Then I dragged him ruthlessly by his feet the length of the workshop and out into the pure air of the garden. He lolled like a dead man, his arms trailing limply behind.

I stooped over him to loosen his shirt collar. Though his breathing was faint, his skin was warm and the pulse beat strongly in his powerful neck. His lips were blue, his face deathly pale against the rich blackness of his hair. I knelt by his side, fighting my own dizziness. Behind me now was a group of factory women, attracted by the sounds of breaking glass. I sent one of them for Mr Jowker. The shop supervisor and another, both sensible country people, helped me to remove the Captain's jacket and loosen his shirt down to his waist.

Mr Jowker came quickly, took in the situation at a glance, and for once was mercifully free of long words and pontification. "I've seen the like before," he said, "in my days as a pit-head clerk. Fire damp, we called it—a poisoning in the lungs." He began to roll up his sleeves. "The Capting needs to breathe. But he needs warmth and snugness likewise. Bed's the place for him."

I sat back on my heels, thinking to organise a carrying party. But Mr Jowker forestalled me. Astonishingly, in one incredible movement he had hauled the unconscious captain into a sitting position and hoisted him up over one shoulder. He set off steadily towards the stairs, staggering but slightly, Captain Deveraux's pale hands almost touching the ground behind him. Though he was old and skinny, at that moment

Mr Jowker seemed to have the strength of ten. This was not the first time he had surprised me—perhaps he would do so again.

Left below, I arranged with the shop supervisor for a doctor to be sent for. By the time he arrived in a battered pony and trap Captain Deveraux was safe in bed and breathing more easily, his colour much improved. The doctor stared intently at his patient for perhaps thirty seconds. After that he sat heavily by the open window, closed his eyes, and appeared to go to sleep while I described the afternoon's events as best I could. Finally he sighed, opened his eyes, scratched his head, removed his glasses to polish them, replaced his glasses, took snuff untidily, and proposed "gas poisoning, without a doubt."

Questioned as to the nature of the gas, he offered no opinion. And as for treatment, why, none was possible. Either the patient got better or he didn't. For these doubtful professional services the doctor charged five shillings, which Mr Jowker paid on the spot. Then he went cheerfully on his way.

The advantages of being a medical man were clear enough. Clear also was the manner in which Dr Craggan must have amassed a fortune sufficient to finance his other, mechanical interests.

In this case the patient got better. Within the hour Captain Deveraux was conscious, his breathing and complexion quite back to normal. And his spirits also, as I discovered when Mr Jowker summoned me to the sickroom and left me there. He must go, he said heavily, his usual gloom now quite restored, and board up the window I had made such a thorough job of breaking. Clearly he felt himself far too old and frail to undertake such an onerous labour.

I watched him trail dejectedly away down the stairs, then turned and tapped upon Captain Deveraux' door. Hardly had I put my head round its edge before I was greeted by one of his great shouts of laughter. "You don't have to tip-toe, child. Nor yet look so reverend. I'm only still in bed because it's snug here, and a man likes a bit of fussing now and then." Suddenly he became serious. "Though I'll not deny you saved my life by all accounts, and I'm grateful to you for that. *Grateful* . . . what a weak, inadequate word that is! You saved my life, Hester. I shall never forget it."

I advanced into the room and sat quietly by his bed. His words moved me deeply—reminded me also of the terror

I had felt, the terror I had not dared dwell upon, seeing not two hours before his still pale form so near to death.

The moment passed. He rubbed his hands briskly together. "Still, an inventor's way has always been a deuced perilous one. And at least there's a valuable lesson been learned this day."

I was, as always, eager not to appear foolish. "Concerning the vapours put forth by your engine, you mean?"

"Exactly, child—there's a poison contained in them that perhaps I should have guessed at.... But not one, I fancy, that will trouble us once the machine is out of doors and in its proper element.

He tailed off, and leaned back against his pillow. Watching his eyes, I understood that although physically trapped within the confines of the room, they were seeing magic visions of the sky beyond, of ships that sailed majestically within the upper air. I tried in vain to share with him his mind's freedom. Repeatedly the clumsy, clanking, stinking reality of what was in his basement workshop brought my dream crashing.

It was with this mood still upon me that I found myself trying to frame an honest answer to his next question.

"Well now, Hester—you've heard my engine in action. What do you think of it?"

I floundered. "It ... makes a very loud noise, sir," I ventured.

"Which means you don't think very much." He smiled ruefully. "Not a patch on Dr Craggan's, eh, for all his wrong-headed ideas about tube ignition?"

In all truthfulness I could only nod, albeit minutely.

He smiled again. "To be honest, child, I don't think much of it myself, either. There's no guts to it—if you'll pardon the expression. And no speed to be got out of it, none at all...."

I leaned towards him, distressed to have my uninformed opinion so confirmed. "But you have ideas? Plans to make it better?"

"Plans exist. Marvellous plans...." There was an unusual note of caution in his voice. He paused, stared at me calculatingly, took my hand, patted it, came to a decision. "Deuce take it, Hester—you saved my life. I reckon you deserve an honest account of things." He pointed across the room. "There's a pile of stuff you'll recognise on that chest over there. Bring it to me, will you?"

The chest of drawers, like the rest of the furniture in his simple, manly bedroom, was plain varnished deal, well-built but quite without pretensions. On it, in a neat pile, lay my father's papers. I picked them up and took them to him. He hardly glanced at them, but set them against his knees and fixed me with a steady, serious gaze.

"It has been in my mind, child, to cheat you. To steal from you, God forgive me, your birthright." He sighed. "These papers I took last night—it was a cruel pretence to tell you they did not interest me. At that very first glance they intrigued me more than I can say. I read them this morning, every one."

He touched the papers lightly, curled up one corner of the bundle, riffled the sheets. In the quiet of the room the sound was like a cat purring. "They opened my eyes, Hester. They made such sense as I dared not recognize ... for they told me my theories were wrong, had been wrong for years. I resisted such an idea, tried to go on believing that my way was the best. And then, Hester, this afternoon—the longer I experimented on my engine the more clearly I saw just how wrong I was. And just how right, child, your father had been."

He looked away. "The thought came to me then to admit nothing. To copy the idea laid out in the papers and tell you nothing. Just return them to you later, casually, as if of no more than passing interest...."

Silence fell. I waited. Finally, though words were difficult, I prompted him. "It's more than six years since my father died, sir. Surely any theory he might have had would be long out of date by now?"

He shrugged. "Clearly your father was a brilliant man, Hester. A genius. For such as he to be six years—or sixty—ahead of their fellows is nothing. You must know that engineers have been working on the petroleum engine far longer than that. The Germans in particular, of course—a man called Benz, for one."

His enthusiasm was mounting. He gazed at me doubtfully. Then suddenly his excitement bubbled over and he sat forward, clasping his arms round his knees. "You see, Hester, the problem is really so very simple"—Simple or not, it was evidently going to be explained to me. I tried to focus my attention. "You see," he went on, "every engine has a cylinder. Inside every cylinder is petroleum vapour. This petroleum vapour must in some manner be ignited so that it will expand and push down the piston and make the engine turn. That, then, is the problem. And the solution? Well, Craggan would ignite it with a red-hot tube introduced into the cylinder. For myself, I have always believed in using an external flame, sucked into the cylinder through a series of valves."

His hands made incomprehensible shapes and movements in the air. Then he saw my bewilderment, laughed, and abandoned them. "Anyway, Hester, the thing is we are both wrong. All those years ago your father saw the solution that has so long eluded us. The electrical spark, Hester. It can be turned on—then off again. It's clean... precise... controllable... reliable. A stroke, my dear, of purest genius!"

Though I had understood but a part of what he said, at least the final words were clear enough. Pride in that strangely inspired man, my father, warmed me right down to my toes. "Then this electrical spark is what his papers are all about?"

"Exactly, child. Exactly. There are even notes of a correspondence he had with the maestro of electricity, Werner Siemens in Austria. The idea was sound, the maestro reported—yet clearly himself thought no more about it. This was back in '77. But for your father this support was all that he needed...."

Suddenly my Captain grabbed the sheaf of papers and brandished them above his head. "Three years' work, Hester! Theory... experiment... perfection... and it's all here. If your father bequeathed you nothing other than this, then he bequeathed you a treasure indeed."

Then he was still, his voice soft, almost beseeching. "Do you understand what I'm asking, child? The system, you see, it's here, worked out down to the smallest detail. But it needs to be constructed. It needs to be applied to an existing viable engine...." He paused, laid the papers aside, and reached out to take my hands. "I'm asking that the task of construction may be granted to me. I'm asking that the engine may be mine. I'm asking for a share in the fruits of your father's genius."

His words distressed me more than I could say. For a moment I sat frozen, unable to move, unable to think even. A strange dizziness affected me. I wrenched away and stumbled to my feet.

The Captain mistook the cause of my distress. "All rights in the device would remain yours, Hester. A patent would be obtained in your name. Only the basic engine mechanism would be mine. And the task of development...."

I hardly heard him. The room, the furniture, even my own hands and feet, everything seemed impossibly distant, as if viewed down the wrong end of a telescope. There was buzzing in my head, and the chill of sudden sweat upon my body. And in my ears, haunting me, the voice of Mordello, following me as if down a long tunnel: *... the secret Orme seeks is yours and none other's ... see that you do not share it unwisely ... share it unwisely ... unwisely....*

See that you do not share it unwisely. Always I had sensed that the man possessed uncanny powers. But that he should have foreseen this moment so precisely—that was a wonder terrifyingly beyond my comprehension.

Gradually I returned to my senses. Captain Deveraux lay just as before, propped up on his pillows against the simple wooden head of his narrow bed. The room also was unchanged, late afternoon sun slanting in onto bare boards and the corner of a worn Turkey rug. From outside the window came the neighing of a horse on the canal towpath, angry shouts, the slither of hooves. The world continued, comfortingly unimpressed. There had been wonders before, and there would doubtless be wonders again.

Captain Deveraux held out his hands to me. "You are upset, Hester. Yet still I have one more thing to beg of you. And though there are many saner men than I who would bid me hold my peace, would say that now is not the time nor the place, yet I must beg it and be hanged."

I should have stopped him then, had not my heart so painfully longed for him to continue. His shoulders rested naked and muscular against the pillow. Though he had lain so recently at the very point of death there was a strength about him that quite took my breath away. I knew what he would say, and I knew what my answer must be. Yet I could not have stopped him for the world.

"I love you, Hester. I have loved you since the first moment I saw you, so serene and so beautiful, behind that wretched counter. You sensed it, did you not? And see, my dear, how Fate has drawn us together. You are here now, and—"

I could bear it no longer. Though words such as these were all I might desire, yet I could not endure to hear them. For Mordello's warning stood irrevocably between me and them. I must deny my heart and body. "No—please, Captain Deveraux, no more. I...."

"You fear it is for some tawdry business advantage that I plead. Of course you do. Yet it is not so—I swear it. Here

—take your father's papers. Do what you will with them. Marry me, Hester. Marry me...."

He thrust out the bundle of documents. I backed away. "No. No, Captain... please I must... I must...."

His arms fell limply down onto the covers. "You're promised to another, then?"

I shook my head.

"Then what is it? It's not that poor trapped animal you found, is it? Friend Jowker seemed to think you did not unduly blame me. I'm not a cruel man, my dear. If you could allow me, I would love you most tenderly."

Again I shook my head. Nothing he could say might challenge seriously the warning that echoed in my head. I gathered my resources and walked as calmly as I might to the door. "You do me a great honour, Captain Deveraux." Formal phrases were needed, phrases to stand as a barrier between us. "Believe me, sir, I am grateful—deeply grateful. But—"

"But you need time, my dear. Of course you do. I know I'm not much of a catch—a rag-a-muffin of a man, really—" I came ridiculously near to rushing to him there and then and enfolding him in my arms, arms that had embraced no lover before and could surely wish to embrace none other after. It was not my will, but Mordello that held me back "—but I can promise you an exciting time of it, my dear. And all the love there is in me to give."

His hair was so dark, and his eyes so fine, and the movement of his lips as he spoke these words to me so utterly beguiling.... I felt behind my back for the door knob. "It would be inexcusable of me long to delay my answer, sir. Yet I am sure you would not have me take such a decision lightly." The door was open behind me, and my heart close to bursting with love. "Two days would seem to be reasonable, Captain Deveraux. Perhaps sooner—"

I could trust myself to say no more, but stumbled back a pace or two and closed the door between us. Instantly my senses reeled and I staggered to one side, leaned against the wall, panting and shuddering as if from the running of some great marathon. I cursed my foolish temporizing. My decision needed no two days in the making. It was singing in my blood at that very moment. Of a surety I loved him, and could think of no greater happiness than to be his wife. Why then should my answer be withheld?

Yet, even as I stood by his door, on the very point of going back to him, a realisation came to me that would not be suppressed. A vile, material thing, unworthy of a moment's honest thought. But it came, and nothing I could do would make it go away: the realization that, if my father's invention was all that the Captain said it was, and if the invention was now mine by right of inheritance, then there was indeed—in the Captain's own words—some tawdry business advantage for him to derive from the marriage he proposed. An advantage all on his side and none on mine. That being so, I told myself I was wise to hesitate. . . .

No—not wise, for wisdom was a soaring, noble thing while my present hesitation came from the merest petty-minded caution. I was, then, being cautious. Thoroughly sensible and cautious.

I sighed, and dragged myself upright from the wall, and made my way slowly downstairs. Hesitation was all very well. But—no matter how sensible and cautious it might be—it had to be resolved eventually. And what in my present situation could possibly happen to bring about such a resolution?

That evening, when Mr Jowker and I were seated in the study passing the hours till bedtime in a largely one-sided discussion of members of the criminal classes with whom he was personally acquainted, Captain Deveraux appeared in the doorway. He was fully dressed and seemed quite recovered, declaring that being snug was all very well, but a fellow could die of the silence up in that bedroom of his. He then brought out the port wine and settled with us to his usual lively conversation. For myself, I was most grateful to him for the easy cheerfulness of his manner, having expected our next meeting to be marked by all manner of dreadful constraints.

So free was the talk that I thought myself able to introduce the subject—long overdue—of my mysterious watcher. At the mention of him the Captain sharply drew in his legs and sat forward in his deep armchair. "A man, Hester? What sort of man?"

I had to admit that the one time I had seen him directly the night had been so dark that I could not tell.

"Craggan, perhaps? Or that pipsqueak ward of his?"

I frowned. "Not Dr Craggan—the man was not as tall, I fancy, and younger. And as for Mr Quennel—I'm sure he'd not do such a thing."

"Ever the loyal Hessie." He smiled at me, not altogether

pleased. "The stakes are high, remember. And the two of them were ready enough to think *you* a spy, were they not?"

For all Peter Quennel's great kindness to me I had no wish to appear in the Captain's eyes greatly partial in my defence of him. "The nature of your work is known to many," I ventured. "Might there not be other rivals who—?"

But the Captain was no longer listening to me. Instead he was attending to the silence of the night beyond the study windows. He rose and went swiftly to the curtains. "Your watcher was there last night, you say. Might he not be there again tonight?"

I had no time to reply before he had abruptly flung the curtains wide. The light of the lamps poured out onto the terrace. I held my breath. Within the lamps' circle nothing moved. But... had it been my imagination, or had there existed in the darkness beyond their range a shifting of black against black, a half-seen something edging away into the night?

Clearly Captain Deveraux had seen nothing. It was easy, then, for me to blame my imagination and say not a word. Mr Jowker joined him, and together they opened the windows and went out onto the terrace. They scouted about, found nothing, and returned. The Captain threw himself down in his chair. "Catching him at it would have been too much to hope for. But no harm's been done. If he was there at all he'll know now that we're on to him. He might even give up and go away."

I kept silent. If my imagination were truly so powerful, then the whole thing might almost be my fancy. Mr. Jowker closed the windows, then drew the curtains. "I've never liked Peeping Toms," he said. "If he's there, and I ever catches up with him, then he'll have a very nasty h'accident. A very nasty h'accident indeed."

There was such venom in his voice as reminded me of the other Mr Jowker, the man with a broken bottle jabbing in his hand, and brought a chill to my spine.

Captain Deveraux shrugged. "We live in exciting times." He regarded me speculatively. "Are you enough alive, Hester? Are you worthy of the age we live in?"

Seeing that I knew not how to answer he leaned back in his chair and began to expound. "All around us, Hester, man's imagination is breaking free. He's daring to dream dreams—and daring to give them the iron sinews of reality. Today, my dear, all things are possible. My vision of machines that will fly is only one among many. Others would drive machines far beneath the oceans. Already messages travel by electricity along wires. Who knows when the power of this electricity may not thrust men's voices, like lightning, through the very air itself?" He stretched his arms wide "We live in the most thrilling times the world has ever known, Hester. Fame, fortune, a shining place in the history books of man's endeavour—all these are there for the asking. That's why I asked you if you were enough alive. Opportunity is yours, my dear. Opportunity such as no woman has ever possessed. Don't be afraid of it, Hester."

Yet I was afraid. I whose ambition had soared no further than the operation of a typewriting machine, I was very afraid of it. I was afraid of my fine and handsome Captain also, when he spoke thus, for his words held a demonic fervour I knew I could never match. I dared not think of marriage to this man. Yet his fascination was such that I knew I could deny him nothing.

I gave him no reply, and the moment quickly passed. But my inner confusion remained, and soon I rose, made my excuses, and retired upstairs towards my bed, needing quiet, and the solace of solitude. As I made my way up through the silent house a candle burned dimly on the landing ahead of me. By the door to Captain Deveraux' room I paused. It stood ajar and I went in, driven by some strange need to regain the papers that had been my father's. They lay on the cover of his tumbled bed, clear in the oblong of light from the open door. I took them up. It seemed that the heat of his hands was still upon them, the heat of his body between the fine white sheets. Almost I returned the papers to where they had lain—my taking of them a shabby, untrustful act. But then I turned, and carried them quickly from the room. Mordello, I knew, would approve my caution. I cried then, as I went away to my bed, yet felt, with the papers in my possession, strangely whole again, all of one piece.

I awoke next morning with my mind made up. The answer to my dilemma was so simple, and so reasonable, that I could not think why it had not come to me before.

At breakfast I asked Captain Deveraux if we might take a walk together: there were things that must be said between us. He agreed without demur, Mr Jowker making with ostentatious discretion, no comment at all. We went out into a morning already grey with the promise of rain. I followed where the Captain led. Our route did not concern me: I merely felt that what had to be said would be best broached while on the move.

We walked along the lane to the bridge over the canal, and then up between the cottages. We walked in silence, the Captain not hurrying me to begin, as patient and gentle as always. Past the cottages he turned to one side and would have conducted me over a stile and up across the meadow beyond. I stopped him. We leaned side by side on the top bar of the stile. Somewhere close by a cuckoo was monotonously chanting its breathy lament. I picked a stem of grass and examined closely the miraculous exactitude of its every seed.

Finally I found my voice. "You asked me to marry you," I said. "I would do so gladly." I choked a little, but persisted. "You asked also for certain documents. For myself, you might have them, and welcome."

I heard his in-drawn breath, felt his arm move beside me, his hand seek to find mine. I evaded his grasp. "Yet I am but eighteen years old, Captain Deveraux, and not wholly mine to give. Neither can the disposal of my father's papers be mine alone."

"If not yours alone, then whose?" Neither the Captain's voice, nor his words, told me what I must know.

"There's a solicitor in Bristol," I said, as casually as I might. "A Mr Margulies. He's my guardian. I would need his consent in the first matter and his advice in the second."

"But why so solemn, child? Is this Margulies then a tyrant?"

"Not a tyrant, sir. A good, kind man. But—"

His answer was instant, and quite without fear. "Then we shall beard the gentleman in his den, you and I together."

Only now could I dare look up, happiness blooming within me like a summer flower. The Captain's face was close to mine, and filled with tender concern. How unworthy the test I had contrived now seemed, my invention of Mr Margulies' guardianship no more than a paltry deception, the product of an untrusting heart. The Captain had baulked at nothing. He feared no enquiry into his affairs, no examination of his motives. His good faith was unquestionable. To have doubted him was a sad thing, best forgotten.

I laughed aloud. I gazed into his eyes and laughed with the pure joy of living. He turned me to him, took me in his arms. I gave myself gladly to his embrace. He held me fast, kissed my lips gently, then with growing passion. A fire engulfed me, a madness of love, so that I clutched his head to me, my fingers deep in his darkly springing hair.

We stood there on the soft grass by that simple stile for a period outside time. The Captain was mine and I his. Nothing else mattered.

It was he at last who eased us gently apart. "We must be off to Bristol at once," he cried. Then he frowned, and snapped his fingers disgustedly. "But I do declare today is Saturday—an afternoon your kind Margulies will surely spend in the bosom of his family. Ride as we may, I doubt we'll catch him before he leaves his office."

I gazed at him, scarcely able to breathe for loving him so much. How typical of the man was this impatience! "Monday comes hard on the heels of Sunday," I said with mock primness. "I think I can survive till then, sir, if you can."

"Survive? Aye, Hester, but hardly more. And my name is Edward—let me hear you call me by it. For my part, I'll never call you 'child' again. You're no child, my dear—by God, you're not."

I blushed at this, though his frankness made me proud. "I'm no more than what my love for you makes me... Edward."

His gaze sought mine and held it, seeming to search my soul. "Say not so, Hester. Above all else you are your own person. You are *you*. Love is but a bonus."

"And love shared?"

"Love shared, my dearest, is the greatest glory of mankind."

For all his sudden seriousness I could have wanted no better an answer. I gave myself into his arms again, feeling, as he kissed me, a new intensity, a solemnity almost, a conscious dedication of myself to him. The fire was there, and stronger than before, but with it a new understanding of the gift that was ours: the gift of shared love.

Our lips parted. He took my hand and led me over the stile. We climbed the steep slopes of the meadow. The air was rich with the heavy smell of summer green. Near to the top he indicated a grassy bank thick with daisies, settled upon it, and flung himself down by my side. Above us the sky was no longer heavy and grey, but set with leisurely clouds that parted miraculously even as I watched, allowing the sun to stream in golden pillars down into our soft, lush valley. It seemed to me the clearest benediction.

My Captain's mood had changed. "Hester—a horrid

thought has just occurred to me. What, I ask you, if the good kind Margulies ain't got quite your taste in whiskery gentlemen? What, in short, if he can't abide me?"

"Then I'll just have to convince him otherwise." Some time before Monday I would have to confess my deception. But not then, not when everything was so new and tender. "I'll remind him it's not he who'll be marrying you. In fact, in the circumstances I'd think it extremely odd if our taste in whiskers agreed, his and mine."

My Captain laughed, and drew me closer to him. "Hester ... Hester ... how soon can we be wed?"

I kissed him then, I myself, for the first time, by way of answer. Then I drew back, interposed my hand between his lips and mine. "Three weeks are needed for the calling of the banns, Edward," I reminded him.

"Calling of the banns?" He raised his eyebrows, mocking me. "Hoity-toity—aren't you the grand lady. And what's the long arm of the law going to be doing all the time the reverend gentleman's crying your name to the four winds?"

The shock of his reminder brought sudden tears to my eyes. How easy it had been to forget the wretched complication of my life! He smiled contritely at his thoughtlessness, and kissed each moist lid. "Don't fret your noddle. There's always ways around these things. If all else fails I'll whisk you off to the sturdy blacksmith at Gretna Green...." His kisses moved down my cheeks. "And tell me, love—how d'you think you'll like it, being mistress of my house? It's not such a bad place really. For the moment, of course—till I can find you the mansion you deserve."

I felt myself responding, to the touch of his lips, to the strength of his body so close against mine. I felt my conscious will slipping away ... and drowsily resisted. "I'll like it very well.... Though I confess I'd rather we had it to ourselves, Edward."

He chuckled. "Your point is well taken, my dear." He was whispering now, his mouth close to my ear. "Friend Jowker must go. I promise I won't grieve for him. He's always left a lot to be desired, one way and another."

My shawl had fallen away, and his hands were on my shoulders, caressing them so that I would have had him never stop. He kissed me again, and his hands moved downwards. "Hester, Hester ... Hester my love—"

I became very still—not from fear, nor yet from outrage. I wished, perhaps, to deny responsibility. I loved him, and

I believed that he loved me. I was—as he had said—no child. In a few weeks we would be man and wife, but already I was his utterly, to do with as his wisdom and his clear desires might determine. My eyes were open, staring at the clean line of his jaw, the curl of his moustaches, the wild fervour of his gaze, and at the patch of blue sky, pale and limitless beyond. I trusted him.

His hands were on my breast. They lingered there, fondled, sought the buttons of my gypsy blouse, paused. And in that moment's hesitation they became still also. I sensed a sudden watchfulness, a new rigidity in his body. And heard, yet did not hear, a curious, inexplicable vibration. The very earth beneath my head transmitted to my brain a curious thudding. It grew, faster than thought, into a fearful thunder. Above me my Captain had lifted his head. I saw in his face something near to fear. In an instant he was on his feet, waving his arms, shouting, shouting. . . .

I screwed myself sideways, up on one elbow. And screamed uncontrollably at the sight before me.

I had always believed cattle to be docile, harmless creatures. Yet the herd I saw pounding down the steep meadow towards me had such a look of panic on their mindless faces that I counted myself already maimed, hideously dying, trampled, unnoticed beneath their sharp, indifferent hooves. I scrambled to my feet, slipped on the grass, and fell. I began to crawl, sobbing in my terror. But the herd was scarcely four yards off, and twelve abreast, and gaining impetus with every stride. I ceased my fevered, useless scrambling and crouched, all hope abandoned.

It was, of course, my Captain who saved me. Now he was on the bank above me, his boots dug firmly into the turf scant inches from my head. He stood there, fearlessly, like a rock, and the sea of cattle parted round him. The closeness of their passing spattered me with mud and stones and sodden clods of turf. They slid and skidded down the slope on either side of us, pressed helplessly on by those behind. One beast, clumsier than the rest, struck him with its shoulder so that he staggered and nearly fell. I screamed again, unheard in the snorting, trampling uproar, and watched him lurch, and find his footing.

Then, suddenly, the herd was gone, its sound and stench diminishing down the sunlit meadow. I was unhurt.

He came to me then, and knelt, and couched me in his

arms. "There, Hester. There, my dear... it's over now. You're safe, quite safe...."

I believe I cried a little. As soon as I was calm again we went together down to the stile. Beside it, in the shadow of the hedge, the herd was gathered, quite still now, their panic quite forgotten, poor stupid things, their sides heaving, staring at us in innocent bewilderment. We skirted them, and climbed the stile. The Captain paused, looking thoughtfully back. "I'd have sworn that field was empty when we entered it. And that gate at the top—I'm sure it was firmly closed."

He stared a moment longer, then shrugged. "At least we're square now, you and I. Yesterday you saved my life. Today —well, I hope you won't think me over-dramatic if I say I've returned the compliment?"

I shook my head. Nothing could over-dramatize the experience I had just been through. And there was something worse, worse even than he knew—something in my mind that I hardly dared give credence to, a recollection that could surely be no more than an impression of the fevered moment, a product of my terror. It troubled me, however, this recollection: I saw again a movement on the skyline behind the surging mass of cattle, a stick brandished, the hand that held this stick, the arm, even a blurred suggestion of the head. For a fleeting moment I saw again the man who had stampeded the cattle down upon us, and then he was gone. Gone as if he had never existed.

I said nothing of this to the Captain—to Edward. It was the merest fantasy, it *had* to be. I could not bear for our loving to have been spied upon, and lip-licked over, and spoiled at last from spite and vile reckless malignancy. It had not happened. The arm I had seen had been but a branch waving in the wind, the stick a wild imagining. It had not happened. Our love was still between the two of us and none other.

We spoke of our ordeal no more that day. Other, happier events piled in to take its place, to fill the sunlit hours with the growing wonder of my love. I moved as if on air. My life was new, each moment a fresh discovery of joy. And my Captain, my Edward, I think he shared in my delight. I think his pleasure, though it ended so soon, was not forced....

TWELVE

Sunday morning a weight lay over the house; an emotional burden having nothing to do with the grey skies beyond my window or the rain that had fallen torrentially during the night. I felt it the moment I waked. It chilled me, bringing with it remembrance of an earlier chill: the one cold disappointment of the day before. I had been aware that to expect joy at our news from the lugubrious Mr Jowker would have been foolish. But an absence of joy was one thing, while in the event Mr Jowker's curious reaction was quite another.

When Edward and I got back to the house after our walk we found him sitting at the kitchen table, polishing silver. He heard my Captain out, his drooping features showing no expression whatsoever. He allowed a long pause after the Captain had finished, rotating his brush slowly and thoughtfully in the tin of polish.

"Getting married, Capting?" he said at last. "That's nice. A fine h'institution marriage, so they tells me."

"The very best!" But my Captain's joviality was by now forced, and cut no ice at all with Ambrose Jowker.

"Finest thing out—for them as has the h'opportunity."

There was such bitter disappointment in his tone that I sought to help. "Did you never marry, Mr. Jowker?" I brightly asked.

The brush ceased its rotating. He lifted it, spat upon it, and returned it to the powder. "Me? Ho yes, I married me the nicest little lady.... If they tells you though, Miss H., as distance lends h'enchantment, don't you believe them. It don't do no such thing." He frowned. "Not that six years ain't a long time, mind. Can't say as I blame her, not really, for the old quick skedaddle."

But he obviously blamed her deeply. I tried to put myself

in her place, to imagine myself married to a man jailed for so long, and for such a crime. Clearly his punishment was far greater than the six years' imprisonment society had exacted.

He gathered his thoughts. "So you're thinking of getting married, Capting. We'll have to see about that, won't we? I said, we'll have to see about that."

The threat was so obvious, and so odious, that I expected the Captain's wrath to break instantly over the old man's head. But no wrath came. "We'll see about all sorts of things, friend Jowker. Each in its place." His tone was level: firm yet guarded. "And now I'd have you wish us happiness."

In this request there was clearly something of a command. For the first time in the conversation Mr Jowker raised his eyes from his work. He regarded us lengthily. "Every happiness to the both of you," he said. "And may your troubles all be little ones."

His words were kind, yet the way he spoke them made their meaning closer to a curse. The Captain drew me away, laughed the incident off. We must be patient, he said, with the poor old man. His days of love and getting wed were long past. We should try to understand his loneliness.

I agreed, of course. Yet it seemed there had been more to the incident than simple envy. It lingered in my mind, and would not easily be dismissed.

It returned to me now, as I lay and listened to the silence of the house. I rose, dispirited, and dressed myself. Besides Mr Jowker's scarcely veiled hostility there were also barriers between the Captain and me—barriers of my own making. I had guilts to expunge: my failure to trust him with my father's papers; above all my cautious invention of a guardian in the person of Mr Margulies who had in fact not concerned himself in the slightest with me for nigh on seven years. Yet this caution, inspired by my good friend Mordello, had been wise and necessary. Now I could go to my Captain in fullest confidence of his sincerity and love. I could take to him my small confession. I could meet his honesty with a similar honesty of my own, and make my mind easy.

I left my room, taking with me as a peace offering the bundle of documents that had been my father's. The breakfast table was deserted. Mr Jowker was pumping water in the scullery. I went to him, and greeted him timidly. His frame of mind seemed much improved, so that I dared ask him where Captain Deveraux might be found.

He sighed. "Well may you ask, Miss H. When there's one of his moods on the Capting he might be anywheres. Anywheres at all."

"Moods?" I could hardly believe moods of my fine and handsome Captain.

"Ho yes. Things ain't always sunshine and laughter with his lordship, not by a long chalk."

I ignored the slight tone of triumph with which this was spoken. "If he's depressed, then I must go to him. Have you *no* idea where he might be?"

"I'd say you'd do well to let him be, Miss H. Even the darkest clouds has a way of passing—h'if you follow my intention."

"Nonsense." I followed his intention very well. But with gentleness and love such clouds could surely be speeded on their way. "If you won't help me, I shall just have to search until I find him."

I strode to the courtyard door and flung it open. Behind me Mr Jowker made a great and unnecessary clatter with his bucket. "I'll tell you one thing—if the fact'ry doors open it might mean he's there, miss H. And then again, it might not.... But I'll tell you something else—" he came towards me, slopping water on the pale stone floor "—I'll tell you this much: when you was gone, all lost at sea like we thought, he spent hours alone in his office then. Shut up in his office. Hours 'n' hours...."

For some reason this piece of information, that touched my heart, seemed to Mr Jowker quite enormously funny. He set down his bucket and leaned against the wall, quite helpless with laughter. "Heart-broken, he was...shut up in his office...hours 'n' hours...."

Angrily I left him and stalked across the mossy cobbles to the factory door. It was indeed open. I entered, walked between the silent, deserted machines. At one end of the workroom there was a low platform on which long strips of scarlet silk, clearly sections of a balloon, had been laid out for varnishing. The smell of the shellac lay heavily in the still air. The only sound was the gentle slush of the water wheel, running free on greased bearings.

Edward was in his office. He seemed not to have heard my approach, for he sat unmoving, his head bowed over his desk, resting on his folded arms. Such was his attitude that I might have thought him asleep, had there not been an air of desperate tension about his motionless figure. I stood in the doorway, watching him. When he did not look up I tapped meekly upon the glass door panels.

Slowly he raised his head. "You, Hester?" He hardly seemed to know me. "What do you want with me?"

I hesitated, then presented the bundle of my father's papers. "I took these from your room, sir. Two nights ago."

"I know that, child. What of it?"

His tone was so remote. Now was no time to remind him he was never to call me "child" again. "I . . . I thought you might want them back."

He frowned, then gestured wearily. "Put them there, child. Put the wretched things there."

I did as I was told—put the wretched things, my peace offering, on a cabinet—then stood, twisting the fullness of my skirt between my unhappy fingers. Now was the moment when I was to have confessed to him my deceptions. He was to have kissed away my shame. We were to have laughed together over my foolishness. . . . The scene had been played like this in my head a dozen times and more. And always with the happiest, the tenderest of endings.

But the scene's beginning had been much different from this. In my imagination it had always been as happy and tender as its end. I sought for words, but found none.

Suddenly he buried his face in his hands. "Go away, Hester. Go away—don't stare at me so. Those eyes of yours—they'd break a man's heart."

I did not go, I could not. Rather I took a step nearer his desk. "It pains me to see you so unhappy, Edward. Is there nothing I can do to—?"

He jerked back his head. There were tears in his eyes. "Unhappy? What does a simple little soul like you know about unhappiness? What can she know?"

He gazed at me, beseeching I knew not what, then took sudden refuge in violence, pounded the top of his desk so that the pens rattled in their stand. "Go away, I say. I have work to do—can't you see the work that is everywhere for me? Must you brood and blubber and wring your hands?"

I made no protest, though it was surely he who was nearer to blubbering than I.

"Get yourself back to the house, child. Find Jowker. Make yourself useful for once. Isn't that what we agreed—that you should make yourself useful?"

Such unfairness was more than I could endure. "We agreed that we should be married, sir," I said. "If that agreement stands, then my usefulness should be to you rather than to Mr Jowker."

For a moment I thought his fury would explode in my face. But almost at once a terrible sadness seemed to engulf him and he lowered his eyes. He fussed absently with the clutter of invoices on his desk. Only after a long while did he speak, and then so softly that I could scarce make out his words. "I wonder, Hester, if a man can really learn to love another before he has learned to love himself?"

It was a question far outside my competence, for I had been brought up to think love for another God-given and self-love a sin. Yet his question held a reasonableness I could not deny. . . .

He picked up a bill of sale and began checking items on it one by one. He took a pencil, made a note, then referred to an almanac beside him on his desk. Clearly my interview with him, not of his asking, was ended. I made no further sign nor sound, but turned away and departed through the empty workroom. I could easily have raged against my Captain for treating me so. But his utter desolation tore at my heart, and the haunting pathos of his final question left me deeply thoughtful. I loved myself as well as most, no doubt better than many. Was that why I found no lack of love to give to him, to give my fine and handsome Captain? Love—and forgiveness also?

By lunch time Edward was quite transformed. He came to the table with ink on his fingers and a hectic brightness in his eye. "I tell you what, Hessie—I've been looking again through your father's papers. We must take 'em to London —take 'em to the Patent Office there. Once they're registered there'll be nothing to worry about." He spread his arms. "Nothing except maybe how to spend all our money!"

His brightness was too forced to be catching, but I joined in as best I could. For if he was a man of moods, then I must learn to live with them as well as him.

The meal progressed. In a moment when Mr Jowker was out of the room, taking dishes through into the scullery, Edward leaned across the table to me. "By the way," he said, "friend Jowker has kindly offered—indeed, he's quite determined—to stay on here with us after we're wed."

I could hardly believe my ears. But he must have seen the rebellion flaring in my eyes, for he held up a pacifying hand. "I know we agreed otherwise. I've told him it's far more than we'd ever dare ask of him, but he seems most firmly decided...."

At this point Mr Jowker, clearly having heard every word, returned smugly to the room. My Captain smiled at me encouragingly. "And you must admit, Hester, we'll find his services uncommon convenient as pressure of work on the new engine builds up. There'll be business meetings, week-end guests, all sorts of bothers."

I smiled thinly but said not a word, knowing that I would never find anything about Mr Ambrose Jowker in the least convenient.

I was silent for another reason also, wondering why the Captain had gone back on his undertaking to rid us of the dreadful old man. Was there some hold Mr Jowker possessed over him? Was this then the cause of his depression that morning? The fear that I might discover perhaps some long past indiscretion and think the worse of him for it? Did he really believe my love so shallow?

These fears of mine found in fact some confirmation shortly after lunch was over, when Captain Deveraux departed with Mr Jowker on the pretext of taking a stroll together. Even allowing for the eccentricities of Sunday behaviour, I doubted if Ambrose Jowker had willingly taken a stroll in his life. There must be matters for them to discuss, matters in which I should have no part.

I washed the dishes and tidied the kitchen. Then I went out into the courtyard. I looked about, trying to guess what path the two men might have taken. Edward's distrust of me hurt—there was nothing I dared not know of him, and I had determined to find him and tell him so, him and the sly old man together. I saw that the factory door stood open. Thinking they might be inside, I crossed the stones and entered. They were nowhere to be seen, either in the workroom or in the office. Then, as I was about to leave, their voices came to me, faintly audible above the soft murmur of the wheel. Following their direction, I went to the windows on the far side of the workroom and looked out through the bars. Captain Deveraux was there, on the bank beside the mill-race, and Mr Jowker with him.

I could hear nothing of their words. After the night's torrential rain the stream was in noisy spate, and besides, they were too distant. As I watched they began to move away, still talking. I raised my hand to beat upon the glass and attract their attention, but then—for no adequate reason that I could afterwards think of—changed my mind. And thus, so easily, so lightly, made possible the whole disastrous chain of events that was to mark that momentous Sunday afternoon.

The two men walked away, still talking. And almost immediately I heard behind me the clatter of a carriage briskly driven. It entered the courtyard and came to a snorting halt. By the time I had reached the factory door its driver was down from his seat, tethering his horse. It was a small closed carriage, smart and to the point. And its driver—equally smart in slim-trousered country tweeds and square-crowned bowler—was to be recognized at once as Mr Peter Quennel.

Astonished and quite delighted, I called to him. He turned, saw me, waved impulsively, and advanced towards me. As he approached, however, so his pace slowed—as if the first simple pleasure of meeting became replaced by some more complicated emotion.

At length he stopped in front of me, his smile now hardly more than manners might require, removed his hat, and held out his hand. "Mrs Deveraux... how d'you do. I see you did reach home safely after all."

It was a curious greeting. And it raised at once the difficult question of my identity. I took his out-stretched hand. "Mr Quennel—I'm truly pleased to see you. Yet there's a confession I must—"

"I almost hoped you hadn't, you see." Clearly he'd not heard me. Awkwardly he scuffled his feet. "Hadn't reached home, I mean. Then this whole project would have fizzled out almost before it had begun." He essayed a nervous laugh.

I was bewildered. "Project? I'm afraid I do not understand you, Mr Quennel."

He glanced quickly round the courtyard. "May I speak to you, Mrs Deveraux? In private?"

This placed me in a quandary, for I doubted if the Captain would be pleased to find me entertaining the ward of his hated enemy in the study or the grand front parlour. Hoping for the best, I stood to one side and invited him into the factory workroom instead. It was not the finest hospitality, but it was the best I dared offer.

He entered without comment and I closed the door. He hesitated, turning his hat brim anxiously in his fingers. "Mrs Deveraux—I'd best come straight to the point. It's fully five days now since you escaped from Orme. My guardian has been expecting some announcement of your safe arrival. He's very surprised that none has been made."

I stared at him. This was a circumstance I should have been prepared for. "No announcement?" I countered, attack being often the best form of defence. "How can he possibly know that no announcement has been made?"

"You were thought dead, ma'am, and now you are alive. He is a magistrate. He would quickly hear if—"

"In that case I would expect him to be grateful for our silence. As a magistrate, his behaviour has hardly been—"

"Please. . . ." Mr Quennel dropped his hat in his confusion, took some seconds recovering it. "Please understand, Mrs Deveraux, that I have little influence over my guardian. If challenged he would say that he had not read the newspaper announcing your death. It would be hard to prove otherwise. He would say that he treated you in all good faith for a damaged ankle, that you left his house in a normal manner. Nurse Bucky would support him. He is a man of considerable position. He would be believed."

It was hard to be angry with this young man, so disarmingly honest and shamefaced was he. "But you still have not explained the reason for this visit," I said. "It can hardly be for the sake of the money or the clothes that I admit I should have returned to you by now."

He waved these away. "Bucky's cloak and bonnet are but a tiny part of it. And the money he doesn't know of. The truth is . . ." distractedly he took a pace or two away, then back again ". . . the truth is that the guv'nor suspects the Captain of some greater deception. Insurance, perhaps. Some legal trickery."

His eyes were pleading that I disassociate him from his guardian's crude suspicions. And yet. . . . "In that case, Mr Quennel, why does not your guardian himself go at once to the police? As a magistrate is that not his clear duty?"

Mr Quennel stared at his boots, his reply almost inaudible. "I'd rather not say."

"Then I'll say it for you. The answer is short, and ugly." I approached very close to where he stood, and spoke with great distinctness. "The answer is blackmail, Mr Quennel. Clearly your guardian hopes to gain some personal advantage from this wicked suspicion of his." I could be brave on the safe ground of my Captain's reputation. Beside that my own fate was nothing. "You can tell him he's had a wasted journey."

Peter Quennel stepped back a pace. "That's why I insisted that he let me come in first. The guv'nor's out in the carriage at this very moment. But I wanted to ... to...."

"To break the news gently?" My tone was harsh. But I did not force him to answer me, for I had played with him long enough. It was time now for truth between us. "You can tell Dr Craggan that his suspicions are quite unfounded. What little deception there was has been mine entirely. You see, I'm not Kitty Deveraux. I let you believe I was because I thought it gave me protection. My name is really Hester Malpass, and I'm wanted for petty theft by the police. And if it's of any interest to you, I swear I'm innocent."

At the mention of my name Peter Quennel's head jerked up from its downcast position. "Malpass? Wasn't that—?"

But I was still in full and righteous flood. "And if Dr Craggan thinks he can blackmail me for that, then just let him try. I'll give myself up to the police this very day, and trust to the Queen's justice."

My heroism went unheeded. Young Peter Quennel was staring at me, amazed, with something near to joy dawning in his face. Finally he actually burst out laughing. "You mean you're truly not the Captain's wife?"

"Not yet."

He passed this over. "I should have known. I really should have known. ... I thought it funny from the start, you see, there being no wedding ring upon your finger. But Bucky said—oh, who cares what Bucky said?"

He strode away from me the full width of the workroom, clearly unable to contain himself. I followed in some puzzlement. "Dr Craggan may not be quite so delighted," I observed. "Don't you think you should go and tell him you've both wasted a journey?"

"The guv'nor? Oh, he won't mind. He's a friendly old cove really—it's as if there's something driving him to do these things, almost against his will. He's always happier when circumstances force his better nature to get the upper hand." He leaned by the window. "It was like that the morning he discovered you'd gone. Oh, he chewed me up a bit, of course. But...."

He tailed off, his eye caught by something beyond the glass. "Isn't that Captain Deveraux out there?"

I followed his gaze. And surely, there was my Captain, still talking with Mr Jowker, some hundred yards away, on the bank by the mill stream. Sunlight shone upon them, outlining them clearly against the dark foliage of the surrounding trees. And this, this was the eerie sunlit moment when the events of that strange Sunday suddenly lost all reason and plummetted into utter terror.

For as we watched through the barred window, Mr Quennel and I, the two men seemed to finish their conversation and part. Mr Jowker turned, and began to make his way back to the mill. My Captain waited a second, then came rapidly after the old man. Raising both his arms high above his head, he brought them down, hands clenched together, with terrible ferocity upon the back of the other's neck. His victim fell instantly, as if pole-axed. With a quick heave of his foot Captain Deveraux (my Captain?) rolled the body off the bank, down into the rushing stream. Caught at once in the current, it floated towards us at fearful speed, turning limply over and over, clothes trailing, head lolling, till it slid into broken water and passed at last out of sight down the side of the mill to the wheel's thrashing paddles.

Though there was in truth no more to be seen, I covered my eyes in horror. Peter Quennel put his arm round my shoulder, comforting me. We stayed like this I know not how long, my mind a total blank, refusing to accept, refusing even to think about the truth of what I had just seen. If my Captain was indeed the callous murderer he seemed to be, then anything might be possible. Anything at all.

When I opened my eyes Captain Deveraux had gone from beside the stream. Almost at once, though, I heard the sound of a key in the lock of the outside door to the floor below, by the padlocked entrance to the engine workshop. And still I could not move, could not break the frozen horror of the moment. I watched, as motionless as stone, and Peter with me, as Captain Deveraux ran lightly up the stairs towards us, humming cheerfully to himself as he came.

When he saw us there was that in our faces which extinguished instantly his merry tune. At once he was electrically alert, moving slowly now, poised like a stalking leopard. His hand darted to his pocket. His eyes flicked from us to the door out into the courtyard and back. Only then, reading his mind, did we run, but already it was too late. He reached the door three strides ahead of us, slammed his back against it, faced about. A pistol was in his hand as he turned, a wicked, long-barrelled, gleaming thing.

He drew a deep breath, then smoothed his dark, disordered hair. "We seem to have a visitor, Hester. Pray introduce me."

Such play-acting caused me momentarily to lose my fear. "I'm sure you know very well who this is, Edward. I positively refuse to...."

The revolver rose till its death-dark eye stared unwinkingly into my face. The Captain's voice was oily soft. "Introduce me, I said. There's a good girl."

Under the steady gaze of his gun I made the introduction. A charade this might be, but a charade on the five letter word called death. The Captain had killed already—there seemed little doubt of his willingness to kill again. He listened to my introduction, then bowed stiffly, and Peter Quennel also. Then the young man took a small pace forward. "You should know that my guardian is close at hand, Captain Deveraux. And armed. If he hears a shot, he...."

The Captain smiled almost apologetically, and gestured round the workroom. "The walls are thick, the windows small.... Besides, you misjudge me if you think me afraid of one man, whether armed or not."

He jerked himself upright from the door and advanced towards us. It gave him much pleasure, I saw, to watch our stumbling retreat before him, shuffling, blundering into obstacles, until finally we were hard up against the back wall and could retreat no farther. He stopped then, perhaps eight feet from us, and perched himself negligently on a work table. The way he handled his gun, however, was not negligent in the least.

He smiled again. "Hester—I told you once that I wasn't a cruel man. That was true. Therefore I'll not spin this out. It seems that you both saw me dispose of a foolish, grasping old man. For as long as you live, then, a death that might have been simply the sad end of a buffer who went for a walk alone by a stream and tumbled in, must be a hanging matter. And you cannot be surprised that I do not wish to hang. So just let us get it over with, and quick.

He had spoken quietly, sensibly, even regretfully. Now he took his revolver in both his hands and raised it, straight-armed, before him, pointed directly at Peter Quennel's heart. Never before in my life had anyone's intention been clearer. Yet I could not believe it—not of him, not of my fine and handsome Captain. It must all be a game, a trick, an illusion, some ill-conceived joke. Even as I saw my Captain's finger tighten, and the hammer rise, even then the unreality remained—indeed, intensified till the whole affair was but a play, and I expected to act out my part.

It was therefore with no sense of danger, and thus no great bravery, that I darted forward, and thrust the weapon upwards, and shrieked my melodramatic, "No, Edward! No!"

The concussion that followed, however, the blast of heat and stench, the report that rang in my ears, all these dispelled in an instant all notions of play-acting. The bullet tore at my hair as it passed, struck an iron girder inches above Peter Quennel's head, and sang away like a train whistle across the workroom. The Captain's face was close to mine, the face that I had kissed and thought so handsome, now convulsed and hideous with fury. He released one hand from his revolver and raised it high to strike me. Then he paused, and lowered it again, and his expression changed, and the smile that returned to his lips was far worse than the hatred that had twisted them before.

He shook himself free of me and backed away a pace. I fell to my knees. His eyes darted round the low-ceilinged room, making calculations I understood not. Then they settled on Peter where he stood by the wall, still rigid in the face of a death that had passed him so closely by. "Mr Quennel—it seems that you have been granted a brief reprieve. I congratulate you. In return, I wonder if you would be good enough to perform a small errand for me. On the filing cabinet in my office you'll find a sheaf of papers. Would you kindly bring them to me?" He stooped and hauled me roughly to my feet. "I need hardly remind you what would happen to little Hester should you play me false."

Peter relaxed. For a moment he hesitated, then he walked steadily across the workroom and into Captain Deveraux' office. A second later he reappeared, carrying my father's documents. All this while the Captain did not move a muscle. "Bring them here. Give them to me."

Peter obeyed curtly, with a brave show of insolence. My captor affected not to notice. He released me and took the papers. He motioned us both back against the wall. As he glanced quickly through the papers his expression softened to a travesty of sadness.

"Poor Hessie ... I wish things could have been other. You saved my life. You beguiled me till I was fool enough to be tempted, fool enough to dream impossible dreams...." He sighed. "But it could never have been. I could never have married you, not while my marriage to Kitty still stood. One of you had to go."

So he had lied to me, even about Kitty—in spite of my deadly peril I gasped at his shocking admission. He heard me, and smiled ruefully "Oh yes, we're man and wife... birds of a feather, Kitty and I. When we found that the authorities believed her dead I lodged her in an old, half-ruined cottage up in the woods beyond the quarry while we decided what advantages could best be gained from the situation. It worked out very well, of course. When you turned up again, there I was with a free hand. Losing you had been hard—especially after the trouble I'd been to, finding you and... making friends. With you back again and Kitty safely out of the way I had a good chance of getting your father's papers after all."

After all...? Then my father's papers had been his target right from the very beginning? The horror in my face must have moved even his disordered spirit, for he took a pace towards me, almost as if pleading.

"But it wasn't all play-acting, Hester. You must believe that. I came to love you. I came to believe that a future was possible for the two of us.... How different things would have been if only you hadn't threatened me with your solicitor." His tone sharpened. "And if only friend Jowker hadn't been so greedy. If only he had trusted me. If only both of you had trusted me...."

He tossed his head restlessly, as if trying to rid it of worrysome midges. I thought of the trust I had squandered on him, the blind faith in his love, even as he had nightly been visiting his Kitty. And I remembered with sick distaste that it had indeed been after my mention of Mr Margulies—when he had known his case hopeless—that we had gone up into the meadow together and he had sought to use my trust cruelly to his own delight.

He began to back away from us, moving with strange clumsiness. An oil lamp stood on a shelf—he reached for it, took it up, and tossed it across the floor. It rolled to stillness, its chimney shattered, oil leaking from it in a steady stream.

"I'm glad you prevented my foolishness with the gun, Hester. A fire looks so much more accidental than a bullet through the heart." He was speaking wildly now, scarcely forming his words. "But then, did I tell you, Hester—improvisation has always been my forte. Did I tell you that?"

He lurched away to a second lamp on a table by the door. Quite without warning Peter darted from my side, snatched a bolt of calico and sent it curling across the room, straight at Captain Deveraux' head. But the distance was too great and the other saw it in the air, and side-stepped easily. "I can quite well shoot you now, Mr Quennel, if you prefer. I doubt very much if the bullet would be found in what little is left of you after the fire."

Peter stood very still, breathing heavily, his arms loose by his sides. "Are you such a monster, Deveraux, that you would burn alive the girl you claimed you loved?"

"Monster?" The Captain's laugh was high-pitched, inhuman. "No monster, lad. Just a man with a vision. A man with the courage to bring that vision about. One day, lad, my aerial fleets will patrol the skies of the whole world. The man who controls them will be king indeed.... What, I ask you, is mere sentiment in the face of such a dream?"

He snatched the lamp from the table and hurled it so that it burst across the cut-out segments of silk. The smell of oil mingled with the varnish already heavy in the air. I watched, petrified, unable to speak or move, as he produced a box of vestas from his breeches pocket. Peter took my hand. Together we faced the madman. "I shan't try to bargain with you, Deveraux," he said. "Neither shall I plead. Men like you destroy everything they touch. You'll never build your dream. You'll achieve nothing in your life—nothing but misery and an unmarked, shameful grave. Your name shall be forgotten, Deveraux, as if it had never been."

Captain Deveraux paused. Briefly Peter's words seemed to reach some sane corner of his mind. Then he shook his head again, tucked the precious sheaf of documents more firmly beneath his arm, took out a match, and struck it firmly, purposefully down the side of the box. Flame blossomed, and was cast in one quick movement onto an oil-sodden bundle of silk cuttings. The silk smoked for a second, then caught. Fire ran quickly along the floor.

Captain Deveraux moved idly, almost casually, to the door, his gun still trained unwaveringly in our direction. He leaned upon the door, easing it open a crack behind him, watching with childish delight the spread of the flames. They were at the cutting table now, and instantly the whole end of the room was ablaze, the shellac flaring almost to the ceiling. He waited a moment longer, then bowed to us regretfully and was gone.

The door snapped shut behind him. I ran to it, beat vainly upon the boards. Behind me Peter was in his shirt sleeves, thrashing the eager flames with his jacket. Even as some died beneath his blows, dozens more licked hungrily about him. I left the door and ran wildly from window to window—each one was closely barred, the iron rods set stoutly in the stone. I dared not even break the glass, for fear of letting in a wind to fan the fire.

Peering out, I saw the doctor's carriage standing in the courtyard, half across the entrance gate. I smashed the glass then, recklessly enough, and screamed for help. I screamed and screamed. Around me the flames were gaining hold with terrifying speed. Already the air was hot and smoke tore at my lungs. I screamed again.... With painful slowness the door of the carriage opened and Dr Craggan descended. He turned to seek the direction of my screaming. He had, I noticed, noticing everything in the vivid immediacy of my terror, he had in his right hand a walking cane and his left arm was in a sling.

A wave of heat engulfed me and I fell back from the window. Peter was at my side now, his jacket no more than a charred rag in his hand. He snatched up calico, ripped at it. "Your face," he shouted. "Cover your face and hands." While on every side the flames bit into the dried-out ancient timbers, consuming them, sending streams of smoke hissing like steam jets across the laden air. There was pounding on the door now, and Dr Craggan's voice shouting indistinguishably. Peter stumbled in its direction, dragging me after him. He was coughing so that he could hardly speak. "The key, Guv'nor," he bellowed. "Find the key!"

His guardian's voice came to us clearly. "Ye dreckit loon—d'ye reckon I'd be dragglin' here if yon scoundrel hadna gone off with the sainted key?"

Peter mopped his eyes. "Then for God's sake break the door down."

"Aye lad—me and what ten others?"

I collapsed to the floor, and Peter beside me. The heat was less there, and the smoke also. Above us the pounding continued steadily, the brave, ineffectual lunging of an old man's shoulder against three-inch oak. Then it stopped.

"He's gone to get something to batter with," Peter gasped.

I nodded, despair already heavy upon me. One-handed, old, what could he do? Our time was running out. Overhead the floor joists were burning fast, the floor boards curling and charring in the heat. Fully one half of the workroom, fed by exploding cans of shellac, was a raging furnace.

Smouldering fragments spurted and fell upon my clothes. Peter knocked them from me. In a screaming thunder of tortured woodwork the staircase up to the first floor collapsed. Sparks flew, and glowed in every place they settled, like fiery ulcers.

I held Peter close to me, and closed my eyes, and prayed.

My prayer was answered. New sounds bore in upon my fading senses—a fresher, stronger pounding, and a voice... a voice I dared not recognize, a voice from a different life, a different world.

"Together now, Doctor. We'll swing he together. *Now*, Doctor. And again, *now!*" Wood splintered. Screws tore from their sockets. "*Now*, Doctor. And again, *now*...."

The door burst open, crashed flat to the floor. Light flooded in, light not of the hellish raging flames, and air not sulphurous from the pit. I crawled towards it, and Peter with me, coughing and sobbing. Strong legs were close, a strong arm bore me up. I stumbled forwards blindly, out into the blessed cool of the day.

"There now, Miss Hester. There now... you'm fine now, Miss Hester. Doing fine...."

I reeled. Perhaps I fainted. Certainly I believed myself in a dream. For where else but in a dream would I hear the calm, infinitely capable tones of Barty Hambro?

My dizziness quickly left me. Barty was no dream—shabbier perhaps than I had known him, and less well shaven, but as real as the trees and the hillsides around. Close by him a massive rough-trimmed gatepost by way of battering ram lay upon the paving. While a short way off Peter leaned against the courtyard wall as his guardian, top hat firm on the back of his head, cleaned sweat and grime from his blistered face. And around us glass splintered from factory windows, smoke billowed, and curling tongues of flame gushed upwards from the inferno within.

Barty dragged me, staggering, to a safer distance. Through all that moment's horror the mystery of his presence clamoured in my head. Wildly I peered up at him. "How, Barty?" I gasped. "Why aren't you... the station... Mrs Skues... how is it that...?"

Though I was clearly beyond coherent expression he understood me very well. "Don't fret yourself, Miss Hester. I been keeping an eye on you all along. Living rough. Right since Mordello got word to me where you was." He hesitated. "Before that even, if the truth be known. Set me on to you, he did, right after your Daddy got himself killed."

His full meaning hardly penetrated. Was this then how Mordello could say he was near, even when he was far? "But Mrs Skues... she..."

"She give me the sack, God bless her. Didn't take to my going off to the Fete that day. Nor yet to the other times when I wasn't where I ought to been, on account of trying to sort out where you was. Put a Bible-bashing Plymouth brother in my place—good luck to the both of them."

From within the factory a thunderous roar was heard as the floor joists collapsed. Tendrils of smoke began to weave up through the roof stones. In the courtyard gateway a crowd of villagers had gathered, two of them leading away the doctor's rearing, panic-stricken horse. Peter limped over to where we stood. "Captain Deveraux," he cried, "we must stop him! He mustn't be allowed to get away."

Momentarily fear had driven all thoughts of the Captain from my head. Barty pointed. "I saw him go that way—up to the balloon field behind the house."

Peter started away at a stumbling run. "Quickly—he'll escape. We must stop him!"

Barty held me back from following. "I'd not say as there's all that much rush and scurry. He'll never get that balloon away all on his own. Besides, there's that gun of his I reckon he won't be too fussy 'bout using."

A new sick fear filled me. I'd forgotten the gun—had Peter forgotten it also? "Peter—" I shrieked "remember he's armed. Take care!"

He must have heard me, for I saw him check his stride. His guardian joined him, and together they went with greater caution round the end of the house and out of my sight. Barty left me, ascertained from the villagers that a policeman was on his way, and the Chalford fire brigade also. A hundred questions jangled in my head. And still the shocks of the day were by no means ended.

From the corner of the courtyard a flight of steps led down to the millstream below the wheel. And just at that moment up these steps staggered the sodden, bedraggled, impossible figure of Mr Jowker. His spindly frame must indeed have been indomitable, so to have survived the Captain's murderous attack, and the slow flailing paddles of the water wheel. I rushed to him, I who would have thought myself happy never to see his mournful face again, and embraced him joyously.

He brushed my tender welcome distractedly aside. "Them papers," he muttered, making straight for the flame-filled factory doorway. "I must get them papers. It'll all be for nowt if I don't get them papers...."

I held him back. Barty came and helped me. "The Captain has the papers safe," I told him. "We think he hopes to escape in the balloon."

Mr Jowker rounded on us. "Then stop him, the swine. Them papers is mine, I tell you! Oh, the double-dyed swine —he'd never of knowed a thing about them, but for me. Fool that I was, I dealt him in, and trusted him to see me right."

I gaped at him. His reason, I thought, had been taken from him by his ordeal. Barty tried to calm his agitation. "Let the Captain go," he said. "Even if he gets away, wherever he comes to earth he'll be picked up easy. The papers won't do him no good, no good at all."

"But them papers is mine. I didn't suffer no six years in jail just to be cheated at the last."

He broke away from us, started a shambling run.

"We'd better go with him," Barty said, looking up at the doomed factory building. "It'll not be safe much longer in this yard, anyways."

Up in the field behind the house it seemed that Captain Deveraux had indeed performed the impossible. Somehow he had dragged the balloon down on its mooring ropes, and now he was in the basket, making frantic preparations to ascend. The banner advertising *Deveraux Balloon and Tent Manufactury* he had jettisoned—it lay across a nearby hedge. We went to Peter and Dr Craggan where they stood, out in the open, several hundred yards from the place where the balloon was tethered.

"I'd advise ye to keep your distance," the doctor told us. "Go much nearer and he looses off that gun of his. And he's no a bad shot, for all he's bouncing around like a bean in a barrel."

Calmly he showed us his stove pipe hat, with a bullet hole clean through its high polished crown. Mr Jowker took no heed of this, but started recklessly across the grass. Ahead of him Captain Deveraux was hacking with a small chopper at the balloon's mooring ropes. One by one they parted. As the last one fell away he gave an exultant shout. The basket leapt beneath him, causing him to stagger. Somehow he held his footing, laughing now, and waving in triumph as he rose away from us into the sky. Mr Jowker stumbled on a grassy tussock and fell, cursing horribly. Briefly the shadow of the balloon passed across his sodden, crumpled body.

But the Captain's triumph did not last. Even as the old man was still scrambling to his feet the balloon lurched sideways, caught by the great blast of hot air rising from the burning mill. Desperately the Captain slashed at sandbags, shedding ballast in a last minute bid for height. He was clear of the factory roof now, and climbing with dizzy speed. But the roof was smouldering fast, and heavy with the weight of years. As we watched it sagged, and buckled, then collapsed. At once the volcano within erupted, gouting spark and flame and fiery fragments like a monstrous roman candle.

For hideous moments the Captain seemed to hang unscathed within the crimson torrent's centre. He rose, indeed, faster even than before. Yet all of us who waited on the ground below knew that his doom was certain.

It came at last in a withering blast of fire as the gas in his balloon ignited. Instantly the huge silken globe was gone, blasted into tiny molten pieces. I watched no more, but heard from those around me a groan of purest animal horror. A groan, and then silence: a silence as deeply shocking as anything I have seen or heard in all my life before or since.

THIRTEEN

The men were talking now quietly among themselves. I left them and wandered away across the rough grass of the field. I needed to be alone. I needed time to think. Captain Deveraux was dead. The man who had so betrayed me was gone, and with him my father's papers. Of these but one charred sheet remained, whisked high above me and drifting down through the troubled air to land on a tussock close by my feet. I sank down onto my knees and took it gently in my hands. On it the blocks of figures marched and countermarched, just as I had seen them do so many times before. Was it for such as these that my Captain had in his madness died? Was it for such as these that he had attempted vile murder? Was it for such as these that old Mr Jowker was now weeping openly, standing alone in the middle of the field, beating his sides in the impotence of his rage and misery?

I crumpled the sheet slowly, carefully, into a tiny ball and ground it with my fist deep into the turf. Nothing, nothing in the world was worth such cruelty, such misery, such destruction.

Below us a fire engine's bell sounded loudly. Peter came to me, helped me to my feet. "Come away, Hester. There's nothing more for any of us here."

But there was so much more, so many things I needed to understand. I disengaged myself from him and went slowly across the grass to Mr Jowker. He was quiet now, head bent, shivering a little in his sodden clothes. Around us lay the severed ends of mooring ropes, and a little distance off the crumpled scarlet banner, mute reminders of the horror but recently concluded. I took his arm. If what he had said about him and the Captain were true, then I had but little sympathy for him. But there was still much I needed to know.

I spoke to him firmly. "You talked about my father's papers—you said they were yours. What did you mean by that?"

He lifted his head. Briefly defiance flared in his haggard, ancient face. Then it faded. He shrugged. "What's the harm in telling? It's all gone now, everything what could of made or broke me...." He sat down wearily upon the grass, and I beside him. He took a sopping handkerchief from his pocket, squeezed it out, and mopped his eyes. Then he began. "I was a clerk in them days, you must know. Respected. A h'onest man. Did clerking for your father, Miss H. All sorts of little jobs—wrote his letters, kept his books.... You might say I believed in Edmund Malpass. Understood his problems too—especially the money ones. Never been easy for the man in a small way of business to make a go of things.... Broke my heart, it did, when he come up with the big idea, the engine thing, and needed a pound or two, and couldn't raise the wind."

He shifted uncomfortably inside his wet clothes. "I tell

you—it got so bad he did what he'd swore he'd never do. He went a-begging to Orme. Did it proper through solicitors and all. Got the thumbs-down too, and no mistake. Even tried the gypsy geezer, bloke called Gypsy Mordello. No funds there though as I could of told him."

Orme? Mordello? What did my father have to do with these? I stifled the question. The old man must tell his story any way he could.

Mr Jowker sighed. "So off we went to this money man up in the Midlands. Iron master, he was—big bank balance, big belly, no imagination.... Got the thumbs-down there as well. There we was then, your mother, him and me, rattling down from Manchester on the old London, Midland and Scottish.... I reckon you knows only too well what happened then—the bridge as wasn't there when it ought to of been. It's not a day as I like to think about. Wasn't many of us lived to tell the tale." He peered at me sideways. "And don't you go upsetting yourself, Miss H. It's all h'ancient history now. And it wasn't that bad. Your Mama died quick, and your Pa weren't in no pain the last time I saw him. Thinking of you, he was, as he laid there on the river bank. Going fast, but thinking of you all the while."

He paused, as if picturing the scene. I had pictured it myself often enough. But he had actually been there—there should have been a dozen questions for me to ask him. I asked none of them. His words had so moved me that I could scarcely keep from open tears.

If he noticed my distress, he made no comment. "You see, Miss H., the case of plans he'd took with him up to Manchester—the plans that was to have made him rich— they was gone in the river. What fussed him was the second set back in his office safe. They'd come to you all right, he didn't have no fears of that. But knowing what they was, knowing what to do with them—that was a different kettle of kippers altogether. That was where I come in: I was to see them plans got treated proper. They was yours, he said— all he had to leave you. The rest was up to me. And then he give me a letter what he'd just had from his solicitor—I'd need something, he said, to prove me good faith...."

He drew breath. People were coming up the lane into the field, the local vicar, it seemed, and two policemen.... So *that* was the letter I had seen Captain Deveraux burn in the restaurant—addressed to Ted, being short not for Edward Deveraux as I had thought, but for Edmund Malpass, my

205

father. Mr Jowker's only proof of respectability, and the Captain had burned it. In the circumstances the old man's anger—if not his extreme violence—was understandable enough.

"So I took your Pa's letter the way he said. And I promised to do everything I could. I meant it, too...." He paused doubtfully, and rubbed his sagging jowls, seemingly afflicted with shame concerning what was to come next. "It was about then, Miss H., as I sees this rich young toff, dead as they come, floating by in the river. I thinks of his wallet and his fine gold ticker what he ain't going to be needing never no more—and I thinks of myself, out of a job now, what with one thing and another."

He fetched his own gunmetal timepiece out of his waistcoat pocket, shook it mournfully, then opened its back. Water poured out in surprisingly large quantities. He closed the watch carefully, and put it back in his pocket.

"Anyways, you knows the rest—how I was nabbed redhanded and sent on down the line. 'I'm going to make a h'example of you,' said the stinking judge.... and he kep' his word. Six stinking years he give me. Still, I got to thinking—and what I thought was as the good Lord helps them as helps theirselves. I still had the letter, y'see —what I needed was some engineering gent as might take kindly to a certain proposition.... Tracing you wasn't no problem—a note to your old school marm saw to that." He sighed. "Only mistake I made was going to the Capting with my little scheme. Not that he didn't seem my best hope, though, mad on engines like he was, and none too partickler besides. Known well for that, he was, by certain gents inside —certain gents as had done jobs for him, one time and another."

He shrugged his sodden shoulders. "I should have known better, mind—them as ain't too partickler over one thing ain't too partickler over another. And I'll tell you somethink else—he wasn't no Capting, neither, as I found out soon enough. Not a military man at all. Never served Her Majesty —never served nobody but hisself, not in his whole life long. Proud of it too, he was."

He began to get stiffly to his feet. "So that's how it is, Miss H. I'd of diddled you solid, there's no denying it. And the Capting would of diddled us both. And now there's none of us got nothink...."

He looked away across the field, frowned slightly at what

he saw there. Then he hitched up his soggy trousers resignedly, gestured to me in wry farewell, and started back in the direction of the gate. I watched him go, a small, damp figure, all in black. Halfway to the gate he passed the vicar and the two policemen talking with Dr Craggan and Peter, Barty Hambro standing respectfully in the background. Mr Jowker nodded discreetly, and went on his way. The people of importance regarded him with some curiosity, but he seemed so civil, and so sure of where he was going, that not one of them stopped him.

I let him go. I could think of nothing that I might charge him with, but even if I could have done, I would have kept silent. He was a loser: he had been all his life. It was not for me to add to his sad burden.

I sat on after he was gone, tearing absent-mindedly at the grass on which I rested. The events of the last hour had left me dazed, incapable of any great feeling, filled only with a sick-hearted weariness. All that lingered in my mind with any real clarity was the bitter realization of how cruelly I'd been manipulated. Captain Deveraux had come to the refreshments, knowing he would find me there. How easily had he got me to identify myself! From that very first moment I had been scarcely more than a puppet in his hands. No doubt Kitty's visit, her pretended flight from him, had been a part of his plan. Only the theft of the money and the silver cup, with its inconvenient outcome, had been hers, and none of his.

I'd been the only means he had of laying his hands on my father's papers. How understandable, then, was his despair once he believed me dead. How understandable also Mr Jowker's cynical laughter as he told me of it. And how understandable his joy at my return, and his eagerness to help me regain my few possessions. While all the time he enmeshed me tighter and tighter in the irresistible charms of his person.

Fine and handsome.... "Handsome is as handsome does," I remembered remarking to Amy. And fine?—well, hardly. And now, it seemed, no Captain either.... Yet I had seen in him the stuff of greatness, and I could not have been too seriously mistaken. He had had a vision, and a zest for life also. He had had courage, and strength, and a virility surely no woman could deny.... My hand stilled, the grass thin and cold against my fingers. I recalled with shame a certain meadow, and the passion of his kisses—what might not be my situation now, all honour lost, should Barty not have loosed the cattle down upon us when he did? I thanked the silent watcher then, as I had never thanked him before. His solution may have been desperate, but then, so had been my plight. And no doubt he, a countryman, would know the danger to be more imagined than real. Considered now in tranquillity, the surge of cattle had parted readily enough, almost gratefully, about us.

Barty had watched over me well. Even, he said, since I first went to Mrs Skues, for it was then that Mordello had sent him. Yet how could that be? What could the old gypsy in those days have known of Hester Malpass, or cared? Unless he had in some way been privy to my father's troubles, as Mr Jowker had implied.

A shadow fell across the grass close by me. In my new confusion I had not been aware of anyone's approach. I looked up. One of the policemen stood over me, very stiff and stern in silver-buttoned splendour.

"Miss Malpass?"

I nodded, and scrambled to my feet, fear catching at my heart. Clearly I was to be led away now, under shameful arrest.

"Miss Malpass—your grandpa tells us you've been victim of a serious misunderstanding. Had we known of the relationship I . . . I reckon we'd've been a mite more careful."

Grandpa? Had I heard him right? Uncomprehendingly I scanned the field for such a man.

"I'm to say as we'll get things sorted out, Miss, never fear." He leaned a little closer, favouring me with an unofficial confidence. "You see, Miss, nobody ever told us that Madam Kitty was in on things. If that's the case then there shouldn't be much trouble—we've had our eye on Madam for a long time. There's men on their way up to that old cottage by the quarry this very minute."

I clutched his arm. Suddenly Kitty, and the theft, and proving my innocence, seemed to be of little importance. "Grandpa? You said Grandpa? My grandfather, you meant?"

He smiled gently. "That's right, Miss. Dr Craggan—he says you saved the young gentleman's life. Right proud of you, he is."

I questioned no more. Quite slowly the earth beneath me tipped, sliding me into grateful oblivion. The day had dealt me one astonishment too many and my senses rebelled. My last recollection, even as I began to fall, is of the strong arms of the constabulary supporting me.

Looking back now, with the wisdom of twenty years' hindsight, I cannot say I feel great regret that my father was denied a place in history as the perfector of the petroleum engine. Captain Deveraux' vision of an aerial fleet may be still no more than a distant dream, but already on the ground the more prosaic contrivances of Dr Craggan and his like render the highways of the nation hideous with their noise and fumes and bustle. Already the amiable horse, the graceful carriage, are being swept aside to make way for rowdy motor cars of every shape and colour. Already even the peace of those quiet country lanes Mordello and I travelled on that sunny summer morning is seriously threatened.

My father's secret may have died with the Captain, but it was after all but a very few months after then that the ingenious Mr Benz first appeared with his wife on the public road in a petroleum engined device. If the present noise and danger is the result of but twenty years' progress, I hesitate to think what horrors the future may provide. And I cannot but be thankful that my poor father was prevented from having any part in all of this. To be surrounded by Malpass motor cars, by Malpass runabouts, by Malpass flying sixes, would scarcely cause me any great pride.

At the time, of course, I knew nothing of all this. I apprehended neither what the world had lost nor what I myself had gained. After my uncharacteristic swoon in the field behind Captain Deveraux' house, I regained my senses on a sofa in the fusty bachelor parlour of what turned out to be the nearby vicarage. The vicar, an excellent man no doubt, was spooning immoderate quantities of brandy between my lips, so that I must surely have choked and died had not Dr Craggan entered then. He thrust the reverend gentleman brusquely aside, and sat me up, and beat me soundly upon the back.

For a while I could not find breath for the many questions that crowded into my head with the return of consciousness. The doctor, however, required no great medical skill to divine the deep uncertainties of my mind. Briskly, still beating me as he did so, he set about putting them at rest.

"I'm no man to mince my words, Hester. You're a brave young woman, and you saved young Peter's life, and there's much for me to make up for. I treated you ill, y'see. Very ill..."

The thumping faltered, then continued fiercer than ever. "But I'd have you know, Hester, that your father was a wilful, headstrong creature. Where Edmund got it from I cannot tell—certainly not from me, his father." He glared at me, defying me to comment. I held my peace. "Aye ... I tell you, lass, I stood more from him than I have stood from any man. It's said a lad seldom fares well in his father's employ—and I'll grant mebbe I rode him hard. But his marriage to yon Mary Squires, and her a gypsy girl, was more than even I could stomach. High words were spoken. Very high.... He left my house that very day. Left my employ too—set up for himself with the wee bit his poor mother'd left him. He took her name also, wanting none of mine...."

He tailed off. Silence descended on the room. My choking had long ceased, and now the beating also. Yet still I was bemused, no more than half aware. The vicar lingered, as vicars will, beaming by the window. Dr Craggan seemed oblivious of him, oblivious of me even, listening only to his memories.

"High words, I say, on both our sides.... I never saw him again, ye ken. If I was hard, then so was he. Father and son, living in the same city, and never a word passing tween us, not in twelve long years." He frowned, his bushy white eyebrows descending fearsomely over his eyes. "I lie—there came a letter once, just before he died. A letter through some solicitor, begging money. A son who could address his father so, through some bow-legged, hollow-chested clerk ... such a son, I thought, was no son of mine. I never answered the letter. And then he was dead, and his gypsy wife with him. And only the little girl was left."

He had moved from my side, and his great bony frame was hunched over the fireplace, head on his arms on the fringed overmantel. "It may be that I hated her. Hated her for being alive while my son was dead. Hated her for the guilt she made me feel, now that it was too late. Issue of a pairing I'd have moved heaven and earth to prevent. Half-gypsy—was that what we Craggans were come to? But I'd filled my life with another, a fine laddie, long before. So I bought freedom for this girl, and bought it cheaply—thirty sovereigns, it cost me. Thirty pieces of gold...." His voice broke. "After that, God help me, I never thought to hear of her again."

Half-gypsy... the word lingered. My mother had been of Mordello's tribe. Myself with such blood in my veins? In sudden horror I looked down at my hands, half-expecting to see them swarthy, thick-fingered, but discovering with relief only the pale fine skin of my father. While close upon this relief came shame, that I should so wish to deny my heritage, the blood that joined me to such fine, gentle people as Barty, and even the mysterious old fortune-teller himself. If I was truly of mixed race then I must learn pride in all my people, dark as well as fair. And I must earn their pride in me also. These, then, were the brothers and sisters Mordello had said even an only child might have.

I looked up from my hands, up to the bowed, gaunt figure of Dr Craggan, my grandfather—and, with his thirty sovereigns, my secret benefactor also. Once he had spurned me, had become for me as good as dead. Now he was asking my forgiveness, which was easily given. Yet I did not know what I truly felt for him, nor he for me. Except that the policeman had said he was proud of me, proud of my courage. And that now, in the pain of his memories, he sought to soften past reality by speaking of that girl he had treated so ill as someone other, someone quite strange from me. My heart went out to him. He had guilt enough, without my trying to increase it.

I spoke to him gently. He lifted his head, and there were tears in the sharp blue eyes I had once feared. He returned to me then, gruff and almost shy in the genuineness of his gratitude. He took one of my hands and patted it, saying "Aye," and "Whisht now," and "You're a good girl, a forgiving girl, for all you're naught but a gypsy lass...."

It was the vicar, beaming still, who intervened, sparing us any great excess of emotion with a pious quotation—something concerning the prodigal son, I believe, and not wholly apposite. But I fancy we were both thankful to him all the same.

Soon I insisted upon rising from my sofa, being much invigorated by the vicar's generous dosages of brandy. Peter was waiting to be allowed to enter, and Barty also. I stood in the bay window to receive them, steady enough, though in something of a spirituous haze.

Dr Craggan's ward was the first to enter. He was still in his soot-smudged shirt sleeves, and ointment glistened on a sorry weal across one cheek. He excitedly brushed aside my words of concern. "It's nothing, nothing.... But how about you? My goodness, I've never known such a girl for surprises!" He strode about the room, waving his arms. "First of all there's this Madam Kitty who turns out to be nothing of the sort. Then there's this Hessie Malpass who saves my life and nearly gets herself shot in the process. And now we find she's not just Hessie Malpass, but a Diddakoi as well—a genuine Diddakoi! I declare it's just about the most thrilling thing I ever heard."

I frowned at him muzzily. "A Diddakoi?" It was a strange-sounding thing to be. "I don't know what you mean."

"It's what they call someone who's half a gypsy, so Hambro here tells me. Your mother was a gypsy, Hessie Malpass. That makes you a Diddakoi."

"And you do not mind?"

"Mind? Why should I mind?"

I considered. Why indeed? Come to that, why should I care *what* he minded? Why should I care what anybody minded? I put a hand to my aching head. The day's events were confusing me still. I turned to Barty—he was standing quietly just inside the doorway. He had smartened himself up since I had seen him last, and his short, soldier's haircut stood up wetly from the vigour of his washing.

I went to him. "Barty! Dear Barty, where would I be now if it hadn't been for you. How can I ever thank—"

But Peter broke in on us, quite irrepressible. "Not just you, Hessie—where would either of us be?" He laughed, and clapped Barty on the shoulder. "But the guv'nor's seen to all that—he's done what's right."

Barty's eyes were on the ground. Behind us Dr Craggan cleared his throat. "I should tell you, my dear, that Mr Hambro has done me a great favour. There's a wee estate of mine in Monmouthshire that's sorely in need of a factor. We've—ah—no gone into the details, but he's been good enough to agree to put his experience at my disposal. I'm very grateful to him."

"Is this true, Barty?" I took his hand. "Will you mind going to Monmouth?"

He looked up now, meeting my gaze squarely. "There's a cottage comes with the post, Miss Hester. And my sister's in service just over the border. If I can give good value then I reckon it's the best thing that's happened to me in many a year."

I felt a glow of happiness for him. "Oh Barty—how shall I ever be able to thank you for all you've done for me? The way you've looked after me all these years...." Impulsively I leaned forward and kissed his rough, unshaven cheek. He blushed like a school boy. But he did not shrink away.

"Mostly you looked after yourself, Miss Hester," he said. "Then again, the boss wouldn't have wanted me making things too easy. He's a great believer in folks finding their own way, the boss is."

"The boss? Is that what you call Mordello?"

He nodded. "Your mother's uncle. He's not the leader exactly—we don't really have one. But we call him the boss because mostly he knows what's to be done. He has the Gift, you see."

I did see. I owed much to that gift of his. So Mordello was my mother's uncle.... But perhaps that was just Barty's way of putting things—I remembered being told the gypsy feeling about relationships. Still, it pleased me to think, in my non-gypsy manner, of Mordello as literally my mother's uncle. With blood such as his in my veins I did not see that I could come to much harm.

Dr Craggan came forward. "Time's getting on," he said. "And I reckon we've made free with this good dominie's house quite long enough."

As the meaning of his words sank in my happiness abruptly faded. Up to that moment I had lived entirely in the present, content simply to be alive, and to be with friends, to listen to Peter's boyish enthusiasms, and to know that dear Barty would never need to go back to the like of Mrs Skues again. The cottage he had dreamed of would be his, and a job in the countryside he so loved. Now, suddenly, Dr Craggan's intervention reminded me that I too had a future, the course of which I hardly dared guess at.

I tried to organize my thoughts. "I'll be on my way, then," I said. "I'm very grateful to you, Dr Craggan. Now I must—"

"What havers is this, child? You're coming with Peter and me, and there's an end of it."

"No, sir." I squared my shoulders. "I would not have you think, sir, that because you are my grandfather there's any obligation now for you to—"

He strode angrily to the door, thrust Barty aside, opened it, and pointed imperiously. "Get you into the carriage, miss. I'll not be crossed. You're coming with us, d'ye hear?"

Peter laughed and took my arm. "You'd better do what the guv'nor says, Hessie. He's a terrible man when he's roused."

That was a fact of which I scarcely needed reminding. Yet I hung back still, looking desperately from him to the doctor to Barty Hambro. The gypsy tilted his head. "Go with them, Miss Hester. They're your father's people. It's where you belong."

I hesitated no longer. I could not fight the three of them. Indeed, to be honest, I was grateful then to have others make the decisions for me. The day had left me weary, with little will of my own. I went with Peter and Dr Craggan out of the vicarage and down the lane to where their carriage was waiting by the mill. Barty did not come with us—he stood by the vicarage door, talking with the vicar, and waved but once, briefly, when I looked back.

Around the balloon factory all was confusion. The fire brigade had its machine in the courtyard, six burly firemen at the pump handles, lifting water from the canal to send in bright jets high into the smouldering ruins. The mill itself no more than a gaunt blackened shell, but the house had been saved, and the surrounding cottages of the village. The scene was unreal, and faintly menacing, like the memory of a nightmare best forgotten.

With my foot on the carriage step I paused. People were moving down the path from the quarry between the trees on the hillside opposite. They crossed a small clearing—so many policemen, I thought, for just one poor misguided young woman. I felt a flare of anger, remembering the words of Patrick on the barge: *'Tis a wicked world, though, when you'm poor and got nobody to stick up for you. . . .* Nobody to stick up for her—with the magisterial might of Dr Craggan arrayed against her, what chance did wretched Kitty Deveraux have? She'd lost a husband that day, and with his going her whole life must have tumbled about her ears.

Tears flooded down my cheeks. How close we were, she and I! For if she had lost a husband, then what had been my loss? And what was left for either of us to make of the future? Blindly I turned from the sight of her and climbed into the blessed oblivion of the carriage. Peter whipped up the horse and we clattered away.

We spent that night at the best hotel in Stroud, the first time I had ever been in such a grand establishment. I cannot say I relished the fuss. I had been a servant myself too long to accept easily the service of others. Was this, then, to be the pattern of my future life?

If the evening was long and much occupied with the explanations Dr Craggan demanded of me—explanations of his granddaughter's unseemly behaviour as a fairground *artiste*—then the night alone in my mausoleum of a hotel room was longer still. Kitty's lot haunted me—her foolishness and my own. With the pandemonium of the day now passed, the full betrayals of my fine and handsome Captain bore agonisingly in upon me. Not fine, nor handsome in deed, nor even a Captain—just an unscrupulous cheat, and I like putty in his hands. Only once, on the path up to the quarry, had I come near to discovering his iniquities: and even then, so eager had I been to see good in him where no good lay, that I had abandoned my quest at the poorest excuse, some rabbit in a poacher's snare, and turned back within perhaps a few yards of its true resolution. A rabbit in a poacher's snare... had that not been I myself? And were not men poachers all? And I a fool ever to hope to love or trust again?

The night was long, I say, and my weeping compounded as much of shame as of grief for the loss of a love that had been but childish folly.

Next morning we continued on our way to Bristol. Word had been sent on ahead to Nurse Buckingham at Orme—I wondered wryly what phrases Dr Craggan had found to explain the new situation, and the complete reversal of his opinion of me. I did not envy her the radical changes necessary in her attitudes. Must she welcome me now, the girl she had so abused?

We made good time on the road, the horse now rested and Dr Craggan's neat equipage far sounder on its springs than Captain Deveraux' mouldering affair. In the city we made a small detour, for errands that the men made much play of secrecy about. I waited in the carriage patiently enough, being in no hurry whatsoever to take up the new life that would be mine when finally we reached Orme. Though Dr Craggan might be my grandfather, and gentler now than I had ever seen him, being much chastened in his dealings with me, yet I would not easily forget his callousness six long years before, nor his treatment of the young woman he had believed to be Madam Kitty. These acts betrayed the man quite as much as his present mildness.

When they returned to the carriage they were loaded down with substantial packages that Peter insisted on having up on the box beside him. Once these were secured we set off again. But our progress now was deadly slow on the streets I had once flown lightly over as fast as any bird being crowded and hot. At last, however, the outskirts of the city were reached, and roads with grassy verges, and houses expensively private within their own walled acres. And so, for a second time, I came to Orme.

The house was as greyly forbidding as ever, its entrance hall the same grisly graveyard of slaughtered beasts, its staircase as vast. The room they gave me, however, was different from before, lighter, altogether sunnier, overlooking lawns and a fine avenue of elms. Nurse Buckingham too was different from before, lighter, sunnier, seemingly truly eager to make amends.

The packages were brought up to my room, and carefully unpacked till all but one, the largest and heaviest, remained. Their contents, spread out on the bed, were enough to take my breath away—a dress of pale green watered silk, bewitching petticoats, a velvet skirt and puff-sleeved jacket, blouses, a little waistcoat in stripes of the highest fashion, clothes from the finest shops in Bristol. And if they did not fit me, Dr Craggan said, they could all be changed within the hour. . . . I touched the rich materials timidly, not knowing what to say, not knowing how the Hessie Malpass I had lived with all these years might ever grow accustomed to such finery.

Peter it was who understood my diffidence. "I expect we're rushing you," he said. "But we couldn't resist it. Just let us have our fun—you'll settle down here soon enough."

The doctor too was hearty. "After all, lassie, it's not every day a man discovers a long-lost granddaughter."

There were bitter things I could have said to that, for he'd known my whereabouts for fully six long years. But their pleasure in giving was such that I could not bring myself to spoil it.

At last they were leaving me. At the door Peter turned. "There's one parcel left," he reminded me. "I hope you'll like it. I remembered what you once said, you see."

He smiled conspiratorially, then went away, closing the door softly behind him.

The package stood on a table in the big bay window. It was large and square. To tell the truth, I did not want to open it. So much had been given me already. The transformation was more than I could readily accommodate. I approached the table warily, fingered the string upon the package, took as long as possible over the knots. Within the paper was a sturdy box. And within the box... I sat down weakly, staring in utter amazement. Peter had indeed remembered what I once had said. Within the box was a gleaming, gold-lined typewriter. A typewriter of my very own.

My new life was as strange as I had feared, but I settled to it well enough. How could I do otherwise, surrounded as I was by Dr Craggan's generosity and his ward's unfailing friendliness? I settled, I say, yet very much as a bird may settle in a rich field of grain, and guiltily fatten itself, ever watchful for the moment when it must be up and away. I felt myself a thief, you see. The element was not mine, the pampered life of Orme no part of what I'd ever longed for.

As the weeks passed Dr Craggan cooled a little and became less uncritical of this long lost granddaughter of his. I could not blame him, for I fitted ill the social role he asked of me. If I tried to discuss matters of a serious nature with his guests I found myself exceeding the limits he placed on my sex. And when I could not bring myself to flirt adequately with his more useful business associates I offended also. The truth was that, having had no daughter of his own, and indeed no wife for more than forty years, he was left with only confused notions as to what he might expect of me. In consequence his temper shortened, and his patience also. And although his generosity continued, it became increasingly selective—particularly he resisted the lessons I desired on my newly-acquired typewriter.

"What reason have ye, child, for wishing so to demean yourself? You're no thinking of robbing the city's clerks of their honest toil, I take it?"

I could hardly tell him yes, that was exactly what I thought to do. Yet to give me the machine and then deny me the skill with which to use it seemed the very height of folly. For a while I pecked daily at the keys in the privacy of my room. But I soon desisted—the results of my efforts were shabby things, and slower than the writings of a five-year-old. So many keys there were, and so few fingers to hit them with. And what anyway was the use of preparing myself for a career I would never in the end be permitted to undertake?

The occasions grew more frequent, also, when Dr Craggan would emerge from Orme's troubled workshops to question me insistently about my father's papers. His own experiments were not going well, it seemed, and the vagueness of my information was a source of sore frustration to him.

"An electric spark, ye say? And how is such a thing to be delivered?"

He'd frown, and pace the room, then come to tower over me. "Think harder, girl! Yon wicked Captain must have told ye more than that. And the papers—there must have been drawings among them. Did you never take a peek at them yourself?"

Often he'd grasp my shoulders, and appear tempted to shake the secrets out of me. And still all I could do was bow my head, and confess again and again my shameful ignorance. How could I explain to him what had filled my head in all those wild, tempestuous days? Surely not thoughts of how an electrical spark might be delivered....

I grew restless. I knew myself to be ungrateful. My life at Orme was far indeed from the day-long drudgery of Mrs Skues' employ. But for all that there were times when it seemed almost as much of an imprisonment as poor Kitty's now must be. In truth, I was bored. And lonely too, for Nurse Buckingham—would I ever learn to call her Bucky? —was at best a poor companion, and Peter much absent, working at his guardian's side.

Neither would my grandfather hear of my visiting Amy or Kate—they were by no means fitting companions, he said, for the young lady he wished me to become. And Peter, even when he was allowed a few hours to himself, and spent an afternoon perhaps with me, and walked me cheerfully about the grounds, even then his unfailing friendliness only served to emphasize the careful distance that he kept between us. If a steep slope were to be negotiated he'd take my hand readily enough to help me to the top. But he'd release it equally readily the moment it was no longer needed. And if we seated ourselves upon the grass he'd keep himself most properly separate....

I thought about his behaviour much—brooded even having time upon my hands—and came at last to the conclusion that it was fear that kept him so distant. Fear of being thought to care. For as long as I had been safely another man's wife it had pleased him to pay me his decent attentions. But now that I was nothing of the sort, and sharing the very same house with him, he shied away. It was an arrangement that should have been exactly to my liking. For had I not loved and lost, and vowed never to love again?... And yet there was an ache in me that I recognized not, nor knew how to fill.

My summons one afternoon to Dr Craggan's study, therefore, and its import, found me vulnerable and quite unprepared. The room was as impressive as its owner, its walls lined with massive medical books, and framed diplomas, as well as shelves of engineering models, miniature bicycles and the like, its mullioned windows looking grandly down the gravelled drive. I could never see that drive without a shiver, remembering my headlong flight down its noisy stones, the baying of dogs seeming already close upon my heels. I shivered now, and fixed my gaze instead upon my grandfather where he sat at the leather acres of his desk. He motioned me to an upright chair in front of this desk and I sat, suddenly as nervous as a serving maid at her first interview with the master.

My grandfather leaned back in his creaking swivel chair. His back was to the window, and of his face I could see but little. He seemed to be examining me intently. "I believe you're soon to be nineteen years of age, Hester," he observed.

I nodded. My nineteenth birthday was scarcely two months away.

"And quite without personal fortune other than I may see fit to provide."

"That is true, sir." I sat forward. "But I would not wish you to—"

"Kindly let me finish. You are then, Hester, clearly of a marriageable age. Yet your birth is no exactly a fine recommendation, and your financial prospects aren't of the best."

I flushed. "The marriage market has never appealed to me, sir. If I am to be wed, then I would far rather it were for myself than for the money I might bring."

"A noble sentiment, child." He coughed drily. "Then you've given some thought to matrimony, I may take it?"

"Not really, sir." His steady gaze discomfitted me. Where were the fine ambitions of the typewriting girl? "Only such thought as any girl in the general way may make."

At this he laughed aloud. "These thoughts 'in the general way', may I know them?" He paused, but only briefly, certainly far too briefly for me to assemble any adequate reply. "Nay, lassie, I'll warrant I know them well enough.

You've been in my house now four full weeks.... You're nobbut flesh and blood—and my ward is gey well-favoured, though I say it myself."

His meaning was instantly clear. "No, sir." I denied it hotly, then floundered, seeing how he might mistake me and think me uncivil. "That is—I mean, well of course your ward is... handsome and all that. But—"

"No, you say? Well, well, I'll no blame you for protesting. Such modesty is becoming in your years. But I'm a doctor, lass, and not easily to be shocked. And my ward being flesh and blood also, and in the full flower of his manhood, I doubt but that he finds you... well enough to his taste, shall we say?"

Looking back, I'd never have thought it. Unless his shyness indeed had this other cause. The room seemed suddenly very quiet. "Has he told you as much?" I queried softly.

"It surprises you?" He leaned forward now, elbows upon the desk. I noticed nevertheless how my question had been parried by another, answering nothing. "Mark you, child, yon Peter is no man to wear his heart upon his sleeve. But the match would suit... it would suit very well."

He stopped then, leaving his words to hang heavily in the air between us. Possibly the match would suit. Possibly it would suit my grandfather very well. It would, after all, afford him considerable economies. And, that being so, it would doubtless be found to suit his ward also. But what of me?

Distracted I looked about me. I should have been horrified at the bargain being proposed. Certainly Peter was in his own way handsome. And certainly I had never seen him be other than brave and kind. I liked him—I even liked him very much. So much so that I had been piqued by his coolness towards me. But, in a husband, were these tame recommendations enough?

The word "love" entered my mind, and was immediately pounced upon. What had love ever brought me but pain and misery? Had I not set it firmly to one side for all my future reckoning? Had I not in fact been preparing myself for just this very moment, when a good match would be offered me, and security, and the care of a man both virtuous and kind?

And yet....

"You'll be wanting time," Dr Craggan was observing. "Time to make up your mind. It's no a matter to be decided just like that. But I'll have a word with the boy meanwhiles.

I've no doubt you'll both come round to my way of thinking. People usually do."

The truth of his last three words was bitter. The man was no less a tyrant for all his present mildness. The marriage he proposed would keep me within his house for as long as he lived. And even afterwards I could readily picture his jealous spirit never leaving the uneasy corridors of Orme. The secret he sought had been denied him—was he to have me instead?

I stumbled to my feet. My decision, my refusal to accede to his wishes, must be made now or never. If I consented to go away and think about it, then the pressures would grow, and the house itself would get to work on me, and I would be lost for ever. But how ... how to find words brave enough to face him with? How to find courage against his inevitable wrath?

The window was behind him. And beyond the window was the gravelled drive. And in that moment of my direst need, just as my eyes were wandering every which way in my distraction, I saw, coming up the drive towards me, a green and yellow gypsy caravan. And driving it, Mordello.

I was never to learn how he got past the great iron gates of Orme. I was never to learn why the guards did not challenge him. I know not even what words I used, how I got myself from Dr Craggan's study, how he came to let me go. The next thing I remember is running down the drive, my feet hardly touching the gravel, startling the horse so that it nearly bolted, and halting, suddenly timid, below the place where the old gypsy sat. He had come, as he had come before, when he was needed most. I knew he would help me. I knew I was safe.

He steadied the rearing horse, then sat very still, looking thoughtfully down at me. "There is fear in your running, Hester Malpass. Do you run to me? Or do you simply run away from another?"

"Take me away, Mordello." My hands were twisting the cloth of my skirt. He could not refuse me. "Please take me away."

He shook his head. "Running *away* provides no answers. It's running *to* that shows the greater wisdom."

My reply came quickly, quicker than thought. "Take me to Barty...."

Time stood still, fixing us, he on his worn leather seat with the curved iron rail, I staring up from the gravel below. The birds were silent, the air quite without motion. Then thought caught up with the words of my heart, tumultuous joy that a truth so obvious should have become clear to me at last.

"Take me to Barty. He said once that I belonged with all these grand people. But I don't—there's nothing grand about me at all. I'm a Diddakoi; I belong with him. If he'll have me, Mordello, please take me to Barty."

The old man asked no question, no questions at all. But he smiled for once as he began slowly to turn the caravan. "He'll have you," he said. "You're your mother all over again, as pretty as a picture, and gentle with it. He's been eating his heart out for you these two years and more. I told him all you needed was time to grow."

I wish it could all have been so utterly simple. I wish we could just have driven off then, Mordello and I, at that very moment, easily, peacefully into the summer afternoon. But life is rarely simple, and peace seldom so easily accomplished. We got away at last, of course, but not before Dr Craggan had spoken many angry words and threatened many things, and Mordello had heard him out and spoken soberly in his turn. Peter was summoned too, to beg me urgently to stay. But I took little heed of him, seeing his enthusiasm for me to be much increased, now that I was clearly determined upon departure.

We got away at last, I say, the doctor's threats now blunted to the grudging admission that all was "mebbe for the best," and clip-clopped joyously away into the gathering dusk. I took but little with me—none of my finery, not even my gleaming typewriter Its mechanical ingenuities I knew now to be no more than a poor substitute for the life of the heart to which I was journeying.

We travelled in the unhurried gypsy way, camping nightly in gentle fields by dusty, unfrequented lanes. I felt no impatience, needing the time to renew myself, to make myself ready. We entered Monmouthshire, Mordello and I. Sometimes he spoke to me, more often we were silent, and even in his silences there was communication between us, deep and satisfying.

We skirted purple mountains, crossed steep stone bridges over rushing streams. We came at last to a wooded valley between rolling hills, entered it, and wound our grassy way up between the pines. A cottage lay beside the track, four-square in rough-hewn, whitewashed granite. Already a garden was dug around its walls, and points of winter cabbage sprouted in neat rows. And, leaning on its gate—as if in the mysterious way of his people (my people) expecting us—stood Barty.

Secretly I had feared this moment. The understanding of my love for him had come to me so suddenly out on the gravelled driveway of Orme—secretly I had feared that this love might turn out to be no more than some sad romantic dream. I had feared that Barty would be a stranger to me, and I nothing to him. But now, seeing him, recognizing him, recognizing the quietly radiant happiness on his face, I knew my love for him and his for me to be no dream. It was as real as the golden evening sunlight on the mellow hills. My heart went out to him. I who had longed for excitement in my life was starting now on the greatest adventure of all, the adventure of loving and sharing and building a proud future. For all his one arm and his humble ways, Barty Hambro was more a man than any I had ever known, or might ever know.

I climbed down slowly from the caravan and went to him. Behind me I heard Mordello talking softly with the horse, talking Romany words of reassurance now that the long journey was over. Barty opened the gate and took my hand. We went contentedly up the path together. He led me through the low doorway. My growing time was over. At long last I had come home.

Romantic Suspense

Here are the stories you love best. Tales about love, intrigue, wealth, power and of course romance. Books that will keep the reader turning pages deep into the night.

☐ CROCODILE ON THE SANDBANK—Peters	Q2752	1.50
☐ DARK INHERITANCE—Salisbury	23064-3	1.50
☐ THE DEVIL OF ASKE—P. Hill	23160-7	1.75
☐ THE HEATHERTON HERITAGE—P. Hill	23106-2	1.75
(Published in England as The Incumbent)		
☐ THE HOUSE BY EXMOOR—Stafford	23058-9	1.50
☐ IRONWOOD—Melville	22894-0	1.50
☐ LEGEND IN GREEN VELVET—Peters	23109-7	1.50
☐ THE LEGEND OF THE GREEN MAN—Hely	23029-5	1.50
☐ THE MALVIE INHERITANCE—P. Hill	23161-5	1.75
☐ MICHAEL'S WIFE—Millhiser	22903-3	1.50
☐ MONCRIEFF—Holland	23089-9	1.50
☐ THE NIGHT CHILD—DeBlasis	22941-6	1.50
☐ NUN'S CASTLE—Melville	P2412	1.25
☐ THE PEACOCK SPRING—Godden	23105-4	1.75
☐ THE PLACE OF SAPPHIRES—Randall	Q2853	1.50
☐ THE PRIDE OF THE TREVALLIONS— Salisbury	P2751	1.25
☐ THE SEVERING LINE—Cardiff	P2528	1.25
☐ STRANGER AT WILDINGS—Brent	23085-6	1.95
(Published in England as Kirkby's Changeling)		
☐ VELVET SHADOWS—Norton	23135-6	1.50
☐ THE WHITE JADE FOX—Norton	Q2865	1.50
☐ WHITTON'S FOLLY—Hill	X2863	1.75

Buy them at your local bookstores or use this handy coupon for ordering:

FAWCETT PUBLICATIONS, P.O. Box 1014, Greenwich Conn. 06830

Please send me the books I have checked above. Orders for less than 5 books must include 60c for the first book and 25c for each additional book to cover mailing and handling. Orders of 5 or more books postage is Free. I enclose $_____ in check or money order.

Mr/Mrs/Miss_____

Address_____

City_____ State/Zip_____

Please allow 4 to 5 weeks for delivery. This offer expires 6/78

A-18